Love Stories Are...

Written By

Katharine M Sweet

Julia
Thank you so much
Hope you enjoy the Book

Book Two of the Goodroe Brother's Duet

Distributed by Sweet Tales With Spice

ISBN: 978-1-7371078-2-8 (eBook)
ISBN: 978-1-7371078-8-0 (paperback)

Table of Contents

Katharine M Sweet

This book is dedicated to writers. Whether published or not, please know that your words have worth and value and should be shared. Writing is a daunting and occasionally grueling task, but it is worth it. The world needs your words. Somewhere out there is a person who needs your story. Write your truth; write for yourself and trust that the person who needs to see your soul bleed onto those pages will.

This project is a labor of love. It rose from the ashes of my broken heart and became a glowing example to me of how incredible and caring people can truly be.

To Nikki for 40 pages and brilliant fires, Jordan Celine for resetting my brain and keeping me out of empty rooms, Angela for so many grammar corrections, Ruby my gorgeous comma and word choice queen, Ash for their unwavering support, Hannah for her cheerleading, Megan for so many jokes, Jordan for another pair of eyes, Juna for design help, and to all the other lovelies at Second Cup Writer's Café.

– THANK YOU

Without you all this book would not exist.

Please Note: There are references to abuse (physical and psychological) to minors and adults, blood, character death, domestic violence, general violence, misogyny, murder, panic attacks, PTSD, and sexism.

"There is no mistaking a real story when one meets it. Even when not romantic leaning, it is like falling in love."

- Anonymous

Chapter 1: Prologues are Pointless

Vincent Got Ahead of Himself

March 4th

Anna Kane took a sip of the cheap wine her date had ordered for her, forcing herself not to grimace at the acidic taste. She would've preferred a Lynchburg Lemonade, but her date had changed plans at the last minute and asked her to meet him at a restaurant that she hadn't realized was a barbeque place. Now, if her last three meetings hadn't run late, she would've had time to research the location, but since they had, she'd barely made it here on time.

The only thing that lessened her annoyance was that it was within walking distance of her office. And while she agreed to the wine for the sake of civility, she had put her foot down when he tried to order her meal. He scowled when she refused to eat the steak he all but demanded she try.

He made a show of flicking his wrist again to expose his oversized, fake gold Rolex from under his suit jacket. When she'd arrived, he'd shaken her hand for an extended time, although he held it like he was worried it would break. He was showcasing that knock-off because he thought she wouldn't know better. He'd commented on her watch saying that he'd never heard of the brand, but the pink gold was cute for a lady. Her 'cute' watch cost a third of the hundred-thousand-dollar annual salary he claimed on his LinkedIn profile.

He was still talking. He hadn't stopped since he'd taken the first sip of his drink. "Finance is a challenging industry. You have to stay ahead of the curve and swim in front of the pack like a killer shark. Otherwise, you get eaten like a guppy fish. Know what I'm saying?"

A guppy is a fish - why are you so repetitive? Anna took a longer sip of her drink. It wasn't her favorite, but it was alcoholic. "It can certainly be a challenge."

"I'm sure you're glad you don't have to worry about any of that. I mean, you're just an editor. All you do is read books all day. Must be nice to simply put commas in between words randomly and daydream the rest of the time." He laughed at his own joke and attempted to put his hand over hers, but Anna moved it back to her wine glass. "I'm only kidding, of course. I'm sure what you do is so important."

The smile she forced made her face hurt, so she excused herself to the restroom. *Strike fucking three.* On habit, she checked her purse for cigarettes. This was proving to be a bad year to quit. She retrieved her phone and texted her assistant.

Anna: Wait 10-15 minutes then call me. Ignore what I say.

The stall door opened, and the waitress that had taken their orders nodded as she moved past Anna to wash her hands.

"First date?" she questioned as she scrubbed.

Anna looked at the woman's name tag: Clara. Clara was pretty. She had curly brown hair pulled back in a high ponytail, friendly brown eyes, and a dusting of freckles over the bridge of her pierced nose.

"First and last," Anna confirmed.

"Good plan, he asked me to change your order to a steak. I told him I couldn't, and he offered me an extra five dollars in my tip."

Anna arched her eyebrow. She had told her date that she didn't eat red meat. "Do you have a side door that leads into the alley?"

Clara nodded as she dried her hands. "If you're feelin' ick about 'im, I can let you out that way."

"No need for that." Anna dismissed the notion, before making her request. "Could you go tell him that you changed your mind, about the steak?"

"Are you sure?"

"Yes. Then bring me the bill for the salad I ordered, so I can pay you for it. I'll meet you at the side door to pick it up after I leave the restaurant. Then you can bring him both steaks."

She clapped her hands together. "Oh, heck yes! This'll be fantastic. Gimme a minute."

Clara brought the bill back to Anna immediately, and Anna handed her a hundred-dollar bill to keep.

"Whoa, this is too much." Clara attempted to hand it back.

Anna shook her head. "In case he stiffs you on his check or throws a fit. You deserve to get paid for your work."

The waitress finally agreed, and Anna went back to her table, sitting across from her date who was checking his phone. Anna was about to thank him for waiting since she'd been gone so long, but he interrupted before she could speak.

"Is this not the week for this?" He motioned between them, a piece of lettuce from his side salad was stuck in his front teeth. "'This is a nice place, and I'm spending a lot on you if it's just going to be dinner we're enjoying tonight."

Her phone rang and she answered it without apologizing or breaking eye contact. "Hello. He wants to move the meeting up to tonight? What time? Of course, he's one of our largest overseas clients. I'll see you in about," she checked her watch, "fifteen or twenty minutes. Bye."

"We're in the middle of dinner." Her date looked exasperated. "I paid for..."

Anna dropped a fifty-dollar bill on his plate, condescendingly offering concern. "Well, since you are worried about affording it, that should cover my half. Have the evening you've earned."

Nearly everyone in the restaurant stared at her as she strutted out of the restaurant. She rounded the corner and stepped into the alleyway, finding Clara by an open door, holding out a to-go bag.

"That was epic! I put a piece of pie in there for you too. Cause you freakin' rock."

Anna took the bag from Clara and flashed her a flirtatious smile. She knew this was a shot in the dark, but she had a thing for dark-haired beauties. "Are you interested in having a drink with me after you get done with work?"

Clara blushed and tucked a lock of curly, brown hair behind her ear. "Sorry, I'm seeing someone. Otherwise, I'd totally say yes."

"Thank you for the easy letdown, Clara. Have a good night." Anna gave her a wave and continued through the alleyway. If she remembered correctly, it connected to the street where her building was located.

Her phone vibrated in her pocket, and she answered it without a greeting. "I'm already out of the restaurant. Yes, alone, but not for lack of trying...No, not him. I invited my waitress out for drinks...We can talk about it on Monday, I'm tired. Make sure you add an hour to your PTO bank for helping me when you're off the clock. I shouldn't be interrupting your weekend."

Anna glanced behind her to make sure no one was following as she left the alleyway. Her boots clacked as she walked heel to toe, stretching out her strides. She crossed the intersection and paced up the street to get to her building.

She rolled her eyes as Alysha, god bless her for being the world's best assistant, admonished her to not go back to work. "I'm going home, not to the office." She punched in her code at the double doors and let herself into the building, turning right to go into her office to retrieve her apartment keys. "Goodnight, Alysha, and thank you."

There was enough light from the streetlights coming through the windows for her to weave her way through the waiting area without turning on the overhead lights. Her jacket was still hanging on the back of the chair, which she accidentally bumped into her desk. The force took her computer out of sleep mode. She scowled at the machine, certain she'd turned it off before she'd left.

Maybe she'd eat down here? She could look over the overseas reports quickly and save herself some time on Monday morning. Might as well. Anna sighed and paced out of her office and into the small kitchenette. She tapped a cup against the ice machine to partially fill her cup and grabbed a napkin-rolled set of silverware.

Anna was irritated. Another Friday night, eating while working alone in the dark. This year was supposed to be about finding a relationship and balance, not hooking up with the pretty waitress who'd made her night a little less awful. She navigated through the desks in the main office area, nearly tripping over the trash can that was halfway out into the pathway.

She glared at the desk - it was Greg's. Of course, it was. He could never seem to keep his space clean, though to be fair, neither could she. But, her space wasn't a trip hazard for anyone other than herself. She put the silverware in the same hand she held her cup with, and went to move the trash can, she noticed the manuscript that had been thrown into it.

Anna cursed out breaking the silence of the empty office. Throwing manuscripts away was a liability — they should always be mailed back with a rejection, shredded, or returned to the author when they met them in person. Her intention was to simply shred it, but as she pulled it out of the trash she noticed the cover.

The cover wasn't blank with only a title and author's name printed on it, like most manuscripts that were sent in by amateur writers. There was an image printed on it, protected by a clear cover. Anna took it with her into her office to inspect it closer.

She turned on her lights and set it onto her desk. After pouring herself a double shot of whiskey, she sat down and picked the printed pages back up.

Upon closer examination, what she thought was a printed image was hand-drawn. She could feel the graphite under her finger. The image was of a couple back to back, the woman obviously pregnant and the man grimacing with his fist on his forehead. The art wasn't spectacular, but it was detailed, he'd taken his time with this. She appreciated time and effort.

Anna flipped the cover back and looked at the summary provided on the first page.

"Have you ever heard the one about the small-town girl, who had a baby with an ex-con who never wanted kids? No? You should, it's a good one."

She chuckled, she could take her dinner upstairs and spend her weekend reading this. There was a little voice nagging her that if it wasn't worth publishing, she would be wasting her time, and she had an entire to-be-read list on her e-reader. Anna rolled her eyes. If it wasn't worth reading, she'd stop. She carefully put the pages into her food bag, her drink into a tumbler from her collection, and started her walk home.

It wasn't like reading a book was going to upend her entire world. Especially a self-declared dramatic romantic comedy titled: Love Is… written by unknown author Vincent Goodroe.

March 7th

Vincent Goodroe wasn't one for drama, please ignore anything his older brother had to say on the topic. He couldn't always phrase things correctly, and it bothered him. He pushed open the heavy fire door and stepped out into the hidden garden patio. The smoke and lights of the club had become *almost* as comfortable as solitude, but even being in the respite of the courtyard couldn't still his brain when it was in overdrive. He lowered himself to sit in one of the cool metal chairs and let out a long sigh. Unconsciously, his hand moved to his shirt pocket to look for his cigarettes, despite the fact that he'd quit years ago.

The accepted calendar invite was flashing on his phone. How had he agreed so simply? Then again, he often agreed to things without putting full thought into them first.

The Playhouse had been built as a money laundering front for, Hector Azura, the original owner of this place. Hector had run it solo for a year, but it was complicated business. Hector had a heavy *entanglement* with Jim, the man Vinnie *collected* for during his prior life of crime. Jim was the only reason Vinnie even knew about this club. What had been a promise to his brother to not spend his first birthday after prison miserably had changed the path of his life. Hector had recognized him and waved him over to the VIP booth in the corner, offering him a business opportunity, while Hector's wife gave him a lap dance that left him feeling more than a little uncomfortable. Hector wanted a partner to split liability, but he needed someone who knew how to look the other way and understood how to stay on Jim's good side.

The lights had been low in the club and Vinnie's attention had been split between listening to Hector's offer and noticing the darkened marks on the woman's slender wrists and the reddened handprint on her thigh. Hector had excused himself to take a call, telling Vinnie to have fun with her, but not too much. She looked frightened beneath the act she was putting on, and as much as Vinnie wanted her to stop, he was aware that stopping might put her in danger. He asked her if she needed help in Spanish, and her nearly black eyes filled up instantly with tears.

He touched her chin and told her that his name was Vinnie and his Spanish was very, very bad, but he wanted to help her if he could. She perched on his lap and slid his hand to a small scar on her lower back. Quiet as breathing, she whispered into his neck that her name was Leila, and she wanted help but didn't think it was possible with Hector alive. Vinnie told her to ignore anything he said to Hector and that he'd find a way to help her. He'd explained that accidents in Hector's line of work were common, and to be patient.

A truck backfiring in the parking lot startled him out of the memory. The club was overly busy for a Monday night. Why was half of Houston here? He could go upstairs and check to see if his business partner and former girlfriend had things under control. Not that he didn't think she could handle it, but he didn't want her to be overwhelmed.

He took the side interior door to leave the courtyard and entered directly onto the main floor. It wasn't as busy as the parking lot looked. Was there an event going on upstairs? He didn't remember that being on the schedule. He nodded to security and took the elevator up to his office.

The private second floor was busier than the main floor, and now he knew he'd forgotten something?

He slipped into his office and found Leila sitting at her desk and tying her hair back, looking not too happy.

"What did I miss?"

"Why are you here?" The exasperation was clear in her tone.

They spoke at nearly the same time and then both stopped. Leila sighed and questioned. "Why are you here? You are supposed to be home. You have not taken a day off in two weeks."

"The parking lot looked too full for a weekday. What's going on?"

"Officially, it's a bachelor party." She scribbled notes onto a deposit slip, put it into a cash bag with a wad of cash, and placed it into the safe.

Hmm. 'Officially' meant rowdier guests that didn't play by the rules. He wouldn't feel safe leaving until he knew what the event actually was. "Unofficially?"

"Lobbyists and politicians. I moved them up here, so it's easier to keep an eye on them."

Leila's eyes had a keen intelligence that he'd recognized even through her tears the first time they'd met. She flourished since Hector's untimely passing. She moved through a dark phase of her life and came out the other side in control. No one hurt her anymore, and no one saw her without clothes unless she permitted it. In his mind's eye there was a technicolor memory of Leila having the moon phases tattooed down her spine, an outside illustration of her inside change.

He kept the special memory of holding her hand while a family friend, Bree, had tattooed the moon phases down her spine close to his heart.

He trusted her, but he always had to ask things out loud. "Good plan. Did you add extra security?"

"I called, but they aren't here yet."

Vinnie grabbed his spare sportcoat that he kept in their office. "I'll stay. At least, until they get here."

"You need a night off." Leila insisted, "I can handle it tonight."

"I wouldn't ever doubt you." He understood what she was saying, but he wasn't going to leave her high and dry.

"Then why are you here?" she countered. "Are you here to help or here to not be home?"

"Huh?"

Leila shook her head. "Vincent, whenever you don't want to deal with whatever is going on at home, you come in and work extra."

"No. I don't."

"Yes, you do." Her hand grabbed his and they made eye contact. "Vincent, you don't seem fine. I'm here to listen."

"Don't use your customer voice on me!" he snapped, not meaning the level of malice that coated his words.

She blinked at his reaction.

"Sit." She pointed to his desk and sat at hers as he silently complied. "¿Qué tienes?" Her brows furrowed, asking him what was wrong. "You know I would've called you if I needed you."

When Leila needed his help all those years ago, he was more than willing to give it. His uncle Rex had handled the details behind the scenes, while he escaped with Leila to Las Vegas. No way to trace anything back to them. He'd never forget watching her eyes light up with relief when he told her the situation was handled, and he'd surrendered to her exuberant gratitude later that night. He shouldn't be thinking of her like this. His eyes fell to the photo on her desk of her recent wedding. She wasn't his. Never truly had been. Some things were only for a moment, then they passed.

"Are you here?" Leila asked, pulling him out of the memories.

"Sorry. Yes, I'm here." He sighed heavily.

"Is this about what we talked about on Saturday, when you decided you weren't talking to me, but thinking out loud?"

"Oh, that?" Vinnie wasn't sure how to rephrase what he'd let slip out. "It's nothing you have to worry about. I'm likely getting ahead of myself, and it isn't something we need to handle at this moment. Everything's fine. It was thinking out loud. Honestly, 80% of adults think out loud as they are performing tasks, and the American Psychological Association now associates thinking out loud with intelligence and creativity instead of insanity and mental illness as it was once considered. So, I'm fine. Did you know…" The facts spilled from his lips in a single breath until she interrupted him.

"Vincent." She was the only person on earth who called him by his full name. Leila didn't like nicknames, so he ignored the deep shudder that would often run down his spine when she used it. "I don't think you were thinking out loud. We've talked about me buying out your share of this place before. You've had one foot out of the door for a while. What has you ready to go now?"

"I'm nothing without someone else," he admitted, the words heavy as they left his mouth. Vinnie hated the admission.

The Playhouse was the first thing that was his without his family involved, yet he was still a part of someone else's sentence. Here, he wasn't Mat's brother, Rex's nephew, or Nathan's crazy kid, but he wasn't Vinnie, either. He was Vincent, Leila's ex and business partner. This still wasn't his.

"This place isn't mine and it never was. I was a way for your former husband to limit liability, and a way for you to stay protected after he died. It's another way for me to play a part but not truly have anything. I'm floating, and I hate it."

Leila's depthless eyes misted over, "Vincent, you have redesigned every aspect of this place. It would not be what it is without you. This is as much yours as it is mine. Why haven't you told me about how you've felt?"

"You and Violet have a lot on your plates. I," He trailed off, hand moving to his phone, and his mind to the accepted calendar invite. "I'm not burning to leave, but I have to pull back. I need your help with something and it's going to require money."

"You're finally going to let me buy you out? I noticed you've had papers with you the past few days. Is that what those papers were that you were bringing in the last few weeks? The contract of sale? We know each other better than to need a whole novel of a contract."

"It's not a contract, it's a novel."

"What?"

Vinnie cleared his throat, "I wrote a book. That's what I want to do. I want to write books. I'm tired of the stories being written around me."

She smiled, "What's it about? A true-crime thriller told from the criminal's eyes?"

"And just like that, you've given an amazing new idea." He chuckled and wiped his glasses on his shirt. "It's a romantic comedy actually."

"You never cease to surprise me."

"Well, technically it's a fictionalization of how Mat and Kass got together."

"Mat will kill you." She warned.

He laughed out loud. "I mean, yeah. So let's keep this between us. Now, if I could get the Lost Horizon away from John, that would be a suitable distraction."

"The Lost Horizon in Galveston that John Allomos owns?"

Vinnie blinked, "You know John?"

"From when Hector was alive, yes. John used to supply the club with drugs." She shrugged as she retrieved her phone from her desk drawer. "You didn't know?"

Vinnie couldn't keep the grin off his face. Jim definitely didn't know that, and knowledge equaled leverage. "Fantastic. How would you feel about helping me acquire a restaurant?"

"Fine with me, but I get to read the book."

"I don't know if it'll even get published. The odds are not with me."

"Then count the cards, use what's been played, and bet accordingly." Leila quoted his own words from their past and took a drink from her water bottle. "Have you sent the book anywhere?"

"I did." He tapped his heel against the floor. "Then I discovered that I should have gotten an agent and approached it differently. And yet...And yet, I got a call scheduling a meeting tomorrow with a local publisher. That's not supposed to happen."

"It sounds like fate. I'm serious about reading your book. I will make time."

"At some point. But don't tell Kass when she comes for class on Saturday."

"My lips are sealed." She pantomimed the motion. "Now, take the night off like you were supposed to. Everything will be fine without you looming."

"I do not loom."

"Of course, you don't."

The door opened, and Violet let herself into the office, closing the door behind her. "When is that extra security getting here?"

"What's wrong?" Vinnie and Leila both questioned.

"Yeesh." Violet held up her hands. "I hate it when you two do that. And nothing's wrong, yet."

"Yet meaning?" Vinnie pressed.

"Yet meaning 'the family man of the hour' is having a hard time keeping his hands to himself and understanding that, 'no,' is a full sentence." Violet supplied air quotes as she spoke.

Vinnie folded his arms over his chest. "We should throw them out and be done."

"No." Leila shook her head. "I'll be on the floor until extra security arrives. As long as they aren't completely out of control, I'll let them stay. What they paid for tonight covers our monthly expenses."

"So money gives them a pass to do whatever they want?" Vinnie grumbled.

"I didn't say that. I'm going on the floor myself to keep an eye on them." Leila narrowed her eyes at him before asking her wife, "Can you get my jacket and tie out of the closet for me, Vi?" Violet was an exception to Leila's nickname rule.

"Sure, baby." Violet handed Leila the items requested and helped knot Leila's tie, sliding it up slowly. She grinned at Leila and brushed her hair back over her shoulders. "I love this on you."

Leila smiled in return, muted but genuine. Nothing like the one she used on customers. "Thank you. Can you go help with the bar downstairs, without your fists?"

Violet rolled her eyes. "You punch one five-piece suit and no one lets you hear the end of it."

"He sued." Vinnie reminded her.

"We won," she dismissed and gave Leila's hand a squeeze before opening the door. "Besides, Vin, you aren't supposed to be here. Go home, we ain't paying you." She slammed the door closed.

Vinnie sighed. "Can you please tell your wife not to call me that?"
"I can try, but no promises. She's very stubborn." Leila put her radio in her right ear and attached the wireless mic to her lapel. She held the office for him and pointed to the elevator. "Go home."
He opened his mouth to argue but reconsidered. He should get some rest before his meeting tomorrow. "Be safe." Vinnie said.
"I will be smart."
Vinnie stopped for a moment, watching Leila transform from the controlled, quiet person she really was into the role she played here in front of clients. Her wide smile and exaggerated accent played into the expectations of the crowd.
"Gentlemen and even a few ladies I see, welcome to The Playhouse. If I can direct your eyes to the stage…"
The rowdy crowd settled as Leila stepped up onto the stage and began to weave her story. Leila had a magnetic presence when she was "on" for lack of a better description. He always liked the quieter part of her personality, the part of her she kept away from the world. As much as he knew he made the right decision to remove himself from their relationship, part of him ached for the connected moments they shared. He was good at pretending to be part of a relationship, and maybe with everything he'd done in the past, it was all he really deserved.
He was going to do what he would control. Help his brother get his dream back so he'd finally marry Kass. Get distance from the club and try to have a life truly his own. His book was the start. It was his, and someone thought it was good enough to consider for publication.
His meeting with Miss Anna Kane tomorrow was the first step. One book could change his whole life.

March 8th; 276 Days Until…

"You don't even know what you have! You have everything in that house. It got handed to you, it was put into your damn lap. You have a sweet girl that cares about you and a kid on the way, but all you want to do is run around like you're Jessie-Fucking-James. You have something that I'm never going to get my hands on. I don't know how you managed to get your head so far up your ass that you can't see that, but you better get it out before I…"

Anna tapped the corner of the printed pages. She snagged a star-shaped tab and secured it to the page she was currently on before flipping to the closest matching tab. There was something familiar in the syntax of this section. This was a clear pivot point of the story's third act. It highlighted the conflict in the male protagonist's character, but there was something unstated with the side character's reaction. It was almost like this writer was on the outside looking in on the feelings he was writing about.

She scanned the lines as she bit down on the end of her pen. She had seen that slight disconnection in another section, something so longing in this writer's words. Almost like a plea to fate about wanting to find this kind of affection; this kind of belonging…She shook her head, she was more than a little tired if she was romanticizing his prose like this. And yet, wasn't there a moment… Maybe in the scene in the doctor's office? She flipped to the passage marked with a square-shaped tab. It had been written in an unnecessary POV.

"You're family, and we take care of each other.' His brother was an idiot for missing this; for not being here with the girl, and for missing the opportunity to see and hear his child. He was gonna have a discussion with his brother about this situation tonight. Regardless of how the child had been conceived, he or she was a part of the family already."

There was this agonizing jealousy, not about the girl herself, but about aching for that kind of love. She narrowed her eyes and underlined the section. This was the writer divulging himself in his work and it likely hadn't been intentional. "What happened to make you think you weren't worthy of being loved?" She cursed out loud, realizing that she'd been chewing on the end of her pen.

She closed the rough-drafted book, "Love Is…" She wasn't fond of the title, it was too plain. It needed to be simpler, but still make an impact. The genre was flooded with thousands of titles. The book would need a hook to stand out and a splashy cover. She'd gotten ahead of herself, reading and critiquing when it wasn't in her financial interest yet.

At best, it might work for one of the subsidiary imprints that was under the umbrella of the main company. The story had an unusual charm. It had caught her by surprise, which was rare with how many books she consumed. She had read it cover to cover in one long sitting on a Saturday. The writer's voice had captivated her and without her permission, melted her heart. Then again, she was also pretty lonely in the love department.

The more unfortunate part was the timing of finding it. She had a plethora of things going on — one more thing might pull her in too many directions to ensure her quality of work. She had to finalize the six imprints they were launching, finish Alysha's training, and conduct all of the meetings with the boards and investors. She still had marketing plans to go over and needed to cement the focus books for each imprint with those who would be running them. Her eyes strayed back to the manuscript on her desk.

A few sections needed work, which was normal for any writer. There were grammatical errors: typos, wrong homonyms, misplaced commas, and incorrectly-tensed verbs here and there, but less than the average manuscript. The meticulous writing had been crafted with affection, like a soul bled out on the pages. *She needed more coffee, she was losing herself again.* One of the imprints was focused on independent authors who transitioned to traditional publishing, so if they went with a couple of writers for that one then perhaps it had a place. *Why was she fighting so hard for this piece?*

Her office door opened and closed with a slam, the wall rattling as Alysha let herself into the office. "Did building maintenance not fix that door yet? I'm gonna call again." She set a bag with their breakfasts down on the desk and rattle one of the iced coffees.

As busy as she was, Alysha stretched beyond the level of efficient, firmly placing herself in the category of irreplaceable — sometimes being the only reason Anna remembered to eat during the day. Her rich brown skin was complimented by her sleeveless black pantsuit, half-calf boots, and accented by her intricate, silver evil-eye pendent. Her naturally dark, tightly coiled curls framed her heart-shaped face and while holding Anna's coffee hostage, she offered a smirk. "Will this be your second or third cup today? Don't lie."

"Third. I've been up since 4 AM." She gratefully accepted the drink and took a sip from the straw. "I was talking to..."

"Not the guy you went out with Friday. Please do not say you answered his texts after I had to rescue you from dinner." Alysha unwrapped her breakfast sandwich and took a bite.

"No. God, no. I blocked him right after I left the restaurant." She unwrapped her own sandwich, pulling off the bacon and putting it into the trash. "I was talking to Minji. She's stressed with the wedding planning."

"I can imagine. You're clocking out early today, right? Since you're flying out tomorrow morning for a twenty-five-hour trip."

"That five-hour layover in San Francisco is going to be miserable. Thankfully my return flight on the 16th is more direct and should have me back in Houston in seventeen hours." She pulled up her calendar. "I'll be available by phone if you need anything."

"I'm not worried about it." She patted a napkin against her lips, leaving a bright red imprint. "I can handle whatever."

Alysha had been a great assistant for the last four years and a real asset to the busy publishing office. In fact, the dark-haired woman had paused in the middle of her interview because Anna's former assistant was having trouble with the internet company. By the time Alysha was done, the office had a thirty-dollar monthly discount, and Alysha had a new job. She took perfect messages, wasn't intimidated or star-struck by their celebrity clients, and had this peculiar magic of making things fall into place. That drive and poise were why she was going to be managing one of the new subsidiary imprints. Anna was glad to let her flourish, but she was going to miss her. Finding a replacement was proving impossible.

"I know you can." Anna sighed, tapping the calendar ahead to the upcoming months. "I think I'm done dating for the year."

"It's March and your New Year's resolution was to attempt a relationship. Remember you want a life outside this building."

"Just because you're going to achieve your resolutions, doesn't mean you get to nitpick mine." Anna closed her eyes. "There are just so many social events for these imprint launches. Going alone is miserable and makes me a target for uncomfortable conversations. Being in a relationship would have made those events easier." Her phone lit up, and she glanced at the alert from the dating app, announcing a new match.

"Relationships are work, too." Alysha stretched her arms over her head. "Do we have time to go over the budget paperwork? I want to look at marketing tools, and I need my final numbers on what I have to spend."

Anna was looking at her phone and the flurry of messages from the potential match. It went from 'Hello Beautiful' to 'You're ugly and not worth my time if you're going to ignore me' in less than twenty minutes, but the messages came in one after another. The wifi must be acting up again; the old building was infamous for connection problems on the ground floor. "No. I have a meeting when we open at nine. Let's plan on eleven to go over your budget, and if we're slow for the rest of today, I might clock out early. Oh, and by Friday you need to get your final author list together, I want a strong start for you."

"So you can look at it while you're supposed to be helping at your friend's wedding?"

"I'll have downtime." She looked at the obnoxious messages again, alternating between being angry and disheartened by them. Maybe Emily had been right about staying single; her mother had always prioritized herself over any relationship.

But Anna didn't want to be alone for the rest of her life. She had a career, but she was allowed to want more than that. She wanted someone who wanted her but didn't hold her back. She wanted children. She wanted to be a mother, but she also wanted to be who she was.

Alysha tossed her wrapper in the trashcan and glanced at the clock. "You aren't playing favorites now, are you? Ben's already raising hell about the extra time you're spending on me."

"Ben, like myself, has his job more based on who he's related to than personal skills. The difference is that I've been willing to sacrifice to succeed, and he wants it for free. You get extra time with me because you make yourself available." Anna showed her phone to Alysha. "This is why I'm done with dating."

"Don't give up because of some douche. There's someone out there for you." Alysha stood up but glanced back at her. "You mixed up your closet again."

Anna looked down at her outfit. "I thought it looked fine."

"You're wearing a turquoise top and forest-green pants. Those colors are second-cousins twice-removed. They shouldn't even be in the same room together without a mediator or alcohol." She laughed at her own observation before reminding her. "Send me pictures in the morning if you aren't sure. I've got you, I'll snag my black and white sweater that'll break up the intensity."

"I'll die of heatstroke."

"Girl, it's fifty."

"I grew up in Chicago, fifty is not cold." Anna took another long drink from her coffee and straightened out the clutter on her desk.

The door buzzer announced that someone was at the front door. "That's your nine o'clock, I'll grab him a coffee and you the sweater. Is this the no-agent guy?"

"Yeah. I just need to figure out his mindset. And *maybe*, see if he'd be a match for one of the imprints."

"Sounds good." Alysha disappeared, turning on the lights on her way to the door.

Anna moved the budget files to the cabinet and jumped as the door slammed closed. Alysha's black eyes were glittering with excitement, as she insisted, "Put on the sweater!"

"What did I miss?" Anna took the offered sweater. She'd learned to trust Alysha when she was buzzing with this much energy.

"Remember yesterday's meeting when you went through that whole spiel about picking authors based on talent, not looks, even with the different imprint focuses? If I didn't know you the way that I do, I would think that whole bit was bullshit."

Anna cocked her head to the side, "I'm still confused. I need more words."

"Come here and look." Alysha grabbed her hand, tugging her away from her clutter and up to the blind-covered window in the door. She pushed down on one of the blind slats and turned her head to the opening. "*That* is your nine o'clock."

Her eyes scanned the waiting area before falling on the dark-haired man in the dark suit sitting on the couch in the corner. He was wearing black-framed glasses that only seemed to accentuate his handsome features, and his light eyes were magnetic. She snapped the opening closed and leaned against the door. *Oh, that was what Alysha was talking about.*

"You didn't know what he looked like?" Alysha gave her a long look, "Oh my god, you didn't!"

"I didn't even google his name. I only checked a couple of phrases from the book to make sure it wasn't plagiarized." She needed more coffee. Or water at this point?

"He's cute, kinda quiet but not in a creepy way." She grinned, "Maybe you skip the book meeting and take him out for a coffee instead? Wait, are you blushing?"

"I am not." *But she was, she could feel the heat in her cheeks.* Anna spun on her heel; moving a pile of file folder to hide in a desk drawer and gathering up various books to shove into the shelves lining her walls. She needed to take better care of her space, this was not the impression she should be giving clients, "This is just a meeting, it's not some fate-orchestrated meet-cute in a romance novella."

"Oh! You think he's hot!" Alysha laughed. "You use fancier syntax when you think a guy's good-looking."

Anna bit her lip; Alysha wasn't wrong. Books highlight perfect little meet-cutes, but those meet-cutes weren't reality. The reality was the guy from the dating app throwing a fit because she didn't respond fast enough or Friday night's disastrous blind date. It wasn't a quiet, attractive man who wrote beautifully-heartbreaking emotions in his first book just strolling into her life.

"Let me fix your hair. Your bun is crooked." Anna bent her knees so Alysha could fix her hair, "This hair of yours — baby soft and won't hold a style for anything." Alysha combed through Anna's hair quickly with her coffin-tipped nails, opting to leave it down, "There, that's better. Maybe you get laid and sign him?"

Anna rolled her eyes. "I don't sleep with clients."

"Sleep with him then sign him?" She held her hands up defensively. "I'm kidding, I'm kidding. I just know it's been a while."

"Professional meeting only."

"You are no fun."Anna smoothed out the sweater over her button-down, "I'll remember this when we see a cute author we interview for your imprint."

"Haha. Deal. I'll go get him." Alysha swept out of the office, but left the door open, "She's all ready for you, sir."

Alysha showed him in and Anna smiled, offering her hand to the slightly taller man, "Mr. Goodroe, it's so nice to meet you. I'm Anna Kane."

Vinnie cursed as he pulled his car into the driveway, he was late and Mat was already home.

He hated breaking his promises. Not being here at 10:30 when he said he would be was not okay. He unlocked the door with one hand and loosened his tie with the other. This was gonna be an earful.

"I'm sorry. I got caught up," he apologized, kicking off his shoes.

"Caught up with what? The club closed at seven, it's almost noon," Mat growled, coming around the corner.

Vinnie sighed. "I already apologized. I was in a meeting and I lost track of time. Don't be so dramatic about it."

"I'm not being dramatic, but me having to come home on my lunch when I thought you had it handled…" Mat's rant abruptly trailed off and he narrowed his eyes at Vinnie, "why does it look like you're trying not to laugh?"

"Because I am." Vinnie confirmed, tapping his temple. "You have a unicorn barrette in your hair."

"She put glitter all over you yesterday."

"I've worked at the club long enough to be fully versed in how to get rid of glitter."

"UNCLE VEENEE!" Lizzie squealed from where she was sitting on the living room floor with her building blocks. "I is here!"

"Hey, Nugget, how are you?" He sat down next to her and handed her a triangle-shaped block. "Do you need this one for your tower?"

"Oh yes!" She took the offered shape and put it on top. "Daddy here too! He so preddy!"

Vinnie chuckled. "I saw that."

Mat sat on the couch. "Lizzie, do you wanna eat lunch before I go back to work?"

"Like headens!" She nodded emphatically.

"No, not like heathens. Up in your highchair where you won't make such a mess," Mat corrected and held out his hands for his daughter, who was already tearing up.

"Daddy, pwease, here with Uncle Veenee?" she implored.

Mat sighed and was likely about to give in, but Vinnie interrupted. "Well, I'm going to have lunch at the table. Don't you want to eat with me?"

Lizzie looked between the two of them, her lighter colored eye looking more gray than blue today, probably due to the colors in her outfit. "Okee."

"I had it," Mat snipped at Vinnie, before picking up his daughter and addressing her. "Come on little lady, you want mac and cheese?"

"Nugs and Nanas, pweese!" she requested, hugging Mat.

"Alright. We can handle that, it's healthy enough I guess. We'll give you some carrot crackers too."

Mat settled her into her highchair, and Lizzie stole his phone from his shirt pocket. She flattened her hand against the black screen. "Oh hi, Mommy! Hi, Hi! We lunch!"

"You can play with it until you get your food." Mat rolled his eyes.

Vinnie had pushed himself back up off the ground and was already cutting up the banana his niece wanted. "I've got the dangerous part handled."

"What are the odds that one of her favorite foods is something that'll kill me?" Mat put the plate into the microwave.

"With your track record, pretty high. Statistically, your life does seem to follow the path of most resistance and potholes," he snickered.

"Fucking joker." Mat's comment was barely audible.

"Sorry, what was that? I couldn't hear you?"

Mat glared. "You heard what the *french-toast* I said."

"HA!" Vinnie barked a laugh, and Lizzie echoed him as the patio door opened, and Rex came inside.

"What's so funny, Lil Bean? What are those two going on about, huh?" The older man unzipped his jacket, hung it over the back of the barstool, and sat next to Lizzie. "Nice of you to come home, Vinnie."

Vinnie sighed and held out his phone. "If you were all so worried about me, why don't I have a single missed call or text?"

"Hi Mommy!" Lizzie waved to his phone. She loved using facetime talks. She would wave and chatter at whosever phone she claimed until she drained the battery.

In true toddler fashion she would have a meltdown if any of them attempted an in-person conversation with her when she was dead set on talking to them with the phone. There had been a number of nights Lizzie had bullied him behind the couch so she and Rex could call him. She truly did have all of them wrapped around her tiny finger.

Rex glanced over his glasses. "I can see a bunch of missed calls from here. Better look again."

Mat scraped the bananas from the cutting board, adding them to the chicken nuggets and carrot slices before offering the plate to Lizzie. "Time to trade. Nugs for Dad's phone."

"OKEE! Byeee, Mommy!"

Vinnie looked down at his phone, there were a handful of missed calls, texts, and alerts. The publishing office must have low coverage. The construction of the building, thicker walls, and older building materials must have blocked the signal. "Sorry, I didn't realize. I got back as soon as I could. I just lost track of time."

"So what was the meeting about?" Rex questioned. "Hey Mat, make a sandwich for me too while you're making yours."

"No prob. You want one too, Vinnie?"

"Yeah, no mustard."

"I've been making you sandwiches since you were five, I know." Mat rolled his eyes.

Rex cracked his knuckles, and Lizzie tried to imitate him. "Lil Bean, you're too young to be aching like me." He turned to Vinnie, "What was the meeting about? Didn't think you guys were making any major changes for a while."

Vinnie didn't want to lie to his uncle, he really didn't. But he also really, really didn't want to tell him what he had been up to. *Lie, with a lowercase 'L' — no harm in a white lie.* He cleared his throat. "Just budget things. Leila wants to change some of the cross-marketing."

"*Does* she now?" The way Rex enunciated that made Vinnie nervous.

Was that more integration than actual question? Had his uncle just asked him a question that he already knew the answer to? It was impossible. There was no way he knew about the book. Vinnie had kept it so close to his chest. He hadn't trusted anyone with the information, except for Leila last night. She wouldn't have said anything. She would have had to go out of her way to tell his brother and uncle.

Mat set their plates on the island but leaned back against the counter to eat his without a plate. He noticed Rex's eyes on him. "Vinnie'll sweep before Kass gets home. He owes me one."

"Oh yeah, I owe you for bending my schedule to watch your kid."

"Nope. Just for not keeping your promise," Mat corrected, then asked with an annoyed tone, "What's your ex trying to change about the club now? I thought the pole dancing lessons on Saturday mornings were the only thing she wanted to do this year. I ain't doing any more construction for free."

Both his brother and his uncle were looking at him and waiting for a response.

Vinnie chewed his bite slowly. This entire conversation felt a bit like a trap. "I know, I know, and for the thousandth time, thank you for the help. I would like to remind you that you got a non-monetary bonus for that work. Kass thinks Saturday is a great time."

"Don't." Mat snapped his finger, "that's not table talk."

Rex gruff laugh echoed in the room. "You're one to go on about inappropriate language."

"I haven't taught Lizzie any of the bad words, I'm doing just fine." Mat defended himself.

"To answer your question, Rex, we're just working with some online advertising. Nothing to write home about." Vinnie took another bite of his sandwich before addressing his uncle again. "If you want to go back to the shop after you eat, I'm here."

"Mhmm." Rex finished his sandwich and walked by him to put away his plate, but paused to pick something off the floor.

"Kass said she'll be back by three, so you'll have time to sleep before work," Mat confirmed. "You still good to watch Lizzie on the 18th?"

Vinnie nodded and took a drink from the bottle of water he'd retrieved from the package on the floor. "I took the weekend off. You gonna manage to pull off the proposal this time?"

"Who's Anna?"

Vinnie nearly spat out his water as Rex asked. He looked over to his uncle, who was holding the white business card in his hand. It must have fallen out of his pocket when he pulled out his phone. "Umm."

"I'm sorry, did you lose track of time because of a date?" Mat snickered.

"She's no one," Vinnie sputtered and rushed to get out of his chair, "and I'm certainly not dating her. I'm going to change before you both leave."

Rex offered him the card as he walked by. "Don't lose that now."

"Shut up."

Chapter 2: First Chapter Estblish

Anna Is Not A Side Character

March 18th; 266 Days Until…

Vinnie parallel parked his car with relative ease. One of the perks of a sports car vs the four-door boat his brother drove. He loved a classic car as much as the next guy, but the amenities of a modern vehicle had won him over despite the crap he got at home about it. This entire block was dark, but it wasn't flooded so he'd take the win on that one. *Maybe that's why her office number hadn't connected?*

"We ged huss-EL-ing, yes?" his niece questioned from the backseat.

He looked back at Lizzie, a smile forming on his lips despite his present discomfort. "Well, yes. But when we execute this plan, it needs to run as smoothly as possible. So we need to be on our best behavior and there is no room for improvisation. Do we have an understanding?"

"Oh yay! Leds go! We do it!" she squealed, her black curls already a mess. She kicked her legs excitedly.

"Alright." He climbed out of the car and settled Lizzie on his hip. "Let's go see Miss Anna."

He felt like an idiot. He should have called her and rescheduled, but somehow it had slipped his mind. Now after attempting to call several times and getting no answer, he was forced to stop by the publishing office to try and explain the situation to Anna in person. He paused, the windows of the office were darkened. That wasn't a good sign, but he was already here so might as well try.

"Okee, okee." Lizzie pushed her black sunglasses up on her nose, which she insisted on wearing despite the rain.

He walked into the building and paused, letting his lenses adjust to the darker light. "I can handle this."

"Uncle Vee-Nee."

"Yes, Lizzie?"

"Is okee, I says so."

"Only because you said so." He kissed the side of her head and let himself into the dark office. "Hello?"

"Thank god, this whole side of the building is out and…" Anna's assistant came around the corner, holding a cellphone she was obviously using as a flashlight.

Vinnie couldn't remember her name, but he recognized her face. He normally remembered names, but his memory of being here last time was consumed with talking about his book and Anna.

She sighed as they made eye contact, "Not the power guy."

"No, unfortunately not."

"I Lizzie!" his niece volunteered, taking off her glasses and handing them over to him. "Hello, Miss Anna!"

"Well hi, cutie-pie. I'm Miss Alysha, but Miss Anna is here. Is that who your daddy is looking for?"

Vinnie wasn't stupid, Alysha was talking to Lizzie, but that question was for him. "This is Lizzie, my niece. And yes, I am looking for Anna. I tried to call both the office and her cellphone, but I didn't have any luck."

"Her phone is sitting in a bowl of rice. She had an interesting trip back yesterday, to say the least. I'll see if she can see you." Alysha disappeared into Anna's office.

"She find Anna?" Lizzie asked.

"I think so. Then we'll go have lunch."

"Oh YESH! Cwackers, pease!" She grinned broadly.

Vinnie adjusted her on his hip, "I think we can do something like that." If you called the food you put in front of her whatever-crackers, she'd at least attempt to eat it. Kass had started it when Lizzie got food fussy last month, and it worked. Most of the time.

Anna came out of her office dressed in a pale pink suit, her hair piled up in curls, and her make-up was clearly done for an evening event. He recognized a one-hour make-up look when he saw it.

"Mr. Goodroe, my apologies for not reaching out sooner. It's been a day and I'm afraid I'll have to reschedule our meeting. I…"

"Miss ANNA!" Lizzie waved empathically, nearly knocking off his glasses. "We finds you!"

"Easy there, Nugget." He straightened his glasses and confirmed to Anna. "I can see you have your hands full. I forgot that I have company this afternoon. So I was attempting to reschedule as well."

Anna's expression was neutral and he wasn't sure what to make of it. Maybe she was stressed by whatever was going on before he got here?

"Well between the day I've had and your company. Why don't we make this easier on ourselves and reschedule for the same time next week? When we get power back, I'll update the appointment."

"That sounds like a plan," he confirmed, then addressed his niece, "Say goodbye to Miss Anna and Miss Alysha."

"No come with us?" Lizzie questioned.

"No, they have things to do here."

"Okee. Bye-Bye!"

His hand was on the doorknob as Alysha started speaking to Anna. "The locksmith just texted me, he says it's going to be at least two hours until he can get over here."

"I'm going to have to buy a new dress for tonight, I don't have time for this. This has been the worst 48 hours of my life. How could I have been so stupid? Locking myself out," Anna huffed, the frustration clear in her voice.

Vinnie opened the door. *Normal people don't know how to pick locks.* Only locksmiths picked locks and weren't seen as criminals. He didn't want to out himself as a former criminal. He wanted to work with Anna. He didn't want to be known for past mistakes. He wanted to move forward.

"We go lunch?" Lizzie interrupted his thoughts. No doubt drawing attention to the fact that he was still standing in the doorway.

He spun around before he could stop himself. "If you locked your keys in your car, I can probably help. I have a tool in my car."

Both women were now staring at him like he had a red flag inked on his shirt. He should have kept his stupid mouth shut. Alysha recovered quicker. "She locked herself out of her apartment, not her car."

"I can still help. I have tools for that too." Vinnie had to physically restrain himself from slapping his forehead. Step one of not looking like a criminal: don't tell people that you own lock picking tools. Step two: remember step fucking one. He elaborated, "My brother and I locked ourselves out of the house all the time when we were kids. Learning how to pick locks was a survival skill of sorts."

"Goodroe Chime Schools. Ged ins and outs." Lizzie 'helped' by mimicking what she'd heard at the dinner table. He had never wished for her vocabulary to be limited, until right now.

"We like gangster movies." His ears were hot. He had to get out of here. *Why had he opened his mouth?*

Anna looked at Alysha then back at him. "You really think you can help me?"

"Yes. Or I can at least try. Save you from having to buy a dress when it sounds like you already have one." He managed to keep an even tone. "I can follow you home and give it a try."

"I live upstairs. The building has apartments on the upper floors." Anna pointed up.

"I'll go get my kit and be right back." He ducked out of the office, and while he couldn't hear what was being said, he knew the two women were definitely talking about him.

He unlocked his car and sat Lizzie down on the passenger seat while he retrieved the kit from the glove box.

"We go lunch now?" She inclined her head to the side.

"Soon. I need you to be patient for me, okay?" He stretched himself over the seat and snagged a package of crackers from her bag.

"Okee!"

He slipped the kit into his pocket and handed Lizzie the snack before hoisting her back up onto his hip. "Let's go help Miss Anna."

He let himself back into the office, and Alshya immediately *requested*, "Cell phone number, please." He relayed it and she texted him to confirm. "Make sure she calls me before you leave."

He nodded. Fully understanding the thinly veiled threat. He worked with mostly female-identifying persons, and he knew the rules about going somewhere with a man and the potential risks.

Anna came around the corner with a folder and a notebook in hand. "The elevator on the other side of the building is working. We'll take that up." She glanced back at her assistant. "I'll talk to you soon."

"Yup."

Lizzie was crinkling the package in her hands, babbling about her favorite colors. Vinnie was glad she was with him, she made him look like less of a threat.

Anna's heels made a staccato rhythm as they passed through the hallway. She was taller than he'd first assessed when they'd met two weeks ago, in heels she was taller than he was. She had to be six feet tall at least. *Why was he examining her like this? Stop it.*

She paused at the welcome desk and the doorman recognized her, calling the elevator down. When they stepped into the space she explained, "You have to have a key to access the elevator and stairway."

"Safe building." He nodded, watching her hit the button for the 31st floor. There was a stairway adjacent to the elevator with no keypad. The building was as safe as avoiding the guy at the desk and being unable to pick a lock. So safe enough in this neighborhood.

"WEE!" Lizzie giggled as the elevator ascended to almost the top floor.

Anna laughed. "I suppose it is fun, isn't it?"

"Oh yesh! We meets!" Lizzie held out her hand to Anna over him. "Hello I is Lizzie and you is Miss Anna."

Anna shook her little hand as she smiled. "It's nice to meet you, Lizzie. Are you on an adventure with your uncle today?"

"Uh-huh! Mommy and Daddy is gones on trip. Gan'pa Rex is homes for stories."

"That sounds like a lot of fun." Anna's expression changed and as the door opened she asked him, "Is the book you wrote based on a true story?"

"True-ish." He smirked without intending to.

"That's why you want to keep it a secret." She deduced, motioning for him to follow.

Lizzie's fingers gripped at his shirt and he glanced down noticing that her eyes had gone huge. "Monssers?"

"No. No, monsters." He flicked his wrist, turning on the flashlight app on his phone, and handed it to her. "Here you keep that."

"Okee." She nodded, shining it directly in his eyes almost immediately.

"Point it down, please," he directed. He caught up to Anna and set Lizzie on the ground. "Hold Miss Anna's hand."

"Miss Anna! I scares away Monssers!"

"Oh, thank you so much."

The lock wasn't anything fancy, just a pin and tumbler. No codes or other complications. Should be simple enough. He just needed to fill in the gaps between the pin gaps and the sheerline. He slipped his torsion wrench and go-to three ridge rake out of his small kit and tapped his foot for a rhythm. His jaw twitched, he hadn't picked a lock since he quit smoking, it felt off to not having something in his mouth. Not wanting to put the only pen he had on him in his mouth, he settled for one of the other rakes. He kept the light pressure on the wrench as he moved the rake back and forth. It would have been easier to concentrate if Lizzie wasn't randomly shining the light into his eyes. His tongue flicked the rake up against his teeth, mirroring the tools in the lock. Tap. Tap. Tap. Click.

The cylinder turned and the lock released. "There you are."

Relief flooded Anna's features. "You are a lifesaver! Thank you so much! Let me go grab my purse."

Vinnie was going to argue what was likely an attempt to pay him, but Lizzie interrupted.

"I hava potty."

He grimaced. "Are you sure?"

"Yes."

He sighed. Lizzie was so young that by the time she asked that, it was an emergency. Of course, she had to pee.

Anna appeared back in the doorway. "There's nothing useful in my purse. I don't even know why I did that. I…What's wrong?"

"I hava potty." Lizzie explained, wiggling restlessly.

Anna opened her door, beckoning them inside. "Come on in, my bathroom's right here."

He took his phone from Lizzie and handed it to Anna as he picked up his niece and went through the door Anna indicated. He settled Lizzie on the toilet, thankful they'd made it in time.

"I do good."

"Sure did." He got her cleaned up, washed her hands, and set her on her feet so he could wash his own. The sink was cluttered with skincare products, make-up, and…

"Issa pwincess dess!"

Vinnie doubted he'd ever moved faster, sweeping Lizzie up into his arms and making her giggle as he kept her from touching the ball gown hanging on a hook on the wall.

"Is peddy." Lizzie pointed at the dress.

He used a towel to dry their hands. The dress looked to be made of silk in various shades of green, the shoulder strap was adorned with pink flowers. This wasn't a cheap dress. It was couture, but not a designer he recognized. "It's a very pretty dress."

Vinnie looked around the bathroom again, noticing the size and design. This wasn't a cookie cutter apartment bathroom, it had been intentionally designed. The counters were higher than the standard, and the floor tiles were heated. He wasn't aware editors were paid that well. Maybe he should think about doing that instead of writing.

"We're going to say goodbye to Miss Anna, then go home. Okay?"

"Noes we geds cwackers!"

Vinnie opened the door. "Sure. We can do that."

"Everything okay?" Anna was holding out his phone and Lizzie held out her hands.

"Oh, thanks you. Hi Mommy!" The toddler took the phone from Anna, then waved at his phone.

Vinnie shifted Lizzie on his hip. "Yes, we're good. Thank you for letting us use your bathroom."

"Thank you for getting me into my apartment."

Rain hit against the windows, and Vinnie glanced into the apartment to see the floor-to-ceiling windows. Thunder clapped and Lizzie squealed happily.

"Is fi-works!!"

"Well, at least she isn't scared." Anna chuckled.

"She isn't scared of much." He shifted on his feet and realized that he needed to leave and get out of Anna's hair. "We'll get out of here and let you get ready for your event."

"Well, I have significantly more time now. I have access to my things."

"That does help."

Neither of them moved any closer to the door or further into the apartment. He should go. She should want him to go. Had her mentioning more time been an offer to stay longer? That would be odd; wouldn't it? He should leave. Lizzie needed food and to go to bed at a decent hour. He should leave.

"I feel bad that I don't have any cash to pay you. I can order us dinner on my tablet. I don't have to leave for three hours and I haven't eaten today. Alysha keeps reminding me that coffee isn't food. What are you in the mood for? Or should I ask Miss Lizzie?"

"We don't want to cause a problem."

"It wouldn't be a problem at all. If you don't want to stay though, I completely understand."

"Are we having an 'after you' escalation?"

Anna laughed. "I think we are. Come in and sit, we can review what you sent me last week. It's the least I can do."

He nodded and followed her further into the apartment. It was clearly designed for a single adult. The windows extended the length of the entire wall and partially around the adjoining wall, giving a panoramic view of the city skyline. It had a vaulted ceiling, high enough that it looked like it could have had an additional floor, and a wide, gray sectional by a line of bookshelves Vinnie sat with Lizzie, who immediately bailed out of his arms to press her face to the glass.

"Isso high!"

He leaned over her shoulder. "It is, isn't it."

"Any requests for dinner?" Anna sat in the recliner across from them with a tablet in her hands.

He didn't know why it caught his eye, but the chair she was sitting in wasn't the same shade of gray as the sectional he was on. For an apartment so impeccably styled with such a modern skew, it seemed odd that the colors wouldn't match exactly. Looking beyond her, he could see there was a set of stairs that led up to the partial second floor, but no wall to block it off. The layout was odd, it felt like something from Europe maybe?

He turned his attention back before he went any further down that rabbit hole. "As long as it resembles chicken nuggets or crackers in some regard, she'll be good. And I'm fine with most anything as long as it isn't tofu trying to be something other than tofu."

"Spicy food alright?"

"For me." He nodded, and Anna started swiping on her tablet.

"I have something in mind."

Lizzie excitedly pointed to the window again, blabbing about how small things were below, and successfully keeping his phone hostage.

After the food arrived, Anna retrieved a blanket that they laid over the couch so they could limit Lizzie's mess.

"Like headens!" The little girl chewed on the piece of chicken.

Struggling a bit with the chopsticks, Vinnie took a bite of the spiced, crispy tofu. "I feel like you ordered this to prove a point."

"Probably." Anna smirked effortlessly using her chopsticks to take another bite. "So, I have to ask and I'll be careful with our audience, but I need to clarify a few things."

He took a long drink from the coffee she'd given him and made an affirming sound.

"Hi Mommy! Oh hi's DADDY!" Lizzie flattened her hand against his phone again, then kissed the dark screen. He'd already explained to Anna about Lizzie's fascination with phones.

"So the novel is about your brother, his wife, and little miss there?"

"There are some similarities. One of those truths is stranger than the fictionalization. I started writing it, and it was done before I realized it."

"You need to get more distance from it. Think of the characters as separate entities rather than who inspired them."

"To make cuts."

"To add a bedroom scene."

Vinnie choked on his bite. "Fade to black is a perfectly valid way to handle a scene like that. In fact..."

Anna cleared her throat. "You aren't going to explain writing statistics to someone in publishing, are you?"

"No, that would be very stupid." Oh, he almost had, though. Sometimes his mouth overrode his brain; always got him in trouble.

"Fading to black is valid, in a cleaner book. But if you want to keep the *colorful* language, you need to have the pay-off scene." She shifted her tablet on the arm of her chair. "If you truly want to keep it away from your family. It's going to make marketing difficult."

"I have co-workers, and I'm sure they would be willing to help."

"If you're marketing your romance book with dancers, you really can't fade to black."

Vinnie arched his eyebrow. "Did we talk about that?"

"No. But one of the documents that you signed at our first meeting, consented to a background check."

"I should have read that more carefully." He shifted. That explained the longer looks that Alysha had given him. Well, that saved the awkward conversation of explaining that he was a criminal. Juvenile records were sealed, so...

"I like to be thorough; I have to protect my company's reputation. Honestly, it gave me pause, but I think having a gun you weren't supposed to have isn't the end of the world. I'm surprised you did any time for it here in Texas, to be honest."

Vinnie shifted in his seat. "It was…I think the best way to describe the whole situation was the wrong place, wrong time and a sister-in-law who didn't understand her right to remain silent."

"From the transcripts, it seemed like she was more focused on self-preservation."

"You have no idea the accuracy of that statement. It took discipline not to have the character based on her meet a tragic end."

"What happened to her?"

Vinnie shrugged. "Don't know and don't particularly care."

Anna took a sip of her multi-colored drink. "Fair enough. To be honest, I Googled you and you've been mentioned in a few articles about the Playhouse. It seems like a fascinating place."

"Let me know if you want a tour, I'd be happy to guide you."

Lizzie yawned and Vinnie noticed that she'd sprawled out on the floor, now barely awake. If he kept talking with Anna for a few more minutes, she'd probably stay asleep through the drive home.

Anna seemed to have followed his eye line and nodded, seeming to pick up on his thought. "The only major thing that concerns me about the book is the one-night stand thing has been done a lot. But the rest of it is amazing."

"Well, this is a case where facts are stranger than fiction."

She looked curiously at him, "Can you elaborate?"

"If you want the technical explanation, my brother's ex-wife caused his now girlfriend to become pregnant with his kid despite the fact that the one-night stand he had was with this ex-wife."

Anna blinked, then blinked again. "What?"

He chuckled. "It's a long story."

"I think I need to hear it. We should have dinner tomorrow night."

"Sounds like a plan."

March 19th; 265 Days Until…

Anna was drained. There had to be a better, more accurate word, but all she could come up with was drained. She was jet lagged, and had she been a phone, the light in her eyes would have been flashing at 1%.

Resisting the urge to lean on, the wall but still closing her eyes, she jumped as the elevator dinged announcing she'd reached her floor.

She retrieved her keys from her clutch and swept out of the elevator into the hallway, finding herself face to face with Vincent Goodroe. Her eyebrow arched as she assessed her situation. A man who knew she didn't have a working phone and picked the lock on her apartment door earlier that day, got by her building's security, and was standing in the hallway on the floor where only her apartment was.

The regret of not getting a room at the hotel where the event had been held was mounting very quickly.

He'd seemed so normal, despite the criminal record. She only had prepper spray in her purse. Would that be enough if she had completely misread him?

Needing to buy time and further analyze the situation, she inclined her head to the side and tried to disguise her concern. "Oh, hello?"

"Hi."

There was a long pause as neither of them knew how to proceed. Vincent cleared his throat. "This is awkward."

"Considering how things went earlier today, yes, it is."

"I'm sorry, I had an odd evening and I impulsively drove up here. I was about to knock, thought better of it, and I was going to leave, but now you're here in front of me and I can't escape." His mannerisms were nothing short of an awkward panic.

He was worried he was going to scare her, and it put her more at ease considering their prior interactions. Once inside, however, she was going to use her tablet to message Alysha about Vinnie simply showing up. Anna wasn't stupid. On the other hand, she was aching for contact, and he was an attractive, interesting person. Perhaps this evening could end on a higher note than it started on?

"It sounds like you had an evening like my last 48 hours. Come in, we'll have a drink."

"Are you sure?" He looked startled.

"Are we going to play this again?"

"No, after you."

Anna unlocked her door and slipped off her shoes, and he followed suit as they stepped inside. "The dress is a rental. Give me a moment to change, go make yourself comfortable."

She'd changed in the bathroom, so she took off her dress and changed back into her suit. If she hadn't been so all over the place today, she would have put on her robe, gone upstairs, and gotten comfortable. This would have to do for now.

As she pulled the hairpins out of her updo, she heard the thump-thud of Jackal descending the stairs. Anna finished with the pins and grabbed her brush as she leaned out of the bathroom to see her little black cat jumping up on the chaise with Vincent.

"Hi there." He greeted her.

"Jackal, don't be a pest." Anna continued to brush out her hair. "Sorry, she's excited to be home after being boarded. I was planning on whiskey for my drink. Do you have a brand preference? Or can I get you something else?"

"She's fine. I think she's trying to be friends. I think tea might be the way to go, I don't want to stay all night and impose."

"Honestly, I'd like some company."

"You might not after I tell you why I came." He scratched under Jackal's chin.

Anna didn't like the sound of that, but maybe it was something simple. If she went off his writing style, he was an overthinker. "That bad, huh? Did your family find out what you've been up to?"

"Not exactly."

Anna pulled down two glasses and retrieved a bottle of whiskey. Ice cubes clattered loudly against the crystal drinkware in the quiet apartment as she prepared their drinks. She handed him one glass and sat at the far end of the sectional, quickly messaging Alysha with her tablet. "And on that cryptic note, I think you should have that drink and explain."

"They think we're dating and I didn't correct them." He closed his eyes, likely waiting for her to freak out.

She paused before saying anything at first, rolling the logistics around in her head. This was a good thing in disguise. Vincent didn't want his family to know about the book, so if they were dating, it would explain the time they would be spending together. Anna didn't want to deal with the upcoming year of attending parties, making small talk, and dodging unwanted advances. Vinnie by comparison, was a breath of fresh air. They could help each other out and both win. She couldn't keep the grin off her face. "I think it's a fantastic idea."

He looked unhappy about her answer. "I suppose it is a funny joke."

Why did men so often think that if a plan wasn't theirs, it wasn't a good one? "I'm not joking. I think letting the outside world think we're dating is a great idea. It will explain why you're spending time with me without admitting to the book." She took a long drink from her glass and itched Jackal's ears. "What?"

"I'm not sure what you would get out of it." He looked genuinely confused.

Anna pursed her lips, trying to think of how to explain this without sounding desperate or pathetic. "By this time next year, I want to travel and spend time at the international publishing houses my company is linked to. Starting this summer, I'm going to be part of six imprints launches and that's a lot of parties, meetings, and trips. It would be convenient for me to have someone on my arm."

He swirled the drink in his hand, clinking the ice. "I'm not especially social, I'm odd."

"You're going to be selling a book. Some social energy is required and being with me would open doors. Also for the record, you aren't the bad kind of odd."

Vincent cleared his throat, "My family is a lot."

"My company contacts are a lot."

He blinked. "The Pretty Woman scenario, so to speak."

Anna smiled behind her glass, "If you want to phrase it that way, I think it fits. And in more ways than one, if you want. Let me go get changed into something comfortable and we'll figure out the details."

"Are you sure about this?"

"Vincent, if I'm not sure, I don't ask."

He leaned back and finished his glass. "You can call me Vinnie."

"Alright then."

Vinnie explained that one of the times his niece had been talking to his phone, she had actually unlocked it and Facetimed her parents. They hadn't been able to hear Anna and Vinnie's conversation but assumed by their body language that they were dating. When Vinnie tried to explain the truth, they thought he was deflecting. His intent of coming here had been to see if she would play along with the rouse then thought better of it. Had she come home any later, she would have missed him and she was glad she hadn't. Vinnie seemed shy with her despite the fact that he worked at a strip club. *Was he awkward there as well? Or was it her?*

He was animated and articulate as he told stories – even if he stretched things out by adding random trivia to *enhance* what he was talking about. After the third story about one of his family's adventures with Lizzie, Anna decided that they were going to have to do major rewrites to the book. Vinnie had written to the style he had read, not what was in his head. The flashes of his real voice that she'd taken notice of were the moments he let himself speak authentically.

Anna couldn't contain her laughter despite how much her sides ached. One quick glance at the clock on the wall revealed it to be well past 2 A.M. She couldn't remember the last time she'd lost track of time talking to someone. What had started as a very awkward meeting in her building's hallway had turned into one of the best nights she'd had in a long time.

"I don't think he can blame her for not hearing him, she'd just had a baby."

"It's not a blame thing. He just can't figure out how to get around himself. Mat's so worried that Kass will say no for some reason that he keeps sabotaging himself." Vinnie shifted on the chaise as he continued to explain. "Part of it is a bit sexist. He's a mechanic and doesn't make that much. He's worried that he won't be able to take care of them. But I'm working on that."

"Sounds like you two are close."

"I'd be lying if I said no. Our parents are both gone so he and my Uncle Rex were my only family for the longest time. Kass came in like a hurricane, but she and Lizzie have made his and our lives better."

"It's good you had family to take you in." Anna ran her hand over Jackal's back. The cat had fallen asleep in her lap. His life was so entwined with his family, and she wasn't jealous, but she wondered what that must be like from a practical standpoint. She hadn't cohabited with anyone in the last four years. The way he described the chaos in his house it sounded overwhelming, but not unpleasant. Sitting like this with someone and talking through the events of a day held a measure of appeal in contrast to her daily solitude.

"Technically, Rex was a friend of my mother's, and he worked with my father. So while we're not related by blood, I couldn't have been raised better," Vinnie corrected. "Something your background check wouldn't have uncovered would be my parent's criminal history. There probably isn't much out there about my mother in general, but my father wasn't good, even by criminal standards. He…he just wasn't good."

He rolled his shoulders as if trying to rid himself of tension. Anna made a mental note not to bring up his father unless absolutely necessary. Even his voice had changed, his conversational tone had shifted to dark and stressed. His lack of elaboration led her to make assumptions likely an abuse situation.

Anna twisted her earring. *Stop letting your imagination run away with you.*

"Well, then your uncle deserves a lot of credit; you're wonderful."

Vinnie cleared his throat and rubbed his glasses on his shirt. "I don't know about all of that. I'm useful though."

"I said what I said." Anna smiled. She noticed his cheeks had flushed slightly. He was nervous at the compliment. Did that not happen often? He was clearly attractive. She thought he was good-looking the first time she saw him. The way he spoke and wrote only made him more interesting.

She felt comfortable around Vinnie, he wasn't the type of guy who'd send insulting messages if she didn't respond quickly enough. Even as they sat on her chaise together laughing and talking, he didn't force his way into her space.

Logic demanded that she get some sleep and continue their 'relationship' planning in a day or two, but the rest of her wanted him to stay and not for conversation.

"I should go," Vinnie offered, stretching his arms over his head.

He caught her off guard, and she had this sudden urge to prevent him from leaving. "Not unless you're calling a ride-share. You've had too much to drink."

"Neither of us has had a drink in over an hour and it's almost three. Plus, it's too late for me to be here."

Anna looked at her clock again. No wonder her eyes were burning. Her contacts had been in for almost 24 hours. "It's been so long since I've enjoyed another person's company this much."

He nodded. "I completely agree."

She excused herself to go to the bathroom and took out her contacts after washing her hands. Thankfully, she didn't need her glasses to functionally see, only for reading and fine details. The outfit she was wearing was about as casual as it got — black yoga pants and her White Sox T-shirt, but her undergarments closely matched the dress she'd worn earlier. She didn't think that Vinnie would try to peek at her when she changed, but there wasn't a wall to block off the view of her lofted bedroom. She considered washing off her make-up again, but she was worried about what she looked like under the make-up.

Anna opened the door to find Vinnie putting on his shoes.

"I figured I'd just let myself out. You've had a long couple of days, probably need sleep."

She touched his shoulder. "If you want to stay, you're welcome to. I'd love the company actually. We can talk upstairs."

Vinnie stumbled back and laughed nervously. "I'm gonna head home. You have a great night, and I'll call you tomorrow."

Anna didn't even have time to respond to his retreat before he'd ducked out of her door, still putting on his second shoe as the door closed behind him.

"I mean, email. I'll email you tomorrow," he called out before his footsteps sounded his retreat.

Jackal yowled from the kitchen, rubbing up against her cabinets and trying to get her attention.

"Jackal, I think you're going to have to wait. Your mother is going to have an existential crisis shower." Anna sighed, stripping as she plodded back into her bathroom. She had clearly gauged his interest in her inaccurately.

March 19th; 265 Days Until…

Vinnie let himself into the house through the patio door. He was going to grab something to eat then hide in his apartment. He didn't want to talk to anyone and felt like a complete moron.

"You're home very late."

Vinnie jumped at Kass' comment from the kitchen table. He looked past her to see if anyone else was there. "Is everyone up or just you?"

"Just me. Lizzie had a nightmare. All she wants is Daddy, but that's normal at her age and Mat's a pushover." She highlighted a line in her textbook.

He chuckled in agreement and leaned against the kitchen island. "I thought you finished your last class."

"I have NCLEX testing, then my licensing, and *then* I'm done."

"You should probably try and go back to sleep. I believe the plan was for you to take a break this weekend." He fished his keys out of his pocket and set them on the counter.

Kass capped her highlighter. "I slept half the day away. I can nap in the afternoon if I get tired."

"I don't think I've seen you nap since before Lizzie was born."

"You didn't know me before Lizzie."

"Are you implying that you napped before we met?" He quirked his eyebrow.

Kass laughed. "No, not at all."

"Good. I'da called you a liar." He snagged an apple and a water bottle. He should get out of the house and to his apartment above the garage before Kass circled back to the time and why he'd only just gotten home.

"I should probably make breakfast." Kass sighed. "Lizzie will be up by six anyway."

He hesitated. If he stayed and helped Kass would likely make one of her fantastic breakfasts, but he also didn't want to get cornered again. "I can start coffee for you. You want the fancy stuff?"

"Yes, please. I'm bummed Mat and I didn't get to have our breakfast on the beach. He was all about it."

Vinnie was glad he had his back turned to hide his smirk. "On the beach is the only time he likes mornings, otherwise he whines."

"I think he had other things on his mind." Kass opened the pantry across from the kitchen, probably looking for ingredients. "He was in jittery mode."

"When is he not?" Vinnie filled the coffee pot with water.

"True. So back to it, why are you home so late?" Kass pushed herself up on the island to sit, swinging her legs in the open space next to him.

"I thought we were picking on my brother."

"He's not awake and *you* are trying to distract me." She grinned, "So about this new girlfriend? You never gave us a straight answer. I already texted Violet to see if she worked at the Playhouse."

"No dating policy there," he reminded her.

What felt like a lifetime ago, he'd taken Kass with him to borrow Leila's wife's truck to set up a surprise for his brother's birthday. *His life was far too entangled.*

"Right, one of the many off-limits D's," she said before laughing as he attempted to disguise his own laughter. "Crap. I'm more tired than I realize if I'm making jokes like that."

"More like you've been around us far too long," Vinnie teased, starting the coffee machine. "What would your father say?"

"Daddy's heard worse. Gram talked worse than that all the time."

"Should we make one of her rated-R recipes?" One more attempt to distract Kass.

"Maybe, but I still want to know who your girlfriend is. Mat says Leila was your last girlfriend, which was before we even met," Kass prodded, before switching to bargain mode. "I'll make Creamy-Nut Waffles if you give me details."

"I wouldn't tell Mat about who I date; I like my privacy. And no fair, tempting me with waffles. Besides, I think I've already ruined my chance before it went anywhere." He moved to leave the kitchen, but Kass hopped down and got in front of him. "Sister Christian, I am tired. I watched your kiddo yesterday and I still haven't slept."

She cocked her head to the side, "Vinnie, I was just picking on you. I'm sorry. What happened?

"Don't worry about it." He took a step back and took a bite from his apple. "Things would have crashed and burned at some point. I'm not the guy women text their friends about meeting."

Vinnie had described Kass as 'small but mighty' more than once, and to be fair, her five feet and four inches versus his six feet and two inches made her small by comparison.

She hugged him, "Don't sell yourself short. You are great. If I wasn't in love with Mat, I'd text my friends about you."

He hugged her back, before stepping out of her space. "Thanks, Kass. I'm pretty sure ducking and running from a sexual advance puts a nail in the coffin."

She folded her arms over her chest, "If you weren't ready to sleep with her, then you shouldn't. Why wouldn't you be allowed to make that decision? And if you say because you're the guy…"

"I yield. I yield." He held up his hands. "Kass, she was obviously too tired and we'd both been drinking. But I was literally putting on my shoes as I was running out the door. I told her I'd email her, in the hallway."

"Oh yeah, you're never getting into her bed or anything else." Mat chuckled, plodding out of the hallway.

"Mathew." Kass gasped and pointed to her own ears.

"She's still sleeping and none of those words were bad." His brother brushed by him and picked Kass up by the waist flipping her up onto his shoulder.

"Mat! Where are we going?" she squealed.

"Back to bed. The monster is back in her bed and I was supposed to get a weekend with you. I'm gonna steal the time I can. Say goodnight."

"It's morning," she argued as the door closed behind them.

Vinnie shook his head. He was glad his brother was happy, but sometimes he wished he didn't live under the same roof. One of these days, he needed to move out, but that would leave Rex alone. Mat and Kass were moving as soon as she decided on one of the three jobs she'd been provisionally offered. Leave it to Kass to make friends in nursing school, something that would lead to premium employment post-graduation.

He checked his phone and noticed the email that had come in from Anna. It was simple: a meeting time, place, and Monday's date. Well, that was likely the end of even the chance to work with her. *So much for that.* Another had popped into his email as he was reading the first one, it was Anna again, correcting the date to Sunday.

Or maybe not.

Whatever was happening on Sunday, he needed to get some sleep. He switched off the coffeemaker before slipping out the patio door, making his way to his small apartment. He liked that he had space from the rest of the crazy but was close enough to help if needed. After his shower, he grabbed his phone to set the alarm and saw the unopened text.

Leila: Can you come in tonight? No manager for the 2nd floor event. Starts at 10.

Vinnie: Sure. But I'm not staying for clean-up

Leila: Thank you Vincent.

Putting the phone on the charger, he rolled over to sleep. It wouldn't be that long of a shift. Just a couple of hours.

March 19th; 265 Days Until...

Anna woke up to a yowling cat and her front door unlocking. Her head wasn't hurting, due to the water she drank after Vinnie left, but she really needed to pee.

"If anyone is naked up there, warn me or put on clothes," Alysha called out from below. "Hi Jackal, there's a sweet-girl. Where's your momma, huh? Still in bed?"

Anna grumbled and pulled the covers over her face before forcing herself to get up and out of bed. She put on her hoodie and plodded down the stairs, raising a hand towards Alysha before ducking into the bathroom.

"I have breakfast and an interesting tidbit. Preston from the local news left three messages on the office line. *After* the party."

She heard Alysha moving in the kitchen. The layout of her apartment made it easier to hear everything that happened in it. After washing her face and brushing out her hair, she dared to leave the bathroom. "Thank you for bringing me breakfast. You aren't supposed to work on Saturdays. Why are you here?"

"Good Morning to you too. Have coffee, be a human." Alysha handed her a cup of iced coffee and strode into the living room, making herself at home. "Why is that Preston guy calling? Did something happen?"

Anna scrunched up her nose as she sat down. "Not recently. We've been strictly business for years."

"So you weren't at one point? How do I not know that you dated that walking country club advertisement? He's all red flags."

"Still colorblind." Anna deadpanned.

Alysha called her out, "But you *can* see red."

"Apparently, I couldn't see it that day." Anna took a long drink, relishing the cool liquid. "To clarify, I didn't date him. I slept with him once, it was a mistake, and it was years ago. It was right after Sincere and I went our separate ways. I was not in a good place."

"I remember that, I met you right after she left you."

"*They,* and we're still acquaintances."

"Sorry, my bad." Alysha apologized before continuing with her reason for being there. "Your phone is officially dead, the rice didn't work. I thought you'd want to get it replaced before Monday. Also, I wanted to talk to you about the *other* guy from last night. Or, *very* early this morning technically. I'm gonna need all of the tea on that."

Anna buried her face in her hands and groaned. "It was a spectacular debacle. After being awake for over twenty-four hours I thought it would be a good idea to throw myself at him."

"What? You did not!"

"I certainly did." She sipped from the straw. "He practically ran out the door. It was mortifying. I'm meeting him tomorrow to save face and derail what was a stupid plan anyway."

Alysha folded her legs under her to sit criss-cross. "What plan?"

"His niece turned on his phone when he helped me get into my apartment and now his family thinks we're dating. Originally, I told him I'd play along to help him work on his book without them knowing, and in return, he'd be on my arm for all the events for the rest of the year."

Alysha blinked several times before breaking out into laughter. "You were going to do like, Decoy Bride?"

"Essentially, yes. Not that it matters. I don't think I could look him in the eye now." She retrieved her tablet and scheduled an appointment to replace her phone.

"So you aren't going forward with the book?"

"The book." Anna closed her eyes and let out a long breath. "I still want the book. It'll sell, and once changes are made, it'll sell better. The real story is far crazier than what he wrote."

She arched her eyebrow, "I read the first three chapters, it's immediately a lot. It's crazier than that? Are you meeting him on Monday? I can log it into the system for you."

"I emailed him to see him on Sunday. Did I tell you he co-owns the Playhouse?"

"The what?"

"It's a strip club on the east side of town."

"I'm gonna repeat...the what? The hot guy who writes books, picks locks, obviously loves kids, and is a former criminal co-owns a strip club? I'm not sure if we've fallen into mafia romance or Rated-R Hallmark territory." Alysha picked up Jackal. "Wait a minute you tried to sleep with him after all of that fussing when y'all met?"

"Yes, but it doesn't matter. I'm not going to embarrass myself again. He clearly wasn't interested." Anna took a bite of pastry. "I can handle things myself today. You don't need to waste your Saturday."

"You don't have any ID or credit cards. Any word from the airport?"

"Yes, they successfully found my empty wallet. I can't believe I got pickpocketed at an airport of all places. It's going to be a pain in the ass to get my ID's back. I looked everywhere and I don't have a copy of my birth certificate anymore. My driver's license will just be money, but the passport is going to be difficult."

Alysha tapped her phone. "I don't think you have any upcoming international travel plans. So you won't have to rush that one. But you should get dressed so we can go get your new phone."

"And more coffee."

"Seriously? I'm glad you quit smoking, but you're gonna have a heart attack with all the caffeine in your system."

"I'll be fine. Thankfully, I have my company ID and one of my credit cards that I didn't take with me. I do need to replace some of the things I lost, if you have time to help."

"Sure thing. But you're gonna owe me more than dinner if I'm acting chauffeur all day."

"Whatever you want."

"Be careful throwing that phrase around, I still want more in my advertising budget."

"We'll see."

Chapter 3: Add Conflict

There Is A Lot Happening

April 22nd; 231 Days Until…

The bass from the music pulsed, but the closed door muffled the sound as Vinnie updated the budget spreadsheets with the food supply orders placed earlier today. He meant to finish this earlier, but he'd gotten distracted. He glanced at his phone and swiped away the incomplete meeting on his calendar. He'd rescheduled for the fifth time with Anna. He was a coward; he should just meet with her and cut his losses. He was embarrassed by the fact that he'd all but run out of her apartment and what he'd asked her to do. He'd also managed to avoid his family for most of the month, but the times he hadn't, they kept asking about his girlfriend. Mat was right about them all being too much in each other's business.

Vinnie took a drink from his coffee cup and pulled the notebook out of his pocket. He'd been trying to rewrite sections of the book according to the notes Anna made on the digital copy he'd given her. Why was he doing this? Her edits weren't relevant; he wasn't going to work with her. He'd ruined any potential chance of working with her, but he didn't want to see the door closed. He knew the meeting she was trying to have with him was just to let him know she didn't want to pursue things any further. He should go back to researching indie publishing.

It was almost ten, and he needed to walk the floor. He'd been up in the office for almost an hour. The security images didn't show anything outside of the ordinary, and with the second floor booked for a private event, it cut down on occupancy for the night. He should make an appearance at the party with the organizer; it was better for business. The office door opened as Dixon let herself in without knocking. He hated when she did that.

He held out his hand, assuming the reason for her intrusion. "What did you break?"

"I come in here when I don't break things," she defended, hands on her hips.

"*Who* did you break then? I'm not ready for another lawsuit. Please just come get me when clients get rowdy. I'm always going to take your side." He cleaned his glasses with the cloth on his desk.

"Rude. I promised you no more punching, and I meant it." She looked annoyed but continued with her reason for interrupting. "You have a guest asking for you at the bar, by name, and she just taught Becki how to make her a custom Soju drink."

"We just started carrying Soju, so it's not unusual that Becki doesn't have all the mixology knowledge on the drink yet. And it could be something that's only popular with the Kpop crowd."

"Did you miss the part where I said the *hot blonde* asked for you by name?"

"Didn't miss it, but you didn't give the prior physical descriptions of her." Vinnie stood up, twisting to crack his back. "Did she mention her name by chance?"

"Anna Kane." Dixon confirmed his suspicions.

Great. He motioned for Dixon to lead the way. "Fantastic. Let's go."

"Do you have a girlfriend we don't know about, Boss?"

"Don't start."

Dixon laughed and angled her head to look into the room. "Looks like a quiet group up here tonight."

"It's a sales meeting of sorts: adult entertainment products and furniture."

"Kinky."

He held the elevator door. "By definition, yes."

She examined her rose-gold flecked nails. "So any chance for money up there?"

"Not until after midnight."

"Lame. I got carpool duty tomorrow; gotta leave around eleven." They moved past the privacy curtain, and Dixon pointed to Anna sitting with her back to him.

Vinnie walked through the crowd, scanning to make sure everyone looked safe. The music was so much louder down here. It was too crowded on the floor, which was why he stayed upstairs whenever he could.

Perched up on a barstool, Anna animatedly talked with the head bartender, Becki. The mirrored backsplash was composed of mosaic tiles, so the reflection wasn't holistically accurate, but it was enough for him to assess that she hadn't come straight from her office. Anna's hair was down, but it had been curled.

She'd prepared to come to meet him here. Her outfit, hair, and make-up were club attire. In an odd way, it gave him the impression of armor as if getting his attention was her current battle. She was tired of being avoided, so now she was here with a sword and shield via golden highlighter and red lipstick. Maybe he was thinking too far into this?

"Good Evening, Vinnie." Becki grinned at him, her pink-lace bodysuit contrasted with the black leather harness over her chest. She'd been on a harness kick lately after they'd hosted an adults-only steampunk show last month.

"Good Evening indeed." Anna turned effortless to face him, offering a coy smile. "I finally caught up with you. Can we chat somewhere private, please?"

"Uh-oh, sounds like you're in trouble. Don't be too hard on him, hun. It's been a while since he had a girl in his life."

"She's..." Vinnie started to explain but Becki cut him off.

"She's sweet and has some great drink recipes. I think I could give Soju another shot and move some of that backstock with her tips." Becki motioned the glass in Anna's hand, before asking him. "Should I comp it?"

He nodded to Becki and offered his hand to Anna. He didn't want to have their chat here.

Anna handed Becki a bill, told her to keep it as a tip, and finished her drink. She took Vinnie's hand and allowed him to lead her.

He would have preferred the courtyard, but one of the doors was being replaced. Currently, the only way to get into the courtyard from inside of the club was to go through the dressing room. Vinnie wasn't going to lead her through the dressing room when she wasn't an employee; his employees deserved their privacy. The balcony upstairs would be quiet, but they'd be walking through the party and that might get awkward. Maybe he'd get lucky and the elevator would fail, and they'd end up in hospital instead. Then he'd be in a coma from his injuries and could avoid the situation as a whole.

Resigning himself, he decided the balcony was the better option. He activated the elevator with his phone and passcode, offering for Anna to enter first. Her dress was two-toned, a gray skirt with a pattern of silver sequins and a white top with a wide-open neck revealing a peek of her green lingerie. He averted his eyes, he hated being tall. It made him feel like a pervert.

"Are we going up, or is the elevator where you wanted to take me?" Anna interrupted his train of thought.

He muttered an apology and hit the second-floor button. The elevator lurched up, making Anna falter on her heels. He caught her arms before she actually fell, the fabric of her satin dress cool and soft.

Her hand was still on his chest when the elevator doors opened.

Miguel looked up from the security desk and smirked but didn't say anything.

"Sorry about that. I've had it looked at a dozen times, but sometimes it just has a mind of its own." This was embarrassing. He moved forward and was surprised when Anna slipped her hand into his. His face flushed at the casual contact, while Anna seemed unfazed occupying herself looking around the room.

"Lead the way." The lights caught her diamond earrings giving off a slight gray in the reflection; they were real. Fake diamonds would reflect rainbows in the light. It was an easy giveaway.

"My office is a little cramped, but there's a balcony up here. There's a party going on, so just excuse anything you see."

She laughed. "I'm not sheltered, and I was downstairs when you came to get me. Are the member's rules much different?"

It shouldn't have surprised him that she'd researched the club before showing up to find him. He doubted she left much to chance. "Private parties are more flexible, but the attendees have to sign a waiver for their guest to bypass the background check."

"You're very thorough."

"This is often dangerous work. I want my employees to be safe. They deserve to be safe." They passed by the bar and he nodded to the extra security on his way past.

"This would be a fun place for a launch party for an erotica book. I love the architecture, it reminds me of a speakeasy but it's more modern." She angled her head, examining the decor.

The room's aesthetic she was complimenting, was his design and the fact that she was on the nose about the speakeasy vibe gave him a sense of pride. It had taken him months to plan and execute the layout. This was his preferred floor of the club.

"There's the owner!" a jovial voice laced with a strong Texas drawl called out. "Vincent! Come over here and meet my better half."

To Vinnie's surprise, Anna kept holding his hand as he approached Sergio Vannicho, the organizer of this event and owner of an adult furniture company. Vinnie offered his hand as he greeted him. "Sergio, nice to see you."

Sergio shook Vinnie's hand and motioned to the tall, black man next to him. "This is Erik, my husband."

"Nice to meet you, Erik. Make sure to keep Sergio on a leash, he kept trying to go over budget for this event." Vinnie winced, instantly regretting his phrasing.

"He's only on the leash in the bedroom, but believe me, I know he runs expensive." Erik laughed and offered his hand to Anna. "Love your bag, Gorgeous. Authentic?"

Anna shook his hand and held out her bag. "Yes, it was a gift. From an unnamed influencer whose autobiography I ghost wrote."

"You're kidding! It's stunning. Sure you can't tell me who it was?" Erik raised his eyebrows as he prodded teasingly.

"The airtight NDA says I can't. I take my contracts seriously." She offered her hand to Sergio. "Your event looks amazing and so do both you and your husband, Sergio. I'm Anna Kane, Independent Director of Expanding Sales for On & Off the Margins Printing. It's a pleasure to meet you both."

"Pleasure to meet you as well, I'm Sergio Vannicho, owner of Folded 'n' Flipped Designs. What's a book publisher doing here?"

"On my boy's arm for the night." Anna lifted her and Vinnie's connected hands. "It's the least I could do since he's working late."

"Leila and Violet are holding out on us. I figured we'd know as soon as you found someone," Sergio teased. "Vincent, she's a cutie. Better not mess this up."

Vinnie found his voice. "Working on it. If you'll excuse us, we're going to get some fresh air."

"Have fun, kids." Erik flashed them a cheeky smile.

"Don't do anything we wouldn't do."

As they walked away Vinnie realized that Sergio and Erik, believed they were a couple. Maybe it was the fact that Anna sold it so effortlessly, as they were still hand in hand. That was odd, wasn't it? Shouldn't she have let go to reclaim her personal space?

He unlocked the patio door and locked it behind them to ensure they wouldn't be interrupted. The balcony was lined with tempered glass and offered two tables to sit at. He used to smoke out here on busy nights when he needed to escape the noise. Anna kept away from the railing and sat in the closest seat to the door, opening her purse, closing it, and sighing before setting it on the table.

"I quit smoking after New Year and I'm still looking for my lighter and pack."

"I quit the year my niece was born and I check my pockets from time to time." He chuckled, leaning against the railing noting Anna stiffening in her seat. "Don't like heights?"

"They are fine, as long as I'm not near them." She kept her eyes on him, avoiding looking out over the view behind him.

He stretched his arms over his head lazily trying to get the crick out of his spine. "So, I'm guessing you're here to...Wait. You just said that you were my girlfriend back there. Why would you...? I haven't... I'm so confused. I thought you were here because I've been avoiding you."

Anna laughed, before explaining the reason for her visit. "I am here because you're avoiding me, and I *did* say that I was your girlfriend. I wanted to make it harder to get rid of me."

He blinked, trying to think of what to say other than 'why' again. He was speechless, and that didn't happen often.

"Mr. Goodroe..."

"Vinnie, please. I'm not a fan of the formalities. Did you know that women didn't have prefixes assigned to their names until the 19th century, unless they were married and upper class? And the root of Miss was from Mistress and was primarily used for young girls. Referring to an adult woman as Miss used to be equating her to a prostitute."

"Alright, Vinnie, that's some information to know." She looked amused instead of annoyed as he expected her to be. *Why couldn't he ever shut his mouth?* She motioned to the chair across from her. "Sit, please. I want to talk to you."

He sat across from her and it might have been the light, but her eye-makeup didn't look like it matched. Her lavender shadow contrasted against emerald green cat-eye liner and brown lashes — it made him think of a peacock. Why would she use those colors? She didn't seem to be overly artistic with her make-up. Perhaps she'd done it, thinking the edgier look would help her blend in?

"Why are you avoiding me? If you don't want to work with me, that's alright. And if I offended you the night you came over when I made a pass at you, I apologize. I don't want to be on poor terms with you or part ways, I genuinely enjoy your company."

Anna was to the point, but not angry. He honestly expected her to be angry with how he'd run out of her apartment. He'd no doubt embarrassed her, yet here she was, far from angry. She was attractive, but he wasn't sure if he was attracted to her, and even if he was, he wasn't boyfriend material with his over-involved family and lack of relationship experience. To be completely honest, Leila had been his first and only girlfriend, and that relationship hadn't ever been totally without asterisks. Having someone seemingly attracted to him without really knowing him was outside of his comfort zone. But he liked Anna's company and did want to work with her. Having her continue the farce they'd talked about would get his family off his back about his lack of social life.

Metal scraped against glass as Anna slid an odd-looking coin across the table to him. He wordlessly took it from her, the cool of her fingers contrasted with the heat from his. The coin was a quarter, but the center had been stamped out and replaced by a penny.

"26 cents for your thoughts?"

"My thoughts are worth more than that, I have an editor, who's much more than an editor trying to convince me to work with her." Vinnie dropped the coin and winced.

Of all the arrogant nonsense he could have spewed… Maybe he'd buy a gag before the conference wrapped up. He clearly needed it.

Anna laughed, covering her mouth with her hand to muffle the sound. "You have me there. Should I write you a check? What's your hourly rate for conversation? I just thought I was being clever."

"You are. You are very clever." He drew in a deep breath and let it out slowly. "I wasn't offended by your invitation the other night. I was caught off guard. You were tired and on top of that I'm not casual with physical encounters."

"Fair enough. Still, I am sorry. Honestly, I'm thankful you had a clearer head. I needed to rest that night."

He nodded, unsure of what to say, touching the coin on the table. "Where did you find this? It's very unique."

"I had a client make it for me as a thank you. It's supposed to be a penny for your thoughts and a quarter for the call, back when payphones existed."

A police car roared by on the nearby highway, the siren breaking through the quiet.

"I want your book. How do I convince you to work with me?"

"I don't want my family to know it was me that wrote it." Vinnie pulled a pen out of his pocket and rolled it between his fingers.

"Well, we can figure out a pseudonym and focus marketing on social media. I've made more notes on the copy you gave me. I think it'll be a bestseller and that will make hiding more difficult. Texas loves to brag." Anna checked her phone before putting it back into her purse.

"Future-me problem, I suppose."

"Current-you question: do you want to keep this?" She motioned between them. "I meant it when I said that it would make my life easier. I have a handful of events this year, and you'd be doing me a favor in exchange for my help to get your book out there. I'm willing to play along with your family and friends, as well. Is anything major happening in the next few weeks? When's your birthday?"

"It was the first of this month."

"You were born on April Fools'?"

He smirked. "Yes, there is a joke in there somewhere. My next major event would be the Christmas in August party that we throw here. Unless my brother finally manages to propose to his girlfriend. Then I suppose a wedding could be possible."

"Sounds like fun."

June 25th; 167 Days Until...

Meeting your significant other's family at a wedding had to be some sort of social faux pas, even if the relationship wasn't real. Anna wasn't entirely sure she was comfortable roleplaying scenes from *The Wedding Date* with Vinnie's family. Give her a board room full of executives or out-for-blood reporters, and she wouldn't break a sweat, but this was entirely out of her comfort zone.

Since Vinnie's brother Mat had been dating, living, and raising their daughter together with his partner, he and Kassarah decided that a simple beach wedding was all they needed. Kass was a preacher's daughter, so her father was performing the ceremony, and they had friends helping with everything else. Becki, the bartender that Anna had met at The Playhouse, was doing Kass' hair and make-up for the day.

She drove herself to the event, as Vinnie was helping his brother get ready. Feeling lost, Anna looked over the list of people that Vinnie had given her. Rex Abster was Vinnie and Mat's un-biological uncle, Jacob Shatan was Kass' father, Noah was Kass' brother, and her best friend Izzy was standing up with her. Anna adjusted the air conditioner in her car, she should have demanded pictures. She hated not having more complete information about the crowd. It would be difficult to blend in without it.

It didn't help that she felt out of sorts with all the little details for the day. Vinnie had emailed her an invite so she'd have the location, and she'd texted him asking what BYOC meant. He explained it meant bring your own chair. The beach didn't technically offer wedding services so the family was handling it on their own. Anna hadn't owned a folding chair, but as of this morning, there was one in her trunk.

The contrast from Minji's wedding was stark. Minji's wedding had been a formal luncheon with family and business contacts, as both of their families were prominent in their respective industries. It had been traditional — quiet and reserved. The couple had hosted an after party for their friends from all parts of the world. She'd drank Soju with her friend and toasted her good fortune.

Anna slipped her phone into her purse, turned off her car, and popped her trunk, thankful for the updo and sleeveless dress that kept her cool. Anna grabbed the gift she'd purchased for the couple and put on her sunglasses. It was at least 90 degrees, which for Texas, was cooler in June, but her skin instantly prickled at the temperature difference from her car.

She got the chair out and balanced it on her leg as she closed the trunk.

A truck pulled into the spot next to her and a hispanic woman in a light-colored romper hopped out of the driver's seat. She rushed around the cab and offered her hand to the tanned skinned woman in the passenger seat. "I think we're a little early. I thought we were running late."

"Vi, I lied to you about when the wedding started. I wanted a good seat." The other woman smirked, her diamond ring reflecting the sunlight.

The driver pulled two chairs out of the bed of the truck. "I see how it is. No faith in my time management."

"You thought we were late. I win. Here, I can carry mine."

"Baby, I don't mind carrying your chair. Come on, let's go get your good seat so you can make fun of me for being a crybaby."

"I would never."

The couple passed her and both women nodded as they made their way down the boardwalk, following the signs for the ceremony space. The wind blew the taller woman's hair over her shoulder, exposing the moon phase tattoo running down her spine. That must be Vinnie's business partner Leila and her wife Violet. He'd mentioned Leila's tattoo. Anna made a mental note to chat with them after the wedding and get to know them better.

Anna kept a few paces back, but was thankful she wasn't walking down completely alone. She was almost to the stairs that led down to the beach when she saw a young man struggling with a handful of papers. He was singing to himself as he organized what Anna recognized as wedding programs. Maybe this was one of Kass' friends? He looked younger and Kass was in her early twenties. He was singing in Korean. If he was someone that Kass had met in school and wasn't from Texas, he likely felt just as out of place.

Without giving it further thought, she waved to get his attention and as he took out one of his earbuds, she greeted him in Korean.

He inclined his head. "Sorry? What was that?"

She flushed red to her ears. He didn't understand her, and looked at her confused. She sputtered out an apology and introduction. "Oh, I'm sorry. I thought, um… that you…Never mind, I'm Anna, Vinnie's girlfriend."

"Oh cool, I'm Noah, Kass' brother. The printer messed these up and I'm fixing them before things get started. Did you need something? The ceremony is down on the beach. You'll see the roped off section where we set up a couple of chairs already." If it bothered him that she just assumed what language he spoke, he didn't vocalize it.

"I can help if you like," she offered. It would be better than standing awkwardly by herself.

She wished she would have asked Vinnie more questions about who would be here. She hated not knowing how to handle herself appropriately in a given crowd.

He grinned as he countered her offer. "You would be a lifesaver if you could take over. I've got a ton to get done still. We're running behind."

"Of course." Anna moved closer. "What should I do?"

"They're folded, but the insert is upside down so just flip that, put it back, and set them down in the basket. Got it?" he asked and Anna nodded, so he continued. "My girlfriend, Izzy, will be up to get them soon-ish? Probably? She's blonde, happy-loud, and wearing a bridesmaid dress. You won't be able to miss her."

"Sounds good."

"Thanks so much. See ya." Noah jogged down the stairs and ducked into a large tent.

On her own, Anna moved further into the shade of the umbrella and rested her chair against it. Even with sunscreen, she was probably going to burn before the day was done. She could smell the ocean and feel the breeze blowing up from the water. The wind wasn't strong, but it was enough to make the heat feel less oppressive. She couldn't recall the last time she'd gone to the beach, in the States anyway. She had deliberately scheduled extra time in Korea to walk the beaches before Minji's wedding.

Spending time there had been good for her. It put into perspective how much she wanted to change her life from being soley focused on work. She didn't want to give up her job, but she needed balance.

Two tiny hands grabbed her legs, nearly knocking her to the ground.

"Ethan! Be careful. I'm so sorry, Ma'am." A man with dark hair and brown skin called out and motioned for the child to come to him, admonishing him in Spanish while trying to balance the chairs under his arm.

Anna wasn't fluent but she knew a few phrases, and she recognized a parent's tone when she heard one.

"I'm Léo Guzman, a friend of the couple, and the human cyclone there is Ethan. Say hi to the nice lady."

"Hola." Ethan smiled, showing off a missing front tooth. He looked about Lizzie's age. He had a mess of dark curls he'd likely inherited from his mother, based on his father's appearance.

"Hello." She smiled at Ethan first, then offered a hand to Léo. "I'm Anna Kane, Vinnie's girlfriend."

Léo chuckled. "We kinda thought he made you up there for a second."

Anna might have responded, but an older man interrupted, commenting with a kind but teasing smile. "I saw her business card, but you can print anything nowadays."

"Hey, Rex. How's it going? Kass looking for a getaway car yet?" Léo greeted the other man, and Anna took immediate attention.

"Not from a ranger, that's for sure."

Of all the people that Vinnie talked about, Rex was the person that garnered the highest amount of respect. This was the man that had raised Vinnie after he'd lost both of his parents. She'd heard a lot of stories from Vinnie, but the ones about Rex always had more color and emotion. Vinnie wanted to make his Uncle proud.

The two men were joking about Léo's wife barking at everyone for pictures, but so far everything was running pretty smoothly, even if they were behind schedule. Rex offered Ethan a serious handshake, but the boy opted to hug him instead then asked where Lizzie was. Anna continued to fix the wedding programs, these still needed to get done.

Léo and Ethan bid them both a see-ya-later and headed down towards the beach.

"So you're the Anna I've heard only a little bit about." Rex's blue eyes were bright and friendly but his handshake was firm. He didn't look at her as fragile, and that was welcomed.

"And you're Rex, whom I've heard a great deal about."

"Well, you have me at a disadvantage and some of it was probably exaggerated."

"So you weren't running with Butch Cassidy and the Sundance Kid?" She smirked.

Rex shook his head. "He thinks messing with me about my age is so funny. I'm gonna trip him down the stairs today if he doesn't watch it."

"That might be a bit extreme."

"Sounds like he didn't tell you any of the best stories." Rex straightened his tie. "I don't think a good story starts without something off the wall happening."

"If the…" Anna stopped and blinked as she almost put her foot in her mouth and faked a cough. She'd almost said something about Vinnie's book. She needed to refocus and remember that she was here to be supportive, and giving away secrets wasn't supportive.

"You alright?" He looked concerned. "Need some water? It's hot as hell out here."

"I'm fine." She retrieved a mint from her purse. "In the publishing industry, all good stories have an inciting moment that grabs attention and keeps the reader wanting more."

"I noticed you were in the publishing business. Is that how you met my nephew? He's been cagey about how you two met."

Anna smiled. She and Vinnie had discussed this in advance, in case Rex tried to get information out of her. "I needed an authenticity check for a crime novel."

"Oh, so he mentioned that part of his life." Rex smirked, almost looking impressed at her answer.

"I do background checks. I'm thorough."

Rex let out a full belly laugh. "I suppose you are then." His phone rang out, and he took it out of his pocket. "Yeah, yeah. I'll be right back down. Ya girl's here. Uh-huh. Tell your brother to calm the fuck down."

Anna finished the last two programs as Rex finished his call.

"Sorry about the swearing. I'm better about it when Lizzie's about."

"No worries at all." She felt good about how this went. This was a good impression. She didn't even know why she'd been so tense before. If she could handle investors and crowds of hundreds, she could handle a small family wedding.

"I'll be getting back to the boys then. Just one thing."

"Of course, how can I help?"

Rex lowered his voice as he brushed by her. "Get a better story about how y'all met. You wouldn't know he was a criminal without the background check or unless he told you. Vinnie doesn't tell just anyone about that part of his life. I best not find out you're honey-potting him for some reason."

Vinnie took a sip from the tumbler, the ice cubes clinking together as he finished what was left of his drink. He didn't get drunk very often, but this was a celebration and he'd been maintaining a buzz since the conclusion of the ceremony.

This was a good day and seeing his brother happy was the best part. His brother had always got the short end of the stick when it came to relationships. Hell, Mat's ex-wife Natalie was a case study in gaslighting and verbal abuse. Kass and Lizzie couldn't have been better for him. Making it easier for him to show that he actually cared.

The wedding was simple, but lovely considering it was put together in about 45 days. It was a testament to the ingenuity of the people they knew and how creative they could be.

If Kass had dreamed of a big wedding as a little girl, she didn't appear the least bit disappointed in how the day had turned out. She was all smiles next to Mat, who had a sleeping Lizzie on his shoulder.

The guests had cleared out and it was just a handful of them sitting at a table chatting and sharing snacks. Anna had been quiet at his side, but he supposed that made sense. He was the only one that she really knew. He'd noticed her eyes following Rex at dinner, almost like he made her nervous which was odd. Everyone always loved Rex.

"They were not joking about forgetting to eat." Kass took a bit of her dinner roll. "Thank you for hiding food for us, Izzy."

Izzy mocked-saluted Kass and snuggled closer to Noah as the breeze picked up. "Do you need a blanket for Lizzie?"

Mat shook his head. "She's warm enough. She'd wake up if she wasn't."

"It was a beautiful wedding." Anna sipped from her glass. "I love your dress."

"Thank you so much." Kass shimmied her shoulders, "I got it second hand and one of the ladies from my old church helped me alter it. I'm just glad Lizzie didn't make too much of a fuss about having to wear her dress for the ceremony. We made her dress from the extra fabric off of mine."

"She looked adorable. Does she not like dresses?" Anna asked.

Vinnie shook his head. "She loves dresses, but she wants to be in a suit like her dad when he wears one."

"Sood up." Lizzie's mummer in her father's shoulder.

Mat chuckled and kissed the top of her head. "That's my little lady, matchin' Daddy."

"Not so little now," Rex pointed out. "She's about outgrown those pants."

"She had another growth spurt, think she grew three inches overnight." Mat took the bite that Kass held up for him.

"Watch out, she might get taller than you, Mat." Noah warned as Mat flipped him off.

"I think I'm the only one that got the tall gene from Nathan." Vinnie rubbed his glasses off on his shirt.

"Nathan wasn't much taller than your mother. Still not sure how you ended up so tall." Rex shook his head. "Think we're out of luck figuring anything out. Neither of them kept much family information laying around."

"I keep forgetting you aren't their blood relative." Izzy motioned between the Goodroe brothers and Rex. She yawned and looked up at Noah. "I have no info about my birth parents, so you're out of luck knowing the crazy I might become one day."

He rubbed his hand over Izzy's arm. "Ah, the curse of being in the adopted-kid club."

"Oh, I'm in that club too." Anna pointed to herself. "I was adopted after my mother died."

Kass held up her hand, "Wait, I think Izzy and Lizzie are the only two at the table that aren't in the mother-passed-away club. Does that make us Disney characters? Should we be able to talk to animals?"

"Explicit versions maybe. We'd only be able to talk to trash pandas and poisonous things." Mat switched Lizzie to his other shoulder, and Kass kissed her daughter's cheek.

"What are the odds of that? So many of us adopted and/or with parents deceased." Vinnie cracked his neck.

"To be fair Izzy, and I don't know if our biological parents are deceased. They could be out there somewhere," Noah stated.

Anna asked, "Have you ever thought of looking for them?"

"I wouldn't know where to start. My adoption paperwork is in Korean."

"I could translate if you wanted," She offered, shifting in her chair as if she was nervous.

Noah questioned, "Is that what you were speaking earlier?"

"Yes. I taught English in Korea for almost two years. My apologies for assuming earlier."

Noah waved her off as Kass interjected. "Your parents must be so proud of you, Anna. Teaching in a foreign country is an accomplishment."

Anna bit her lip before answering. "Emily, my adoptive parent, wasn't easy to impress. I hope she was proud of me. She passed away before I finished college."

"Orphaned twice. Yeesh, bad luck."

"Mathew!"

"What? Ouch!" Mat winced. Kass no doubt pinched his leg under the table. "Sorry; phrased that wrong. I'm sure that was rough."

Vinnie glared at his brother over his glasses. Mat didn't mean any harm in it, but would it kill him to be a little more sensitive?

"Not really." Anna shrugged, and her tone was casual as she explained. "Emily was older when she adopted me, and I think she liked the idea of being a parent more than actually being one. She had money, put me in good schools, and I never wanted for anything. She wasn't unkind, but she wasn't affectionate. So while I miss her, it's not the same kind of pain normally associated with the loss of a parent."

"Do you have much other family?" Rex asked.

Had he missed something? Vinnie was beginning to wonder if Rex and Anna had a weird run-in before the wedding.

Rex kept his eyes focused on Anna. He was watching her like he'd gauge an opponent while playing chess. Had Anna told him about the book?

No, Rex would have confronted him, or maybe not yet since it was Mat and Kass' wedding. Was he in for an earful tomorrow?

"I don't have any other family." Anna finished her drink. "Unless my biological father is alive somewhere. I'm pretty sure my original birth certificate had John Doe on it, but I only saw it once before it was misplaced."

"Good luck finding an original without your name change form or knowing which hospital you were born in." Izzy sighed. "Getting mine for my passport application was a nightmare."

"You two going somewhere?" Kass questioned.

Noah stood up and stretched, offering Izzy his hand. "Yes, we're gonna run away and have a destination wedding to avoid all the crying that happened today."

"Sorry baby, I want my daddy there, and I'm sure he's gonna cry."

"The thought of your dad crying is terrifying." Noah tugged at her hand. "We're gonna go back to our room for the night. I'm exhausted. 'Night guys."

Everyone started saying their goodbyes, and Mat and Kass left with Rex to put Lizzie in his car. Rex and Vinnie were babysitting Lizzie while they took a short honeymoon. They'd all tried to convince the couple to spend a full week away from the world, but they couldn't be convinced. They didn't want to be apart from their daughter for more than a couple of days, plus there were a lot of changes upcoming, and Kass was all about plans and executing them. Mat had work to do with Lost Horizon officially being his again, and Kass wanted to find a house in Galveston, close to the doctor's office where she'd be working. Vinnie was left alone with Anna, and she let out a long sigh, leaning her head on her folded arms on the table.

"Sorry, this day was probably longer than you bargained for," He apologized. "I hope it wasn't too miserable."

Anna shifted as she sat up. "Don't worry about it. The day was fun. Really, your family is amazing. So welcoming for the most part."

"I'm sensing there's an unfallen shoe."

"Rex does not like me," Anna explained, pulling out her phone to check her messages. "He didn't believe the story about how we met and he thinks I'm a liar."

"Well, if we were really dating that would be a problem. It's about impossible to change that man's mind."

"Fantastic."

Vinnie chuckled. "I'll talk to him. I'll make something up and smooth it over."

"He doesn't strike me as someone who gets tricked too often." Anna reached down and pulled off her shoes, flexing her toes.

"Paying attention is essential for survival when you live off the books." He leaned back in his chair and stared out over the water.

"I wish I could've thought of a way to get out of the wedding photos Kass had me in. I couldn't think of a way to say no with Rex right there. When we end our ruse, it might make her regret them."

"My ex-girlfriend and her wife were in attendance today. My family believes me when I say I part on good terms with a partner."

Anna smiled. "They were so sweet. I'm looking forward to seeing them at the not-Christmas, Christmas party in August."

They sat in companionable silence for a spell as Anna quietly observed. "This wedding couldn't have been more different than Minji's. Her wedding was incredibly formal, but there was an afterparty on a rooftop bar, which was loud for lack of better description. Minji and her husband both attended college overseas, so the afterparty was more for their non-Korean friends. Today was…" She trailed off as if looking for the correct word, "it was comfortable. I know there was stress behind the scenes, but no one was trying to make things perfect. Mat and Kass seemed content to celebrate with Lizzie and everyone else was a bonus."

"They are shockingly perfect for each other."

Anna yawned and stretched her arms over her head. "Do you want to walk for a bit?"

"Honestly, I'd normally say yes, but I'm exhausted, and I still need to drive back to Houston tonight. But I'll walk you to your room." Vinnie forced himself to stand. He should have ridden home with Rex. He didn't feel like sobering up in his car, he was going to have to get a room for the night.

Anna started up the stairs, and he followed close behind. The boardwalk was full of rowdy drunks from the bars and he didn't want her to be alone. She turned onto the lower walkway that paralleled the rooms on the beach and continued until she reached one of the suites.

"There's a second bed in my suite if you want to sleep here tonight," she offered.

It would be nice to just lay down and not have to deal with walking to the front desk. "If it's not imposing, that would be appreciated."

"One of these days, you're going to take up my offer the first time I ask instead of volleying back." She unlocked the door, and he excused himself to go fetch the change of clothes that were in his car.

Vinnie grabbed his bag and double-checked his car doors to ensure they were locked. He pulled his cellphone from his pocket and scrolled through the messages on his phone – Leila's, in particular, caught his eye, as it was a picture, and she didn't normally send those.

The image in the thread was of him and Anna, dancing with Lizzie on his hip, all three of them laughing and smiling.

Leila: Looks like Anna won the most important person over
Leila: Also she's wonderful. It's good to see you happy

He paused and re-read the messages. Leila wasn't wrong. Today was a joyful day. The opposite of Mat's prior wedding to Natalie, which had essentially been them coming back from Las Vegas married, and him and Rex wanting to commit Mat to a mental facility. Today, everyone came together and had a family celebration. In a few of those pictures, Anna was present, because she was introduced as his girlfriend. Kass welcomed her with open arms, and Lizzie was so excited to see her again. Anna and Mat had talked whiskey, and she offered to put him in contact with a good account for the bar. Vinnie hadn't thought much of Rex not talking to her, but now that he knew the reason why, it might be a problem.

Twirling his keys around his index finger, he paused to look up at the stars. He'd been out here with Mat working on the bar and working at The Playhouse; he was exhausted. He wanted a long shower, and to collapse for about twenty hours of sleep, but that wasn't in the cards. Rex wasn't as young as he used to be and Lizzie was going to be full of energy tomorrow. He was going to have to force himself up and out of bed early.

Vinnie knocked on Anna's door, hearing a jingle as it opened, which was an out-of-place sound. Anna motioned for him to come in, her hair already down from the updo.

He noticed the Christmas-style sleighbell hanging from the doorknob. "Was that on the doorknob when you got here?"

Anna laughed. "No. I travel alone as a woman. It's an easy way to know if someone is messing with my door before they potentially get into my room."

Vinnie knew those statistics all too well, and it put an ache in his stomach.

"The answer to your unasked question is no. No one's ever broken into my room and taken advantage, but it has happened to people I know." She moved closer to him. "Do you mind starting the zipper on my dress?"

"No trouble."

Anna turned her back to him and twisted her arm up her back, tapping where she wanted the dress unzipped to. He obliged her and she strode the connecting door in the living room. "I'll grab us a drink. Feel free to use the bathroom on this side of the room."

He took off his suit jacket and hung it over the chair, pacing to the bathroom while unbuttoning the top buttons of his dress shirt. He washed his hands and walked back into the living room as Anna entered from the other direction, two glasses in one hand and her phone in the other.

"I should send you some of these candid pictures. I got some good ones. Your brother is sweet with his wife and daughter."

"He thinks that's the only time he's any good." Vinnie took the offered drink and sat on the chair while Anna sat on the couch.

She looked up from her phone. "That's sad. I take it the background of your characters having a *rough* upbringing comes from experience?"

He shifted, not wanting to go in-depth about his past. What was in the book was more than enough. "More or less, some of it is a touch exaggerated. Where's the black-tie dinner you need me for? I remember it's next week but I can't remember where we're going."

"Boston, next Saturday night. It's an Independence Day fundraiser for a literacy campaign. We fly out at six in the morning."

Vinnie sipped from the drink she'd given him. "That'll be my first time in Boston. Too bad we're only there for a day and a night."

"My schedule for the Friday before and the Monday after are full."

"Isn't Monday the 4th?"

"In this country."

"Ah, I see. International meetings on Monday."

"I don't stop working very well or often, even when I should. It's a character flaw." Anna sipped from her own glass. "Next year, my plan is to take more time for myself. I'm successful, and I've done the things that I want to do. I don't want to stop working, but I do want a life outside of it."

"Makes sense. It's hard finding that balance and still having enough to keep your head above water, but the latter isn't so much a problem for you."

During their planning session of their little charade for the outside world, they had learned a lot about each other's backgrounds. Anna had left out that she'd been adopted, but had told him that her mother died ten years ago. He just hadn't realized that had been her second mother. Emily's death had left Anna with a stake in the company that she worked for and as she described it, more money than she'd ever had to worry about spending.

She didn't seem to care that he didn't have money or that he sold his stake in The Playhouse to help his brother. She wanted to help him be successful with his book and make money for her company.

Anna chuckled and swung her legs up on the couch, flexing her toes. Her feet probably hurt from the heels she'd worn earlier. "I should let you get some sleep. You've had a busy day."

"Yeah. Thank you for the drink. I'm going to take a shower and leave early in the morning. But I'll text you this week to confirm the Boston trip."

"Sounds good. G'dnight."

"Night."

Anna walked through the connecting door and locked the deadbolt behind her. Vinnie was left alone in the quiet. His phone lit up to show the text from Anna – a picture of himself and Rex. He chuckled remembering how Dara kept making everyone laugh while she was snapping pictures. She said it was easier to use photoshop than it was to get a whole wedding party to give natural smiles.

He plugged his phone into the USB charging port after setting the alarm. He needed to finish up the edits Anna requested for the book. After this book was done, he'd focus on a new story. One that was completely his own.

But how could he ever write a twist better than a hijacked surrogacy? He didn't want to tempt fate, but it was going to be a struggle.

Chapter 4: First Twists Should Be Intense

No One Saw This Coming

August 23rd; 108 Days Until…

Vinnie stifled his yawn as he parked his car and pulled up the parking app on his phone to pay for a couple of hours. He might not need the entire two hours, but he didn't want to fuss with this phone if he was to talk to Anna. He'd driven around the block three times before deciding to follow through on the whim to bring Anna lunch. Maggie's Diner was one of his staple breakfast places after work until Kass had moved into Rex's and food at home had more appeal. The takeout bag in the passenger seat smelled fantastic. His stomach started growling; he'd only had a snack earlier and it was half past three.

He grabbed the two bags, stretching his stride as he crossed the street and entered the building. The air conditioned lobby was a welcome change to oppressive Texas summer heat, but waiting for the fog to clear from his glasses wasn't. He should investigate Lasik. It would make his life easier. The studies showed that…*Focus.*

Anna's office was the first office inside the building. The publishing house logo was installed on the frosted glass of the reflective door. He hadn't messaged her — again, this was a spontaneous idea — but this wouldn't seem as odd. Bringing someone food was a perfectly, socially acceptable way to show gratitude. He let himself in the office, and Alysha looked up from the reception desk holding up her finger while she finished her phone call. She repeated the address for a second time and tapped her earpiece definitively.

"Good Afternoon. She's not here." She offered him a crooked smile.

Vinnie resisted the urge to sigh, but noticed Alysha eyeing the bags in his hand.

"Who told you about Maggie's?"

"I've lived in Houston my whole life. Also did you recognise the bag from there? It's fairly generic."

"I know Maggie's take out when I see it. But it isn't a place everyone knows about. Who took you?" She arched her eyebrow.

"One of the girls that worked at my club requested it for her going away party. I got hooked on the Croissant French Toast they serve for brunch." He shifted on his feet. "I can leave this for her. I just wanted to do something nice since I was in the area."

"Mhmm." Alysha rounded the desk.

He went to hand her the bags but paused. "I don't suppose you'd tell me when she'll be back."

"If you have shrimp and grits in that bag, and it appears on my desk, I'll tell you where she is."

Vinnie chuckled. "Ah, so you can be bribed. With the right food, I can get access to secrets."

"Mine. Not Anna's, except a couple if you play your cards right." She glanced back into the rest of the office where muffled conversations could be heard over the white noise machine.

"You are welcome to anything in the bag, but the butternut squash, since Anna's a vegetarian. I can't bring her lunch without lunch to bring her." He liked Alysha; she was quick-witted and while cautious, she didn't seem to judge him for his oddities. Or, if she did, she had an impeccable poker face.

Alysha took the bags and looked through them for what she wanted. "She's not a vegetarian. She just avoids red meat."

"Not ideal for living in Texas." He glanced at his watch out of habit.

"Bacon is always a hazard. I get us breakfast some mornings and half the time, even when I ask them to leave it off, they still put bacon in it." She pulled out one container and smiled triumphantly. "Thanks for lunch."

"Thank you for telling me where Anna is."

Alysha snickered. "She works out every other Tuesday afternoon. There's a gym at the opposite end of the building. Eric's at the security desk; I'll message him to buzz you through. But listen, if she asks how you figured it out, I didn't tell you."

"If I don't tell her that it was you, then she's going to think I'm stalking her." He took the bags back.

"That, is a *you* problem." Triumphantly she took her lunch back to her desk.

Vinnie left the office and stopped by the security desk where a younger man greeted him. "Good Afternoon, Sir."

He winced at the honorific. "Vinnie's fine."

"If it's just us, then cool, but otherwise, I kinda gotta." Eric tapped his name tag, then snapped his fingers. "I've seen you with Miss Kane. You drive a black Roadster, sweet car."

"Thanks. It wasn't in the best condition when I got it, so my brother and I fixed it up. It was worth the work. It's a smooth ride."

He grinned. "I'll own a car like that someday. I'm already savin'."

Vinnie nodded. "Good to have a goal. I was trying to find the gym and Miss Kane."

"Sure." Eric looked down on his screens and tapped a couple of keys. "Alysha just approved your pass. Miss Kane's really punctual about her workouts."

"That doesn't surprise me in the slightest."

Eric laughed and explained how to get to the gym as he handed him a temporary entry badge.

The architecture of the building was historical, with black and white marble floors that made his steps echo off the vaulted ceilings. Vinnie waved the badge over the sensor when he reached the door to the gym area. An LED screen built into the wall flashed advertisements for yoga classes in gym room A, spin classes in gym room B, open swim hours, and when the masseuse was available on site. He never regretted growing up poor, but clearly there were advantages to the other side.

The muffled music amplified as he got closer. The first room was stocked with equipment, but the second was an open space with a wall of mirrors. Anna, wore a black sports bra and shorts, dancing to the music in a choreography he didn't recognize. Judging on what he knew about Anna's younger years, he'd wager a guess that both the song and the dance were from a Kpop group. It was high energy, and her enjoyment was clear by the sheen of sweat on her skin, making her glow under the lights.

The song was winding down, and Anna flicked her wrists over her head as she twisted her body, making eye contact with him. He closed his eyes on instinct, hoping irrationally that if he couldn't see her, she couldn't see him. He opened one eye and noticed that Anna had gone back to her routine, seemingly unbothered. She pivoted as she bounced to a beat which was so impossibly loud, that he felt it in his feet. As Anna completed her turn, he noticed the tattoo on her lower back – had it been centered, it might have been what was commonly known as a tramp stamp. He knew better than to stare, but his curiosity wouldn't let him off the hook until he identified it. She spun around again, hair flying as she rolled her shoulders and neck. It was a quote. Her tattoo was a quote from Dr. Who.

What were the odds that she enjoyed one of his favorite shows? His eyebrow arched more at that fact than in her music taste. He realized he was still watching her and was about to step back when Anna motioned for him to come in.

She tapped on a tablet, and the music stopped suddenly. But clearly she was speaking to someone with bluetooth; the light flashed under her hair.

"We'll see how good your English is the next time I visit. Be well, Minji." Anna retrieved a towel from a cabinet and unplugged her tablet from the wall.

"Well, hello."

"Hi."

She arched her back to crack it. "This is a surprise. What did you bribe Alysha with for her to give me up?"

"Shrimp and grits. But one, please don't tell her I told you, and two, I did bring food for you as well."

"Hmmm." She toweled off her neck and shoulders, before going to retrieve her bag.

Vinnie was getting nervous, as she didn't seem angry to see him, but she also didn't seem happy. He shouldn't have interrupted her routine. This had been a colossal mistake.

"Mother fucking bitch," Anna growled.

He jumped at the venom in her voice. Thankfully she was looking at her phone and not at him. "Problem?"

She averted her eyes, seemingly more embarrassed by her outburst than at him being here while she was working out. "I thought…" she sighed and lowered her shoulders, physically making herself relax. " I found the hospital where my birth record was, but after a week of back and forth, I'm back to the drawing board."

"Do you want help?" he offered. Data, he could handle.

"I appreciate the offer, but I have to make the calls myself." She pulled on a pair of flats.

"Well, you said you were born in '87. I can compile a list of what hospitals were open that year and put them in a spreadsheet with the phone numbers. It would be an easy way to keep track of things."

She blinked, then smiled as she tied her hair up into a messy bun. "Thank you. That would be immensely helpful. Are you sure you don't mind?"

"I have time here and there. My pleasure to help."

"Alright then." She pulled on a t-shirt and started to the exit.

Vinnie held the door open for her and let her lead the way.

He followed her out into the courtyard, pausing for a moment to allow his lenses to darken and block to the sunshine. "You have a tattoo."

"Oh, that's why you were staring at me." Anna laughed and motioned for him to sit at one of the small tables with her. "I got it when I was in college. My one and only wild spring break."

"It's a perfect quote. I mean, the show is amazing! For it to still be relevant over such a span of time – the concepts, the talent that's been a part of it over the years, a reboot after so many years, and for it to grow even more successful with age, is just inconvincible." Vinnie wanted to pick her brain about the show, but he didn't want to freak her out with the plethora of knowledge about the British show.

"I…"

"I'm not gonna bore you with trivia, although I promise you, I could. I do have to know who your favorite doctor is."

"Um…" Anna paused, biting down on her lower lip before answering. "I think the one from the reboot."

"Really? That's fascinating. I'll have to pick your brain about why another day." He pulled the food out of the bags. "This one is butternut squash. I thought you were a vegetarian, but Alysha explained that you only avoid red meat."

"Where did you get it from?"

"Maggie's. I only found out about it a couple of years ago, but it's a great place."

"We'll see." Anna took the covered dish he offered.

"Are you picky?"

She let out a staccato laugh. "What about me says otherwise? You must view me in a very optimistic light. I'm very particular about most things. Living with roommates was a nightmare when I was younger."

He took a bite of his sweet potato waffle. "That's the advantage of fake dating. We don't need to worry about living together."

"That's very true. Also, this is very good. Thank you for randomly bringing me lunch. Such a nice thing to do. I'll have to return the favor sometime."

September 15th; 85 Days Until…

"Stop pacing for gods' sake," Alysha implored, pointing to the floor beneath them. "You're gonna grind a hole in my new floor. The builders just finished laying the tile on Monday. Why are you freaking out?"

Anna stopped moving and bit down on her thumb. “Rex is very important to Vinnie and he does not like me. He knows there’s something fishy going on between us, and he won’t let it go. We’re having a party for his birthday tonight and I have a gift, but now I don’t know if I should bring it. What if he thinks it’s too much? Or he hates it?”

“Whoa, settle down. You do remember that you’re not actually dating Vinnie. Right?” Alysha clicked her tongue against the roof of her mouth. “Because, not to re-stir this pot, but you two are awfully chummy when you’re together.”

“Don’t.” Anna sighed. “I’m attracted to him the more time I spend with him. And I would date him, but he isn’t interested in anything beyond my professional help and friendship. Although I’m not gonna lie, the way we talk, it seems like he’s interested in me sometimes, but he never crosses any lines.”

“Could he be not straight?”

“I suppose. But I know he dated a woman before, and he runs that club with her now. They’re fine around each other.” Anna checked the time on her phone. Vinnie was going to pick her up for the party soon. “But she’s married to a woman now. I met them at that weird Christmas party I went to last month.”

“You’ve dated women, but clearly lean more towards men. The past doesn’t guarantee the future.”

“My past relationships weren’t exactly healthy or conventional. Men don’t want a woman who’s in a higher tax bracket and won’t be treated like she’s not. I don’t want to be alone, but I’m unwilling to compromise my goals to make someone feel less threatened by my success.”

Alysha pulled the cord on the shades to let more light into the under-construction office. “Vinnie thinks you're amazing. He was talking about you when he was wiring the office sound system for me. He’s not threatened by who you are, but he’s sneaky. Tryin’ to get information about you without me noticin’.”

“That’s a family default setting. His whole family was involved in crime, and knowledge can save your life.” She leaned against one of the boxes. “They have some very interesting stories. What’s funny is that while money talks in that world, there’s more loyalty between them than there is in the *respectable* business world.”

“You expect people with money to play by the rules? Money makes the law irrelevant.”

“I suppose.”

Alysha looked at her phone. “Preston from channel 10 just emailed. He wants to set up an interview for next month. Horror books by Texas authors. He said you get the first segment if you respond in the hour.”

"Confirm it."

"You hate him."

"No. I think he's a misogynistic prick who gets what he wants because he's got a pretty face and local fame. I dislike him because he thinks he has power over me since we slept together." Anna rarely craved cigarettes since she quit, but right now she wanted one. She retrieved a piece of gum from her purse and put it in her mouth. "Just because we fucked, doesn't mean he gets to fuck me over."

Her dark-skinned co-worker laughed. "Preston is a burr under your skin. You normally don't swear unless you've been drinking. Are you only taking the slot to prove that you can be professional?"

"I am professional. If men can sleep with women and act like it's nothing, then why can't women do the same? The hypocrisy is nauseating," Anna growled.

"Because western society has double standards due to patriarchal values. And it's never examined as a whole because it's too closely linked to religion, and people don't like to talk about religion or politics unless they are trying to oppress someone who doesn't think like them," Vinnie interrupted from the open doorway, he pointed above him to the empty frame. "You're missing a door."

"They broke it when they were installing it, but they're in the parking lot figuring out an emergency replacement," Alysha explained. She'd obviously gotten accustomed to Vinnie randomly spilling facts.

"Do you want us to stay until they finish up?" Vinnie offered.

"Naw." Alysha shook her head. "They should finish up soon. You two get going; I've got this."

"Still, I…" Anna started.

"No. My office and my responsibility. Trust me," Alysha interrupted.

Anna nodded. "I do. Text me if you need anything though."

"I will, but I won't. Bye-bye, love-birds."

Anna and Vinnie waved goodbye to Alysha and made their way to his car. It must have started raining when they'd been in the building because it was pouring outside.

Vinnie opened an umbrella for them. "I thought Alysha knew about our arrangement."

"She does, but she also thinks she's funny."

Vinnie held the door for her and kept the umbrella over her until she was fully inside the car. He paused to sweep up the tail of her coat, so it didn't get closed in the door. He was always so thoughtful about her space when they were together. He climbed in the driver's seat and made their way to Rex's house.

"Are we picking Lizzie up?" Anna questioned, noticing the empty car seat.

"Naw. Rex wanted to pick her up. No doubt getting her ice cream and spoiling her dinner. Kass'll be thrilled."

"I suppose that is his prerogative as a grandparent. How's the house hunting going for Kass and Mat?"

"They have offers on two houses. Hopefully, one gets accepted, they aren't enjoying their two-hour daily commutes." Vinnie pulled onto the highway and shifted gears as he merged into traffic. "Mat's been a *joy* with less sleep."

Anna flexed her hand on the door handle as he increased the car's speed. "I think your brother has more bark than bite."

"Ha!" Vinnie barked out a laugh, his eyes closing for a moment as he threw his head back with exaggerated agreement. "Very true, just don't tell him that. And while I don't like listening to his bitching, watching him bend over backwards to not swear is always hilarious."

"Any luck talking to Rex about me?" She didn't like the wrench thrown into the works of being the unliked girlfriend.

"Kinda. I talked to him about you just being private about how we really met, but he's being him. It doesn't help that Kass gave him a wedding picture with you in the shot as a gift to try and encourage him to like you. He's stubborn and he doesn't like being pushed." Vinnie shrugged his shoulders. "He'll come around."

"I hope so. He seems to like Kass so much. Maybe he doesn't like me because I don't act like she does."

"Kass was thrown into the works in a different way. She had the advantage of Natalie messing with her, it gave her instant sympathy points."

They discussed the recent edits of the book and ideas for the cover as they drove, eventually reaching Rex's house at the same time Mat did from the opposite direction. Vinnie motioned for Mat to pull in first and he followed in behind. Mat made his way into the house, sprinting to get out of the rain. Kass' car wasn't here, so she was likely still on her way.

Anna took a deep breath, but Vinnie assured her. "It'll be fine. It's a birthday dinner, nothing to worry about."

"If you say so."

"I say so."

"What if he hates the gift I bought him?"

"I'll say it was my idea. I appreciate everything you've done for me. I have your back. Knowing you is the first time that I've been me first, and someone's relative second. You believe in me and not who I know. It means a lot to me."

They made eye contact and Vinnie's light eyes were misty. She wished she could see what color they actually were. She touched his cheek and turned him to face her. She wanted to encourage him. She hated that he felt less than, and she wished she could figure out why he did. "You are very special. And your work speaks for itself."

Vinnie almost touched her hand on his cheek, but stopped and flashed her a smirk. "If you keep being this nice to me, I'm going to think you want to date me for real. Sit tight, I'll get the door for you."

Anna blinked as he bailed out of the car and retrieved the bags from the trunk. Maybe she was wrong, and Vinnie was attracted to her in some way. After the book came out in December, she'd revisit this conversation with him.

Everything would be fine tonight. This was just dinner. Vinnie opened the door and waited for her to get out of the car, and they walked up to the front door under the umbrella.

"Mat's got three umbrellas in that car, you'd think he'd be capable of finding one." Vinnie snickered, and Anna opened the door for them to get inside.

Instead of being warmly greeted, it was eerily quiet in the house. Before either of them could call out and say hi, Mat came around the corner with Lizzie in his arms.

"What's wr…" Vinnie started but Mat cut him off.

"Can Anna take her for a bit? We have some family business to take care of *right now.*"

Anna had only interacted with Mat a handful of times, and even though he was rough around the edges, he'd never seemed dangerous until right now. His mouth was set in a thin line and he seemed to be shaking, attempting to control himself.

"Yeah. I have a carseat in my car." Vinnie nodded, and grabbed Lizzie's coat, helping get her into it as she put on her shoes. He handed Anna a purple backpack and took Lizzie from Mat.

"Be good for Miss Anna, Lizzie. Daddy loves you." Mat kissed his daughter's cheek.

Whatever was happening, it didn't seem like Lizzie was affected by it. She was as happy as she always seemed to be. "Okee! Love 'OU, Daddy! Bye-BYE!!"

Vinnie gave her the umbrella as they left the house, and she held it over him as he buckled Lizzie into the carseat. He hit the remote start on the car and gave Anna the keys. She could feel the tension in his hand as he folded her fingers over the fob. "I can't explain what's going on and I don't know how long it's going to be before someone comes and gets Lizzie. I need you to trust me and just leave."

"Did something happen to Rex?" Honestly, it was the only thing Anna could think of that would be causing this much distress. What if he'd had a heart attack or something?

Vinnie opened the driver's door and motioned for her to get inside. "No. Mat would have called an ambulance and told us. Please trust me and go. I'll text you as soon as I know more. Can you make sure she eats?"

"Of course. Remind me, does she have any allergies?"

"No. She likes chicken nuggets though, and she's normally not too picky if you call whatever you give her crackers." He leaned into the car and kissed her cheek. "Thank you."

"You're welcome. I hope everything is alright."

"Unfortunately, it rarely is." He waved to Lizzie in the back. "Be good for Miss Anna, Nugget."

"Okee! Bys-bye!!!"

Vinnie closed the car door and marched back to the house. Even his pace was tense. What on earth had happened?

Anna set the keyfob in the cup holder and pulled out of the driveway. "I guess we're going on an adventure, Lizzie."

"YEE! It 'venture times!" The toddler excitedly kicked her legs.

She opted to not take the highway. Vinnie's sports car was light, and she didn't want to risk the highway with the rain still pouring down. She knew a drive-thru spot she could stop for chicken nuggets and a salad for herself. That would take care of dinner, and she could sign up for whichever streaming service was hosting Lizzie's current favorite movie.

Lizzie was happily chattering in the back. Some of it, Anna understood and some of it, she didn't, but she kept nodding along to keep the child occupied.

"Lizzie, did something happen to make your daddy unhappy?" Anna knew better than to ask, but she hated feeling completely out of the loop on whatever was happening.

"Nuh-uh. G'andpa Rex has a f'end and I meets her. Her eyes like my eyes." Lizzie explained.

Lizzie's eyes were different, the heterochromia was stark, one dark brown and one noticeably lighter, probably blue-ish gray if she were to guess. Vinnie had mentioned that Lizzie had inherited them from a relative, but Anna couldn't remember which relative. It was on the edge of her memory, just out of reach. She could recall the rest of the conversation but not the name.

"Have you met your grandpa's friend before? Do you know her?"

"Noes. But she peddy with silver and dark hairs"

A woman with dark and gray hair would have been in Rex's dating age bracket. But she was sure it would have been mentioned if Rex had a girlfriend.

It just concerned her because she didn't want Vinnie to be involved with anything else criminal. That part of his life was fine, as long as it was in the past.

"Was she nice?"

"Oh yes! G'andpa Rex gived her a kiss and she looks at my pictures." Lizzie answered. "I likes her."

So Rex did have a girlfriend, potentially. One who Mat didn't like and might be roping the family back into crime. She was jumping to conclusions. She shouldn't assume.

Anna picked up food and parked Vinnie's car in the garage, snapping a picture for the front desk. Lizzie was well behaved enough to keep at Anna's side through the parking lot and building's lobby. Anna paused by the security desk, showing the picture of the license plate and explaining the situation so Vinnie wouldn't get ticketed or towed.

Lizzie was happy to walk next to her, but the hidden elevator had her dancing as they went up. "Issa magic el'lator."

"It is. Do you remember going up before?"

Oddly Lizzie shook her head despite what she'd just said. The little girl held her hand as the elevator stopped at the top floor.

The hallway was often dark and while it didn't bother her, Lizzie's eyes got big. "Can you hold my phone for me, Lizzie?" She flicked on the flashlight app and offered it.

"Oh yeahs!" False bravery intact, the girl followed her to the door, and Anna opened it carefully, watching for Jackal.

The black cat yowled at her as they got inside, and Anna closed and locked the door.

"KIDDY!" Lizzie screeched, dropping the phone and making Jackal skid to a stop.

Anna knelt down and motioned for Jackel to come. "Here Jackal, here kitty, kitty. Lizzie, be gentle. This is Jackal, she's my kitty."

"Is so peddy!" Her voice was excited but she stayed still holding her hand out. "Heres 'ackel. Here kiddy, kiddy. So peddy."

Jackal slowly approached sniffing the air cautiously, finally allowing herself to be petted by the girl.

Anna was grateful for the quiet moment, watching the two as she and picked up her phone: no new messages. "Why don't we pick a cartoon and eat in the living room?"

"Like 'eathens?"

She wasn't sure what Lizzie meant by that, but she nodded anyway. Arguably, her apartment wasn't the most kid-friendly, but it would be alright for a few hours. No toys here unfortunately. The only thing she could give Lizzie to cuddle, would be a throw pillow.

Thankfully Jackal seemed to be happy to keep the little girl's attention.

She hadn't planned for Lizzie to be here, but she should have stopped and bought her something to play with. If a movie wasn't sufficient entertainment, maybe Anna could download a game on her tablet?

The skyline was already lighting up as the sun was setting on the opposite of the building. "Wow! We isso high!" Lizzie climbed up on the chaise and pressed her face to the glass. "Looks at all the cars!" She angled her head trying to get a better look at the traffic.

Anna pulled a blanket down from one of her cupboards and laid it on the floor. "We'll have a picnic."

"And cartoons!"

"Yes and cartoons."

Vinnie had done several self-studies into the psychological damage of verbal and physical abuse on children and how those traumas impacted those children as they grew into adults. He understood that it went beyond flight, fight, and fawn. Mat was quick to lose his temper, but thought in some twisted way, he deserved what happened to him. Vinnie deduced that he hid behind facts and logic, but he still blamed himself for causing the abuse. For all the fucking unpacking he'd done with what had happened to him when his father, Nathan Goodroe, had been alive, nothing had prepared him for what was in the living room after he'd sent Anna away with Lizzie.

The phrase Mat used, 'we have family business to take care of right now' was code for danger. He expected to see Jim or John in the living room, ready to take revenge for some prior perceived slight. He was terrified that it was going to be Rex beaten to absolute hell by someone who just got out of prison. He'd flat out lied to Anna when he told her they would have called an ambulance if they needed one. What stuck out was how calm Lizzie was, so maybe it was something else. Something only Mat recognized as a threat.

Rex looked just fine, but Mat was clearly pissed. Standing off to the side was a short woman with dark brown hair streaked with silver. It took him only a fraction of a second to realize that he was looking at Jane Elizabeth McCroy, his mother.

Mat folded his arms over his chest. "I'm gonna ask you one more goddamn time, what the fuck are you doing here?"

"You ain't gonna talk to her like that!" Rex hollered back.

"Talk to who like what? She's nothing to me!" Mat snapped, pointing at Jane.

Rex tapped his foot on the floor, his tone was almost accusatory. "This isn't the attitude you had when I told you what happened."

"Because she was dead and not just someone who walked away!"

Jane finally spoke, her voice even and quiet. "I didn't just walk away."

"Well, you sure the fuck weren't around!" Mat clearly wasn't impressed by her composure.

Rex took a step towards Mat. The room felt warmer, like a match too close to a powder keg. "I am not gonna tell you again!"

Vinnie could feel a ringing pierce his eardrums. It was sharp, breaking through the pulsing of his heartbeat. He'd always thought books with scenes of a character's hearing going in and out from stress were cliche, but here he was experiencing it. Rex didn't lose his temper often, but he was trying to protect Jane, who was standing up for herself but without yelling. Unlike Mat, Vinnie didn't have any memories of Jane. Despite the picture he had of her, she was a stranger.

"Where were you all these years?" His own voice sounded far away and detached. He'd been a child the last time he'd disassociated this badly from the space he was in.

Jane turned to face him. She had light crow's feet by her eyes and laugh lines by the corners of her mouth. "Hopkinsville."

Vinnie did the math in his head, here to the club, club to the prison, and subtract the miles between a and c. "That's thirty-seven miles from here."

"Thirty-seven and half miles from gate to front door," she clarified. "I walked it every day I could."

"Did you know what happened to us?"

"Not until after it happened." She maintained eye contact with him.

So she'd known but hadn't done anything about it. "Did you know Rex had us?"

"I assumed he did, but I couldn't check."

"Didn't — the correct word is didn't. You *didn't* check, but you *could* have." Vinnie was starting to shake, but he kept his voice neutral. A grammar lesson was preferable to losing his temper completely.

Rex and Mat had stopped mid-argument to listen to their conversation.

She looked away, finally showing some kind of guilt. Remorse? "It wasn't as simple as you're making it. I needed to keep you safe."

"By abandoning us with fucking Nathan?" Vinnie clenched his fist. He hated that she was trying to lessen her responsibility. She'd left him and Mat to their fate and they hadn't deserved that. Nathan didn't give a shit about them, but he gave a shit when they were in his way, and *magically* they were always in his way. Until an accident that saved them from late night screaming sessions and unclaimed injuries, their lives had been hell. After Nathan died, he and Mat overnight became less clumsy, less hungry, and less scared; after being placed with Rex, they were actually safe.

Mat cleared his throat. "Yeah, that wasn't exactly a picnic."

"I know and I'm sorry." She shifted on her feet, her eyes darting between them, then to the patio door. "I should go. I never should have come back. It was stupid of me to come here." She seemed sad, but she was a grifter so seeming sad was close to meaningless.

"Why did she come back?" Mat asked Rex, apparently deciding to ignore Jane.

Rex sighed. "We hadn't gotten that far."

"Does it have to do with that picture? She keeps looking at it," Vinnie questioned. Mat might have been the talker when they were on the job, but he was the planner — he didn't miss the details. Jane's eyes had strayed to that painting no less than a dozen times during this heated discussion.

"I hid my last score in the wall behind it," She stated, glancing at Rex. "And I know you didn't find it, because you're still living here."

"We should see…" Vinnie started, but Mat interrupted again.

"No. I don't give a shit about that. I want you gone."

"Mat, this ain't your house and that ain't your call," Rex pointed out.

"If you think I'm going to let her anywhere near Lizzie and Kass, you're outta your goddamn mind. We're not staying here if she is. We won't…"

"I never said I was staying." Jane interjected.

"Where would you go? I'm not losing you again." Rex's voice was quiet and for a moment, shifting the perspective.

Jane might have been the mother that chose to walk away from her children, but she was also the woman who Rex had loved and lost. It wasn't fair, what she had done, but it also wasn't fair to drag them apart. Rex didn't deserve this.

"We should let them have some time to talk." Vinnie tapped Mat's shoulder. "We're both mad. Let's go take a drive and calm down. Text Kass and let her know that Lizzie's with Anna"

Mat hesitated, but nodded and followed him toward the door. Vinnie didn't miss Rex's nod of gratitude. The brothers stood under the lip of the roof, staying out of the rain while Mat texted Kass.

He grumbled, "I have three umbrellas in my car."

"Yup," Vinnie affirmed. "But you only think about using one when you have one of your girls with you. You never minded getting caught in the rain."

"And you always hated it."

"I don't like being cold. Reminds me of the trailer."

Mat patted Vinnie's closer arm. "I'm pissed she's just standing there, but I also wanted to fucking hug her. That's pretty fucked up."

Vinnie shook his head. "No, that's normal. For once in your life, you are reacting within societal norms."

"How are you feeling?" The question likely felt as foreign as it sounded coming from Mat.

The positive force Kass had on his brother would never cease to amaze Vinnie. Mat always cared about his family, but until Kass, he was shit at vocalizing it.

"Less passionate than you, either way. I don't have any memories of her. She's a stranger to me. It's like watching through a film of plastic, I can see it, but I'm not as connected."

"Are you sure you aren't…"

"I'm not." Vinnie didn't want anyone else to know or point out how off-kilter he felt about the situation. He was retreading old habits of dealing with intense emotions. He was better at that now, had better control.

Mat looked at his phone. "Kass is still at work. Someone didn't show up. I don't know what to do. But I know I don't want to be here."

"Let's get you guys a hotel room for the night at least. I'll tell Rex to get a bag around for the three of ya and he can meet Kass somewhere with it. He won't mind, and you know Kass, she'll want to get his side of this mess."

"This was gonna be such a good night." Mat shoved his hands in his pockets. "The seller approved me and Kass' offer on one of the houses. We wouldn't be able to move in until the middle of November, but that was the only condition. I was gonna tell Rex that his birthday present was getting his house back. Now this…"

"Congratulations. You should still celebrate that. Business and homeowner, look at you moving up in the world." Vinnie snickered. "Hallmark style family."

Mat shook his head, laughing humorlessly. "Don't give Kass any ideas. She's already chomping at the bit to have creative freedom decorating a whole house. Speaking of which, those stars in Lizzie's room."

"I'll find my notes and set it up again." Vinnie chuckled. "Can't deny my niece her stars. I've got ideas on how to make them better this time around."

"I appreciate it." He sighed. "What am I gonna do if Rex lets her stay? You know he's going to offer and even if I want to, I don't know if I can blame him for that."

Vinnie considered what Mat said, and his brother was right, Rex was going to offer. And if Jane had truly been locked up the entire time, she wouldn't have anything and would need a permanent address if she had any type of probation. Rex would give almost anyone a second chance, and the love of his life wasn't going to be an exception to that.

One of the easiest parts of writing the book was the scenes about Rex and Jane. Tragedy was easier to write, as it was a supercharged emotion and practically wrote itself. Those words had poured onto the pages like water. Anna had given him push back on the section as it wasn't a traditional break in the flow of the book, but he'd won over his point with her. That was a story that needed to be told – the tragedy of the wrong choice made and the love slipping away. With Jane being alive it changed everything. Why had she never reached out? What was she trying to protect them from? He would have to cut it. On top of everything else, she was impacting his fucking book.

"I suppose if Rex lets her stay, you could look for a place to rent or deal with it like an adult. We should have a conversation with her, hear her out."

"Yelling isn't talking?"

"Not successful talking."

"If you say so, let's go save Anna from my tiny terror."

"Thanks for watching her." Mat shifted a sleeping Lizzie on his shoulder. "I hope she wasn't too much trouble."

"Not at all, but Jackal will probably sleep for a week. She hasn't had anyone play with her like that since she was a kitten," Anna laughed.

Vinnie offered a warning, "I'd invest in a stuffed cat pretty quick or she'll be hounding you for a real one."

"No kidding." Mat nodded goodbye and Vinnie closed the door behind his brother.

Anna started tidying up the living room. Nothing too intense, as the maid service was scheduled for tomorrow.

She wanted to get the food containers thrown out and the dishes in the sink. Mat and Vinnie had gone to get something to eat before picking up Lizzie, who truly hadn't been that difficult to watch.

They had been vague as to what happened earlier and Anna had been content to wait until Mat left, but now she wanted answers.

"Where's your vacuum?" Vinnie asked as he poked his head into her coat closet.

"I don't own one."

"How can you not own a vacuum? You have a cat."

Anna tapped her foot on the floor. "My floors are temperature-regulated tiles, I have a handheld machine for my furniture, and my apartment gets cleaned once a week by a professional service. Do you want something to drink?"

"Sure, something not caffeinated, not alcoholic, but not water. Because I'm *not* being picky at all tonight." Vinnie took a few steps from the entryway that led to her small kitchen.

"You're allowed to be picky. Whatever happened, it seems like it was a lot." Anna pulled down two coffee mugs and started her coffee pot with a decaf blend. She leaned against the counter, looking up at Vinnie. Trivial as it was, she liked that he was only a little taller than she was. "Am I allowed to know what happened? Or at least how you're doing? You're very tense."

Vinnie averted his eyes and looked around her apartment instead. "You pay someone to clean your apartment? It's so small."

"I have better things to do with my downtime and I have the money to do so. I'm not ashamed of it."

"Sorry, that sounded judgmental." He fidgeted with his phone.

"I didn't take it that way. Did you actually eat with your brother?" Anna noticed that when Vinnie got stressed he didn't eat, and she was the opposite. As much as she hated the gym, she found herself there quite often to combat that bad habit. That habit also kept her out of the size zero category.

"Yeah. We only had one drink. That might change for Mat once he meets up Kass at their hotel room."

Interesting. Whatever happened had Mat and Kass not staying elsewhere for the night. So it was serious. Rex was only in his fifties, but if he'd done drugs or drank heavily in his youth, that could change how fast his body aged. Something happening to Rex was the only thing that made sense. If something had broken in the house, they would have banded together and fixed it, not gone in different directions. The Goodroes were tight-knit; even if everything was falling apart, they held onto each other. Anna never had that before; it took some getting used to. She wasn't accustomed to so many people being interested in her well-being.

Vinnie was so quiet. He was usually busy with something when he wasn't talking. But now, he was standing still with his head down and his hands shoved in his pockets, looking between miserable and one minor inconvenience away from crying.

The coffee pot beeped, and Anna poured them both a cup, motioning for him to follow her to the living room. She pulled the coffee table closer to her chaise, and they sat on it together. The shades automatically dropped down on their timer, covering the windows and giving the apartment a softer light.

"I get the feeling you don't want to talk about what happened. But why is your brother going to a hotel for the night? Am I allowed to know that?" She didn't want to bully him, but there was a limit to the uncertainty that she was comfortable with, even if their relationship was a ruse. Off-handedly she wondered about the gentle kiss he'd placed on her cheek before she'd left with Lizzie. Mat was touch-orientated but Vinnie didn't seem to be as much.

Vinnie sipped from his cup and set it down on the table. "My mother is alive. She was at Rex's house. That's what happened."

Anna blinked. She'd asked about his mother when going through edits of his book. He'd told her that 'disappeared' in her line of work meant no longer alive. He didn't seem to have any doubts that her fate was certain. She reclined against the arm of the chaise and observed Vinnie's more than tense posture. He was in pain.

"Did she say where she's been?" She couldn't think of anything else to ask.

Vinnie unlocked his phone, opened a text thread, and handed it to her without a word.

Kass: She's still with Rex. Tell Mat I have bags for a couple of days
Kass: She got out of jail two days ago
Kass: I think you should at least try and talk to her
Kass: She might need to stay here

Vinnie: I'll let Mat know. And thanks, Sis.

Kass: No problem :)
Kass: We're family, we'll get through this. Hugs!

Vinnie: Indeed.

Anna did some fast math from Vinnie's age to when he said his mother left to his current age and it was over twenty years. It was a lifetime. It was the lifetime of her children. Why would she just show up? Had those two days been spent trying to find them?

"Oh."

"That is a full sentence." Vinnie set his glasses on the table and flexed his fingers at his hairline. "She was there the whole time. Less than forty miles from where I spent most of my life. And she never even tried."

Anna set Vinnie's phone down next to his glasses, before reaching for her phone to turn on the white noise through her apartment's surround sound. "Did she say why she didn't try?"

"Something about protecting us." His voice was muffled by his hands. "My head is killing me."

"Here." Anna tugged his arm, coaxing him to lie down. "Lay down on my lap, I'll massage your head."

"I don't want..."

"You won't make me uncomfortable. I want to try something to help you feel better, physically at least."

She knew he couldn't really see her without his glasses, but he complied, letting out a sigh as her nails started moving through his dark hair. She moved her fingers lightly in a circular pattern at first then slowly added more pressure.

Vinnie let out a sound of appreciation. Anna would have smiled but he was shaking, his breath slightly uneven. Betrayal was a deep feeling, and having his mother go from an idolized memory to someone real and flawed must be gut-wrenching.

She noticed that he was being careful not to touch her legs, his wrists were crossed, hands clasped and pulled tightly to his chest. The relationships she'd had in the past had been more physical, but this felt intimate.

He was so careful of her space. She continued to move her hands, lightening the pressure behind his ear. His body relaxed slightly, and he breathed more deeply. He trusted her.

"I used to get migraines in college. I had an almost-lover do this for me all the time until I got my daith piercing."

"I've never noticed your piercing."

"I have a very small, custom piece in it. You'd have to get very close to my right ear to notice it." Anna had to resist the urge to touch it as she often did when she referenced it. "Is this helping?"

"It is." He was quiet, contrasting his normally animated nature. "I'm not used to being touched. It's not my go-to for comfort."

"I've noticed, especially since you kissed my cheek before I left with Lizzie." She closed her eyes, wishing she could edit herself in real-time.

"You said almost-lover. I didn't miss that." Vinnie changed the subject, so she'd go with it.

"Her family was conservative, so even if she felt what I did, she never would have acted on it." Anna let out a slow breath, before admitting.

"I was so lovesick. But she wasn't ever mine. It was only a dream, and other than my current relationship, it was the best I ever had."

"I hate to break this to you, but your current relationship isn't real either." His shoulders relaxed more fully and there was a touch of humor in his voice.

Anna smiled, letting her fingers trail down to the nape of his neck. "But it's an honest one, and I'm very fond of the person I'm in it with."

"Thank you, Anna."

Chapter 5: Change The Setting & Pace

Take A Breath and Assess

September 18th; 82 Days until…

"You know, a couple of years ago, I stood in this kitchen and got fuck all to say about someone moving in here, and while it was the best thing that ever happened to me, I'm not trying to repeat history here." Mat rolled the glass in his hand clinking the ice together.

"Nice save," Vinnie grunted as Mat elbowed him. "Seriously?"

"Knock it off you two," Kass admonished. She looked exhausted. Between her new day job, raising a toddler, and all of this drama, it was clearly starting to wear her down. "Please just hear him out."

Rex took a sip from his coffee cup. "It's not permanent. It's a couple of months until I can get all her paperwork around and then we'll go up to the cabin and get out of your hair."

"Kass and I will be gone by November." Mat questioned, "Can't you just take her up to the cabin and get papers for her up there?"

"Ah, yes the universal language of criminals is so connected. One Tom, Dick, or Harry is just as trustworthy as another so no reason to be cautious. That's definitely something we learned growing up – not to vet everyone we worked with." There were times that Vinnie thought his brother might actually have brain damage from the stupid shit they'd gotten into.

He was grateful that Anna was still at the office, there were things he didn't want her to know about. They were friends, but their relationship was fake and the fourth rule of crime school was to never involve those you don't have to.

"Guys please." Kass sighed before addressing Rex. "I know why you're letting Jane stay here, and I'm not trying to change your mind, but I'm not comfortable with her being alone with Lizzie. *I* don't know her that well yet."

"That's a very big yet," Mat countered. "I don't really want her around Lizzie in general. Where is she anyway?"

"My room. She wanted to let us talk to Rex without the volume going up ten decibels." Vinnie turned the coffee pot back on, he was working at the club tonight, and he needed more caffeine.

"I don't see why we're bending over backward for her," Mat insisted.

"Because I'm asking you to." Rex cleared his throat. "I know things aren't okay between you two, but I can't just…I don't want her to disappear again. I'm not sure my heart could handle it."

Mat sighed. "I get it, but don't ask me to like it."

"I won't. Let's go sit on the patio and have a drink." Rex motioned for Mat to follow.

"You coming, Sweetheart?"

Kass nodded, "Go. I'll finish up the dishes and be out in a couple of minutes."

Vinnie turned on the faucet to get the hot water moving and retrieved the drying rack. Kass started on the dishes as he wiped down the counter.

"What am I gonna do when I have to do this on my own?" she wondered out loud.

"Make your lazy husband do it." Vinnie scoffed.

She chuckled. "I suppose. My new house is gonna have an actual dishwasher."

"Fancy. Look at you two moving up in the world."

She flicked water at him, and he returned the favor, so she stuck out her tongue at him.

Vinnie admonished her as they worked on their task. "Mind your manners, Sis, you're supposed to be keeping our clan on the straight and narrow."

"I'll make you a deal, Brother Thief, stop bringing nonsense into my life, and I'll see what I can do." Kass finished scrubbing the pan in her hand and passed it to him to rinse.

He was going to miss this when they didn't live under the same roof. From the moment he and Kass had shaken hands, they'd been instant friends. She was the sister he'd never had, and even if things hadn't worked out between her and Mat, he would've stayed friends with her. Kass was sassy, funny, and kind enough to make anyone's day better.

"It's exciting that your offer on the house got accepted."

"Technically, one got accepted, and we got a counteroffer on the other." Kass looked up at him. "The second one came back stating we can move in immediately, but they want thirty-thousand more. I don't want to go with my second choice for more money because Mat doesn't want to be here. It's sticky."

Vinnie nodded. “Thirty-thousand is quite a bit more.”

“It’s fifty-thousand more than the first house.” She scrubbed out one of the coffee cups. “Mat liked the first house better too. It’s closer to the restaurant.”

“Just push back and he won’t do anything too stupid. He knows you’ve got the cooler head. He’ll listen to you.” His brother wouldn’t mess with Kass’ happiness, no matter how mad he was.

“How are you feeling?”

Vinnie wasn’t entirely sure how to answer the question. Was he mad that Jane had disappeared and then reappeared? Yes. Was he was curious about the whys and wanted to talk to her? Also yes. “I’m a bit torn. I’m less angry than Mat but less forgiving than Rex. She’s never been real to me, and now she is, my brain’s not sure how to process it.”

“That’s fair. Are you going to Chicago with Anna this weekend?”

“Unless someone starts throwing things around here, yes. She told me I could back out if I needed to, but I don’t want to break my promise.”

He wasn’t lying to Kass at the moment, but he wasn’t being forthcoming either. The trip to Chicago was as much about Anna’s business as it was about his book. Her conference coincided with his cover artist completing the rough draft of his book cover. He and Anna were going to be meeting up with the artist during the day, then attending a black-tie party at night.

“Things seem to be going well with her. Don’t let this craziness get in the way if you can help it.”

“Weren’t you pregnant by drama-incarnate when you met Mat?”

“Let’s not bring my story into this, we’re talking about yours.” Kass rolled her eyes, before commenting. “I really do like Anna, she’s nice, but kinda intimidating. She reminds me a little of Leila, but softer, for lack of a better word.”

He smirked. “Kassarah Goodroe, are you implying that I have a type? A *thing* for strong women?”

She flushed and snapped the towel against his leg, “You’re such a brat. Go get ready for work and outta my hair.”

Vinnie snickered before looking out through the patio doors and scowling. “I think they’re gonna start fighting again. Rock, paper, scissors for who’s going out there to intervene.”

“Sorry, still washing dishes.” Kass showed off her still-wet hands and feigned sorrow at the turn of events.

“Rex bought Jane a phone. Number’s on the fridge so you and/or Mat can text and avoid running into her in the house. If, or, and when she needs to come in.” He strode out onto the patio to interrupt the potential disaster.

Mat and Rex paused and looked at him expectantly.

"Are we getting loud?" Mat questioned.

Vinnie shrugged. "Lizzie's still sleeping, so I'm going with no. I was just going to tell you that I heard a rumor they might be remaking Shane."

"Can those entitled assholes write original movies anymore? Or am I gonna have to suffer through remakes ruining my favorite movies until I die of disappointment?" Rex grumbled and sat down across from Vinnie.

"Not all remakes are bad," Mat argued.

Rex arched his eyebrow. "Name a single good one."

Mat paused for a moment. "The Thing."

"That CGI piece of..."

"Not the prequel. The John Carpenter flick from '82, it was a remark of The Thing from Another World," Mat explained.

"I don't remember that one." Rex took a sip his cold coffee.

"It was from 1951, so it's old, even by your standards." Vinnie smirked as his uncle glared at him.

"Kid, one these days you're gonna end up in cement shoes if you keep talking like that."

"Just put me in the water by Mat's bar so I can haunt him." Vinnie stood back up and stretched.

Mat growled, "Oh fuck off."

"Yeah. Yeah." He waved Mat off and walked through the yard.

"Where are you going?" Rex questioned.

Vinnie kept walking, "Work. I'll see you sometime tomorrow morning." He pulled his phone out and looked at the picture Anna had sent him a picture of her dress for the event on Saturday. *Why hadn't she just told him it was navy blue? Navy blue was a standard color.*

September 23th; 77 Days Until...

Vinnie hadn't traveled very much in his life between monetary and judicial entanglements, and he read about more places than he visited. Plus, flying first class? Not an expense he would have afforded himself, and damn was the legroom nice. Flying out of Houston was one thing, but landing at O'Hare with Anna and Alysha was another thing entirely. Anna moved with purpose, and Alysha, despite her height, seemed to be used to the pace. He had to force himself not to gawk at his surroundings.

"I just don't know why Cypress would have wanted to move up the meeting. She's never been a morning person," Anna remarked, checking her phone as they walked towards the baggage claim.

"Maybe she's turning over a new leaf?" Alysha snickered. "Or I could have requested the reschedule."

"Why would you…" Anna stepped onto the moving sidewalk.

God, he hated these things, they almost made him seasick.

"These tickets were cheaper. You can spend money or time, that's what you taught me."

Anna arched her eyebrow. "And you know my preference is to spend money."

"True, but..." Aylsha looked down at her phone and wiggled her shoulders excitedly. "Yes!"

Anna glanced over her co-worker's shoulder. "Did you fly us in early for donuts?"

"For Stan's donuts? Yes, I did! Remember when you offered me 'anything' in return for helping you when you got back from Korea? My plans for us are my *'anything'* that you promised." Alysha had a Cheshire-Cat grin when she had a scheme in mind. Vinnie had immediately noticed this about the young publishing manager.

Alysha was fully capable of keeping a practiced poker face, but joy seemed to light up her countenance. It was endearing. Her current hairstyle caught his curiosity when they met up at the Houston airport. Long, eye-catching cornrow braids in reds, yellows, and oranges that made her hair look like a living fire. Several of the girls at the club would style their hair in a similar fashion, so he knew the complex style was costly. He often wondered about the intricacies of the process because he liked to know things, but he also didn't want to intrude on a space he wasn't needed in.

"I think she's going to steal me away for part of this trip." Anna broke his train of thought, looking up at him as they stepped off the moving sidewalk.

He smirked. "I'm capable of entertaining myself without getting into too much trouble. There's a few touristy places I'd be interested in seeing. Although, I might have to check out this donut place if Alysha thinks so highly of it."

"You can order a dozen and have them shipped." Anna shook her head.

"Not at seventy bucks a dozen."

"Are these donuts or drugs?" Vinnie questioned.

Alysha let out a laugh. "Both. Play your cards right and I might share."

"Much appreciated." He held the elevator so they could go down to the baggage claim. He hadn't even had time to read the signs, so he just kept up with Anna, who clearly knew the way.

They got into the elevator with several other people, and Vinnie pressed himself to the wall to avoid crowding into anyone's space. *File this under tall person problems: accidental intimidation/looming.* Anna and Alysha were chatting about tomorrow evening's party and he was content to listen in versus participate. He should have left The Playhouse earlier last night/this morning, but he hadn't and he was exhausted.

"What pretty braids." A woman to his left complimented, and Vinnie realized the older woman was reaching for Alysha's hair.

He caught the woman's hand in his before she could follow through with the action. "What a unique ring. Is it turquoise?"

The woman blinked up at him, and to be fair he could feel the eyes of everyone in the elevator on him. Maybe his next book should be 'how to be awkward for fun and profit.'

"It is. But young man, you should be careful just touching someone." She clicked her tongue disapprovingly and took back her hand.

If he were Mat, he would have snapped about how he stopped her from doing just that, but he wasn't Mat, so instead he simply smiled. "Indeed. We should all remember our personal space."

"I don't need someone like you to tell me that." The older woman turned up her nose.

The elevator doors opened and he followed behind Anna and Alysha towards the baggage carousel. Anna excused herself to take a call and he and Alysha stood side by side watching for their bags.

"What kind of donut do you want?" She stepped forward to grab her suitcase, and he let her, despite his instinct to intervene.

He yawned, unable to help it. "I'm not too picky. I have a sweet tooth."

"You really do – extra flavor shot, cream, and sugar." She popped up the handle of sleek, forest green bag, the silver accents were scratched no doubt from frequent travel.

He was genuinely confused. Had Alysha gotten him coffee before? "You know my coffee order?"

"No, but Anna texted it to me before." She held up her phone.

"Good memory."

"I keep telling you guys, I'm magic."

He chuckled, grabbing Anna's suitcase. "I have no doubt."

Vinnie glanced over at Anna, who was animatedly talking on the phone, not noticing the man in a powder-blue suit who approached her and tapped her on the shoulder. She held her hand up to him and continued talking, turning away from him. He didn't seem to get the hint and stepped around her, putting himself in her eyeline again. Anna's brows knitted together and she pivoted to get away from him a second time.

His own simple black suitcase was coming up, so he snagged it and marched towards Anna. Vinnie put himself squarely between the 'gentleman,' and Anna. "Help you?"

"Sorry, man. I didn't know she was with you." The blonde man's brown eyes widened and he took a step back.

"Well, you know now." Vinnie narrowed his eyes, hoping it came across as intimidating. *Tall person advantage: easier to be imposing when you could look down on someone.* The man quickly stepped in the opposite direction.

"We'll see you soon, Cypress." Anna completed her call, threading her arm through his as Alysha passed her, a coco-brown, Louis Vuitton suitcase with Anna's initials monogrammed in cream.

The three of them continued toward the pick-up area, and Alysha mimicked in a mock-lower voice, "You know now."

Vinnie's cheeks warmed, but before he could defend himself Anna leaned against him. Her cool, slender fingers threaded through his before squeezing reassuringly. "Thank you."

He expected her to pull away, but she didn't. Instead, she stayed tucked at his side.

"Of course."

They dropped off Alysha at the hotel with the luggage but stayed in the cab so they could make their meeting. He couldn't help but crane his neck up as he looked out the window to see the buildings towering overhead. The air in the city smelled fresher than he imagined it would, Boston had smelled older and saltier.

"Cypress' office is in the West Loop. It shouldn't take us too long to get there, even with the traffic."

"Fifteen minutes tops, Ma'am." The driver chimed in, adjusting his mirror.

Anna nodded and checked her phone. "Thank you."

"I expected the city to feel more congested," Vinnie commented as he surveyed the moving traffic, then turned to Anna. "You'll have to show me your old haunts, since you grew up here."

She blinked as if trying to remember what those places would be, which was fair considering she hadn't lived here in a few years. Cities changed fast. Businesses that had stood for thirty years could close overnight. Nothing stayed the same forever.

"Not asking you to reveal any dark secrets, just curious about your favorite places before you moved to Houston. I do want to get a slice of Chicago pizza before we go back. I've heard stories. I think Giordano's was the name I heard most. Also, I was reading up on the history of prohibition and there all bars all over this city with a speakeasy vibe, some you even need a membership to enter."

He continued, "of course, the Green Door is one of the most well-known, but I think I read about one on the West Loop."

"The Office is on the West Loop, but if you want to see a speakeasy, I know the one you'd like better. We can start at the Green Door but then I'll show you around a bit. As for pizza, I can find you the taste of the city. We should be..." Anna trailed off. As they pulled to a stop in front of a brick building, she paid the cab driver, sabotaging his attempt to try.

Vinnie hopped out of the cab and got around quickly enough to offer his hand and help her up onto the curb.

She smiled as she took it. "The airport interception was appreciated, but this is spoiling me a bit."

"I like to live up to the roles I play." He grinned back at her and let go of her hand as they stepped into the office building.

The exposed brick and pipes had been painted white and there were bright pops of green and pale wood floors, giving the space an inviting atmosphere. There were people working on laptops at the various tables and on couches against one of the walls.

"Anna!"

Vinnie looked to his left where the voice called from, but didn't see the speaker immediately. Anna offered her hand down, and he realized the woman who called Anna's name was in a wheelchair.

"Good morning, Cypress. I love the space. It suits you. Very optimistic."

She shook Anna's hand first then reached for his. "Accessible and stylish, who knew? You must be Mr. Goodroe. It's a pleasure to meet you. I'm Cypress Summers."

He shook her hand. "Vinnie's just fine."

"Sure. Follow me. I love the concept art you did for your cover."

"Well, my creative skills are more word-focused, but I made an attempt." He shoved his hands into his pockets as they made their way down the hallway.

Cypress glanced up at him as she unlocked her office door. "Good attempt, the sketch had great bones. I think you'll like what I came up with."

Her office looked more like a conference room, but Vinnie supposed since she was in a wheelchair, an open concept would be necessary. It was exceptionally neat with nothing on the walls, in fact; the only part of the office that looked used was the far end of the table where a lap and stretch pads were visible.

"You'll have to tell me your secret for maintaining such a clean environment. I'm horrible about keeping things, it drives my business partner crazy." He took a seat beside her, making certain to give her enough space.

"Oh, I only rent this space a month or two out of the year for meetings. The rest of the year I work out of my cramped little studio, where the L shakes my windows and I'm in constant fear of fires."

"Houston has a better housing market." Anna sat on Cypress's other side.

"Anna, if I *ever* leave Chicago, I'm going to the Northwest, not Texas." Cypress's fingers flew across her keyboard.

"The winters are mostly mild," Anna countered.

"And risk my wheels melting to the sidewalk in hundred-degree heat? Naw, pass. Don't tell me you've acclimated."

"Chicago will always be in my heart and I do miss the seasons, especially winter parties on Navy Pier." Anna's smile was soft, and Vinnie wondered what she was remembering.

He hated the cold. He couldn't imagine willingly being in the midwest in the winter and near the water. That was the type of chill he'd pass on experiencing. The Christmas trips up to Rex's cabin in Kansas were cold enough for him. He rubbed his arm, instinctively.

"Should we start with his cover?" Cypress rested her hands on the sketchpad in front of her.

He fought the urge to answer for Anna, but this was her world and overstepping would be rude.

"I thought you were designing all the covers digitally now," Anna questioned as she set down her phone, then addressed him. "She's designed about a dozen covers for me for other upcoming books."

He couldn't keep the smirk off his face. "I feel decidedly less special now."

Cypress clicked her tongue. "You shouldn't. Yours is the only one she asked me to go old school on."

Anna cleared her throat and snatched up her phone, excusing herself to go make a call. "Cypress, could you go over his cover with him first? I'll be right back."

"Of course." The artist grinned and opened her sketchpad, flipping through the pages.

Vinnie should have been focused on seeing his cover, but he was curious as to why Anna had singled out his cover.

"It's been a while since I've seen her flustered. You two must be getting along."

He would have contested the assumption, but as far as the world was concerned he was Anna's boyfriend, so he simply nodded.

"You could have shared the suite with me and made Vinnie stay in the other room." Anna sipped on her glass of champagne as the woman doing her pedicure rubbed her calves.

Alysha checked her Apple watch. "I've got calls for the rest of the afternoon and I'm ducking out of the party early tomorrow."

"Why are you leaving early? Is everything alright?"

"I'm good. But I found a writer here in Chicago that I want. I want her so much, I'm subjecting myself to church." Alysha shook her head.

"That's a serious detour for you." Anna observed, "why not meet her before or after? Or call her?"

"Because she ghosted me after getting cold feet about publishing her manuscript."

"So she's the actual reason you rescheduled our flights?"

Alysha smirked. "Technically, yes. But the donuts were a solid bonus."

"Fair enough. Tell me about this writer. Why is she worth chasing?"

"This YA book of hers is diverse and empowering and joyful. It's about growing towards something better and teaching how it's possible." She twisted one of her braids around her finger. "I freaking cried when I read it. The world needs it. The little girl I used to be, needed it."

The salon was quiet as soft music played to compliment the zen aesthetic, with only the sounds of filing of nails and muted conversations interrupting.

Alysha shifted and cracked her back, "No, the neutral and white for her, not the pink. The pink is for me."

The younger nail tech rolled her eyes at the correction, but the older woman shook her head and wordlessly exchanged their bottles. She started painting Anna's toes carefully applying the white tips and pointed for the other woman to start on Alysha's.

"Thank you." Anna nodded and sipped from her glass. "This was a good idea."

"I'm always full of good ideas."

"You are. What's the writer's hang up with having the book out in the world?"

"She's worried about her family finding out. She doesn't think they'd approve of the magic system and gods she made up."

"She created a mythology and a magic system? How old is she?"

"Eighteen, just turned."

"And it's solid?"

"She wrote a separate mythology book. She's so organized."

"That's incredible. I'm sure you'll convince her. I've never known you to fail at anything you've put your mind to."

"Seriously, Anna, thank you for everything."

"You have earned every opportunity I've given you."

The younger nail tech cleaned up the supplies, while the older woman addressed them with a practiced smile. "You ladies are all set. It's been a pleasure to have you visit our spa."

Anna signed off on having the spa treatments charged to her room, but handed both women cash tips. As they walked out she checked her phone again. There was a message from Ben asking about expanding his budget and how his father was open to the discussion.

"Son of a Bitch," she snarled as she answered the message, agreeing to speak to them tomorrow.

"What's wrong?"

"Ben."

"Is he trying to get more money?"

"Yes, and now he's getting this father involved."

"Must be nice to have that advantage."

"If I could get his father off the board, I would. Richard has been dead weight for years. I should have told Vinnie that all the executives on the board and their families will be attending this party. I can't believe I didn't mention that. It'll be fine, he can handle himself." Anna was more speaking to herself as she continued walking towards the elevator. She stopped short as Alysha grabbed her arm, jerking her to an abrupt stop and squashing them together.

She let out a low whisper. "Hot damn, he's been hiding a body under those long sleeves."

"What?"

Alysha turned Anna's head towards the fitness center they'd just walked by. Vinnie had his back to the window as he lifted himself up, performing a chin-up on gym's equipment.

He wasn't shirtless, but he was wearing a sleeveless white top and well-fitting gray shorts. His grip was wide as he slowly pulled himself up and lowered back down without planting his feet. The muscles in his back flexed as he lifted his chin over the bar again and remained tense as he lowered himself. His measured pace made a shiver run down Anna's spine as her brain equated his rhythmic movements to something more torrid.

Her tongue darted out to moisten her lips. He was stronger than Anna thought. She needed to get pictures of him in a casual outfit for marketing purposes, of course.

"Do you need water, whiskey, or a cold shower? Maybe a towel at least for the drool there?" Alysha teased.

"Hush. What I *need* is to get laid. This has been the longest I've been celibate in a decade." Anna rolled her shoulders, attempting to loosen the tension building there, and forced herself to look away from Vinnie.

"Well, if you dated him for real..."

"Hush, and go start your calls. I know you're why my schedule was mysteriously cleared." She started towards the elevator.

Alysha mashed the up button. "I just figured you'd want to spend some one on one time with him without all his family drama."

Anna stepped onto the elevator with Alysha on her heels. "He thinks I have haunts here to show him."

"He's so smart. How has he not figured out that work is your life?" She checked her phone.

"I honestly have no idea."

Vinnie held his hand out for Anna as they exited the Lyft once they reached the destination he planned.

"I could have paid. This trip is for me, not you." She shouldered her bag over her houndstooth jacket and allowed him to help her.

"I think we need to establish a rule. If I suggest it, then I pay, and if you suggest it, then you pay, unless you request otherwise."

"Leaving room for chivalry?"

"Listen, I'm aware that Rex is rough around the edges, but he did make a valiant attempt to make good men of Mat and myself."

"I think he did a fine job," She glanced around.

He hadn't intended for them to match, but his chocolate brown pants and wine colored sweater mirrored the colors in her jacket. He was grateful he'd picked the white collared shirt to go under versus the black he'd originally picked out. Even with Anna in jeans, it would have looked far too intentional. The mirrored windows of the buildings reflected them hand in hand – oh god, they looked like preppy catalog models. He needed to be more careful. He didn't want to embarrass her.

"If you were aiming for Giordano's, you missed it by about a block." Anna still had a flush in her cheeks. Going to the spa with Alysha must have been good for her.

He twisted his watch on his wrist. "Pizza is on the agenda, but there is a tourist trap in Willis Tower that I have to see."

"The Skydeck at *Sears* Tower," she deduced, then shook her head. "I'll go up to the floor with you, but I'm not getting anywhere near that glass box."

"It would be a safe place for you to face your fear."

"You'd get a front row seat for a panic attack. I've argued with my therapist about this. I'm not interested in immersion therapy." She pulled her hand away and motioned for him to follow.

He fell in step with her brisk pace. "Fair enough. The Skydeck can hold up to ten-thousand pounds. Each box is three layers of half-inch thick glass laminated into one seamless unit, and the fully tempered, low-iron clear glass panels weigh fifteen-hundred pounds. It's fascinating how they created and built such a unique attraction."

"Still not gettin' me anywhere near it." She laughed as they entered the building.

If Anna minded his slow meander through the exhibits on Chicago's history, she didn't give any indication. He barked out a laugh as she flipped off the image of the Cubs stadium when they passed it in the Chicago landmarks.

"White Sox for life, huh?"

"Yes." She smirked as they got onto the elevator to go up the 103rd floor.

Vinnie knew that he probably shouldn't find the information about buildings around the world as interesting as he did, but he couldn't help it. His brain had always worked a bit differently. *No changing it at this point.*

"You have now reached the 103rd floor," the narration informed them, but the panel read 90th floor and they still went up for a bit before 103 illuminated in green.

"It's a bit off," he remarked as the doors opened, and he was pointed in the direction to walk around the tower.

Anna stepped to his inside, keeping him between her and the windows.

"Are you alright? I can hurry if you want."

She put her hands into her pockets. "I'm fine as long as I'm not near the edge or the glass. I get disorientated if I look down."

"It's a common phobia," Vinnie confirmed, but his eyes were fixed on the views in front of him. The sprawling, tight-knit cityscape contrasting against the openness of the lake was poetic. But something suddenly struck him. "Your apartment has two walls of windows, you live on the top floor."

"I certainly don't press my face against the glass. I love the sunshine and moonlight that they provide. I try not to think about heights and I'm accustomed to my own space, so it bothers me less."

She stepped closer to him as a tour group passed. A bunch of teenagers laughing and taking pictures.

He pulled out his cellphone and took a few pictures as they made their way around. They reached the boxes themselves, and Anna stepped back from him so he could stand in one. The city was beneath him, the view wasn't anything like he'd experienced before.

Honestly, he thought he'd get nervous looking down, but it was the opposite. He got a bit of a rush from it, seeing the traffic and buildings beneath him. The line from Titanic about being king of the world rang in his memories.

"I can take your picture if you want." As Anna held out her hand for his phone, someone bumped into her and knocked her forward.

She gasped and closed her eyes. Vinnie dropped his phone, opting to catch her and stop her forward momentum. He shifted his back foot to anchor himself as she crashed into him, instinctively gripping her hips for better control. She had pulled her arms tight to her own chest, her elbows impacted his ribs making him grunt. Anna let out a small squeak, her hands clawing down his chest in controlled desperation as she attempted to center herself.

"It's okay." He lowered his voice. He didn't want to draw more attention to her as she dug her nails into his forearms. She was trembling, her breathing coming in short, shallow bursts. "Just keep your eyes closed and walk backwards."

"I can't." She clenched her jaw. "I can't move."

"Then look at me."

She peaked up at him through her lashes, fear evident in her clear blue eyes. Her grip intensified. She was gonna leave marks at this rate. He pressed his forehead to hers and bumped her toe with his. "Let's scooch that one foot back. Good. Now the other. That's good. Good job."

Anna started to giggle but kept moving with him until he got her feet off of the clear glass. *Why was she laughing? Stress response?* She let go of him and covered her mouth, still laughing, but motioning for him to follow.

Vinnie scooped his phone, grimacing the fractured screen and quickstepped to match Anna's pace. "May I ask what's so funny?"

She looped her arm through his as she fought to keep a straight face, continuing to the elevators with purpose. The doors closed and she doubled over, holding her sides as she burst into laughter. He'd heard her laugh, but not like this. It was a full belly laugh and wasn't something she'd likely let out very often, given her professional nature. But he still wanted to know what was so amusing.

"I can't..." she tried to catch her breath again but kept laughing.

Vinnie wondered if this was just a reaction to the stress of her fear. He didn't think anything he'd said was funny. He'd just tried to reassure her. *What was funny about that?*

Managing to get herself under control, she leaned against the wall of the elevator, wiping tears from her eyes.

"I'm very confused."

She nodded, still grinning ear to ear. "I'm sorry. When you said 'that's good,' I heard 'good girl.' And I couldn't figure out why you were using a praise kink to get me out of a panic attack. But I'm not gonna lie, it worked."

His cheeks burned, but he started laughing along with her. "Jesus Christ! Why would I say anything like that in public?"

"I know. That's why I couldn't stop laughing." She waved her hand trying to maintain control. "Come on, you deserve a real Chicago deep dish, than we're getting drinks, because I need one."

"Me too."

Anna still laughing; caught his hand. "Come on, you."

September 24th; 76 Days Until…

Vinnie adjusted the knot of his tie; the navy-blue and black pattern was complimented the black shirt he'd picked to contrast his lighter gray suit. The event was formal but not black tie, and he was glad to have the option of a little color. He was to meet Anna on the roof in twenty minutes, when he and Alysha went up together. *Safety in numbers or something like that.*

His time with Anna had been a breath of fresh air to get himself out of his own head. With the fallout from Jane basically coming back from the dead, he didn't want to be alone with his thoughts. Throwing himself into the role of dutiful boyfriend was a welcome distraction, one that kept his mind from spiraling.

Even if it was fake. He didn't want to get lost in his head. There was too much there he didn't want to unpack – that's what therapy was for.

After a decidedly embarrassing moment at the Skydeck, Anna had taken him to Pequod's for a slice of pizza. And as was often the case, the little hole in the wall spot offered the best comfort food. Anna had taken him to the Green Door, which had confused him until she motioned for him to follow her down to a hidden gem called, The Drifter.

The eccentric burlesque themed speakeasy was a treat, to say the least, with a tarot card ordering system. The warm, built-in wooden shelves full of bottles, adjacent to exposed brick walls, with black painted piping above were a perfect complement to the vintage bar and stools.

He obviously couldn't make changes to The Playhouse to mirror what he'd seen. Tearing apart the drop ceiling for a cosmetic reason would make Leila considering killing him, but he'd made some notes for private events or a theme night. The environment was simply too extraordinary not to draw inspiration from. Anna had talked about going to private parties at this venue and loving it. She told him she wanted to bring him here when he'd mentioned speakeasies.

They hadn't stayed out late considering Anna had meetings this morning before tonight's party. This was an annual meeting for the executives on her board and their families. He checked his brand-new phone for the tenth time within the minute as his foot tapped incessantly on the carpet. No pressure, just don't embarrass her in front of the most important people at her company.

Before going back to London House, they'd made one stop after The Drifter on the east side of the city where the signs read in both English and what Vinnie assumed was Korean. Anna had gone into the bakery and came out with a small bag containing what she called injeolmi, a rice cake dessert. She offered him a piece, and it was good. It wasn't as sweet as most American desserts and the texture was chewy akin to a stretched out marshmallow. The bag was sitting on the table in the living section of the suite they were sharing, next to the bag from the cellphone store. Anna had insisted on replacing his broken one, purchasing the newest model without giving him much opportunity to argue.

He finished buffing his dress shoes when two quick knocks sounded at the door. Alysha was waiting for him. "Ready to go?" she questioned.

Vinnie motioned for her to come in. "I just need to put on my shoes and wash my hands."

She nodded and stepped inside, walking to the window. "I shoulda made you take the other room. You got a better view."

He finished tying his shoes and excused himself to go to the bathroom to wash his hands One more look in the mirror to assure himself he looked acceptable and their wasn't anything in his teeth. It took him three tries to get his watch latched as his fingers never wanted to cooperate when he was nervous. Cracking into a safe, steady hands; suspended over rafters fixing wiring, no sweat. But social situation – his hands acted like he'd been shot up with novocaine. Nothing to be done for it. He could clean up, but he wasn't anyone's ten.

"Alright." He chuckled. "I'm as ready as I'm going to be."

Alysha was inspecting the bakery bag on the table. "She took you to her bakery?"

Her inquisitive tone piqued his curiosity, but he didn't want to pry. *Her bakery? He had asked about her old haunts, perhaps that place had deeper meaning.* "I mean, she left me in the Lyft, but I was there."

"Huh." She sounded surprised, then shrugged. "Well, you did ask to see her haunts and that bakery is about as close to a haunt as she's got."

"Really?"

"Yeah, it's not for me to talk about, but you should feel honored."

Honored? He didn't want to think too much into that. He already found himself getting lost in Anna's company and it was dangerous territory. He wasn't meant for someone like Anna. She was worthy of so much more than what he was. Vinnie checked his watch. "Time to get going."

Shoulder to mid-bicep they strode to the elevator, to reach the venue on the roof top. Vinnie watched the floor numbers ascend on the lighted panel. "I hope Anna's alright. She really doesn't like heights."

"She'll keep her distance from the edge, and with a drink in her hand, she'll be fine. It's not like the Skydeck where you can see through the floor."

He chuckled, unable to help it. "She wasn't a fan."

"She went up there with you?"

The elevator doors opened, and Anna was waiting for them in her navy-blue dress. There was a science to lighting, how angles could change how people looked under them. He'd helped her with her necklace before she'd come up here, but somehow she looked like a different woman.

The deep navy of satin material clung to Anna, framing her curves. The rouched bodice cascaded down like water from the halter style neckline and flared out at the hip. He knew the back was nearly non-existent, but he hadn't noticed the slit in the skirt or the silver heels that matched her necklace. With their height those heels couldn't be comfortable. She stood confident, clearly at ease in the lavish space and the company she kept. He averted his eyes, realizing he'd been staring for far too long.

Vinnie looked out over the crowd to distract himself: five-piece suits and floor length gowns contrasted the waitstaff in simple white tuxedo tops and black bow-ties. White linen covered, small, high-top conversation tables framed the bar, and set on the large circular tables were placecards on gold accented plates filled the remaining space. This whole event was money – capital M, money.

"You went up on the Skydeck with him? Are you going to try The Tilt at the Hancock Building, next?" Alysha snickered as Anna glared at her. "This boy is turning you into a daredevil."

"I assure you that there is no way I'm stepping foot on the same floor as that attraction. Yesterday was enough daredevil for half a lifetime."

"Well, you're thirty next September, and that's creeping up to the halfway point. It'll be time to try again."

"I will fill your office with black roses on your next birthday," Anna warned.

Alysha laughed. "Eh, age is just a number."

Anna sighed and pointed towards the far end of the party. "That's Emilo Grant, with the polka dot tie, and he wants to have a positive word with you about your imprint. Make sure you introduce yourself. He's big on handshakes and eye contact."

"Thanks." Alysha tossed Vinnie a wink, "Have fun you two." She sauntered toward the man, painting on her 100-watt smile.

"Miss Kane, let's get a picture of you and your friend." A woman, who Vinnie assumed was the event's photographer clicked a few shots, than motioned for them to stand closer together. "Gimme a smile."

"I hate having my picture taken," Anna muttered, her smile tense and forced.

Vinnie put a finger under her chin. "Thank you for sharing your bakery with me. Alysha said it was special to you."

Her awkward smile was replaced by a genuine one as the camera flashed behind him.

"Great picture, Miss Kane. Thank you."

Anna moved closer to him and threaded her arm through his. "You look wonderful."

"That's supposed to be my line."

"You told me earlier, before I left for my meeting." She moved them over to the bar.

"True. Also, when's your birthday? I should know that."

"It was the third." She shrugged before assuring him, "I've never really celebrated my birthday. So don't worry about not doing anything for it."

He should have done something though, they were friends at the very least. She ordered them both a drink and she pointed to where they were sitting at the main table.

"Alysha's not sitting with us?" Vinnie noticed the placecards only had his and Anna's name on them, and the cards to the right and left had names he'd heard but couldn't place.

"No, all the imprint leaders have a table to themselves." Anna explained.

A waitress helped Alysha sit at the head of her table and she was positively beaming despite being the only woman seated there.

Anna's smile intensified as well, seeing Alysha succeed obviously affected her. She sipped from her glass and let Vinnie pull out her chair for her. "Most of tonight is going to be speeches and honoring their achievements along with the company's overall performance going into the fourth quarter. I'm sorry if it's boring."

"I'm here for you. Even if I'm bored, I'm not going to act like it."

"I appreciate that. Oh, if we get separated, feel free to mingle and relax. It's an open bar. I want you on my arm, but I don't need you to bodyguard me."

He chuckled at the idea of Anna needing someone to take care of her. She wasn't helpless in any sense of the word. "Great movie."

"Movie?" She cocked her head to the side.

"The Bodyguard. Whitney Houston," he elaborated, then took a sip of his drink. Whatever was in this it was far too smooth. There wasn't even a trace of burn.

Anna shook her head. "Never seen it. I can barely track modern media to keep up with trends."

"I need to start expanding your movie horizons. The classics are the best."

"Find me the time and I'm in." She sipped from her own drink, smiling at him over the glass.

The dinner started and he settled into a controlled silence, opting to listen to the conversations around him. Easier to keep your foot out of your mouth if you kept it closed. Anna had two speeches this evening, and she shrugged her shoulders when he asked her if she was nervous. It didn't occur to her to be nervous in a crowd like this. Vinnie on the other hand, kept a cocktail glass in hand, attempting to masquerade as normal for the evening.

Anna gave the opening speech, as the imprint project had been her proposal. She told a few jokes and laughed along with the crowd, but the laughter didn't reach her eyes. The man Vinnie was sitting next to, the head of finance, nudged him. "I think her being pretty helps make her jokes funnier. Her mother wasn't ever funny, but Emily was all power and not much personality."

Before he could respond, the man's date elbowed him and handed him a cup of water. How could this guy be drunk already? It was only two hours into the event. Clearly moderation was a concept for people with less money and less power.

Between speeches, Anna kept a hand on his arm as she made small talk with the others at their table. Vinnie sipped on his third cocktail, but again, slow and easy while ensuring to eat a little something every sip.

He needed to keep himself calm, but not get drunk. He wasn't risking getting drunk. He wasn't going to embarrass her.

"Can you do me a favor?" Anna leaned in close and whispered in his ear. She smelled like coffee and vanilla with a floral undertone. They'd been close all evening, but it was the first time he noticed it and now he was very aware of it.

He nodded, not trusting his voice and his pinkie tapping on the table.

"I want drinks for you, me, and Alysha to toast with when they announce her imprint. Can you go request them at the bar for me? If they give you push back, just have the bartender charge them to our room, and I'll handle it later."

He swallowed. "I can handle that."

"Thank you. Mcallan Rare Cask for me, Extra Añejo for Alysha, and Laphroaig 25 year for you." She smirked, "They are above top shelf, and they aren't on the menu for the open bar, for a reason." She smiled, the lights of the city behind her framing her as the picture of modern grace and quiet exceptionalism.

"I don't drink a lot of bourbon. It goes to my head fast."

"You don't have to finish it. But I really think you'll like the smoke and apple flavors. Make sure the staff tells Alysha that I ordered it for her or she might not drink it. I want her to have this moment without any unnecessary concerns."

"I can tell her. I don't mind just going and giving it to her."

Anna's eyes lit up with what he could only translate as joy. "You are a breath of fresh air in my life. What am I going to do when you're not at my side anymore?"

"I suppose you could hire me as your new assistant." He stood, not sure how to handle the compliment she'd just paid him.

"Don't tempt me."

Vinnie ordered the drinks, and the bartender verified the liquors twice, requiring his signature so they could be charged to the room before agreeing to retrieve the spirits. Apparently Anna hadn't been exaggerating about these particular spirits being above top shelf. *How much money he was about to be drinking?*

The executives on the board were all, excluding Anna, in their fifties, sixties, and seventies, so it made it easy to distinguish the partners and imprint leaders.

"I'm Ben Gallows," the younger man had wandered up to the bar leaned closer to him. "I'm running the new true crime imprint."

Vinnie shook Ben's hand. "Vincent Goodroe, Anna's partner."

Ben nodded, his sandy colored hair not budging a centimeter. "Cool. I'd heard she was dating again. She's a hell of a catch with all that money."

His eye twitched behind his glasses and he glanced back to the bar. *Where were those drinks?*

"Her mother set her up when she died. All the shares and all that power transferred to her. My dad says they tried to buy her out because she was twenty-two and they thought she'd just want the money, but she didn't sell. They weren't happy about that, so they tried to squeeze her out by forcing her to come back from whatever country she was in, but that didn't work either." Ben nudged Vinnie with his elbow. "Dude, don't tell my dad how much I've been drinking. He'd be pissed."

Drunks, Vinnie could handle. "Maybe you should slow down so he doesn't notice."

"Naw man. I'm too jacked. The imprint thing I'm in charge of is true crime. I got to sit in on an interview with an actual murderer. It was like I looked into the face of evil." Ben was close enough that Vinnie could smell the gin on his breath. "Like this guy shot and killed someone. How the hell do you just snuff out a life like that? That's gotta be a power trip, living on the other side of the law, being the actual bad guy."

Vinnie's heel bounced up and down as he drew in a slow breath.

"Benjamin. There you are. Come over here, I want a picture with my son." An overweight man with thinning hair called out to Ben.

"Later man. You're a cool-looking dude, I wanna chat you up later." Ben disappeared into the crowd.

"Sorry that took so long, Sir." The bartender set the three drinks in front of him. "Anything else I can get you?"

Vinnie swallowed. "Can I get a shot of whatever your well bourbon is?"

"Chilled?"

"Whatever's easiest."

She nodded and set the shot in front of him, which he threw back immediately. It warmed his chest and softened the sharpness of the memories in his head. Living on the other side of law wasn't glamorous. It was as miserable as any job, there were just more bullets involved.

Vinnie reached for his wallet, but she pointed to the sign that requested no tips to the staff. He inclined his head and offered a warning. "You might want to start servicing non-alcoholic drinks to that Ben guy who was talking to me. He's pretty far gone."

She shrugged. "Most corporate parties are like this. We just get them back to their rooms when they pass out or get too rowdy."

"Take care of yourself then." He gathered the three drinks, but as he reached Anna, she was already on her feet.

"Thank you." She took her drink, "I'm sure she's fine, but can you check on Alysha? This is her first executive event in the spotlight."

"Of course."

Anna kissed his cheek and breezed by him.

That was new. Not out of left field with the roles they played and not unpleasant, but new. Vinnie walked over to Alysha, who didn't look thrilled with the conversation she was having.

"Alysha, I need to steal you for a moment. If you'll excuse us."

She followed him to the edge of the roof and rested her hand on the railing accepting the drink he offered. "From Anna?"

"Yes, to toast your imprint announcement. Are you alright?" At least he could help Alysha feel better.

"You can't be playing knight in shining armor all the time. And while I appreciate the swoop in, I could've handled it." She rolled her eyes and looked out over the city.

Vinnie followed her lead; he hadn't really paused since getting up here. The lights from offices and apartments made the city glow in the dusk light as the sun set. The river carved through the center, bridges lined up in a row with the traffic moving steadily. Again, the freshness of the air caught him off guard, but they were stories above the street. The architecture, a mix of the historic and the modern, blended in a way that he felt only this city could pull off so seamlessly. Chicago was Chicago and it didn't try to be anything else.

He glanced back at the party goers, his eyes finding Anna almost instantly. She held herself open and with a self-assurance he wished he had versus constantly feigning it. Her back was to him, her halter-style dress giving him a view of the freckles speckled across her pale back. Her long hair had been curled and piled up on her head, giving him an unobstructed view from the nape of her neck to the curve of her spine where her dress began.

"So are you undressing her with your eyes or counting her freckles?"

He jumped and adjusted his glasses, taking a sip of his drink reflexively. "I have no idea what you're talking about."

"Yeah okay, Romeo."

Anna Kane pulled off her heels the moment the elevator started descending. She put her hand on Vinnie's shoulder to steady herself as she slipped on the satin fold-up flats she kept in her clutch.

"That bad, huh?" The corner of his mouth tugged up with that crooked smile that made him look instantly like trouble.

And he'd been trouble most of the night. Not by causing it, but by being it. She'd seen him in suits before, and he clearly knew how to dress, but the light-gray suit had made him stand out. Vinnie could also be charming as the devil when he wanted to be. He'd grinned when she stepped out of the bathroom of their hotel suite, tapping his tie as he announced that he'd picked the navy that matched her dress. When she looked curious about his response, he'd simply offered her his arm, explaining that a man should always match his lady when they went out.

Anna straightened, and although surprised by Vinnie's offered hand, she grabbed it.

"Well, I was offering to carry your shoes, but this works too."

She blushed to her ears and attempted to pull her hand back, but he held fast. "I…"

"No, you gave it to me. It's mine now." He chuckled. He lowered his voice as he leaned into her space, bringing her hand to his lips and placing a kiss on her knuckles.

"Are you flirting with me, or are you drunk?" She teased, despite her heart rate picking up as she looked up into his overly-dilated eyes.

"Yes?" He tipped his glass down then chuckled again. "I can't see you without my glasses."

Anna wanted to push his glasses back up, but she didn't have a free hand so she stepped closer and pushed her shoes towards his free hand. He took the heels from her and she touched the bridge of his glasses to move them back into place. "Is that better?"

"Much. I don't think your earrings match."

She jumped back, expecting to feel the cold metal of the doors on her bare back, but they opened, and she fell backward. She winced preparing for the impact, even more so when Vinnie released her hand, but he looped his arm around her waist keeping her on her feet and pulling her flush against him.

He smelled like mahogany and teakwood. She had caught the scent of his cologne earlier and appreciated how much the rich scent fit him. A touch of whiskey and coffee from his last drink lingered on his breath, and she fought the urge to move in closer.

If she hadn't almost fallen out of an elevator, she would've blamed her weak knees on his proximity. She was grateful to have an excuse, but her voice wavered. "Oh. Hello you."

"Hi." His breath was warm against her ear. "Sorry. I shouldn't have mentioned it."

Her feet were still off the ground as he awkwardly stumbled forward, backing her into the wall opposite the elevator.

"It's okay. Are you doing alright?"

He nodded, inhaling slowly. "You look breathtaking tonight. Like the backdrop of nighttime waters."

"That's very sweet of you to say." Anna wasn't sure about moving. She didn't want either of them to fall. He swayed back and forth slightly, far drunker than she thought he was. How had he managed to stay on topic during that last conversation with her colleague?

"No. I'm not sweet, I'm honest." He blinked. "I have your shoes."

"Indeed you do. I can take them, and we'll go back to the room." Anna slipped her shoes out of his hand and motioned for him to follow her down the hall.

"Did you know the hexagonal pattern in the carpet in *The Shining* was based on Chess boards and war planning patterns? Kubrick picked the colors to make it mesmerizing and foreboding, which makes sense with his symmetrical filming style." Vinnie stepped in and out of the pattern on the hallway carpet, almost passing the door she was unlocking. "This isn't as interesting."

"I would hope not. I wouldn't want to be in a horror film. I'm not much of a runner." Anna touched his arm. "Come on, handsome. Let's get you out of those clothes."

He laughed and let her guide him into the room. She locked the door behind them and put on the chain. She dropped her shoes on the floor and set her clutch atop the dresser under the flatscreen. Vinnie sat on the bed and flopped on his back, letting out another breathy laugh. "I'm feeling good." He half sang, half told her.

Anna retrieved a water bottle from the mini-fridge and set it on the nightstand by the bed. "Can you sit back up for me?"

Vinnie complied far too fast, and he almost pitched himself off the bed, but Anna got in front of him with one leg between his knees and her hands on his shoulders.

He leaned into her, resting his forehead against her bare shoulder. "You have freckles on your back. I kept looking away so I wouldn't count them. It's rude to stare at people and normal people don't do that. Your skin smells like vanilla and coffee. That's weird, you're not supposed to tell people how they smell." Apparently drunk he overshared more then normal, was it endearing, even if it was slightly nonsensical.

"You're fine." She helped him sit upright again placing her knee on the outside of his leg, and up on the bed. "Let's get this off first." The satin of his tie was smooth against her fingers as she coaxed the knot loose, sliding it out from under his collar.

He bounced his foot, making her lose her balance and crash onto his knee. He didn't say anything but watched her intently, remaining perfectly still.

His tongue darted out, licking his lips before asking in a hushed tone, "Is this okay?"

"You should drink some water." She might need that water herself. Anna shifted to get up from the bed, but Vinnie clamped his hand down on her hip.

"I bet you can reach it from here."

Anna wasn't one to back down from a challenge, even a drunken one she knew better than to accept. She leaned to the side, stretching until she snagged the water and unscrewed the cap. She took a drink and smirked at him, "Now, I'm going to have to get up and get you another bottle."

Vinnie snatched the bottle from her faster than she would have imagined his reflexes would allow in the state he was in. He guzzled the water down, eyes never leaving hers, until he finished it and tossed the bottle across the room. He returned her prior smirk. "You are far too pretty for anyone to believe you're dating me of your own free will."

"I think you're unaware of how attractive you are." She slipped Vinnie's glasses off and set them on the nightstand.

"Now, I'm at your mercy. I can't see without those and I'm warm."

Anna helped him get out of his suit jacket, dropping it to the floor to get it out of the way. "Is that better?"

"Mhmm." He trailed his finger from her wrist to her shoulder and back again. "Why was your dress in the room when we got here and not in your bag?"

Gooseflesh followed the path of his finger and she shifted slightly on his knee. "Because I rented it. I rarely buy things and keep them. I don't get attached to much of anything."

"I read a psychology article once about detachment, no, it was attachment theory." He corrected himself. He furrowed his eyebrows and despite his unfocused eyes, he attempted to explain further. "The author theorized that sometimes adopted children struggle with attachment. Some of them feel an internal disconnect they can't explain. But conversely some children who feel abandoned by parental figures hoard things, it helps them exercise control."

Anna ran her fingers slowly through his hair. He was far too drunk to remember anything they talked about, and even if he did, it wasn't anything she was worried about him knowing. Vinnie cared about the people around him and was acutely aware of others' boundaries. She didn't want to overstep, but he clearly needed to sleep. She started unbuttoning Vinnie's collared shirt, so he could sleep more comfortably.

"I think I'm drunk." He closed his eyes as she got the second button undone, and he let out a long sigh.

"Leila told me I'm flirty when I'm drunk. I slept with her when we dated, but I'm not sure I wanted it to happen."

She immediately froze, fingers on the fourth button. She didn't want to move away from him, but she didn't know what to do with her hands as he continued his admission.

"I didn't *not* want to sleep with her. She's beautiful and nice, and I helped her. It was like a thank you, a very personal thank you. She's the only person I've ever slept with, and I expected to feel more connected to her after, but I didn't."

Oh, thank god. Anna felt a rush of relief. It was one thing to listen to a drunken confession about regret, it'd be entirely another to hear he'd been taken advantage of. Only one partner. That might explain his reactions when she'd flirted with him prior. Was she allowed to have someone as precious as him? Was she doing too much?

He covered her hands with his, methodically rubbing his thumbs over her knuckles. "I can't ever figure out if I'm attracted to someone or if I just enjoy their company. I should be able to figure that out. I'm all messed up."

"You're not messed up." Her eyes were misty as she kissed his forehead. "You are allowed to take your time figuring out if you're sexually attracted to someone. Not everyone experiences instant attraction. There's nothing wrong with taking your time."

"What if I want to take my time with you?" He bounced his knee, unsettling her, and as she gripped his shoulders he grinned.

"I think you need to sleep off the alcohol before you do or say something you regret." Anna shook her head. She was going to take advantage of a long shower after all of this. She put one foot on the floor, got back onto her feet, and retrieved another bottled water for her companion. "Try to drink some more before you fall asleep."

Chapter 6: Tropes Are Expected

Presenting Forced Proximity

September 27th; 73 Days Until…

The two couples sat on the patio of the Italian restaurant as the music floated in the air from the sound system hooked to the light poles. It wasn't the best use of light or space, but the food was good. Anna had sent her first dish back to the kitchen, explaining that she hadn't ordered the meat sauce on her spaghetti and couldn't eat it.

"Are you a vegetarian?" Kass asked, before taking a bite of her own dinner.

Anna shook her head. "Not exactly. I have trouble digesting red meats, so I avoid them. The last time I ate bacon, I ended up in the hospital."

"Oh! You have alpha-gal syndrome. One of the girls in one of my nursing classes told me about this. You must have gotten bit by a Lone Star tick when you were younger. That's so fascinating. Do you react to dairy based products too, or is it just meat you have problems with digesting? Well, I mean, technically it's an allergy."

"Sweetheart, can we not with the medical stuff at dinner, please? Just have a normal pleasant, non-stressful conversation?" Mat pleaded. "We're out having dinner without the kiddo, and I'd like to enjoy it."

Kass rolled her eyes. "All the things he talks about, and he's gonna give me grief about inappropriate topics."

"You have no one to blame but yourself, Kass. You put him on the straight and narrow," Vinnie teased, taking a sip of his wine.

"Thank you for inviting us out, Anna. This place is great," Kass complimented.

"My co-worker recommended it. It's my first time here too."

Vinnie fought the urge to finish off his glass of wine before bringing up the reason that he and Anna had invited his brother and sister-in-law out to eat. He wasn't going to push the alcohol. He was firmly back on the moderation train. He had gotten far too drunk in Chicago, and while he hadn't made a fool of himself at the party, he could only remember flashes of the rest of his evening with Anna. If he'd done anything too crazy, she didn't mention it, but her smile in the morning made him think he'd done something embarrassing.

What was worse was after getting back from Chicago, Rex's house was a battle royale waiting to happen. It had been fifteen days since Jane appeared like a rabbit out of a hat, and it wasn't getting easier. Vinnie had only seen her twice despite Rex informing him that she was still staying there. Mat had seen her once, and he had stared her down like a cop looking at a man he knew to be guilty but couldn't prove it. Kass had spoken to Jane more than once, but wasn't sure about her, which spoke volumes in and of itself. Rex kept trying to play mediator, and it was wearing on him.

They needed to figure something out, and Mat and Kass buying a house they didn't really want, just to move out faster wasn't it. Anna had offered a solution that he wouldn't have considered, but she shrugged, explaining that she wasn't any more attached to her apartment than she was to anything else. The conversation felt familiar somehow, catching him off guard.

Vinnie cleared his throat. "So we actually wanted to talk to you both about something, in regards to what's going on at home."

"Don't make me ask you for the same thing I just asked my wife for."

Vinnie deadpanned. "Gross. You should never do that."

"Vinnie!" Kass wrinkled her nose. "You're awful."

"I'm hilarious. People tell me all the time," he defended.

Mat scoffed. "If they think it'll make you shut up faster, I'm sure they do."

"Can you make him be nicer?" Vinnie implored Kass.

The waiter brought Anna her new dish, and the table fell quiet while she thanked him. No one said anything for a moment, then Anna cleared her throat and gave him a glance from the corner of her eye.

"Right. So. Things at home are obviously stressful, and the house you two really want isn't ready until November, so we had a thought. Well, Anna had a thought, and I think it's a good one. I mean, there isn't really a good solution to this situation with all the high emotions and..." Vinnie might have continued, but Anna covered his hand with hers and he got back on track.

"To make a long story short, Anna has offered to let you two and Lizzie stay at her apartment until your house is ready."

Mat and Kass both blinked, shock clear on their faces as they turned to each other and then back to him and Anna.

"To be honest, it isn't the most kid-friendly space. But, I can put my things in storage and rent anything that would make it a more comfortable, temporary space for your family," Anna explained, taking a drink of her Old Fashion.

"I…" Kass started, but Mat cut her off.

"Why? Why would you do that? And where would you be?"

Anna patted her mouth with her napkin. "I would help, because you're my partner's brother, and what makes his family happy makes him happy, and that's better for me. And I'll be staying with Vinnie at Rex's."

"What?" Mat managed another question.

"I don't have any attachment to the person who is causing all the stress, so being around her won't be upsetting to me. Offering my space is the easiest way for me to help." Anna rested her hands on the table.

"That's really generous of you," Kass recovered, "but we'd want to pay your rent if we decided to take you up on the offer."

"No. I own the apartment, rent isn't a concern."

"You own…" Kass started but stopped herself. "Oops, my small-town upbringing just snuck out. I forget that people own apartments in cities."

"I bought it and had it redesigned when I moved to Houston."

"No offense…" Mat began as Vinnie braced for whatever offensive thing his brother was about to say, "...it's nice that you can help, but being forced to live with someone you just started dating with *a lot* of additional stress ain't exactly a good way to go."

Anna arched her eyebrow. "Considering Kass started living with you before you two even started dating, I don't think you're in a position to judge."

"You told her about all of that?" Kass blushed. "Vinnie, why?"

"I didn't tell her, she…" Vinnie forced out a cough, to stop himself from continuing. *SHIT!* He almost mentioned his book and now he was fucked. Why did his mouth always get ahead of him?

"Don't be angry with him, please. I interrogated him after attending your wedding. You and Mat seemed so different and I had to know the story." Anna took another sip of her drink. "He's got loose lips after a few drinks."

"That's a fact." Mat glared at him.

Two sides to this coin. On the good side, Mat and Kass weren't accidentally told about the book; on the bad side, Mat was still pissed. Vinnie was surprised how effortlessly Anna lied to his family.

He appreciated at the moment, but it was a bit disconcerting. He muttered a lame apology and took a bite of his dinner.

Kass waved her hand dismissively. "Don't worry, she would have heard it eventually. It's a funny story with a good ending."

"A bestseller the way he tells it." Anna smiled and glanced up at him as she entwined their fingers.

Vinnie wouldn't claim to be church-raised, because even his year in Catholic school had been more sneaking out and playing pranks, but he knew the phrase 'pride goeth before a fall' was serious. Right now, he wasn't sure whose fall Anna's pride was going to cause. Fact of the matter was, she could pull away and vanish at any time. He was the one with real consequences at play. He wasn't stupid. He knew that he'd likely have to come clean at some point about the book. He wanted it to be on his terms – when it was done and something to be proud of. Until it was physical, writing a book was a hobby and didn't really count.

He pulled his hand away from Anna, wanting his space back, and took a long drink from the glass of water next to his wine.

"Hey, my car was making a noise before we got here. Let's let the ladies finish their drinks and we can take a look at it real quick." Mat stood up and motioned for him to follow.

"Really, Mat?" Kass questioned.

Mat tipped up Kass' chin and gave her a quick kiss. "We'll be back like The Flash, Sweetheart. Enjoy your drink."

"Okay." Kass held onto Mat's hand for a moment, longer no doubt trying to figure out what was going on. She let go and offered a warning. "Keep your glasses on, Vinnie."

As they walked out shoulder to mid-bicep, Vinnie heard Anna comment to Kass that he couldn't see without his glasses. As much as Anna's mind was a steel trap, she had missed the reference in his book about the difference between a discussion and a fight. And this was not turning into a fight. Firstly because they were in public, and secondly because he liked this suit. Mat kept his hands to himself and leaned against the trunk of his car, angling his head to look up at the stars. Vinnie copied his brother and waited for him to speak.

"Do you really think this is the best idea?"

Vinnie flipped a coin in his mind, because Mat wasn't dumb, just oblivious sometimes. Mat could have heard the term bestseller, and knowing Anna was an editor, deduced that he'd written a book about how Mat and Kass met. But then this could be just about the living situation. Choosing to play it safe, Vinnie silently shrugged.

Mat sighed. "Is Anna really okay with this, or is she trying to get on Rex's good side?"

Good, Mat hadn't caught his slip up and Anna's damn near admission of guilt. He cracked his neck and echoed his brother's sigh. "Probably a bit of both. It was her idea, not mine. She can't figure out what she did to rub Rex the wrong way. She's hoping if she throws herself into the thick of our family mess, sacrifices her comfort for his grandchild's, then it might earn her brownie points."

"Well, there is that." Mat spun his keyring around his finger, catching his keys in his palm, then spinning them again.

A couple walked by them in the parking lot and they nodded in sync, waiting for the two to pass so they could continue the conversation. The woman was arguing about the potential price, and the man was bragging that he would write it off as a business expense. The company had given him a platinum card and he wasn't afraid to use it. As far as he was concerned, money was simply not a concern.

Mat chuckled as they disappeared. "So, Anna's got money. Like capital, M, money."

"Caught that, huh?" He shoved his hands in his pockets.

It only took him a handful of weeks to realize Anna hadn't been kidding about never worrying about money. From her apartment, to her office, to the way she traveled – Mat hit a bullseye with his observation. Anna wasn't frivolous, but money was never a concern. Unless it was for the company, she didn't ever verify prices.

Vinnie regarded his brother. "Wait until you see her apartment."

"That fancy?"

"Well, it would definitely be the house of the villain in the heist movie, complete with ceiling to floor windows."

"You're fucking with me."

"Nope. That's your wife's job."

"Ha ha."

September 30th; 69 Days Until…

Being tall and relatively capable, Vinnie was always on the short-list whenever a friend or acquaintance moved. Helping Mat and Anna move in a weekend as they played the shell-game with living spaces had even less appeal. Anna needed less help as she hired a service to pack up her things, which was good because when he wasn't at the Playhouse or sleeping, he'd been packing and carrying his brother's family's things into the moving pod for the last two days. Everyone's nerves were frayed by this point.

It didn't help that Kass, the calming effect the house needed, was stuck working during the day until tomorrow.

Vinnie had been lying on the living room floor to stretch out his back for about ten minutes when he felt his brother's footsteps approaching.

"Squish your Uncle and stay out of my way for a bit, Little Lady."

Oh shit! "Ugh." Vinnie grunted as Lizzie belly flopped on his chest. "Hey, Nugget."

"Uncle VeeNee, I squeesh you!" She squealed and pressed her sticky hands onto his face.

He cringed. "Why are you sticky?"

"She shouldn't be. I washed her hands after her snack. It was just peanut butter and jelly crackers, nothing bad," Mat assured him.

Vinnie sat up and settled Lizzie on his lap, looking her over, until noticing the purple under her hair. "Tell dad that he missed the jelly on your neck."

"Lizzie, how did you get jelly on your neck?" Mat questioned with exasperation.

"I dunno." Her big eyes pleaded her case for innocence.

"Go do whatever you were doing. I'll clean her up in the yard. Gotta get it off me, too." Vinnie dismissed him.

"Thanks. Sorry about the mess. She's got a box of clothes on the table that Kass left out so we'd know where it was."

"Momma?"

"Still at work, Nugget. Come on, we're gonna get half naked in the yard and dunk you in a bucket like a monkey." Vinnie managed to pull himself up off the ground, ignoring the protest from his muscles. He snagged the soap from the kitchen on their way.

Lizzie squirmed, eager to be put down the moment they were outside. "Eeee! I play in fowers!"

Vinnie wasn't actually going to dunk her, but Kass had sat out with Lizzie in a kiddie pool last night to keep her out of the way. With nothing in its rightful place at the moment, using the towels hanging on the garden bed rails held more appeal than anything else.

He kept her in his eyeline as he turned on the hose and to fill the pool. It was still in the high seventies, so she'd be fine if he wrapped her up after. Lizzie spun around in circles, singing her current favorite Disney song with made-up words and an almost melody. She zipped around like a hummingbird in the side yard, full of energy and spirit in the sunshine.

"Lizzie, come 'er for a second. Let's get you cleaned up."

"No! Pway!" She raced in the opposite direction, but he caught her and tossed her up in the air, making her laugh.

"I don't think you took a nap today."

"No naps. Helps Daddy," she confirmed, before poking out her lower lip. "Pwease pway."

Vinnie kissed the side of her head. "I know you wanna play, but we've got to get you cleaned up. It's gonna be time for dinner soonish."

"No hungry." She tugged at his shirt. "Uncle VeeNee pwease."

"How about…" he shifted her on his hip, "…we get cleaned up and then we play a game on your tablet?" Maybe if he could get her to sit still, she might take a short nap?

"Okee, okee," She nodded emphatically.

Vinnie set Lizzie down next to the pool and reached to turn off the hose when a blast of cold water hit his back.

"Gots you!" His niece giggled.

He turned off the water and saw that not only did Lizzie have the hose in her hands, she had also gotten into the wading pool fully clothed and was now sopping wet.

"Oh fuck!" Mat barked out a laugh from where he was standing on the ramp, box in hand and observing the whole mess.

"Oh phucks!" Lizzie mirrored, and Vinnie leaned against the house as he broke down laughing.

Vinnie took off his shirt and tossed it towards the rail, but it landed in the remnants of Kass' tomato plants. He knelt by Lizzie as she shook the hose up and down.

"Uh-oh! Watter all gone," she informed him.

He shook his head. "You aren't wrong. Let's get you cleaned up." He got her out of her wet things and set them on the ground. After rubbing soap on his hands, he started washing the giggling toddler.

She being 'super helpful,' wiggling and slapping the surface of the water. His glasses were speckled with water droplets from her antics. As irksome as his now limited vision was, Lizzie was so damn happy, that it was worth putting up with the temporary annoyance. He was going to miss listening to her laughter everyday. Vinnie had spent almost as much time with Lizzie as her parents. The realization she wasn't going to be a be a part of his day-to-day life anymore hit him in the chest.

"Hairs too?" she questioned, pulling his attention back to present. She put her wet hands in her hair.

"Nope, just your body."

"Okees." She rocked from foot to foot and bent down to splash the water.

"When's Rex getting back?" Mat called out.

"Half hour or so, I think. He was grabbing dinner and some snacks so we don't have to cook while we're finishin' up." Vinnie answered before turning back to his niece, who had a death grip on the hose. "I need to see this for a second."

"No thanks you. Is mine." Lizzie swished it back and forth under the water's surface.

Vinnie tipped her chin so she'd look at him. "I need it for ten fingers." He held up both hands so she could see all of his fingers, offering a compromise. "Then we can water the plants. Deal?"

"Only tens." She handed him the hose, distrust in her mismatched eyes. She mean-mugged like Mat sometimes.

He counted outloud as he rinsed the soap off, then flipped the pool over to drain. He wrapped Lizzie up in a towel, hiking her up on his hip and squelching through the newly-created mud as she watered the flowers.

"I think that's good. You wanna help me turn it off now? Be helpful?"

"Okee! Down pweese!!"

Vinnie kept the hose pointed down as he helped Lizzie turn off the water. Rocks crunched in the driveway behind him and he assumed it was Rex, but when he turned he recognized Anna's navy BMW. He bundled Lizzie back in her towel, kicked off his muddy shoes, and immediately slipped into the house.

"Who here?" Lizzie asked.

Mat came in the front door. "Hey, Anna just pulled in. I've got almost everything out of the bedroom. Just got a handful of boxes left."

"Yup, saw that. Can I borrow a shirt?"

Mat cocked his head to the side. "You know we haven't worn the same size clothes since we were – nope, we've never been the same size."

"Mat, please," Vinnie pleaded.

"Alright, alright." Mat whipped out his pocketknife and cut the tape on the box labelled 'M.'

"Put me down pwease. I go pway." Lizzie squirmed under the towel.

"Nope. Daddy's gonna trade Uncle Vinnie a t-shirt for you." Mat handed the black t-shirt to Vinnie and took Lizzie from him.

"Thank you."

Mat nodded and walked away with Lizzie, grabbing an outfit from the 'L' box. "Let's get some lotion and a dry pull-up on you. And not repeat the new word you learned to Momma."

"Issa little lady."

Vinie pulled on the t-shirt as a knock sounded against the screen door. This shirt was tighter than he expected it to be. He didn't think he was that much bigger than Mat, just taller. "Come on in."

"Oh, hello." Anna walked into the room, shoes in hand.

"Hi. We're being less stringent about the no shoes in the house rule with all the back and forth."

She pointed toward the patio. “I saw you kick yours off, so I thought I should.”

“They were muddy. Lizzie gave me a shower with the hose, hence the wet.” He ruffled his hair, sending droplets everywhere.

“*Chili Peppers* fan?”

Vinnie looked down at the shirt Mat had given him with ‘*Californication*’ printed on it. “It’s an older shirt.”

“It looks a little snug on you.”

“Yeah, well who hasn’t gained weight since high school?”

Anna bit her lower lip. “I just meant it looked tight across the chest. I think it fits you nicely.”

“Miss ANNA!!!”

Saved by the toddler. Lizzie barreled into Anna’s leg, dressed in clean clothes and laughing joyously. Anna knelt and hugged her back. “I like your shirt, Lizzie.”

“Issa Pincess shirt.”

Mat came out of the hallway, with a box on his hip, towel on top of it. “This is the last one out of the main bedroom. We have to pack up some of her stuff, but you guys are good to move your sh…” He stopped himself from swearing, “stuff in there.”

“I picked up dinner on my way over. I figured with everything going on, the last thing people wanted to do was cook.” Anna piped up as she disentangled from Lizzie.

“That was nice of you. Rex should be back soon with food, too. I guess we’ll have options.” Vinnie took the towel from Mat and dried his hair better.

“Let me get this into the pod and then Vinnie and I can help you with your boxes.”

“I only have a couple of boxes and two suitcases for my clothes. I won’t be here that long, so it made more sense to put everything in storage.”

Mat and Vinnie both looked at her for a long moment.

Anna cleared her throat. “If I need anything, I can just buy it. I have very few things that have more value beyond what they are at face value.”

“Fair enough,” Mat chuckled. “Guess we could take a break after this box. I’m starving. I think Lizzie’s the only one who got a real meal today. I’m running on coffee and spite at this point.”

“I’m on part of that diet.” Anna waved at Vinnie as she followed Mat out.

“Nugget, I think we just got abandoned.”

“Tabwit pwease.” She held out her hands for the device.

“Not you, too. Okay, only until dinner though.” Vinnie swept her up, handed her the tablet, and set her on the couch.

“Thanks you.”

"You are very welcome." He kissed the top of her head and turned around as Mat and Anna walked back into the house.

"Ain't the first time I've carried this many food bags in the house. Did he tell you he sent me all over town when Kass first moved in because he didn't know what her favorite food was?" Mat recounted.

"You didn't know it already?" Anna was pushing one suitcase and pulling the other.

Mat set the food down on the kitchen island. "I'd just met her. Come on, Little Lady, Miss Anna got ya nuggets."

"Oh, yays!" Lizzie scrambled down from the couch, tablet crashing to the ground as she abandoned it in favour of food.

Vinnie took one of Anna's suitcase and pointed towards the hallway. "It's the second door on the left."

This room wasn't huge, but with their schedules they shouldn't have to share the space often.

"The closet is on the other side of the door here, and the dresser's over there. The top two drawers are open for you. If you need more storage space, we can figure something out." He gave her the layout so she'd know where to put her things.

Anna examined the room as she put her suitcase up on the bed, motioning for him to do the same. She checked the tags and opened the one that he'd helped with first. "What does that door lead to?"

"The main bathroom. It has two doors, this one, and the one that connects to the hallway. Just make sure you lock and unlock both when you use it."

She checked her phone before pulling out her outfits already on hangers. "Which side of the closet is mine?"

"The left. Do you need help?" he offered.

"No, thank you. To confirm, you aren't going to put things on my side of the closet, correct?"

Vinnie was confused, but affirmed. "That's not part of the plan."

Anna was counting the items she'd hung in the closet before returning to her suitcase for the other items. After hanging that grouping, she repeated the same process a third time. "So, this side of the closet is mine, and you aren't going to mix it up or move things around?"

"I just stated that I wasn't planning on doing that."

"You aren't planning on it or you aren't going to?"

He could not figure out why she was so insistent on this point of order. He had no desire to mess up whatever organization system she was using, but it was such an odd thing to focus on. "Is there a concern you have about me touching your clothes? Because if that's the case, we should discuss that."

"I…" Anna kept her eyes averted, and her shoulders slumped in as she grabbed her elbows. "I'm colorblind. Tritanopia affects the blue-yellow spectrum, so if my clothes aren't the order I hang them in, I might go out of the house mismatched."

He shouldn't have laughed, but it seemed such a silly thing to worry about that he couldn't help himself.

The defeated posture Anna had immediately changed to tense, and defensive. She made a decisive stride towards the door, tears in her eyes. *Shit.* He'd never seen her instantly emotional. This was obviously important to her.

He realized it wasn't the vanity of not matching, it was the dependence of needing someone to tell her if she did or not. She'd spent the majority of her life leaning only on herself, and her sight deficiency made her feel vulnerable.

Vinnie caught her hand and closed the door with his foot so they'd be alone. "Anna."

"Don't," she snapped, attempting to pull her hand away, but he held on. "Vincent."

He winced at his full name. "Anna, I'm sorry. I shouldn't have laughed. Please look at me."

Her nostrils were flaring, but her breathing was slow, as if she was unconsciously trying to calm herself. Did Anna have a temper? *Well she would. Everyone had a temper.* He was an asshole for laughing. Even if unintended, he'd hurt her.

"It's fine." Anna's lips were a thin line, her tone clipped.

"It's not fine. It was a dick move to laugh. It's not okay that I did that. You're sacrificing your comfort to help my family, and the last thing I want to do is make you uncomfortable."

She breathed out as she let go of his hand. "Thank you."

"Of course. Other than not touching your things, is there anything I can do to help?"

Anna gathered her hair back into a ponytail. "Let me know if I don't match, but don't make it a joke. It's silly, but it matters to me."

"If it matters to you, it's not silly."

She smiled at him, the expression reaching those brilliant blue eyes of hers. "Let's go get the rest of my boxes."

Anna was about to leave the room with Vinnie when her phone rang. Noticing it was Minji, she wanted to answer, as it had been a while since she'd spoken to her friend.

"If you go out and back towards the kitchen, you can go out the patio doors. The signal is so-so in the house," Vinnie added, and she nodded gratefully.

She answered as she stepped outside, carefully avoiding the mud. Minji was talking a mile a minute about her new home. The construction had taken months, but finally she'd been able to move in with her new husband.

Leaning against one of the garden beds, she mostly listened as her friend recounted all the changes happening in her life. Anna was elated for her friend. Minji deserved to be happy. She deserved the fairytale ending with the handsome prince.

Rex pulled into the driveway, and Kass pulled in behind him. The whole family was here. Anna knew she should get off the phone, but she wanted a few more minutes to pretend her life hadn't been upended.

She'd chosen to do this, and she hadn't hesitated until Mary came to pick up Jackal. Normally, she didn't mind handing her cat over to the boarder, but she felt a pang in her chest as she handed Jackal's crate and bag over this morning.

Minji pulled her attention back to the call, asking about how work was and if she'd found anyone to distract her from it. Anna told her about work, watching Vinnie help his uncle with the bags from his car and Kass steal a box of something from one of them. All three of them, were smiling and laughing.

Anna walked towards her car to retrieve her boxes as she began wrapping up the call, promising to visit once she resolved her passport situation. It wasn't like anyone else spoke Korean, so Minji would be the one person she could speak to unguarded.

She unlocked her car and bid her friend goodbye, noticing that Rex was standing by her car. She clenched her jaw, unsure how this interaction was going to go, but clung to some optimism for the sake of practicality. Whether they liked it or not, they were going to be spending at least some time together.

"Wanted to chat with you."

Good, straight to the point with no false pleasantries. Anna slipped her phone into her back pocket. "Fair enough."

"Firstly, we didn't get off on the right foot and that's just that. But Vinnie's awful fond of you and you're doing us a solid by playin' musical homes, and that's appreciated. So, you can keep those secrets of yours, but let's say we try again with introductions and move forward."

Anna blinked at the unexpected offer, but recovered and offered her hand to him. "Anna Kane, Vinnie's partner. It's nice to meet you, Rex. I've heard nothing but good things about you."

"Rexton Abster, Rex'll do. And Miss Anna, from what I've heard about you, you've captured my nephew's heart. I'd appreciate it if you were careful with it." His handshake was firm and they held eye contact.

She nodded, not trusting her voice. The idea that she had Vinnie's heart hit her harder than she expected. It wasn't real. They were working together and had become friends, but that was it.

"When's the rest of your stuff getting here?" He questioned.

"It's just the couple of boxes in the backseat there. No need to take up a lot of space." She unlocked the car, and Rex opened the door to grab one box, while she grabbed the other.

"Mat!" Rex hollered, "get over here and grab this other box for Anna."

"Two seconds, I gotta fix this strap down!" Mat's voice echoed inside the pod.

"Slowest mover I've ever met."

Mat glared as he stomped down the ramp. "I like to be sure it's done right." He inclined his head towards Anna's car. "Trunk or backseat?"

"Backseat, behind the driver's seat," she answered, keeping pace with Rex.

"So, was it Korean you were speaking on the phone earlier? You said you taught English over there after college, if I remember correct from the wedding."

"It was Korean I was speaking, yes. I taught English for almost two years.."

Rex held the patio door for her and she slipped by him. "So you learned the language while you were teaching?"

"No, I learned before going over." Anna felt her ears getting hot as she anticipated the next question.

"Seems like a unique language to just pick up."

She sighed and glanced over to the dinner table where Vinnie and Kass were setting out plates and entertaining Lizzie. "I learned it to impress a girl." Anna admitted in a rush figuring that it was best to just be honest when it came to Rex.

"Oh."

"HA!" Mat exclaimed, making everyone in the room jump. "I wanna don't hear about the crazy things I've done to impress girls anymore. She learned a whole language."

Kass rolled her eyes. "Baby, you jumped off a roof to impress your ex-wife and it didn't work. Anna acquired a life skill. There's a big difference."

The room broke out in laughter, even Mat, who surprisingly didn't seem to mind the joke at his expense.

"We'll get these in the room and eat some dinner." Rex got them back on track, and they put the boxes in her room.

Anna would worry about unpacking later this evening. She couldn't remember if Vinnie was working or not, but either way she would have plenty of time to unpack her few boxes. As she walked back out into the main room, she noticed the chess board on the computer desk. She picked up one of the pieces. The creature looked familiar, but she couldn't quite place it.

"Gollum from Lord of the Rings." Rex explained, "Had to get it up higher, so *someone* wouldn't put the pieces in her mouth. I have a normal set as well. This one's more for show. Do you play?"

"I do," she confirmed.

"Well, we'll have to play later then. Neither of those knuckleheads are decent opponents. Mat can't sit still, and Vinnie's always trying to play with creative rules."

"My rules make the game more interesting," Vinnie defended.

"No thanks you." Lizzie pushed at the food on her highchair, nearly tipping her plate off the edge, before Kass caught it.

"Lizzie you can get down if you're done, but you can't make a mess." Kass took a sip of her water, but held her daughter's plate with the other hand.

She tried to push her plate away again, but held on when Kass attempted to take it. "NO! PWAY!"

Anna jumped, it was the first time she'd heard Lizzie get angry-loud. She didn't spend a lot of time around children. Most executives hired nannies, and she escaped from crying little children in stores. She shifted in her chair, forcing herself to be still. Even if this wasn't a permanent thing, being part of a family meant dealing with children. Then again she wanted children one day, so this would be part of her world at some point. Best if she learned to get used to this now.

Kass tried to get her attention, "Lizzie," but the toddler screeched something incoherent. The auburn-haired woman turned to Mat, "Did she take a nap?"

"NO! NAPS! I HELP!"

"That answers that." Kass got up, but Mat intercepted her.

"Eat. I got her." Mat lifted Lizzie out of her highchair as she kicked and screeched at him. "Alright Elizabeth, let's go for a walk."

"No, no, no, no! Issa good girl. Izzie good girl!" Lizzie continued to flail as Mat carried her through the patio door and into the yard.

Kass looked a little embarrassed. "Sorry, toddler drama."

"No worries. She's sweet," Anna assured her.

"Nine times out of ten, that is completely true." Kass took a bite of her dinner, and motioned to the seat next to her.

"Careful sitting next to Kass, she's a food thief," Vinnie warned with a laugh as Kass flipped him off. "We've been a terrible influence on her."

Anna chuckled and pointed to the hallway. "I'm gonna change real quick. Get out of my suit."

"Sure."

Anna got into the suitcase that held her lingerie and comfortable clothes. The room didn't have air conditioning, but there was a good cross breeze, so with a fan it should be fine. She got out of her suit, hanging it up backwards so she'd remember to drop it at the dry cleaners.

Opting for leggings instead of jeans, she found her black pair buried under the new sleepwear she'd bought. In her apartment, she had a tendency to be in a bathrobe or naked when not expecting company. She grabbed one of her older t-shirts, shaking it out to make sure it didn't look wrinkled. After pulling it over her head, she opened the bathroom door. She intended to go wash her hands, but she stopped by the window.

Lizzie and Mat's voices could be heard from the open window facing the patio. The toddler was quieting, and Anna paused to listen.

"I know, Little Lady, I know. There's a lot going on right now. Daddy doesn't like it either. But it'll be okay. You've got a lot of big feelings and it's rough. Come on now, deep breaths. Atta girl. Everything's gonna be okay." Mat's voice was low, but it carried.

The metal patio door scraped and while Anna expected to hear Kass, it was Vinnie's voice instead. "Let me take her."

"I got her," Mat responded, slightly muffled.

"But you're gonna miss bein' here, and I'm gonna miss my niece. Go eat with Rex and Kass for one more meal. It'll be a minute before it happens again." Vinnie countered his brother, and the patio door opened and closed again, before Vinnie's voice softened to the tone he used when comforting Lizzie. "Come 'ere, Nugget. No, no, I'm not singin', that's your momma and Grandpa Rex when you're lucky. I'll tell you a story though."

"Hey," Kass called out. She'd come in through the open bathroom door. "They're okay out there."

"Mat's really good with Lizzie. I wouldn't expect him to be the gentle parenting type." Anna hoped Kass didn't take it as judgment on her family.

Kass sighed. "When you grow up with the opposite, you want something different for your kids. You want better. I'm not sure if Vinnie's told you about how he and Mat grew up, but it was rough. And Rex blames himself for part of the pain, so that's why he's so overprotective."

Anna was surprised when Kass suddenly hugged her, which Anna returned reflexively.

"I'm so glad you and Vinnie found each other," Kass pulled back a big grin on her face.

"He's great." She didn't know what else to say.

"He is, and he thinks you hung the moon. I've never heard him talk about anyone the way he talks about you. He never thought he'd find anyone and…" The younger woman waved her hands in front of her face. "Sorry, all the emotions with everything going on right now. I'm glad you're in his life."

There was a knock at the bedroom door. "You ladies ready to eat?"

"Coming, Rex," Kass called out. They walked back into the dining room to join Mat and Rex at the table just as Vinnie came in from the patio with a sleeping Lizzie on his shoulder.

Vinnie reappeared after putting Lizzie in what was now her playroom, and sat down next to her. "Hey you."

"Hi." Anna smiled at him as they passed dishes around the table. It felt odd and welcoming at the same time. The rest of the table pretending this was normal and her taking it all in.

Chapter 7: Tension Comes In Many Forms

Anger Is A Valid Emotion

October 8th; 62 Days Until...

Vinnie cleaned his glasses off on his shirt and yawned as the cleaning crew finished up the last of the early morning duties. He'd taken the trash out, prepped the deposit, and straightened up his office, hoping the cleaning crew would be done before he finished. Instead, he was waiting and trying to be patient with the new guy the cleaning company had sent over this morning.

He wasn't one to make snap judgments, but he listened to his instincts, and his guy had the hairs on the back of his neck standing up. He also understood wanting to get paid, but this guy was milking the clock, taking too much time with everything. Plus, he'd tried to get in the dressing room despite it being red-marked on the cleaning sheet he was provided when he got here.

"Just gotta finish up the bathroom down here and I'm all done, Boss." The guy pushed the mop and bucket towards the aforementioned room.

Vinnie waved him on without a look, trying to not be annoyed at the boss term. The guy sneered, as if Vinnie didn't deserve any respect, but Vinnie knew he might also be tired. He'd gotten here at five last night and it was well past 7 AM. Fourteen-hour shifts felt forever-long. He made a mental note to send Kass lunch later this week. Her normal shifts were ten hours with commuting. He pulled up Kass' Instagram and the family picture she'd taken in Anna's apartment. Anna had rented furniture for Mat, Kass, and Lizzie, including childproofing to make things easier.

Mat had tried three times to pay her or at least figure out what everything had cost, but Anna hadn't budged. Finally, Rex told Mat that he wasn't gonna out-stubborn the spitfire blonde and to let it go.

The positive interaction from Rex had Anna on cloud nine, but it was short-lived with the tension still in the air. During the confusing merry-go-round of moving, Jane had somehow stayed out of sight the entire time, which was a good thing, he guessed. Though there was no telling what she was up to or what trouble could be brewing in her absence.

Despite the fact that they were sharing a room, he and Anna weren't going to have to share the bed because of their differing work schedules. Anna didn't know how to cook, but when Rex asked her to help with dinner, she'd agreed. She ended up asking him so many questions that he'd opted to finish on his own. She wouldn't even look at Vinnie when she was recounting the story, and her media consumption had switched almost entirely to cooking content. She didn't expect it to make her any better at cooking, but if she didn't have to ask as many questions, maybe she could try again with Rex.

It was endearing how much Anna threw herself into the role of loving girlfriend despite the falsehood. She wanted to support him and make things better. Now, if only he could get her to stop trying to cut things out of his book. She was an editor at heart, which meant redlines on manuscripts and removing things he didn't want to remove. There was a certain element of dance to their banter on the topic. She would mark out, he would argue, she would point out her experience, he would argue creativity, and eventually, one of them would win. It was a four-step waltz with a flourish to finish, but he'd never been adept at dancing. He defaulted to her for the most part, as it was her area of expertise, but he loved watching the fire in her eyes when she was making a point. As much as it was 'pulling on her pigtails' to get her attention, he just couldn't help himself.

Vinnie yawned again and checked his phone for the fifth time. *How long did it take to clean a bathroom?* He'd had enough. He'd call the cleaning company a little later today, because this guy was never being assigned here again. Vinnie was not wasting the manpower and money for someone without any urgency. The contract was one hour every day with allowances for extra time if needed, but it had been almost two hours now.

Vinnie walked to the bathroom to see what the hold-up was, but when he opened the door, only the mop and bucket were there. He mentally mapped the layout of the club. He hadn't seen the guy walk by, so he couldn't have gone upstairs, or to the bar, or to the stage area, or VIP, and that left…*FUCK.*

He wasn't one to run, but he sprinted to the dressing room and rushed through the door without knocking. The girls should all be gone. This should just be catching a pervert, which was a simple call to the police. No violence, just indignation.

He heard someone struggling, and he rounded the half wall by the showers to see Dixon fighting to get the cleaning guy off of her.

No thoughts. Only action. Vinnie grabbed the asshole by the collar of his company t-shirt with one hand and slammed his skull against the shower wall, causing him to holler in pain and fear. *Good.*

"Get off me, you freak! She was asking for it!" The greasy-haired man took a swipe at Vinnie but only managed to knock off his glasses.

Vinnie punched the guy in the face so hard he felt the cartilage of the guy's nose give. Blood flowed from his nostrils and the guy tried to cover his face, but Vinnie was faster, hitting him again and again. One of Vinnie's hands held him in place while the other struck with maximum efficiency. Vinnie had height and weight on the guy. He realized he should have stopped hitting, but he didn't want to. He had failed to keep Dixon safe. He was enraged at the thought of what could have happened with him mere feet away.

"Vinnie, he's had enough. Jesus, stop!" Dixon grabbed his arm before he could strike again, and Vinnie dropped the other man to the floor.

Vinnie knelt to make sure the now-unconscious man still had a pulse, and thank god, he did. "Are you okay, Dixon?"

"Yeah Boss, I'm good. Are you?" She got on his level and pulled his hand closer to inspect. "Think you hit the wall as many times as you hit him. You messed up your knuckles real good. But I think you woulda killed him if you'da landed all them hits."

He didn't know how to respond, and couldn't see, so he let her help him stand. Where had his glasses ended up? "Are you sure you're okay?"

"Yeah, he only got in here a couple of minutes ago. Hell, I still got all my clothes on. I wore less dancing last night, no big deal." She talked a big game, but she sounded shaken up nonetheless.

"It's a big deal. I don't care if your clothes are still on. He fucking deserves what he got," Vinnie snarled. He pinched the bridge of his nose. "Can you see my glasses?"

"Oh sure, Boss, I..." Dixon trailed off. "Let me clean these real quick before you put 'em back on. Soap and water okay?"

"Dish soap is fine, nothing with lotion in it." Vinnie blindly moved his hand behind him until he found the shower wall to lean against. He needed to calm down. He shook, his right hand aching as the stinging pain final broke through the rush of adrenaline.

Dixon banged around in the cupboards, the water running as she washed his glasses. He kinda hoped she didn't offer up where they'd landed. "They weren't in his blood were they?" He had to ask. Didn't want to know, but needed to.

"Nope. Do you want to know where they were?"

"No. As long as they weren't in a bodily fluid, I can't care. If they were, please make sure the water is super hot and don't tell me."

"Okay, Boss. Will do."

Vinnie resisted the urge to groan, now positive that his glasses had landed in the trash can next to the shower. There were always used period products in that trash can. Speaking of trash, he needed to figure out what to do with the unconscious asshole. He realized he needed to get the law involved given the circumstances, as much as he loathed the idea. "We need to call the cops. Do you have someone to take your son to school? We're gonna be here for a while."

"It's Becki's turn for carpool. She's already on her way to get Henry." Dixon put his glasses back in his hands. "There you go."

"Thank you." Vinnie noticed the lotion streaks across the lens; he was going to have to clean them again before he could drive home, but this worked for now.

She rubbed her hands together. "Vinnie, I don't wanna press charges. Cops ain't gonna care about me getting roughed up. I'm more worried about them pinning an assault charge on you. Dude's got a broken nose at least and he's unconscious."

"I suppose I can try to press charges on behalf of the club and leave you out of it." Vinnie tried to think through how this was going to look. He had a record – not violent, but still a record. He was an ex-con. He'd done prison time. If this guy didn't have a record and Dixon wasn't willing to talk to the cops, it wouldn't be one man's word against another's. Or, more accurately, would be a citizen's word, against an ex-con's word, even if he was the business owner and the other guy had just committed an assault. Cops realistically hated cons. *Facts of the game, even once you were out.*

"What if they end up arresting you for beating the shit out of him?"

"That is the thought I just had."

"Couldn't we just throw him in the dumpster and call the company to come pick him up?" She braided her mousey brown hair as she asked.

Vinnie chuckled at the idea, "Much as I like the idea on a poetic level, I can't risk this guy cleaning somewhere and attacking a person who can't defend themselves."

"I suppose." She wasn't sold on the idea, and she was looking for her things.

Vinnie conceded and motioned for her to leave. "Please call Leila and let her know what happened so she can come down, just in case. I'll call after you leave, but I'm going to have to give them your phone number."

"Thanks, Boss. Are you sure about this?"
"I'm an upstanding citizen nowadays, what could go wrong?"

October 8th; 62 Days Until...

Anna was finishing her make-up in the bathroom when she heard the house phone ringing, then the ringing then abruptly stop. She didn't hear the answering machine greeting, so Jane must have picked it up. Rex's voice carried throughout the house while Jane's was subdued, but from what Anna observed, it was likely intentional. Anna blended out her eyeshadow and tapped off her brush as a knock sounded on the door.

"Vinnie is on the phone. He needs to speak to you," Jane informed her through the door.

Anna cocked her head to the side and glanced at her cellphone. No missed calls. Why hadn't he tried her cellphone? She wasn't ever without her cellphone. She opened the door, and Jane pointed to the lit up mute button.

"He's calling from a police station. Do not say anything you don't need to. Don't give them anything to stand on. Yes and no answers whenever possible." Jane's instructions were firm, and she kept her hold on the phone until Anna nodded, confirming she understood.

"Should I put it on speakerphone mode so you can hear?" Anna took the phone while asking.

"No. The less background noise the better."

Anna had worked with people who had been intimidating by nature, but Jane was a completely different story. Despite Anna's willingness to help out by living here with Jane, she was honestly a little afraid of the older woman. Her mismatched eyes and muted expressions were a form of control that kept Anna from reading her the way she normally could. Jane didn't give anything away. She seemed to isolate herself whenever possible. The Goodroe's mother was a mystery.

Anna unmuted the phone. "Hello."

"Hi." Vinnie sounded tense, and given the circumstances, it was understandable.

Anna waited for him to continue instead of asking all the questions running through her mind.

The most relevant one being, why was he at the police station and not calling from his own phone? That implied being arrested, or at least held for some kind of questioning. She picked up her phone with her free hand and texted her lawyer to get a recommendation for a criminal attorney that could be available immediately. The response was nearly instant: a law firm, phone number, and name.

"I need you to go to the club and get the surveillance footage from Leila. She should have it on a flashdrive by the time you get there, then bring it to the police station on West Freeway."

"Yes." Anna felt odd answering yes when she would have normally just agreed, but Jane was staring at her.

"Get ahold of Rex and he'll call me a lawyer. He knows who to call."

Anna wanted to say no, whoever Rex knew wasn't going to be as good as the people she could hire. "I think..."

"Just talk to Rex, *please*." Vinnie insisted, as Jane made a face letting her know whatever thought she had, wasn't needed.

Anna nodded, even though she couldn't be seen, as she stumbled through her answer. "I can do that. I mean, yes."

"Thank you. I'll see you soon." The dial tone clicked before Anna had a chance to respond.

Anna handed the home phone back to Jane. She texted her new assistant, Bailey, that she wouldn't be in until later, instructing her to reschedule her morning meetings and to call Alysha if she had any trouble. She considered her options. The club might take longer and Rex was closer. She wanted to be efficient; the faster she did what Vinnie asked, the faster she could get the whole story.

"Are you going to stand there or go do something?" Jane put her hands on her hips.

Anna didn't appreciate the disapproval over her pause in action. "I could text Rex about..."

"How about you go see Rex so there isn't a record? You can walk to the shop from here."

"How about you go talk to him since I have more than one thing to do?" Anna wasn't going to be talked to like a child. She walked back to her bedroom and grabbed her purse. "He's at the police station on West Freeway." She turned up her nose and prepared to leave the house, but Jane moved in front of her to block the door.

"I can't go to the shop. It isn't safe for me to be seen by people that occasionally visit." Jane looked as unhappy delivering the information as Anna was receiving it.

"Fine. I will stop there first then go to The Playhouse." She tapped her foot and Jane moved out of her way. As much as Anna had a genuine fear of what Jane was capable of, she wasn't going to be talked down to.

She popped the trunk of her car and exchanged her half-calf boots for the pair of red-bottom heels she kept there for emergencies.

Pausing only for a second to check for traffic, she backed out of the driveway and flew around the corner to Rex's appliance repair shop. She paused before going into the shop, Rex wasn't likely to be happy to see her with what she was going to tell him.

Uncaffeinated was not her preferred condition, especially when she was stressed. Maybe she'd snag a pack of cigarettes before she got to...*No.* She would not undo months of a broken bad habit over some stress. She was better than that.

Anna tugged on the door, but it didn't budge. Locked. She tapped on the glass portion of the door to get Rex's attention. She received a text message from Bailey about a rescheduling question, and she paused, trying to piece the client together with the project being referenced. *Willows...Willows...True Crime by Gragg Boltens.* She started to reply, when the shop door jerked open, startling Anna as the bells sounded.

"Help you?" Rex, as expected, didn't look thrilled at her presence.

Anna squared her shoulders. "Vinnie's in trouble."

"You related?" The older man really didn't pull any punches when it came to his adopted nephews.

"No. He didn't elaborate, but something happened at the club. I'm supposed to pick up footage from Leila at The Playhouse and ask you about a lawyer before I head over to the police station."

Rex nodded. "I'll call Larry and tell him to meet you at the police station. If you beat him there, wait for him in the parking lot. He drives a purple Plymouth, and I'll tell him to look for your black car."

"No, it's navy. The dealership said it was navy when I bought it."

"Hm. If you say so. Then I'll tell him that." Rex pulled out his phone, admonishing her, "You should get going. Larry's got a lead foot."

Never in her life had she wanted to stomp her foot and scream about her age more than right now. She wasn't a damn child. Despite the twitch she felt in her eye, Anna nodded and climbed back into her car.

Although she did go through a drive-thru to pick up coffee, she drove over the speed limit the entire trip. She wasn't getting a migraine on top of everything. The club's parking lot was empty except for Vinnie's car, a cleaning company's van, and a battered pick-up truck. Without attempting to open the door, she knocked loudly on the glass. To her surprise, Violet, Leila's wife, immediately opened the door.

"Why didn't you just open the door? We've been waiting for you."

"Vinnie didn't elaborate on his instructions. He just told me to come here and pick up the footage," Anna explained.

Violet scoffed. "Gotta be the only time he wouldn't speak a novel without anyone asking him to."

"Generally, he's interesting, so I don't mind the novel."

"Better you than me." Violet smiled and motioned for her to follow. "Leila's getting it ready. Did you get a hold of Larry? He's..."

"A friend of the Goodroes and Rex;" Anna interjected. "I heard. Rex called Larry, and he's supposed to meet me at the police station." Anna shouldn't have cut Violet off, it was rude, and none of what was happening was Violet's fault. Anna just wanted to get to where Vinnie was so she could help him.

"O-kay."

Anna followed Violet into the overly bright space. With all the lights on it looked so much different than it had during previous visits. Leila was sitting at the bar, tapping her painted nails impatiently while staring at her laptop. "This is almost completed. I had to go buy a larger flashdrive for the size of the files. I can't believe they took both of them away. What if they put Vincent in the same cell as that monster?"

"Baby, there's no way that guy isn't at the hospital. Vinnie broke his nose and probably his cheekbone. Dixon says she heard at least two cracks when Vinnie was beating him," Violet explained.

"What happened!" Anna demanded, her voice rising with more urgency than she'd intended.

Her practiced civility slipped as she interrupted the couple. She'd feel bad about it later when she calmed down. She was done; done being talked around. She wanted to know what the hell had happened.

"Our cleaning company sent over a new employee this morning. And he cornered Dixon, one of the dancers, in the dressing room and attempted to assault her. Vincent intervened." Leila explained.

"By breaking the guy's face." Violet humorlessly chuckled, making a face and shaking her own hand. "Did you see how fucked up his knuckles were?"

"Then why were they both taken into custody?" Anna was furious. If Vinnie had stood up for someone, why had the police chosen to take him in too?

Violet arched her eyebrow. "Because they're cops, Vinnie's an ex-con, and they know he is. So, it's cuffs first and questions later."

"Did the woman say anything?"

"Dixon's been in trouble before too. She didn't want to talk to them. Vincent made an excuse for her." Leila pulled out the flashdrive and offered it to Anna."

"This footage should be enough to confirm the story he gave. Larry should be able to get him released with that."

Anna nodded and put the drive in her purse. "Thank you."

"One of us will cover his shift tonight. Tell him to get some rest." Leila took a drink from the water bottle sitting on the bar.

"Thank you both."

"Just go take care of your boy."

By the time Anna arrived at the police station, a man, who she assumed was Larry, was already waiting impatiently outside the front doors. The slightly overweight man, in an ill-fitting pastel suit which was likely a pale green, odd yellow, or some other ridiculous color she couldn't properly identify, completed his look with a crooked bow tie. He took one look at her car and hurried over despite his slight limp. She pushed her door open, and he extended his hand. "You got the footage?" he questioned breathlessly.

Anna pulled the flashdrive from her purse, jumping as he reached across, snatching it from her hands and starting toward the station without so much as a thank you.

Oh, fuck this!

She didn't know who Larry thought he was, but he wasn't leaving her in the parking lot like a damn valet. She stretched her strides and reached the double doors at the same time as he did. She yanked the door open for him, her tone dripping with sarcasm. "After you."

He stormed into the station and while she appreciated his urgency, she bit the inside of cheek to keep from screaming. *Vinnie; she was here to help Vinnie.*

The inside of the station was a buzz of activity. Phones rang and conversations overlapped, one man was struggling in handcuffs as an officer yelled at him, and sitting on a bench was a frightened woman, crying into a cell phone. It was all far too loud for Anna's liking. She'd never been in a police station before, and she didn't think she'd be repeating the experience again.

"Larry Stevens, legal representation for Vincent Goodroe." Larry informed the officer at the front desk before handing him the flashdrive. "I believe this will corroborate my client's story."

"Come on, Larry. Do I look like I have time for this bullshit?" the officer at the front desk complained with a huff.

"I didn't ask you to have time for it, now did I, you prick?" Larry rubbed a hand over his bald head.

Anna arched her eyebrow at Larry's caustic treatment of the officer. She could have gotten a better lawyer than this. At the rate Larry was going, Vinnie was going to be in jail for the rest of the night. Her hand twitched in her pocket.

"Just get the cop who chose to detain Vincent at The Playhouse, and we'll call it even. Or do I need to win another lawsuit against the state of Texas based on this precinct's *upstanding* record?" He smirked as the officer picked the desk phone and requested Officer Jenner come up to speak to them.

Maybe she'd misjudged Larry a smidge. Whatever leverage he had here, he clearly knew how to use it.

Officer Jenner took the footage from the other officer and motioned for them to follow him to his desk. Larry sat down in the only free chair, leaving Anna to stand, which was fine with her. She'd rather not sit in a room where even the air felt sticky.

The sandy-haired officer plugged the USB into his computer and opened the singular video file on it. The footage played on fast forward: Vinnie clearly motioning for the man from the cleaning crew to go the opposite way from the dressing room door, the man mopping while a brunette strutted by him, then him following her into the dressing room, and Vinnie sprinting into the room a few minutes after.

That poor woman. If Vinnie hadn't been there…

"That good enough?" Larry tapped his pen on the officer's desk.

"It'll do for now." The officer grunted, rising from his chair. "Let's get your boy, but you know the drill. Stay close, no skipping town, all that."

The officer gave her a polite nod and pointed towards the front of the station. "Feel free to have a seat on the benches up front. It'll take us a moment to fill out the paperwork."

"No, I…"

Larry held up his hand, interrupting her. "Best if you wait up there, Hun."

Anna's heels smacked against the cheap tile floor as she virtually stomped her way to the front of the station. The crying woman was no longer at the bench, so she resigned herself and sat down, crossing one leg over her knee. The audacity of this entire situation had her one step away from buying a single cigar so she could have nicotine without breaking her resolution. It didn't help that the room smelled like stale cigarettes and body odor. She turned up her nose and retrieved her phone.

Anna: How's your morning?

Alysha: Good??? What did the new girl do?

Anna: Nothing. Just a long morning.

Alysha: Eat something & drink some water.
Alysha: O.o. The boy did something, didn't he?

Anna: No. I just wanted to check on you.

Alysha: Whatever you say

"Nice shoes."

Anna glanced at a woman wearing a skin-tight leopard print bodysuit in handcuffs and a purse falling off her shoulder.

"Keep moving, Goldie." An officer pushed the woman forward. Anna winced, imagining what she'd been arrested for and smoothed out her own jacket.

Patience had never been Anna's strong suit, but here she sat. After thirty-five minutes, she called Bailey and told her to reschedule the rest of her meetings for the day. The young girl sounded nervous as she asked how to view Anna's calendar. Anna slowly explained the process, *requesting* for Bailey to write it down and repeat it back to her. Whatever she needed to get done today, she would get done on her laptop. She was too keyed up to deal with anyone face to face today.

Another forty minutes passed before she heard Vinnie and Larry's voices from down the hall. They sounded almost jovial as they turned the corner. Larry was saying something about how much easier it was dealing with Vinnie's trouble vs. his brother's.

They came into view, and Anna was relieved to see a smile on Vinnie's face. He clapped Larry on the shoulder and thanked him. She stood to her feet, grateful that Vinnie didn't look hurt, only disheveled. But when their eyes met and his face dropped, the light in Vinnie's eyes faded. His shoulders slumped inward and he averted his eyes.

"Look at that, your girl came to your rescue." Larry elbowed Vinnie, and he flinched. "I'll send the bill in the mail. Or better yet tell Rex to get his ass out to the Rusty Nail. It's been over a month since I've seen that Irish asshole."

"We've been busy," Vinnie muttered, barely audible over the din of the station.

"Tell him to be less busy. He owes me a drink especially after all this nonsense," Larry insisted.

They passed through the swinging divider and up to Anna.

"Hello you." Anna touched the back of Vinnie's hand, but he recoiled, shoving his hands in his pockets. She lowered her voice and stepped closer. "Are you alright?"

He shifted away from her and closer to Larry. "My hand's messed up. There's blood on it; you don't want it on you." Vinnie's eyes were still on the ground, his entire body tense.

His logic was sound, but it still stung. Anna acquiesced, "Fair enough. Let's get you home."

The three walked into the parking lot, and Anna unlocked her car with the remote. Vinnie wordlessly climbed into the passenger seat, leaned against the window, and closed his eyes.

Anna blinked, stunned at Vinnie's actions. This was the first time he hadn't insisted on holding a door for her. But this day had been stressful, and maybe he needed time. It just hurt that he seemed to want nothing to do with her. She had bent over backwards to help, and he hadn't even thanked her. It seemed so out of character for him. He was so insistent that his past was behind him. Maybe today had just brought up bad memories. She felt herself scowling. She wasn't going to judge him. She knew what kind of man Vinnie was.

"Don't be too rough on him now." Larry sneezed and blew his nose into a handkerchief. "Lawd knows that boy is hard enough on himself."

She opened her purse. "I can pay you. How much do we owe?"

"I don't mind sending a bill. I've been running around in Goodroes' business since before Vinnie and Mat were crawlin' in diapers."

"I have cash," She offered again. "Will five hundred cover it?"

"Hell, I usually only charge those yahoos two-fifty for somethin' like this." Larry laughed, belly jiggling.

Anna handed three bills over. "Here, I'm sure there'll be more to this mess than just today."

"Well thank you kindly, Hun. You know, you're alright. Think you'll fit right in with 'em."

Larry waved goodbye and paced to his car as Anna got into her car and started it.

"Do you want to go to Urgent Care to have your hand looked at?"

Vinnie buckled his seatbelt and kept himself turned toward the window, rubbing his wrists. "No. Just take me home. I can handle it myself."

Vinnie hadn't ever been one for romance movies, so the irony of him writing a rom-com wasn't lost on him.

He loved the classics, horror, and even some action movies – a mindless good time was a good time. He was particularly attached to the trope of the injured hero or heroine being tended to by the love interest. While he might not consider himself a hero or a love interest, he couldn't stop the warm feeling in his chest as Anna tended to his hands in Rex's bathroom. He told Anna he could handle it himself and yet, her she was.

"Did you knock him out with one hit, then hit the wall with all your other blows?"

So much being heroic in Anna's eyes. She continued cleaning his knuckles as he defended himself. "I know I hit him more than once. But you don't need to do this. I've cleaned up plenty of injuries by myself."

"You won't be cleaning this one yourself." She took the tweezers from the cup on the sink and pulled out what looked like a piece of plaster.

No wonder that knuckle hurt more than the others. He tried to keep his wincing to a minimum as she moved the pieces of his skin around to check further. Anna might have finesse in the boardroom or with the press, but her bedside, or sink-side manner, left a lot to be desired. Had this bathroom always been so narrow? It felt like they were very, very close.

"I can't believe they handcuffed you when you hadn't done anything wrong."

"I got out and no one's pressing charges. I'll take the win."

"What were you thinking?" She shook her head.

"Clear head, moving hands."

"Clear head?"

"Alright, to be fair, it was more empty head and fast fists. It was more reactive than thinking through the consequences."

"Well, it's good you were there. Who knows what might have happened."

He nodded, not sure what else to say on the matter. He watched as she inspected his hands for any additional debris before setting the tweezers on the counter.

Anna took the alcohol bottle and soaked a cotton ball before wiping it over his hand, and he hissed at the stink. "That company deserves to be out of business. I wouldn't mind paying for a lawyer to sue them."

Vinnie pulled his hand back. "What? No. They're good people that took a chance on someone who turned out awful. That's not their fault."

She put her hands on her hips. "Background checks exist."

"He didn't have a record," Vinnie challenged. "And even if he did have a record, that doesn't make him a threat automatically."

"A record means the company should have acted with more caution to keep their reputation intact. Someone like that could cause problems, like what almost happened to that girl. Ultimately, they should have been more careful about who they hired. The company you keep, keeps you."

"Does it now?" Vinnie wanted to be anywhere but in this cramped bathroom with Anna. He couldn't get by her without moving her out of the way, but he didn't want to be where this conversation existed. *Someone like that?* She thought less of him. "What does that say about you?"

Anna blinked, opened her mouth, then closed it, before finally responding. "You're different."

"Why?" He rolled his shoulders to relieve the gathering tension.

"Because you are."

"Because I am." He nodded, the words burned in his mouth. "Because you thought I was good-looking enough to sleep with? Because you thought my book would sell? Because you thought you could drag me along like a puppy? I'm no one's tagalong anymore."

Anna folded her arms over her chest. "I never said anything about you being a puppy or a tagalong. And yes, I found you attractive from the start, but I treat you like an intelligent person, whose writing broke my heart. I'm not going to lie about that, or lie about the fact that I was worried about your record. It was a risk, and I weighed that risk before reaching out to you. And picking you was the right call, but not everyone is."

"You can't just put people up into generalized boxes," he argued.

"I'm not," Anna insisted, now scowling. "I am using common sense. Not everyone deserves trust. There are people who don't deserve a second chance."

He bounced his foot again, wanting to escape the stifling room. He wasn't sure where to go with her. Anna was right, but also wrong. Even if a person messed up, they could change. *You didn't have to be doomed to your past.* Vinnie hated the thought that the past was always going to be just out of sight behind him.

"So he wrote a book, and that's how y'all really met," Rex interrupted their conversation. He was standing just outside the bathroom in the hallway. "I knew that expert tale you spun at the wedding was a load of crap."

Vinnie felt his heart rate spike. He wasn't up for explaining the book he wrote to Rex on a normal day, let alone a day where he'd fought someone, gone to jail, and was having a real argument with his not real girlfriend.

"When do I get to read it?" Rex questioned.

Anna slipped out of the bathroom and addressed Rex. "He asked me to keep it quiet or I wouldn't have spun that tale. It's up to him to give you any details about it. I'm just the editor and he's got work to do before it's ready."

"Can I bribe you into telling me about it?"

Anna smirked. "Not with the whiskey in your cabinet."

Rex barked out a laugh, "I recently got a brand you might like. Got a fancy shaped bottle and everything."

"Oh, did you get it for your birthday?" Anna asked, knowing full well he was referring to the bottle she gifted him.

"Wouldcha know, I did."

"If you two are going to plot against me, could you at least do it behind my back?" Vinnie complained. "I don't need to know the length of the blade until it draws blood."

"Your brother is the drama queen, we only need one of those in the family." Rex rolled his eyes. "How's the hand?"

Anna looked down at her phone and headed towards the patio door. "Excuse me. I need to take this."

"My hand's fine. And as much as I'd like you and Anna to get along, could you not do it at my expense?" He was irked by what Anna had implied and felt justified in his position.

"Why do you think I'm doing it at your expense? 'Cause she ruffled your feathers?" Rex prodded.

Vinnie wound the ace bandage loosely over his hand. "Did you hear what she said?"

"That you have to be careful about the company you keep? Yeah, I heard that. Makes sense to me. Just because she said it with her money accent don't make her wrong."

"It doesn't feel great to have her talk about ex-cons like that when I'm an ex-con."

Rex shook his head. "Kid, you're missing the point."

"And what point is that?" He folded his arms and leaned against the frame of the bathroom door.

"Vinnie, you're the smartest person in the room and somehow still a dumbass. You missed it. She knows your past and *never* put you in the box that you're so worried about being in."

"Yeah. I guess you're right." Vinnie felt stupid and even though he was still unhappy, Rex was right. Every argument Anna had made hadn't been about him. "Come on, we should start dinner."

"I can start dinner. You can tell me about this book, now that I know it exists."

"On second thought, I can go grab us takeout. Who wants to cook with all that went on today?" He could get out of this, he just had to distract Rex for a little bit and he'd forget to bring it back up.

Maybe? Doubtful. Rex was as likely to let it go as pigs were to fly into pea-soup-colored sky. Vinnie patted his pockets, looking for his keyfob.

"Your car is still at the club," Rex reminded him.

"Right, I shouldn't leave it up there. I'll order an Uber and get it."

"Or you could ask your girl when she gets off the phone."

Vinnie tapped the rideshare app on his phone and walked towards the front door, snagging his keys from the hook. "She'll likely be on the phone for a while. No reason to bother her."

He sighed when he got outside and sent Anna a text to cover his bases.

Vinnie: Left to get my car. Thanks for your help today.

Anna: Happy to help.

Vinnie: Don't tell Rex about the book. He'll try and trick you.

The rideshare would be there shortly, and he glanced back at the house. Jane had emerged from wherever she'd been hiding and was helping Rex with dinner. Vinnie still didn't know what to make of his mother's return, but seeing Rex so happy made him smile. One day, maybe he'd be able to find someone like that. His phone vibrated, and he checked the message from Anna.

Anna: I work for you. Not him. My lips are sealed until you say so.

As differently as they looked at the world sometimes, it was nice to have Anna on his side.

Anna finished her phone call and stretched her legs. She reached her hand out instinctively to pet Jackal, only to realize her cat wasn't there. She sat in an oversized adirondack chair on the patio at Rex Abster's house, breathing in the evening air.

"So you have a cat." Jane's voice broke the silence, and Anna jumped, not having heard the door.

"Yes, I have her with a boarder, while I'm here. How did you know?" She wondered if there was cat hair on her clothes or some other sign. The horrific thought of her things smelling like cat and not knowing made her stomach clench.

No. Alysha would tell her if that was the case. She owned a cat, but she wasn't a crazy cat lady.

Jane held her hand out, making sure she was downwind of Anna before lighting a black cigarette. "Knew someone who used to hold her hand out like that all the time. Said it was reflexive from always petting her cat."

The smell of cloves filled the air, and Anna realized this was what she kept smelling in the evenings when she opened the window in the bedroom.

"You want one?" Jane held out the pack to her.

She did. Anna really wanted one, so badly that her fingers twitched at the thought of holding it in her hand. "No. I quit smoking in January. If I try one, I might get a new bad habit."

"Trying to break those? Bad habits, I mean."

"I suppose. Although I'm not giving up coffee or whiskey. There's a lot I want to accomplish in the next ten years and I don't want vices holding me back."

The older woman sat in the chair next to her, taking a long drag of her cigarette. Almost talking to herself more than anything, she admitted, "I think all that's left of me is vices."

Anna wasn't sure how to respond. One part of her wanted to be reassuring and see if Jane would open up; the stories she must have would be amazing. The other part of her was hesitant to engage with someone who seemed not to want to engage with anyone other than Rex. Jane wasn't a mystery for Anna to unravel. It wouldn't be fair to Vinnie if she learned things about his mother and didn't share them, but sharing secrets about Jane might put her in a worse position with Rex. He was finally warming up to her, and Anna didn't want to jeopardize that. It was silly, but she hated it when she couldn't figure out how to effectively communicate with someone.

"Sorry, what?" She opted feign ignorance as a way to give Jane an out, and Jane shrugged in response. They settled into silence, and she waited to see if Jane would continue.

Anna felt a little guilty about how she'd spoken to Vinnie earlier. Not because she was wrong because she wasn't, but she'd sounded callous. She didn't want him to think that she judged him because to his past, and it was obvious he felt that way. He'd looked for an excuse to run and it didn't seem to surprise Rex. Anna wasn't a stranger to burying herself in a project when she needed to think through a problem. Vinnie was the same kind of intelligent she was, maybe smarter if she was being honest, so it would stand to reason they might be similar in other ways as well.

"So what are you looking to accomplish in ten years?" Jane asked, breaking the silence. "That's a specific time frame."

Anna set her phone back to silent before responding. "I've focused all my attention on education and a career for the last ten years. I know I want a family, but I'm not giving up what I've been able to build."

"Rex said he overheard you talking to Vinnie and that you're editing his book. Is editing that intense a career? I don't know too much about books, so that whole process is over my head."

"I edit an occasional book to stay in practice, but I'm part of the executive team of the company I work for. This is my seventh year on the board of directors."

Jane looked her up and down. "You must be older than you look."

"No. I'm privileged," Anna explained. "My adoptive mother passed away when I was eighteen and finishing college. Part of her will was leaving me the shares she held, which essentially handed me a job."

"How does that happen?"

"Money. And no one knew she was sick, so she wrote it that way, and the board didn't flinch. I would have spent more time abroad in South Korea if I hadn't been required to either come back and take my position or risk losing it entirely." She watched the fireflies light up the yard in front of her and smiled. She missed the seasons in Chicago, but it was nice not to deal with a real winter.

"Why Korea? Seems like an odd place to pick. I'd hate being somewhere and not knowing the language." Jane's questions weren't interrogatory. She was trying to learn more. This wasn't exactly small talk.

Anna checked the time on her phone. "I'm fluent. We had a Korean exchange student my freshman year of high school. She was the daughter of one of Emily's business associates, and I chose to live in the international dorms with her for the rest of high school."

"She sent you to boarding school?"

She shook her head. "I asked to go. It made my college course attendance easier. I started college my sophomore year of high school. I liked, and still like to achieve. It was easy to get into the University of Chicago in tandem with high school, based on Emily's donations, my grades, and my drive."

"All that and no sense in the kitchen," Rex teased Ana as he handed Jane a drink.

"I didn't have much use for the kitchen. Emily was always working, and the woman who bought food for our apartment made meals that only needed to be heated up." Anna shrugged.

"Sounds lonely," Jane pointed out.

"I suppose it was, but I never paid it much attention. I was always busy with something," she explained.

"I was adopted when I was five and I don't remember who my birth mother was. My life in Chicago with Emily is the earliest I can remember."

"What about your father?" Rex asked.

"John Doe was written on my birth certificate when I saw it last, but without a DNA test, I wouldn't have any idea. I have to try and get a copy of it again, which is nothing short of a nightmare since I can't remember my birth mother's name."

"You don't have anything from your mother?" Jane's voice wavered slightly, and Rex put his hand on her shoulder.

Anna had never felt any sort of way about not having anything relating, to her mother until this moment, looking at Jane who was obviously affected by the thought. "No. Emily didn't believe in keeping things passed its usefulness. She explained to me that my birth mother had died in an accident, and there wasn't a lot in the car other than a few bags."

"She died in a car accident?" Rex's hand kept moving over Jane's shoulder. He was trying to comfort her without drawing attention.

Anna confirmed, "Here in Houston. Emily was here on business and was a witness to the crash."

"And she just took you home as a souvenir?" Jane clipped.

"What? No. She told me that she moved here temporarily while she filed paperwork, and the state determined if I was really an orphan or not. Then it was just lawyers and money. When she finally got approval to adopt me, we moved to Chicago."

"So she eliminated your mother essentially." Jane stood up, anger creeping into her tone.

"Janey," Rex started.

"I don't think it was intentional," Anna interrupted. "Emily wasn't perfect, but she gave me a home. Whoever my mother was, she died the car accident is what eliminated her, not Emily adopting me."

"I'm gonna go lay down." Jane walked back into the house, closing the door hard behind her.

Anna shifted in her chair. "I didn't mean to upset her."

Rex sat down in the chair that Jane had been in and sipped the drink she'd left behind. "She's got guilt eating her. Ain't your fault."

"I suppose, but I should have thought about the impact my words might have before I continued."

"You are not used to anything other than professional, are ya?"

Anna laughed. "I'm really not. It's become my default over the past few years. I'm not good at relaxing."

"I've noticed." Rex chuckled before clearing his throat. "Thank you for helping with Vinnie's *incident* this morning. Larry said you paid him already. How much do we owe you?"

"You don't," She answered, before nonchalantly clarifying. "If I want the money back, I'll get it from Vinnie."

"But you aren't gonna ask for it."

"It's only money." She stretched as she stood. "It's the one thing I've never had to worry about. Do you want help with dinner?"

"I suppose, but then it's my turn to worry."

Anna held the door open for Rex and he came in behind her. It looked like he'd already started dinner and put on a fresh pot of coffee. "You don't need my help."

"Always need help with the dishes."

Anna took her cue and turned on the hot water. She wasn't the biggest fan of washing dishes, but she was less a fan of the awkward feeling of being the only one in the house not contributing in some way.

"Not sure about the ins and outs of how you met my nephew," Rex held his hand up before Anna could say anything. "The business between you kids is none of mine. Just be good to him and we're straight."

"I promise being good to him is my only plan, Rex."

Vinnie pulled into the parking lot of Lost Horizon and sighed before getting out of his car. He hadn't meant to drive all the way down the Causeway, but here he was in Galveston. The ocean air didn't calm him the way it pacified his brother. He preferred the woods or a quiet room full of books. He clunked up the wooden steps, pausing at the sign on the door indicating that only the patio was open and to walk around. He saw movement and wrapped his knuckles against the glass inset of the door.

What the hell was Mat messing with now? His brother had been fussing at this place since he'd gotten it back. There wasn't a lot of upfront capital, so any renovations had to be done in phases, while the restaurant was still running. Mat appeared in the doorway looking confused, but still opened the door for him.

"Fuck you doing here?"

"Hello to you too." Vinnie rolled his eyes as he walked by Mat as his brother re-locked the door.

"Yeah, hi. Now, what are you doing here?" Mat questioned again. "Don't you normally work on Saturdays?"

"I do. Didn't Rex call you?" Vinnie was genuinely surprised that their Uncle hadn't called Mat about the goings-on this morning.

"We're not really talkin' at the moment," Mat admitted. "And before you start trying to play peacemaker, we didn't fight. I just told him I needed some space."

"Oh. That's surprisingly mature for you. Kass is a good influence on you. You might end up a respectable member of society yet."

"Asshole."

"Dick."

There was noise in the kitchen, and laughter spiked over the music from the patio diners. The silence between them was amplified by the stereo of cheerful noise from every side. Vinnie looked up and noticed the wires hanging down from the ceiling. He followed their pathway with his eyes to the music system at the bar.

"You decide to rewire the music system without me? How am I hearing music if you have this ripped up?"

"Band on the patio; radio in the kitchen," Mat explained, before questioning, "Why do you care if I'm working it?"

"Because, you suck at sound systems. You shoulda called me."

"Well since you're here now, you can help." Mat handed him a pair of wire strippers and motioned to the ladder.

Vinnie took the tool and climbed up on the ladder, inspecting the damage. "Three things: one, you need more light in here, two, you damaged the trim, and three, I'm impressed you could reach this high, even with the ladder."

"I've got no witnesses right now and good liability insurance. It'd be a shame if this ladder fell," Mat snickered, "although it would cover the cost of a few of renovations."

Vinnie scoffed. "I wouldn't suggest it. Anna would sue you and take the restaurant. Can you get me some electrical tape?"

Mat handed him the requested item. "Well, good to know she'd avenge you."

"I suppose."

"You want a drink?"

"Yeah." Vinnie pulled the penlight out of his pocket and put it in his mouth so he could use both hands to fix the issue he found.

Mat always walked heavy, so his steps echoed on the wooden floors. The song on the radio switched to a more Blues-inspired track, and someone let out a whistle. Liquor bottles and glasses clanged together before the telltale clank of the shaker locking in place. Mat announced, "I got a new drink I want you to try."

"Fam-tas-ic," Vinnie managed to respond around the flashlight still in his mouth. He finished the section, put the penlight back in his pocket, and climbed down.

Mat held out the dark-colored drink to him.

He took it without too much concern. Mat generally knew what he was doing with mixology.

The drink was a touch bitter.It tasted like espresso and whiskey with chocolate and vanilla added in. It was more alcoholic than he would normally like his drinks. He had a tendency to acquire holes in his memory when he drank too much.

"Not bad, tastes kinda like a White Russian but with more coffee," He offered feedback on the drink.

"It's a Nutty Irishman."

Vinnie choked on his second sip. "Sorry?" He coughed to clear his throat. "What did you call this?"

"A Nutty Irishman." Mat repeated with a grin, clearly impressed with himself. "It's got Irish cream, Amaretto, whiskey, and espresso in it. Kass and I found it in the back of her Gram's recipes."

"The Rated R Recipe Book strikes again. You better be giving your wife credit for helping you with all these good ideas."

"I'd be nothing without her."

"Dawe, listen to you being all soft and mushy." Vinnie chuckled until Mat cuffed the back of his head. "I ain't cleaning it up if you make me drop this."

"Sit." Mat barked and pointed to a chair before retrieving a bottle of water. "So what the hell happened this morning?"

He waited until Mat sat down, looking at the table to avoid making eye contact. "I got put in cuffs this morning."

"The fuck happened? Why?"

"Cleaning guy attacked one of the girls, and I objected with my fists." Vinnie took off the glove he'd been wearing to show off the bandage he'd been hiding.

"She okay?"

Vinnie nodded. "I got there in time."

Mat folded his arms over his chest. "And the cops arrested you because you were there."

"Technically, I was only brought in for questioning."

"But in cuffs," Mat objected.

"Yeah, Anna showed up with Larry to get me out." He pushed the half-full glass back and forth with his pointer fingers.

Mat sighed. "On a scale of an uncomfortable conversation with Anna to Kass and I having to find a new temporary place to live, how badly did that go?"

"She wanted to sue the cleaning company, blame them for what that asshole tried." Vinnie put his phone on the table, making sure there weren't any missed messages. "She's not gonna do that to you guys. It was just uncomfortable."

"Well, Anna's not from our side of the tracks. Only criminals she's probably met besides us are white-collar creeps."

He tapped his heel. "I'm not a fucking criminal. You always forget the ex-con part, and Kass didn't care when we met her."

"Kass is in a league of her own. She wouldn't judge a match until it started a fire in front of her." Mat took a long drink of his water.

"You aren't even mad about the criminal part. You're still mad because we got caught and ended up with a record. If Anna's gonna judge you for that then she ain't for ya."

"She really isn't," Vinnie muttered.

"Huh?"

"Nothing. You're right."

"So what did she say?" Mat asked.

Vinnie shrugged. "I left to go get my car before we said too much."

"Hmm."

"What? I didn't want to leave my car at club all night."

Mat stood to resume cleaning, gathering the tools scattered throughout the dining room. "You ever notice you get gone when you don't wanna talk about something?"

"I haven't, because I don't," He argued, finishing his drink. "Stepping away to clear my head, rather than staying and throwing a fit, doesn't mean I'm getting gone to get gone."

"Okay, if you say so."

"Come on, Mat."

His brother turned to face him and cocked his head to the side. "What? What did I say now?"

Vinnie really wanted to argue, but was it worth it? If Mat believed it, there wasn't much that was going to change his mind. His brother was nothing if not stubborn to a fault. He didn't leave a fight to simply leave, but he did have a temper that he hated to lose, so sometimes he needed space to calm down. It wasn't his fault that getting a better handle on his emotions occasionally coincided with finding something else that needed to be done.

It wasn't worth fighting about. Vinnie dismissed the topic, deciding he didn't want to dwell on it. "Nothing; don't worry about it. You want a hand sweeping?"

"Broom's in the corner." Mat pointed before continuing to wind up the cord of wires.

"You remember that fast food joint we worked at?" He reminisced as he swept.

"I remember tripping over the camera's power cord to unplug it and you cracking the safe."

"What the hell did we spend that two hundred on?"

"It was a hundred and thirty and we paid some guy at the liquor store a twenty to buy us a bottle of hooch and a pack of smokes. He took forty, you started smoking on the regular, and Rex kicked both our asses." Mat chuckled. "We've come a long way from that."

"You have. I'm still spinning my wheels." Vinnie swept the sawdust into one corner before looking for the dustpan. "Off-topic, but when am I getting *my* bartender back?"

"Look, Kass and I are still trying to find a daycare that doesn't look like garbage. I trust Becki with Lizzie, so it's gonna be another week or so at least." Mat sighed and checked his phone.

"Just don't steal her for your bar."

"No promises."

CHAPTER 8:
BUILD CHARACTER WITH PURPOSE

Balance Strife and Celebration

October 10th; 60 Days Until...

Anna double-checked the excel spreadsheet on her tablet and signed off on the last of the budgetary requests. One of the girls working at the boutique set an iced coffee down on the table, next to the plush chair she was sitting in. Anna thanked her and took a drink before opening an email from Vinnie. He was arguing with her over the changes she wanted for the book. He thought this was the last round of edits before the arc copies went out, and he was fighting tooth and nail for a handful of scenes she told him to cut. She smiled as she replied, agreeing to talk about it over dinner tonight.

She had already let him win; this book was his baby, but she couldn't risk her reputation by being too soft. She knew how happy he was going to be and that was worth being a little soft. The proof copy was in her car, and she couldn't wait to give it to him tonight.

The trick was finding time to be alone. She didn't think it was, going to be as hard as it was living with more people. *Had she been alone too long?* The thought of having a life with someone seemed more impossible every time she had to work around Rex or Jane. But those moments alone with Vinnie swayed her into believing that perhaps there was someone out there for her. Someone that would let her be with them, while remaining independent.

Her phone vibrated, reminding her about the doctor's appointment she had this afternoon. As painful the process of having her IUD replaced was and as little sex as she had this entire year, she still wasn't taking any risks. One of the harder parts of pretending to date Vinnie was always being around him. As good-looking as he was and as close as they often were, it made her ache for physical contact.

She wasn't going to get herself off with his uncle and mother in the other room, or god forbid, Vinnie getting home early and being caught mid-act. Anna took a long drink of her coffee to cool the flush in her cheeks. *What else needed to get done before she finished for the afternoon?*

She had three more covers to approve and four marketing campaigns, that needed more details before she signed for any payments. And if Ben asked her to tour one more office location that was out of his price range she was going to send him a revised budget with a deduction in his salary to reflect the cost of the type of office he wanted. With his father was on the board, she didn't have a choice about putting Ben in charge, but she wasn't going to simply let him run the company into the ground to make his father happy. She was exhausted from dealing with his whining about needing to look the part and his lack of focus on doing the actual work. Alysha's subsidiary was launching in twelve days, and it was no surprise that she was ahead of schedule.

The sunshine from outside reflected off the round mirrors that adorned the walls, catching her attention and bringing her back to the present. The circular, golden displays had dresses hanging from small bars, and grand chandeliers hung overhead, adding extra light and atmosphere. Bright, round lights lit up the recessed displays of shoes, accessories, and bags. Another woman shopping walked behind Anna, her heels clicking on the wood floor. This shop was Anna's favorite places to purchase clothes, there was always a new designer being showcased – they also provided iced coffee, which was a nice bonus.

"I feel like that girl from that Disney movie who doesn't know she's a princess until Mary Poppins is her grandmother and she gets an insane makeover," Alysha called out from inside the dressing room.

Anna chuckled, "Because you feel awkward and out of place?"

Alysha poked just her head out from between the curtains. "Because there are no price tags on anything and you aren't going to let me pay for any of this."

"I'm not. Do you like the dress you have on?"

"It's a lot of money on my body."

Anna arched her eyebrow. "That isn't what I asked."

"I like it," Alysha admitted quietly. "But this has to be a lot of money."

"It's free for you," She smirked, and Alysha made an exasperated noise.

"But it's not free for you."

"I told you that I was treating you for your launch." Anna set her tablet down.

"You were careful with your budget, and even with the black-tie event you're hosting, you are still ahead of what we forecasted. Additionally, the presales for the dozen authors you've signed are four times what two of the others have combined. This is my thank you for that. You have a lot to be proud of."

"I am proud."

"Good. Now since you like the dress, may I please see you in it?"

"I'm not wearing the style I was thinking of for my launch. I want a more traditional look for my launch. But since I'm going to the gala event with you, I tried on one for that. You said fantasy theme, right?"

"I did. This will be a good networking opportunity for you," Anna answered. "the tailor is finishing alterations on my dress. I can get your opinion on mine while we're both here."

Alysha's painted toes curled into the plush rug from under the curtain she was hiding behind. "It's pink."

"I have a general idea of what pink is. I'm not that colorblind."

Alysha was still hiding behind the curtain. "It's ethereal pink and the dress is floaty."

Anna motioned for her to come forward.

"I'm gonna have to change my hair," Alysha muttered, and stepped out from behind the curtain.

Anna might have been unable to see the dress' true color, but she could tell it was iridescent by the way the light hit it. The dress remined her of a flower – puffed sleeves with ruffles accenting the edges, a sweetheart neckline, and the flowy, layered skirt was also ruffled at the hem. It was elegant and whimsical; it would be perfect for the gala.

Alysha stepped onto the round pedestal. She moved from side to side as she looked at herself in the mirror. "It has a slit." She angled her leg to show off the feature. She moved listlessly, but her dark eyes were practically sparkling.

"It's gorgeous and it looks beautiful on you." Anna grinned.

"Miss Kane, I have your…" Beverly, the shop's in-house tailor, emerged with Anna's dress, but stopped in her tracks at the sight of Alysha. "Oh my goodness, my dear, you look like royalty. That piece was made for you! The contrast of your skin against that fabric…well, it's perfect. Oh my goodness!"

"Thank you." Alysha bobbed her head and stood up straighter.

"Miss Kane, I'll hang this up for you in this dressing room here. And I *need* to get the designer to come to see you, Miss Brooks. I'll be right back."

"Thank you." Anna stood up and moved next to Alysha. She looked at both of them in the mirror. "You're going to need new shoes."

"You aren't letting me say no, are you?"

"I can't force you into anything, but if the designer sees you in bad shoes, it wouldn't be good."

"Has anyone ever told you, that you're passively-aggressively manipulative?"

"Only with you. With most people, I trick or force my opinion forward." Anna patted Alysha's shoulder. "Pick out a pair of shoes with the designer. I need to see how my own dress fits."

She entered the indicated dressing room and stripped down to her bra and panties. She unhooked the fasteners at the top of the intricate back that linked it to the shoulders. She was going to need help putting this on before the event. She felt the smooth, cool fabric against her skin as she dropped the gown over her head. She preferred silks to satins, as she was constantly warm.

Despite living in Texas for years, she hadn't acclimated to the heat. She put her heels on relieved that Beverly had let the hem out enough to accommodate her height. She walked out with the back of the undone, holding the bodice up with her hand as she stepped onto the platform next to Alysha's.

"Do you need…"

Anna held her hand up. "Stay put, Beverly can help me in a moment."

"I can. I even brought my step stool." Beverly walked back in with one of the designers that showcased their work here. "Look at Miss Brooks in your piece, Emmet."

Emmet smiled widely. "Oh she was right, it's perfect on you."

"Thank you so much, and you can both call me Alysha, please."

"Anna, we're picking out shoes here, *correct*?" Emmet was halfway between asking and demanding.

Anna bent her knees so Beverly could secure the fasteners. Even with the wooden stool, Anna was too tall for the older woman. "Whatever she wants, Emmet. It's on me."

His grin intensified, whitened teeth contrasting his dark lips, and his night-sky eyes lighting up with what she could only assume was mischief. "Whatever she wants?"

"Go nuts."

"Yes, girl!" and "Anna!" came in perfect synch from the designer and current model respectively.

Beverly had gotten off the stool and inspected the hem of her dress. "Take advantage, Miss Brooks. It'll be worse if you don't. I've seen Miss Kane buy half the store for someone."

"You never did that with my clothes," Emmet mockingly complained.

Anna glanced at him over her shoulder, "You weren't in Houston yet or I would have. They would've loved your creative flare."

"You're too kind." Emmet walked behind her, but Anna could see him analyzing the back of her dress in the reflection. "I haven't seen that one. Did you order that?"

"I did. I wanted something unique. I have a pair of Jimmy Choo's that will accent it perfectly."

"But it's still black," Emmit lamented. "You are constantly in black."

"I've done two events in color this year," Anna defended. "Grab my phone and I'll show you."

Emmet handed her the phone, and as Anna scrolled through the pictures to show him the green dress she'd worn at the beginning of the year, she noticed that Vinnie was in all the pictures from Chicago. In one of the selfies in particular, Vinnie had been adjusting her necklace from behind her.

"Show me that picture. I wanna see the human who is making you smile like that," Emmet demanded, as she hesitated to hand it over. "Ma'am, does he have a brother?"

"Only a married one," Alysha supplied. "Anna went to the wedding in July."

"How have I not heard about this man? You're going to family events? Since when does Anna Kane go to family events with romantic partners? I thought you were a serial dater and…" He cleared his throat. "...late-night rendezvous experiencer. Look at how he looks at you. He is enraptured."

"It's very new." Anna was not explaining the convoluted story to Emmet. Despite how much she liked working with him, they weren't close. They had a professional relationship.

"July is not *very* new."

"Her New Year's resolution was to try for a relationship, but Vinnie is a talker and not one for a lot of action." Alysha snickered as she tried on the white heels Beverly had brought her.

"Beverly, could you go get the silver Vivians from the back? I think that style will be better with Alysha's dress," Emmet requested. As soon as the older woman was out of earshot, he motioned for Anna to come closer. "Have you somehow not slept with this man? And if so, are you alright?"

Anna's cheeks flushed red. "It's complicated. There's a lot going on with this family right now."

"His family ain't the thing. Drag the man to your bed."

Alysha started laughing, bouncing her heels on the platform.

Emmet put his hands on his hips. "What am I missing? Spill."

Anna's jaw was tight as she forced herself to partially explain the situation. "It's complicated. The relationship is more for show." She snatched her phone back. She knew they didn't mean any harm, but she didn't need them ganging up on her.

"Has anyone told him that?"
Alysha clapped her hands together. "That's what I've been saying."

"Home early?" Rex questioned as he came in from the patio.
Vinnie looked up from the vegetables he was chopping in the kitchen. "It's Monday. I don't work on Mondays."
"Hmmm. I guess I lost track of the days."
"They say the first thing to go is the memory."
"Kid…"
"I'm the only one with a knife in hand," Vinnie interrupted.
"Fair enough." Rex retrieved two bottles of water from the refrigerator. "You need help with dinner?"
"If you want," Vinnie shrugged.
"I'll be right back." Rex disappeared for moment, returning with only one bottle in hand. "What do you want me to start with?"
"Either start the rice or brown the chuck that's in the sink. Wash the rice if you pick it." Vinnie continued to dice up the pepper, but slowed his rhythm to quiet the banging against the cutting board.
"Think I'll stick to the meat. Never noticed rice tasting much different with it being washed or not. You want this seasoned?"
"Anna's eaten a lot of rice, so she notices. Also, you should wash it." He explained, "You can season it however you want. I'm gonna keep the elements separate."
Rex pulled out a skillet. "Anna gonna be eating with us tonight?"
"Should be."
The click of the igniter and whoosh of the flame signaled that the burner was on as Rex looked through the cabinets for the oil. "Feels like that hasn't happened too much."
Without a word, Vinnie cleared his throat as he grabbed the remaining vegetables that he needed to cut.
"I think it's a good thing."
"Mhmm." He ran the onion under the water as he peeled back the outer layers.
"She hardly leaves that room when you aren't here and I know she's not shy," Rex pointed out.
Vinnie sighed heavily, chopping the onion under the water and draining a portion of them before handing it to Rex. "She's used to living alone. Been on her own most of her life. You didn't give Mat any of this shit when he brought Kass home."

"Mat brought Kass home? I remember that differently. *We* made him go get her and he was growling and griping the whole time."

The onions sizzled on the pan. The scent mixing with sage and garlic as Rex added the spices.

"You know what I meant."

"We're getting along better now. I just didn't like that she lied to me. Don't like secrets."

"That I understand."

Anna was a lie. The idea that she'd be in a relationship with him was a lie. She was in a green tier and he was in a red one. Their couple-ship was a subterfuge of convenience and cowardice on his part. He should have come clean from the beginning and told his family who Anna really was, but he hadn't, and now she was tied up in his knot. Worse than that, he often forgot that what they shared wasn't real. He hadn't crossed any lines, but it was all too easy to talk about her and pretend. Part of him wanted…*Focus. Dinner.*

Vinnie sped up his cuts. He almost went to the club instead of starting dinner, but Anna said they were going to talk about his book tonight. That meant they had to be alone, unfortunately, as rare as Jane's presence was, she seemed to emerge at the most inopportune times.

He wanted to talk to Jane – at least part of him did –but the rest of him was indifferent. Whatever the reason, she'd left him and Mat with Nathan and that wasn't okay. They didn't deserve to be alone with him as violent as he was. He shouldn't have…*No. Not going down that path tonight.*

Vinnie was going to have dinner with his family and then he and Anna were going to talk about his book. The arcs were about to go out and everything needed to be finalized…at least as much as it was going to be finalized. Anna reminded him over and over that every book had errors, perfection wasn't the end goal — a good story was. He was going to accomplish this, with Anna's help, and then things would settle down.

"I think Jane and I should be set to settle into the cabin by December." The sizzle of the pan almost covered Rex's statement.

Vinnie stopped cutting and turned to look at his uncle. "You're leaving for good?"

"Houston isn't safe for her. I'm selling the shop, and hell, maybe this place. She and I are moving up there. I'm old enough and I've done enough." Rex's shoulders were tense.

Vinnie had seen his uncle fight when he was younger, and this was the type of stance Rex took when preparing to duck a punch.

Rex was ready for a fight. The instinct to physically defend himself was a side effect of the years of violent life he'd lived.

"Vincent."

Shit. He knew that Rex was just trying to be serious, but Vinnie couldn't stop the shiver that ran down his spine at hearing his full name. That was the name he'd hear any time Nathan Goodroe opened his mouth, may that bastard rot in hell. Even when Leila used that name, it would startle him.

Rex continued. "I know you and Mat feel a way about her and I don't blame you. I'm a little raw at her myself for the disappearing act, but I can't... I won't let her go again. I know it's gonna be a trail full of bear traps and quicksand, but I still want the lot of you in my life. Just not sure how that's gonna work."

Vinnie couldn't blame him. He knew how much his mother meant to Rex. Even if Jane screwed up royally, Vinnie believed in second chances and he was dedicated to letting Rex have space with Jane. That was the whole point of playing musical living spaces to get Mat, Kass, and Lizzie out of the house. He knew his own temperament was less explosive. Despite everything, he hadn't expected Rex to leave Houston. Vinnie felt a pit in his stomach at the thought of Rex being gone on top of everything else.

"I know that brain of yours is running like a hamster in a wheel. Say something."

"A hamster in a wheel implies I'm not getting anywhere with my thoughts. I'd prefer to think of it as a racecar on a track. At least this way I'm running towards a goal."

Rex glared at him. "Your brother is right about you sometimes."

"You used to tell us that even blind squirrels find nuts." He scraped the chopped peppers into an empty bowl.

"Tell me what you're thinking dammit!" Rex smacked the counter.

Vinnie jumped, and dropped the bowl into the sink. Thankfully it landed right-side up and away from the peppers.

"I'm sorry," His uncle sighed heavily. "I didn't mean to startle ya."

Vinnie leaned back against the counter, halting his task. "It's fine. But what do you want me to say, Rex? I don't know what to think about my mother being here and suddenly *not* dead. I don't like the idea of not being about to access the only happy place I lived in as a kid. I hate that you and Mat aren't talking. I'm bent out of shape about all of it, and worst of all," He took a deep breath, "I can't talk to you because you're in the middle of it."

Rex's jaw twitched, but he didn't speak, so Vinnie grabbed the bag of rice to portion out and clean.

"I'm sorry, I'm pulling things apart for you."

Both men jumped, at Jane's voice. Vinnie gripped the bowl to the point where plastic bent. Jane had appeared from virtually nowhere and was standing by the dining table. Vinnie was going to rig a tracking system on her – he hated how she would suddenly appear.

Logically, he had been distracted talking while Rex, and it would make sense that she walked quietly given her past grifting. It consistently threw him off to see her dark hair retreating whenever he entered the room. Jane was trying to stay out of the way, but it wasn't helping because she was still here.

She was wearing the pants she had on the first day she'd come back. He recognized the paint splatter on the hems. Her hands tugged at the pockets of her hoodie as if she couldn't keep her hands still. Funny how even a few years with her had influenced him and Mat. They were both always doing something with their hands. Had they learned it from her? Were there subconscious memories of her out of his reach? He didn't like to think about his early childhood. Too much to be afraid of during those days.

Jane stepped closer, her mismatched eyes watery. "I hate that me being here is making you feel like that. I didn't want to hurt anyone. I've never been good at keeping things calm. I'm all chaos and bad choices."

Rex adjusted the stove. "We should talk it through at the table."

Vinnie was torn. There was an appeal in getting these conversations over with, but also he didn't want to have them without Mat here. It felt like a betrayal not to have Mat at the table as they went through this. The grandfather clock chimed out the hour, signifying that Anna would be back here for dinner. Should Anna be a part of this? If they were actually in a relationship, then of course she should. But they weren't. It would look odd to exclude her intentionally. He could text her and tell her to wait to come back to the house. Maybe he should call Mat? Despite everything, they were still a family, weren't they? He wished it was easier to know what the right choice was to fix things.

Anna rubbed her temples. Staring, at the screen was finally getting to her as a headache formed at the base of her skull. Prior to a few weeks ago, if she were working this late, it wasn't a problem.

She'd lock her office, walk to the other side of the building, take the elevator up, and be home. Presently, she wasn't sure what to do with herself; she was in pain from seeing the doctor, and she was ready to be out of her clothes and in the shower.

Maybe she'd get a hotel for the night? It wouldn't strike anyone as odd, she traveled often enough. She also wanted to avoid raising any further suspicions about the contents of Vinnie's book.

Avoiding Rex's questions was one thing, outright lying to him (again) would risk what little footing she'd managed to gain. Getting a hotel for the night would probably be the best strategy. She wasn't part of Vinnie's family. Her presence was a matter of convenience and being a part of whatever unfolded tonight would not be convenient for either of them. She was only sitting at their proverbial table until it was time to move on.

Vinnie had sent her a text that his family was finally having a chat with Jane and asked her to stay late at work if possible. She understood why. They weren't actually a couple, but it still stung a bit. Perhaps she was getting too attached. The gift-wrapped bundle was sitting on her desk, the proof copy of Vinnie's book. She hadn't looked at it herself, but rather made sure it was wrapped so Vinnie could see it first. Now she felt like an idiot. She should open it. She previewed almost every other book that she edited; this wouldn't be any different.

The package felt heavy in her hands. One manicured nail slipped under the folded-over corner, but she stopped herself and set it back down. Agitated as she was, two things were still true: one, that wasn't professional and two, they weren't dating. She had no reason to be upset about being left out.

She wished Jackal was here. Petting her cat always soothed her nerves when she was upset. The bag with her new dress hanging on the hook would have been a tempting target to her black furball. Anna always had to be careful with bags, sometimes, it seemed like, Jackal had a death wish.

Her coffee had grown lukewarm and her stomach growled in protest from skipping dinner. She should have ordered dinner; she could have eaten while she worked. She constantly worked late, this wasn't any different, yet it was. Anna had bent her life out of shape for someone who wasn't interested in dating her. Vinnie wasn't interested her title or her money, instead genuinely fascinated in her as a person. It was so refreshing, but also incredible frustrating. She wasn't used to being kept at arm's length. As much as she wanted Vincent Goodroe, she also kinda of wanted him out of her veins. If he wasn't for her personally, then he was only worth the time investment of a new writer, and she'd given him far too much time in that case.

The memory of him flirting with her in Chicago made her bite down on her lip. Him being too drunk for his own good and confessing his confusion and self-doubt only made his admission of counting her freckles more poignant. Unconscious Vinnie was interested in her, but conscious Vinnie was content to keep their distance.

She thought about grabbing her phone and swiping through tinder. Maybe sex would get her head on straight? This had been one of her longer dry spells, and it had to be having an impact on her state of mind. Shifting in her chair, pain shot through her stomach. *No, in too much pain to go down that road.*

Ping. Ping.

Anna nearly fell out of her chair, as something hit the outside of her window. Mat Goodroe was standing on the sidewalk, keys in one hand as weakly waved at her with the other. Had he locked himself out? She had keys. At least she could help with this.

A quick search through her desk drawers, and she found the spare keys she now kept there. She made sure to lock her office behind her and strode over to the outside door to let Mat inside.

He nodded at her as he came inside but looked confused as she offered him the key. "What's this?"

"Oh, I figured you locked yourself out, saw I was still working, and needed to borrow my key." Anna closed her hand around the key and mirrored Mat's confusion.

"No, I have my key. I was looking for you actually. Can we talk?" He cracked his neck and looked one way then the other.

Was he trying to figure out if he'd been followed or was he being cautious in general? Was she in danger? Was he trying something? Mat hadn't struck her as the unfaithful type. Anna was not going to get into any further drama with this family. She was reflexively hesitant, but still agreed.

Mat hadn't given her a reason not to trust him and he looked upset; not angry, but defeated. From her observations, Mat held himself with confidence regardless of his actual belief in his abilities. Her curiosity overruled caution. Why did he want to talk to her? *She never could resist a mystery.*

"Sure. We can talk in my office." She motioned for him to follow. She left the main lights on, but the dark of the building made her office seem twice as bright as they passed through the open doorway. "Have a seat. The couch is actually comfortable."

"Thanks. You've got a nice office, very...white?"

That sounded like he meant it as a compliment, so Anna decided to respond that way. "Thank you, modern offices are often designed to be minimal. It's cleaner than normal, with my upcoming staff changes and all. I have a tendency to let it get cluttered. Too much going on in too little time, I suppose."

"As the father of a toddler, I get ya." Mat checked his phone and bounced his knee up and down.

So neither of them knew how to be still. Anna pulled out a pair of coffee cups. "Would you like a drink?"

"It's a little late for coffee, but if you've got water or..." Mat trailed off as she pulled out two bottles of whiskey from the mini-fridge built into her desk. "Or two whiskeys so good, if I say no, I won't forgive myself." He picked up one of the bottles to examine it more closely. "You've got good taste."

"I've always been a fan of whiskeys. Everyone expects me to ask for wine, and by asking for whiskey, it gives me a glimpse into what they look like when they're surprised. It helps me not get taken advantage of most of the time."

Anna poured them each a drink and clinked her glass against his without giving it a thought. Mat took a sip and sighed. "That is good whiskey."

"Thank you." She smiled.

He cleared his throat. "I hope you're working and not here because of my brother's text about dinner tonight."

Anna silently took a drink of her whiskey. She didn't know why he was here. She didn't mind his presence, but what was the point? As far as Mat was concerned, she was only the person dating his brother. Why would he be looking out for her in this way? Why was he here?

"Ya know, between the two of us, I'm normally the asshole." Mat sighed and took another drink.

She arched her eyebrow. "Did the dinner go that badly? Should I go rent a hotel room for the night?"

Mat averted his eyes to the floor as he finished off his glass. "I don't know. I didn't show up and he's bent out of shape about it."

"I can see how that would cause problems." Anna held her hand out for Mat's glass, but he set it on her coffee table. "If you don't mind me asking, is there a reason you didn't go?"

"I didn't like that he sprung it on me and I still don't know how to talk to her." His heel was bouncing on the floor again. "Kass had the day off and she's got Lizzie upstairs, but she's gonna ask how the dinner went and I'm not looking forward to that."

"You could try a distraction. Lizzie's birthday is in three days and the party is in four. Maybe ask her about that?"

"Ha!" He barked out a laugh, before shaking his head. "Kass's got a mind like a steel trap. I'm not getting much by her for long."

Anna's phone vibrated and she turned it over reflexively. There was a string of texts from Vinnie. "I would just tell her how you feel. She strikes me as an understanding soul."

"She really is. I should go upstairs." Mat stood up and Anna walked him to the door. They paused as she opened it. "Don't hold this against Vinnie too much. He likes to play peacemaker, but he really likes you." Then he smirked, "But don't let him off too easy either."

She smiled. "Thank you, Mat. I'll keep it in mind. Have a goodnight."

"'Night."

After five unopened texts and a missed call, Vinnie got the hint that Anna wasn't answering him. At least for tonight. He hesitated before laying down in bed. With the mismatched schedules, they'd been able to avoid sleeping at the same time, but it looked like that streak was coming to an end. If she came home. And that's if it wasn't like she couldn't afford a hotel for the night. And maybe it was just as well if she did just that, but he shouldn't have asked her to stay away; it was a shitty call.

Mat hadn't shown up, and while Vinnie wanted to be surprised, he wasn't. Kass texted him an hour ago and told him that Mat made it home safe, but he hadn't wanted to talk about anything. She also requested Jane not accompany Rex and himself to Lizzie's birthday. She didn't want her daughter's birthday ruined by family drama. That was a more than fair request. Put that on a list of future conversations he was going to have, despite his aversion to them.

Dinner hadn't gone badly, but it hadn't gone the way he assumed it would. For some reason, he thought one of them would start speaking and then the conversation would flow from there. Jane answered a few more questions, but her responses were guarded and short. She'd gone to prison for crashing a stolen car; since she was drunk, they'd given her the maximum sentence. From how Rex described her cautious planning in past stories, it didn't make any sense whatsoever. Vinnie had pressed her on the why's, and she suddenly said she wasn't feeling well and needed air. Jane had gone out the patio door, and after an hour, Rex and Vinnie cleared the table in relative silence.

Vinnie was in the bathroom when he'd heard Rex questioning Jane on how she got back in the house, but hadn't been able to hear her answer.

Now he was staring at the ceiling wondering why he'd tried this in the first place. He should do something useful for the book's upcoming release.

There was a quote in the writing world about writing the book you wanted to read. He had a new appreciation for all the books he'd read over his lifetime.

Although he felt like he had his book memorized at times, he'd find himself to be utterly confused as he read over some of the passages, forgetting for a moment that he had written them.

He had questioned Anna about it, but she assured him that her edits were suggestions, and she wouldn't have rewritten things for him. Explaining that was one of the most important reasons to have an editor. As the writer, he could be reading what he wanted and not what was on the page. Writers were apparently infamous for having the story drive them and not the other way around.

The bedroom door opened without a knock, and he jumped, his hand going to the nightstand for a weapon that wasn't there out of habit. Anna nodded, entering without a word and hanging up a bag, probably her dress for Saturday's party, which he was missing because of Lizzie's birthday. She set down her purse before going into the bathroom, locking the door forcibly. A few minutes passed, and he heard the shower turn on – his cue to find somewhere else to be before she was done.

He climbed out of bed and collided with a towel-clad Anna, who had walked back into the room. "Shit." He'd caught her shoulders, but immediately lost his balance as he tired to avoid touching her inappropriately, causing both them to toppled onto the bed. Vinnie closed his eyes, assuming her towel hadn't made it to the bed with them. "I'm so sorry. I'm not looking."

"Thank you," Anna muttered, shifting on the bed. "You're on the towel." She informed him.

Of course he fucking was. Vinnie rolled away from the bathroom and felt the towel go with him. "My eyes are closed. I'm so…"

"Please don't apologize. We're adults and it was an accident. I just need to grab my face lotion from my bag. I can get another towel in the bathroom. Just stay put. We can talk when I get done."

She grunted as she got up, possibly in pain from their collision. He hoped he hadn't hurt her.

Vinnie waited until the bathroom door closed before opening his eyes and getting off the bed. So much for leaving to give her space. She obviously wanted to talk about…the book.

She had wanted to talk about the book tonight. They were supposed to go over the final approvals tonight and he'd blown her off for a useless dinner.

While he waited for Anna, he grabbed his notebook and wrote down a few lines about how he was feeling at the moment. The disjointed lines devolved quickly into melodramatic woe-is-me nonsense. He glared at the paper in front of him. How he'd ever thought that he was good enough to write a book was beyond him. He'd just re-told someone else's story in his first book.

Maybe if he wasn't so screwed up, he could manage to write something of his own instead of plagiarizing reality.

He flipped to an empty page and drew a line down the middle, titling one side 'actions' and the other side 'consequences.' Forgiveness was achievable but, even still, a person was responsible for the fall out. Jane left; abandoning him and Mat with Nathan. Jane stayed away; they thought she was dead. Jane never reached out; Rex was sad, and they still thought she was dead. Jane stayed 'dead;'' they memorialized her and forgave her because she was dead. Jane came back; their family was fractured.

The shower turned off, and he sighed, which seemed loud in the quiet of the room. Despite how many challenges they'd overcome as a family, this one might be the one that broke them. Rex clearly wasn't going to give Jane up, but he was obviously hurting not having Mat and Vinnie in his life as they'd been before Jane's return. This fracture was only going to get worse. Mat wasn't going to forgive Jane for not coming back. Hell, he didn't know if he could forgive her for not coming back. Maybe if she'd come back…It was hard to see the page, and he took off his glasses to clean them. Water dropped onto the page, and Vinnie realized he was crying. *Shit.*

He grabbed a tissue from the nightstand and wiped his eyes. Why the hell was he crying? He wasn't this attached to Jane. He didn't know her as his mother. Why was he upset? She didn't matter.

Vinnie jumped to leave the room when the bathroom door opened, but his glasses were still on the nightstand, and he couldn't see without them. He knew Anna was standing in front of him, but he could only make out her vague shape. He needed to get away from her, but as he tried to get away he felt her hands grip his forearms, her nails pressing into his flesh.

"Are you alright?" Her voice was concerned and not curt as it had been before. "Where are your glasses?"

He pulled away. He couldn't be here. His ears were hot. He was overheated and he couldn't get enough air. As the blood pounded against his eardrums, but he couldn't make out what Anna was saying. He needed to get away.

"Shh. Try and take a breath." Anna let go of his arms and her hands cupped his face, bringing his forehead down to touch hers.

He couldn't breathe. His chest was tight but his arms were limp by his side and despite the tremors, he couldn't stop. He was lightheaded. The world felt like it was tipping over.

"Sit down on the bed. I'm going to grab your glasses."

"Can't…" His throat hurt. He couldn't sit down. If he sat down, he might not be able to get up again.

He couldn't move; his body was rigid. His muscles burned like he'd run a mile.

"Hold my hand." Anna slipped her hand into his. "Come on."

He was blind without his glasses, but he followed behind her, gripping her hand like a hand-hold on a climbing wall. He was sure he'd fall if she let go. He knew they were moving through the house, but he wasn't sure where they were going until he heard the patio door. Metal scraped against metal as the door stuck at the halfway point then lurched forward.

"Keep with me."

Vinnie wasn't wearing shoes. The wood was cool under his feet, but she kept him moving until his feet touched the grass. Anna brought his hand to the side of Kass' raised garden beds, probably to give him something to balance on. Kass had already harvested what she planted this year, and Mat, Kass, and Lizzie weren't here anymore.

Anna guided him until he was flush with the structure the eased him closer to the ground. He fought to stay upright. He didn't want to break down on the ground. He'd break if he was on the ground. He'd be put down hard if he was on the ground.

"Vinnie. Vinnie, you're having a panic attack. I'll be here with you, but you have to sit down. Your breathing is erratic. I'm afraid you're going to faint."

"I can't," He growled, swallowing bile down. Why did it feel so cold? Why was he suddenly cold? He clenched his jaw. Anna was still holding his hand, tugging him towards the earth. "I won't get back up if I go down."

His eyes were closed, but they would have been worthless even open — no glasses, no sight. Anna moved into his space, her body warm and damp from her shower. He released her hand and put his hands on her shoulders, weakly trying to keep her back. His muscles hurt.

"Bullshit! You've gotten up from everything that's ever knocked you down." Anna wrapped her arms around his waist and implored him, "Sit down on the ground with me. I'm right here. Hold onto me."

It was awkward, but he managed to get on the ground with her. But he didn't want to hold on, he wanted to disappear. He pulled his knees to his chest, gripping his own forearms to make himself small. Why was the road so damn loud? Why was everything so loud? He could hear a loud roar, but he couldn't see. He was fucking helpless. He wasn't crying, but a strangled sound escaped his throat.

Cool hands covered his ears. That pressure blocked out any sounds as Anna leaned against him.

"When I was little I was fascinated by baseball."

Her voice broke through the pulsing beat in his eardrums. Anna was calm as she soothed him. "Our apartment was nowhere near Comiskey Park, but I always wanted to go to games. Emily and I went to the opener every year. Those were the only times I can remember us really connecting other than over books. And with books, it was always about what they were worth and not about the books themselves. I wear glasses to read. I know you've never seen me in them, but I don't like wearing them in public. I think they make me look pretentious."

Vinnie breathed in through his nose, the air stinging in his passageways.

"I was ten, and I saw a book in Emily's library about the scandal of the 1919 World Series. I told her I didn't understand why we went to baseball games if the teams could just cheat. What was the point? Emily told me that you can't hold the past against the future. I imagine as long as she'd been in the business world, she'd done underhanded things. I know I'm not proud of every decision that I've made. But once they are made, they're made. We can't go back. And we can't undo. We can only move in the rut left by the river." She continued to speak in the same soft tone.

He felt Anna's nails scrape against the base of his skull, in slow circles. A fixed pattern. He leaned his forehead against his knees. Breathe in. *One. Two. Three. Four.* Hold the breath. *One. Two. Three. Four.* Breathe out. *One. Two. Three. Four.*

"That's good. You're doing good. You're good." Anna laid her head on his shoulder and wrapped her arms around his waist. "I know you don't believe it, but you *are* good. Mistakes are mistakes; they don't define you."

He didn't think she was lying, but he knew better and he fought to keep from shaking. *One. Two. Three. Four.* Breathing was getting easier. But dear god, now his brain was starting to replay how he got out here.

"I never much cared for relationships. I'm independent and I don't like someone else's problems overshadowing mine. I think being an only child made me selfish."

Anna wasn't selfish. She was a little oblivious to how money could impact a situation, but he didn't think she was selfish. She was kind and respected the people around her. He liked her stories, and the way she told them. When he started rambling, she didn't seem annoyed with how long it took him to get to the point.

Vinnie turned his head to look at Anna, and they were nose to nose. Being this close, he couldn't see her smile but he could see the light in her brilliant blue eyes.

Her hands stopped moving as they held eye contact. "Hello, you."

"Hi."

"Penny for your thoughts."

"My editor says my thoughts are worth more than a penny, and she's brilliant."

"She is, a bit." Anna moved up onto her knees and kissed his forehead. "I'm going to get your glasses and bring you some water. Will you be alright?"

He nodded. *God, this was fucking embarrassing.* As, he turned to watch her head back to the house and saw a blur of a shadow pass by the door, blocking the light from the kitchen. Likely Jane. If it had been Rex, his uncle would have checked on him.

His body protested as he got back onto his feet, his muscles stiff from how rigid he'd been for however long that episode had lasted. He inched his foot back until he could feel the cement and considered sitting on one of the patio chairs, but didn't trust himself not to over…well, everything. He hated not having his glasses.

"On your feet, that's good." Anna was in his space again, putting his glasses in one of his hands.

After putting on his glasses, the world came back into focus. He took the water she offered him and nearly finished the entire bottle.

"Can we sit out here for a bit?"

The idea of being alone brought a flurry of emotions and none of them were good. He didn't need her to touch him, but he didn't want her to leave. He wanted her presence. He didn't want to be alone with his thoughts. If he started spiraling again, he didn't know if he'd be able to get out. The patio furniture was between where they were standing and the door. It was only a couple of steps, then they could relax out here, if Anna was alright with it.

"Sure." She had a package tucked under her arm and she set it down on the arm of the chair.

"What's this?" he asked.

"Your book. I got the proof copy today."

It was his book. Oh, that's why she wanted to talk tonight. He thought they were finishing the last of the edits, but clearly, she'd made decisions without him. "But the cutout chapter…"

"Is edited down the way we discussed in light of all that's happened recently. I'm here to make your story better, not steal your voice. Open it."

Vinnie hadn't sat down yet, he still didn't trust his legs entirely. He picked up the package. It felt heavier than the actual weight of the book. "How did it turn out?"

"I haven't looked. I had Bailey wrap it, but I wanted you to see it first." Anna said as she braided her hair.

"Is that normal?"

"Are you stalling?" She countered.

He was stalling a bit. His emotions were all over the place, and he was worried he might start crying again when he opened the package. He felt equal parts excitement and terror about opening it. His book would be real once he laid eyes on it. “Suppose I should rip the bandage off, huh?”

“Or open it and be proud of your accomplishment.”

“Taters and tomaters, I guess.”

Anna cocked her head to the side. “That’s so odd.”

“I know it’s supposed to be tah-mah-toh, toh-may-toe. But Rex always said it the other way.” Vinnie chuckled.

“No, the odd part is that it’s familiar.”

“I’m sure he’s said it since you’ve been here.”

“Probably.” Anna motioned with her hand. “Can you please open it now? I swear, my entire day has been spent waiting for someone else to do something.” She paused, “Sorry, that was bitchy.”

“No worries. Long day.” He cracked his neck and pulled at the package’s seam, carefully pulling the wrapping away to reveal the lavender hardback. He examined – the artfully crafted blurb, the graphic elements that faded across the cover. He turned it over in his hands, pausing at the spine to inspect: his pen name, the book’s new title, and Anna’s publishing house logo.

Vinnie took a deep breath before turning it over, biting down on his lower lip. It was perfect. It was exactly what he had discussed with Cypress. This was real. His book was in his hands.

“It looks great.” Anna rose from her chair, leaning closer to get a better look. She had her back to the patio doors, so she was technically looking at it upside down. “The font change was a good idea, it contrasts better with the art.”

“Yeah.” In print. Real. Completed. His pen name at the bottom was a combination of two movie heroes from his childhood. He smoothed his hand over the cover. It was his. *He’d written a whole ass book.* “I did it.” He grinned, unable to keep the smile off his face.

“You really did. You should be proud of yourself.” She smiled back at him.

He was. Vinnie laughed. The sheer energy from his joy making him as giddy as a freaking kid.

Anna echoed his laugh, although hers was quieter. “I’m glad you're happy with it.”

“I’m happy.” He said the words out loud, and they hit him in the chest. He was happy; for this moment right now, he was happy. Anna was the reason for that. “Thank you, Anna. Thank you for making this happen.”

“This is all you, I just helped.”

The kitchen light turned on and Vinnie realized that Rex was awake.

Wait… Rex was in the kitchen, it was nearly midnight, he was standing outside with no shoes, Anna was barely dressed, and the book he didn't want Rex to know the contents of was in his hands. *FUCK!*

His face must have given away his panic because Anna's brows furrowed.

"Rex or Jane?"

"Rex," He muttered as Rex started towards the patio. "Anna, I am not ready to talk to him about this book, especially after everything…"

Anna pushed up further into his space, squishing the book between them, and pulling him down for a kiss. Her thumb was between their lips and she held herself there for a moment before settling back down on her feet. "Is he gone?"

"Yeah." He blinked. "Crisis averted. I get the PDA discomfort factor, but your thumb…"

"Theater kiss," She smirked. "What? Did you want to kiss me for real?"

Vinnie coughed. "That's not what I said."

"True. We should head to bed. Been a long day." Anna's smile was coy.

"Yeah, we…" Vinnie trailed off, realizing that their schedules had finally aligned, and they were going to be sharing a bed. No. He had too many emotions swirling in his brain for this right now. "I think I'm going to look my book over in Lizzie's playroom. I won't be able to sleep before I do."

"Alright. If you say so."

Vinnie watched Anna walk into the house before he sat down and ran his hand over his book. Too many emotions, too fast. If he thought he was mixed up about Anna before, he really didn't know what to think now. They weren't teenagers, and it wouldn't have been the end of the world if she would have crossed that line. So why did it mean so much to him that she hadn't?

Did he want her? The gentleness of her hands, the vanilla and coffee scents that clung to her skin, the kindness of her eyes, and her self-assured calm which made him feel at ease were all points in her favor. He'd been disappointed that she hadn't really kissed him. He needed to think this through before he did something dumb.

Chapter 9: Every Scene Moves The Plot

Pay Attention To Detail

October 14th; 56 Days Until…

Anna finished the last touches of her make-up, turning her head one way and then another to inspect her blending job in the mirror. She didn't mind doing her own make-up and hair for an event, but she preferred to have it professionally done. Scheduling had been a nightmare, so it had been easier to do it herself this time. Thankfully, there were two bathrooms in the house, because she knew how long she'd been trying to get a perfect look. It was dramatic, as the gala's theme was fantasy. It was going to take forever to get this glitter off when she got back.

She also needed to find Vinnie before he and Rex left for Lizzie's birthday party. Could she manage to get her dress on without help? Creatively, with some awkward poses and irksome bends, yes, she could get into her dress without help. Was she going to go through all of that trouble when she had someone that she could ask for help? No, no she wasn't.

Finding him might be a challenge, as he'd made himself as scarce as his mother since the almost kiss they'd shared a few days prior. But, unless he rode to the party with Rex, he was going to have to come into the bedroom before leaving. She'd hidden his keyfob after he'd gotten home this morning.

The bedroom door opened as she finished securing the lift tape that was acting as her bra for the night. Vinnie was rustling through his side of the dresser, muttering something, but she couldn't quite make out what he was saying.

She chuckled and glanced at her phone.

Kass: Thank you for the gift for Lizzie
Kass: I'll send you a picture later of her with it :)
Kass: What was the name of your publishing company again?

Anna: On & Off the Margins Printing
Anna: I hope she enjoys it. Let me know if you need/want to exchange it

The search was getting more intense on the other side of the door. "Is everything alright in there?" She called out, finally giving him a little mercy.

"I can't find my keys. Have you seen them?"

She smirked despite the fact he couldn't see her. "I hid them."

"Did you now?" He sounded amused. "May I ask why?"

"I needed help with my dress. It's hanging up in the closet. Let me know when you're ready."

"Are you naked on the other side of that door?"

She laughed. "I have underwear on, but only tape on the top."

"Are you trying to kill me?" He chuckled, despite his likely discomfort.

"No, I'm trying to get your help with my dress."

"Alright, whenever you're ready."

Anna let herself out of the bathroom and stepped around Vinnie to the closet. She slipped the dress off of the hanger and over her head. She held the bodice against her collarbones with one hand, while gathering the skirt with the other to keep it off the floor. She stepped in front of Vinnie. "All set."

There was a pause. The ticking clock on the wall punctuating the silence. "I'm lost here."

"There are fasteners at the tops of the wings, that connect to the straps on my shoulders."

"Oh, these are wings." He flattened his palm to keep the back piece in place.

The warmth of his hand through the fabric gave her goosebumps. Two fingers slid down over one of her shoulders, pinching the fabric to lift it toward the connection. The fastener wasn't complicated, but it was delicate, and one of Anna's favorite things about Vinnie was how he always took his time.

"It's intricate. I don't think I've ever seen a butterfly shape as the back of a gown." He completed his task, but Anna jumped when he slipped both of his index fingers under the butterfly detail and smoothed edges of the design. "Sorry, didn't mean to startle you. Just wanted to make sure it wasn't twisted."

"No problem." She could feel the heat in her cheeks but tried to maintain a relaxed expression when she turned to face him. "What do you think?"

"Beautiful as always." His expression was less flustered than she wanted.

"I knew it was lacking." Anna was annoyed. She hated when she didn't make an impression.

"The dress isn't lacking, but your makeup is a touch tame for the event theme you described." He touched her chin, narrowing his eyes, as if trying to come up with a plan. "There isn't anything wrong with this look, and again, you do look beautiful."

"I got distracted and forgot to schedule a professional. I'm not inept, but I'm certainly not going to be able to imitate a professional." She folded her arms over her chest.

Vinnie bit his lower lip as if carefully considering what he was about to say. "Do you have lash glue?"

"Yes?" Now she was just confused. "I used it for the lashes I'm wearing. Why?"

"Lash glue will do in a pinch if you aren't sweating too much."

He wasn't suggesting what she thought he was. "I…"

Vinnie lifted his eyebrows. "I've worked in a strip club for over five years. You think I haven't picked up some tricks?"

"Makeup tricks?"

He nodded.

Anna wasn't entirely sure about this, but she didn't have a lot of options short of finding an artist she didn't know, potentially ruining her current look, or worst of all, possibly being late. "The makeup I have is in the second drawer in the bathroom cabinet."

"Go ahead and open the window shade so I can have more light. And sit on the closer side of the bed. I'll be right back." He disappeared from the room and Anna opened the window shade to let in the sunshine.

Before sitting on the bed, she pulled out the box with the shoes she was wearing for the gala. Glancing at her phone she assured herself she was indeed ahead of schedule. Unable to keep still, with a buzz of anticipation running down her spine, she smoothed the skirt as she sat.

Vinnie returned with a dining room chair, her makeup, and a small paintbrush. He held his phone out to her, displaying a Pinterest page with a handful of images.

"You have a Pinterest page about fantasy makeup?"

"What?" He turned his phone back to himself then chuckled. "No, it's a screenshot I've used for reference. Does that look alright?"

"It's very detailed."

The corner of his mouth turned up – that devilish grin he got when he was proud of himself. "I'm good at details. Can you hold my phone for me?"

"Sure."

Anna held the phone at chest level. Since the dress had a modest neckline it shouldn't distract him.

He sorted through her makeup, holding two of her eyeshadow pallets to her face to compare the colors. The browns and golden glitter she used should be fairly simple to match, and she'd used black liner, so there shouldn't be an issue there. He was quiet until he found what he was looking for.

"Using shadows instead of loose glitter will tone down the look, but I think it will up the elegance."

She smirked. "If you pull it off."

"Oh, ye of little faith." Vinnie clicked his tongue. "Close your eyes, please. Let me know if you want to open them or need a break to move. "

"I can handle being still."

"A skill I've never been especially good at. Even when cracking a safe, I always had to tap my foot to make a rhythm." He sounded amused. "Most *experts* in that field need silence."

The brush was cool against her skin as he painted a pattern on the edge of her eyes. He must be using lash glue first as a guide. It was odd, but she wasn't in a position to argue. His thumb and finger pinched her chin, moving her head to the side.

"The second year I worked at the club, one of the girls, her stage name was Calliope, broke her hand. We moved her to the bar, but she wasn't very good at it. Which was fair since she only had one usable hand. But…" he paused and his brush moved to the crease of her eye, extending past the outer corner. "...she couldn't afford not to work."

She should have taken more time to examine that image. She worried it might be too extreme.

Vinnie continued with his task and his story, his voice low and reflective. "Leila altered her outfits so she could remove them one-handed and she came up with new routines. But she struggled with her makeup, and I figured it was like a painting…shadows, highlights, lots of patience…"

"I didn't know you liked to paint." As much as she knew about Vinnie, he was always surprising her.

He chuckled, "I don't. But I used to watch a lot of Bob Ross, it came on late at night."

The makeup brush retraced prior strokes he'd made. *Stroke was the wrong word choice, her brain associated it with other things.* "So she trusted you on your word?" Anna restlessly flexed her toes against the carpet.

"She did. And I suppose you get the benefit of her trial and error. Can you open your eyes for a moment?"

She complied and found Vinnie staring at her or more properly, examining his work. His eyes moved side to side behind his ever-present frames. His tongue slipped out over his lips, wetting them as he moved her head again.

"Look up, please."

He was a breath away from her as he applied liner to the inner corner of her eye. She kept herself from exhaling until he was done. *Had she brushed her teeth?*

After a few more swipes, he sat back and studied her face again. "That's good. Close your eyes again."

Anna let her breath out slowly so he wouldn't realize she'd been holding her breath.

"The best part is that she loved over-the-top makeup, so I got good at patterns. Most things are patterns, you just have to find the pattern beneath the filler. It's just lines, shading, light, and repeat. Things like this follow rules; knowing the rules solves problems."

"Or helps find workarounds." She let him move her head again, trying to keep herself loose and relaxed.

"This is true. This would look better accented with rhinestones, but we'll make do."

They were quiet as he worked, with only a request here and there to close or open her eyes and the occasional unlocking of the phone she was holding.

"I struggle to be quiet," He admitted, unprompted. "I get nervous when I don't know how people will react to situations. When I talk, I can keep their eyes on me then I can often predict their behavior. Even if they just get annoyed it's better to know, than to guess."

"It sounds like you learned by watching your mother." She'd almost said father and caught herself at the last moment. From the few things she'd heard about Nathan Goodroe, it sounded like he'd had an explosive temper, and often children with violent parents often learned to compensate. But she didn't want to bring up such a dark memory at present. Unfortunately, the observation slipped out. Now, could she think of a reason that his mother would have caused the same type of reaction if he asked?

"How's that?"

Anna knew she was on slippery ground here, but she wasn't exactly lying. "You said she was a con-artist, er, grifter. She would have used tactics like that to read people for her benefit."

"I suppose…And I think you're done." He took his phone back, and Anna opened her eyes to look into his eyes again.

This time, he wasn't examining his work. He was looking at her. A smile broke through his contemplative expression, and he held up one of her compacts to show her reflection in the mirror. "I like it. What do you think?"

Her original look had been smokey eyes, but Vinnie had extended the shadow out, making it more dramatic. The simple black, winged liner now connected to a pattern of gold and rose-gold, glittery, filigree created with eyeshadows to further accent the fantasy elements of her dress.

"It almost looks like the butterfly wings." She could feel how far open her mouth was as she stared at herself. "It's beautiful."

"I mirrored it after your dress, but you'd only know if you really looked." He explained before requesting. "Close your eyes, I need to set it."

Anna wasn't often speechless, but she couldn't find any words as she let her lids fall closed. The setting spray was cool on her skin. It was why she picked the product in the first place. Air moved back and forth in front of her. Vinnie no doubt waving his hand to get it to dry faster.

"And open."

She was greeted a genuine smile, almost goofy smile, and she felt herself echo it back.

"Anything else you need help with?"

"Um. Just my shoes." She pointed limply at the box.

The expectation was Vinnie handing her the box and giving her space. Reality was Vinnie leaning in, pulling the box to himself, and opening it. He took one of the shoes out and unbuckled the crystal ankle strap. "I think these are worth more than my first car."

"They were about a thousand." Her mouth was suddenly dry. He caught her foot in one hand and slipped on her heel with the other.

"My first car was fifteen-hundred, so that makes me feel a little better." His fingers were deft and careful as he fastened the first shoe, then reached for the other.

"How do you know so much about shoes?"

"Well, again, strip-club ownership, plus Leila's a fan of shoes. She liked the pair you wore when you came into the club to help me, so I knew you had good taste. After her husband passed, she wore fake red-bottom heels to his funeral, aca."

"A.C.A.?" Ana couldn't think of how the Affordable Care Act would have to do with this conversation. Clearly, she'd missed something.

Vinnie smirked. "Against criminal advice."

Anna laughed, wondering out loud, "Not that I don't appreciate the help, but what are you doing exactly? What's the goal here?"

"I'm thinking," he fastened the second heel ensuring both straps were flat and turned the correct side up. Instead of moving away, he put one hand on either side of her. The bed depressed down and he leaned in, putting them nearly nose to nose. "I'm saying thank you."

He smelled like coffee and his rich, mahogany cologne.

"Helping you is the only way I can think to properly thank you for everything."

There was a feral part of Anna, likely stemming from her unintentional abstinence, that wanted to give him suggestions on creative ways to thank her. None of those suggestions involved space or clothes between them. The other part of her was worried that if she said it out loud, Vinnie would run or laugh it off. She couldn't think of any other way to encourage him. Words might scare him and getting too physical might push past a boundary, so she cupped his cheek, coaxing him closer.

He mirrored her touch, fingers on her neck, thumb under her chin. The warmth of his hand was surpassed by the heat of his stare. His soft, almost boyish smile was gone, replaced by something intense and…hungry. In opposition the ravenous look, he advanced no further seeming to seek permission. She dared to nod, almost terrified the spell would break.

Despite the look in Vinnie's eyes, his kiss was feather-light, almost nervous. His lips brushed over her, testing the boundary but not encroaching past where he was allowed. He hovered there, lips still ghosting over hers as if it was enough to breath in her presence.

The sentiment would have been endearing if Anna hadn't been close to screaming. She moved her hands up his chest, over his shoulders, and splayed them over his neck. As she returned his kiss she could feel the tension in his body, but he was so measured, so she matched it. Slowly moving her lips over his, the moment he relaxed into her touch she deepened the kiss. Much as she would have liked to claim she was ladylike, the moan that erupted from her would have been enough to make her blush. Blushing, however, was reserved for a less pent-up version of herself – presently she just wanted this man, however she could have him.

Vinnie moved his hand away from under her face, gripping the bedspread on either side of her as he responded with the same enthusiasm.

It struck her that he was trying to keep her make-up intact, even with the ever-increasing passionate kiss they were locked in. *She did not want to leave this room. She didn't want to leave this bed.* Small gulps of air were the only pauses in their exploration, and while she never thought of herself as having a denial kink, the fact that he wasn't touching her was making her wet. "Fuck." She breathed out. "I…"

"Rex says he's waiting…" Jane announced as she opened the door without knocking.

Vinnie cursed loudly and stood up straight, nearly throwing Anna off the bed from the shift in weight.

"Sorry. I'll tell him you're busy."

"No!" he barked. "Tell him that I'll be out in a minute and close the door!"

The little credit Anna would give Jane is that she left the room without another word and closed the door. Her pulse was elevated, and she took a few slower breaths to try and even herself out.

Vinnie ran his hands through his hair, looking thoroughly flustered. Good, at least they were on the same page. "I…I'm sorry, about her, not for the other."

She held out her hand, and he helped her stand up. She kissed his cheek. "Good, I would have been upset if you were apologizing for the other. We'll have to *talk* about this later tonight."

With her heels on she was taller than him for the moment, but it didn't seem to phase him. He pressed his lips to the side of her neck while gripping her hands, forcing her to be still. "How late are you going to be out?"

"Much later than I want to be." She closed her eyes. "Don't…"

He continued his exploration, nipping her earlobe. "I wouldn't dream of leaving a mark on you. We'll probably be back after ten. Kass and Mat are having Lizzie's party at Lost Horizon."

She tried to move, but Vinnie chuckled in response while continuing to lock her body in place. "What if I rent us a hotel room for tonight? Then we don't have to worry about being interrupted, whatever we decide to get up to."

"I think you have carnal intentions for me." He attempted to kiss her cheek, but she turned her head and caught his lips again. He breathlessly pulled away, releasing her hands finally. "I'm gonna need a shower at this rate, and Rex is not gonna let me take that long."

Anna couldn't keep the smile off her face. "I'll text you where to meet me."

"Pack a bag. No point in doing a walk of shame," Vinnie snickered and reached the bathroom door, but Anna grabbed his hand stopping him short. "What? I…"

"Vinnie, there is nothing shameful about sleeping with you. I'll do that walk with pride." She grabbed her clutch with her free hand. After giving his hand a final squeeze, she retrieved her phone and keys. "I'll see you later tonight."

Anna bid Rex and Jane goodbye as she breezed out the door. After getting in her car, she checked her makeup, which incredibly was still intact despite the flush in her cheeks. She tapped her phone, reserved a room for the night, and emailed the concierge to have clothes delivered to her room. She had been so excited about the gala, and now she was excited for it to be over so she could see Vinnie again. Even if this thing between them wasn't real, it was going to be real fun.

Lizzie's birthday party was in full swing as Vinnie stepped away from the crowd to get another drink. Mat was leaning on the rail, taking pictures with his cellphone.

"Kass has a camera."

"She's got it on her, but she never gets pictures of herself and Lizzie. It's always just Lizzie, or me and Lizzie. I want to get some of my girls together," Mat countered.

Vinnie agreed, "Kass is always behind the camera."

"She's just trying to be the best mom she can be, not that she isn't a natural at it."

He sipped from the cup in his hand. "Mat, I'm the last person you need to defend your words to. Plus, you know you're doing a good job with Lizzie too. She listens and she's learning faster than most kids her age."

"Mmm." Mat pocketed his phone. "I suppose you're trying to get away with buying her noisy shit as a learning thing?"

"You and Kass said no live animals. I complied."

"Vinnie, you bought her a fucking keyboard and enough magnetic blocks to build a castle. You know she's gonna want me to figure out how to build the castle on that box?" Mat grumbled, watching his volume as he cursed.

Vinnie laughed, unable to help it. "I'll help you figure it out. No need to whine about it." He pulled out his own phone to check the time. Anna had sent him a picture of herself and Alysha at the gala. They looked like they were having a good time. Even in a photo, Anna was breathtaking.

"You gonna be checking out early?"

"Huh?"

Mat chuckled. "Hell, now I don't have to ask how things are going with Anna. That look and *you* being confused says it all."

"Shut up." He put his phone away and looked out over the beach.

"No. There will be zero shutting up from me. I heard you two got caught going at it hot and heavy."

"Damnit, Mat. It's not like you and Kass weren't all over each other when you lived there. I don't need any shit from you. Rex ribbed me the whole drive down." Vinnie's ears were hot.

"Easy. Jeeze. Dish it out, but ya can't take it? I'm just givin' ya shit. You can cut out early if you want. Lizzie ain't gonna know the difference, and I don't wanna be a cock block." Mat laughed at his brother's exasperation. "Chill out, it ain't the first time you've been caught chasing…Wait, hold up, no, I think this is the first time. You didn't go after Leila, she went after you. And then…"

Vinnie had the urge to be anywhere else and took one step back towards the party, but Mat grabbed his arm.

"Was the last person you dated Leila? Is she the only one? No, you had a girl in high school. Robin, er, Rachel." Mat snapped his fingers. "Yeah it was Rachel, you guys dated for a couple of months."

"Her name was Reggie, but you kept calling her Ragan because we just watched the exorcist. And you made gagging noises whenever we hung out."

"I did?"

"Yes. You did."

"Sorry, I was a shithead when I was younger. You still got laid though."

Mat you're still kinda of a shithead. But Vinnie didn't want to respond, so he clenched his jaw.

"No, you did. I remember her talking about it, and you skipped school for three days straight. Rex threw a fit and dragged you to school himself after."

Again silence.

"Did I miss something?"

"She lied. I didn't want to sleep with her, but she didn't want to be embarrassed. So I told her that I didn't care and she could say whatever she wanted."

Mat was quiet for a minute, "Wait, does that mean when you met Leila, you were…?"

"Hey. Can we not? Could we not talk about this? Why do you want to talk about this? No. We aren't talkin' about this. Go, celebrate Lizzie's birthday, hang out with your wife, or attempt to talk to Rex. Anything but this," Vinnie grumbled, folding his arms over his chest. He needed to get Kass' attention. She'd be the best way to distract Mat.

Vinnie made eye contact with Kass, and she nodded at him but didn't smile. What was up with that? Her smile returned immediately as her attention turned back to Dara and Ethan.

"Did I make Kass mad?" he questioned, grateful to be able to shift the subject.

Mat leaned over the balcony and waved at Kass. She waved back but turned her attention to Lizzie when Vinnie tried the same tactic. "Hmm. Maybe you did. Maybe it was fucking keyboard."

"It's good for brain development," He defended.

"I'll go get her and see what's going on." Mat smacked Vinnie's shoulder as he passed by him to join Kass and picked up Lizzie to put her up on his shoulders.

All the whining that Mat had done about not wanting to be a parent in the past was dust in the wind, so to speak.

His brother's life revolved around his wife and child. Lizzie squealed and laughed as Mat spun them both around. Kass kissed Mat's cheek when he paused, then she started up the steps to Vinnie.

As she reached him, he started with the apology to get it out of the way. "I am sorry about the noise level of the keyboard. But in my defense, the only rule I was given was no live animals."

She blinked and shook her head. "It's fine. I'll lose the batteries if it gets too annoying." After getting herself a drink, she leaned against the refreshment table and looked out over the beach.

So whatever she was upset about, it wasn't the toy. He couldn't think of anything else that would have made her angry. From the moment Kass walked into Rex's house, he and Kass had become fast friends, and he couldn't remember ever getting the cold shoulder from her.

She was intentionally not looking in his direction, fiddling with her phone as he tried again.

"Did I do something else to upset you?" He asked.

"You have everything in that house, and you want to run around like you're Jessie-fucking-james."

Kass swearing alone was enough to get his attention, but having a line quoted from his book nearly stopped his heart. "What?"

"You heard me and you know what I meant." Her lips were pursed in a thin line.

He'd seen Kass angry at Mat, but never at him. He did not like her angry. He shifted on his feet. It was impossible. Kass couldn't have known about the book. It was being published under a pen name. It wasn't even coming out for another two months. But she couldn't be quoting it out of thin air. He had the only copy, and Kass hadn't been to the house. If Rex had found it, then he would have confronted him about it, not put Kass in the middle. And even if it had been Rex, he wouldn't have brought it up at Lizzie's party. He missed their nights together as a family. This was the first time they'd all been together since September, which for most families wouldn't have been odd, but they'd been living together since before Lizzie was born. It was hard not being under one roof.

"Say something." Her voice was quiet. Kass was trying not to cause a scene, but she wanted an explanation.

He fidgeted up on the ball of his foot. "I don't know what to say without more information."

She looked down at her phone and turned it to him, showing him the cover of the ebook version of his book. "My coworker is a big reader. She's an arc reader for romance books. And she got this book two days ago from On and Off the Margins Printing Company. The company that Anna works for."

"I..."

"Vincent James Goodroe, how could you do this? You wrote a book about me and Mat. You wrote about how we got together. Why would you do that? Does Anna know that it's about me and Mat? Have you two been joking about us behind our backs?" There were tears in her eyes as she turned to face him.

"What? No! Absolutely not, I'd never do that to you." Vinnie hadn't thought about Kass' reaction to the book, only Mat's. He'd expected violence, not tears. She was so upset. "Kass..."

"The only reason I haven't told Mat is that everything with Jane has been so stressful and I don't want to add one more thing." Kass drew in a deep breath and wiped her eyes. "These are angry tears, by the way. I'm furious with you. And when Rex finds out? Everything that happened between him and Jane in print? What if she wasn't alive? It would have crushed him. I just don't understand."

"I had originally written their story in, but I cut most of it in editing." He stopped short, as the next thing he was going to say was that he didn't want to upset Rex, but given Kass' reaction, it would be best to leave that unsaid.

"Well thank goodness for that at least." She folded her arms over her chest.

"I changed a lot of things about it," He defended.

"I recognized *my* love story from the plot synopsis my coworker gave me, then I confirmed the company that Anna worked for. And it *might* have been a coincidence, but your reaction certainly says otherwise."

Vinnie looked at the boards beneath his feet. What could he say? What could he do? He didn't want Kass to be hurt, but he didn't want to give up his book. He'd poured so much of himself into it, and he didn't even think about it in the context of Kass and Mat anymore.

He'd rehearsed an anecdote about how a popular TV show had inspired the book. The book had some inspiration from what had happened, but it wasn't plagiarized reality anymore. He and Anna had made so many changes to make it perfect. To make the book something to be proud of, something that was his.

"Tell me why. I deserve to know why."

Forget being scared of Mat ever again. Kass was a new level of terrifying. Was she ever going to forgive him for this?

"It started as a journal for my thoughts. I watched you both fall in love, and I knew I'd never get that. I wrote down what I saw and heard, then a couple of months after Lizzie was born, I organized my notes. And last year I put it together into a book."

Vinnie cleared his throat and glanced at Kass, instantly regretting it, as she didn't look impressed. "Kass, I didn't even intend to do anything with it. I thought, what the hell, I'd send it to a publisher, they'd reject it, and that would be that. I'd know writing wasn't for me, and I'd move on. Then maybe I'd give it to you guys as a joke for your wedding."

"That part certainly didn't happen."

"No, it didn't. Anna found my manuscript and liked it, thought it had potential. I re-wrote the conception as a one-night stand, but Anna thought an edited version of reality would be better."

Kass cracked the knuckles on her dominant hand. "And it didn't occur to you to say no to that?"

Was she going to slap him? Unlikely. This was her daughter's party, but judging by the look on her face, the odds were not zero.

"No, it didn't. She believed in my work, and I just went with it. Kassarah, I never meant to hurt you. I made a lot of changes to the protagonists to make sure no one would know it was based on your family."

"Well, I knew it was. I want to read it. I want a full copy, in digital form so Mat doesn't see it by accident. And if it's too much of what happened *to me*, then you will make changes." She checked her phone and sighed. "I need to get back down there."

Vinnie agreed to send her the copy. What else could he do?

Mat tromped up behind Kass and kissed her cheek. "Hey, Sweetheart."

"Hey. Where's Lizzie?"

"She's down with Dara and the other kids." Mat poked Kass' side. "Tell Vinnie goodbye. He's leaving early so he can go get laid."

"Mat!" They both yelped.

Mat laughed and rocked back and forth with Kass, kissing her neck. "What? If he's got a chance, he needs to seize it."

"I can't leave early. Rex and I rode together," Vinnie argued.

"He can ride back with us. We need to sort things out anyhow." Mat shrugged as Kass and Vinnie both looked at him slack jawed. "What?"

"I'm so proud of you." Kass kissed Mat's cheek.

Mat rolled his eyes. "It's nothing to be proud about. I've been bitching too long, and it's time to talk it through. Not ready to talk to *her* yet, though. That'll be later."

"So proud of you."

"You hear that? My wife is proud of me." Mat grinned at his brother.

"She's had a couple of drinks, so I'd take that with a grain of salt." Vinnie smirked until he made eye contact with Kass. She wasn't saying anything because of Mat, but she was still pissed.

Mat swatted at Vinnie, but only half-heartedly, since his other arm was still around Kass' waist. "Get outta here."

"Bye guys. Kass, I'll email you later."

Anna tipped the tumbler to the side, letting the ice tink against the glass as the cold burned against her index finger.

The whiskey cocktail warmed her core in contrast to its form in the glass. She'd never been one to get stood up, and the fact that her fake boyfriend seemed to be moving in that direction made her absolutely furious. She finished off her glass, deciding to head up to her room for a night by herself, when the overpowering scent of something sickly sweet and minty filled her nostrils.

"Did I have a chance to tell you that you look like absolute sin in that dress?"

His voice would have been familiar even if she hadn't known him personally. Preston Walthers was a local TV personality who never missed an opportunity to put himself at a party where the powerful and rich attended, and the man who she had the misfortune of taking to bed in a fit of lunacy.

Tonight's fantasy-themed, charity gala for raising funds for a children's library was a perfect target. He had a habit of getting attendees a little too tipsy and asking just the right questions, off-the-record, to steer the later on-the-record conversation into sensationalist territory.

"You have, twice. And it's the second time you attempted the exact same line. You're slipping." She motioned for another drink, and the bartender nodded at her.

Preston grinned, showing off his overly-whitened teeth. He'd smoked for years and the yellow tar had done its damage; so those must be caps. Why was she staring at his teeth of all things?

"I hosted the morning show today. It has been a long one." He perched on the stool next to her. "I didn't miss your stare just now. Were you thinking about my mouth?"

The retort that Anna wanted to respond with would have been a commentary on his lackluster bedroom performance, but she didn't burn bridges as a rule. Regardless of her feelings about this conceited prick, he had pull in the media, and she wasn't going to war when it wasn't needed.

So instead of venom, she was only a touch prickly. "I was wondering who your new dentist is. Your teeth look great."

"No one you'd know. Out of state." Preston rolled his shoulders and paid for the drink that Anna had just been given.

She hated when he did that. They ran in the same circles, and he knew she didn't like people paying for her drinks. She didn't need to be coddled. His whitened teeth meant he'd gone out to California again to try to get picked up out there, but since he was back home, he'd failed. He'd be bragging otherwise. Preston was the good ole boy that Houston adored, but he was a trust fund baby like she was. He knew that playing the part of the Texas' son made him money, and Preston liked money.

"Stop scowling, Anna. You'll ruin your looks. At your age, it's a dangerous game. I have the names of a few plastic surgeons if you need a recommendation."

Don't throw the drink in his face. Don't waste good whiskey on his tacky suit. Anna sipped from her drink, eyes never leaving his. "I'll let you know if it comes up on my agenda."

"Fair enough. By the way, are you back on women now? Where's your date? She was a chocolate-skinned dream in that pink number."

"She's not food. Watch how you talk about people." Anna checked her phone; no missed calls or texts. "She wasn't my date. She's the manager of a new printing house based here in Houston. It's going to focus on BIPOC voices."

"I'll have to have her on for black history month, if she's still in business then." Preston took a drink from the glass the bartender brought him. Sparkling water meant to look like vodka, if Anna remembered correctly. He liked to look like he was drinking when he wasn't. Sobriety was a tool for him.

"Her imprint is tracking to be the most successful of the six we launched this year. You'll want her on before then, trust me. She'll be booked for February."

"But you'll tell her to come see me either way. Because you know me."

Anna wanted to roll her eyes and argue that his show wasn't worth Alysha's time, but Anna knew it was. Not only would the publicity be good for the new imprint, but Anna wanted the extra airtime at Christmas. She really wanted Vinnie's book to be featured. The preliminary reviews were already coming in overwhelmingly positive. "You know I will."

"That's a good girl."

Anna tightened her grip on her glass and counted backward in her head from one hundred.

"I've missed you, Anna. And you know you missed me." Preston patted her hand that was resting on the bar.

"I've had a very busy year, so I haven't had time to miss myself let alone anyone else." She tried to divert the conversation away from where she was sure it was headed. If she could keep him focused on his fame, maybe he wouldn't try to get her into bed. "I've seen your show, you've been busy as well."

"Never too busy for you." His index finger moved deliberately over her bracelet. "We should go upstairs. I know you have a room. I overheard you earlier."

She wanted to pull away sharply, slap him, and to tell him what she really thought about him. Instead of any of those things, she slipped her hand away slowly. "I'm seeing someone."

"And my wife isn't here." He leaned into her space. "I can be discreet if you can."

Anna straightened her spine. "You know that's not my thing."

Preston let out a loud laugh, the fake one he used all too often on his show. "Well, it's not mine either. I was messing with you. You should have seen your face."

She responded with her own fake laugh, content to act like she believed him on some level. What she needed was a way to get out of this conversation. When her phone lit up, she'd never been so happy to see Vinnie's contact icon on her screen. "Excuse me, I need to take this."

Preston motioned for her to go ahead but didn't give her any space.

"Hello there, I was getting worried." She forced herself to smile as she spoke. The other side of the line was so quiet that Anna wondered if the call had been dropped. "Vinnie, are you there?" The silence persisted until the telltale beep of the call being dropped.

"Maybe you're free after all?" Preston smirked.

She stood up. "Unfortunately not, but have a nice evening, Preston."

"You too, Anna. Call me if you change your mind."

Anna stretched out her strides and reached the elevator as it was about to close, but a hand interrupted the doors from sealing. "Thank you."

"Not a problem." The androgynous person who caught the door smiled at Anna as she got into the elevator. "Which floor?"

"Fourteenth."

"Coincidence. Me too." The smile was now flirtatious as they stretched their arms over their head.

She wasn't in the mood for conversation and Vinnie's dropped call had her concerned. Anna stayed silent but looked at her phone, willing it to ring again.

"Were you at the gala tonight?"

The question was innocent enough, but Anna just needed quiet.

"I was, and at the risk of being rude, I've had a long night and want to be alone with my thoughts."

They shrugged, "Fair enough."

The elevator stopped at the fourteenth floor and they went in opposite directions. Anna glanced behind her to make sure they were going to a room and then continued to her own. She unlocked the door, noting the absence of the sound of the bell that would have normally sounded. Even planning to meet Vinnie here, she should have brought a bell or bought one. *Stupid to not be vigilant.*

She opened door to small balcony and leaned against the frame, careful to keep her feet inside the room. She breathed in the fresh air as she called Vinnie back. It rang once, then the familiar voicemail message connected.

"You've reached Vinnie. Leave a message and I'll return your call. Alternatively, you can feel free to text me at this number." She hung up and sent him a text.

Anna: Are you alright?

Vinnie: . . .

She watched the flashing dots disappear, reappear, and disappear. On a positive note, the apparent indecision meant he likely wasn't in physical danger. On the negative, it meant something had happened, and he didn't want to tell her. Anna could picture him typing a message, analyzing it, deleting it, and then repeating the process. She called again.

He sent her to voicemail immediately.

She reminded herself that they weren't in a relationship but it made her agitated. There was such a thing professional courtesy.

She bent over backward for this man and to have him outright ignore her was infuriating. Vinnie had a particular way of processing things, so there was some leeway for that, but not for brushing her aside.

The evening had been a good time, and Alysha had been every bit the professional, charming woman Anna knew she would be. Tonight had opened even more doors for her, and Anna couldn't be happier about that.

Seeing Preston at the bar afterward wasn't entirely unexpected. Anna had felt his eyes on her all night, but he'd kept his distance. His pregnant wife had been on his arm for part of the evening. Anna wondered if his wife had been sleeping in a room upstairs as Preston was hitting on her, or if she had been taken home by car service. It didn't matter, Preston was a mistake that Anna would never make again.

She sat in the chair found in the office area of the room she'd rented for her and Vinnie. Sighing as she unfastened both of her shoes, and unceremoniously kicked them off. Her brain replayed Vinnie helping her get into them earlier that day and an unwanted shiver ran down her spine. Her phone lit up and it was embarrassing how fast she snatched from where it sat.

It wasn't Vinnie on the other end, it was Minji. She should answer. Part of her wanted to let it ring through to her voicemail. Minji was on Seoul time, and she was used to playing phone-tag with Anna. It wouldn't be the first time she'd ignored her friend's call because she was too overwhelmed with the world. Opting to split the difference, Anna ignored the call but replied with a text.

Anna: I'm at an event. Can't talk. Tomorrow?

She furrowed her brows, reading over the simple message three times before she sent it. Her spoken Korean had always been better than her Hangul.

Minji: Yes. Tomorrow night, your time. Very exciting news!!

Anna looked at the screen, mind racing with what the exciting news might be. *Probably a baby*. The thought hit Anna hard. Minji's family was traditional, and after her marriage at the beginning of the year, children would be an expectation. It could be something else, but she doubted it. Good for Minji. She deserved a baby and a happy life. Anna confirmed a time for tomorrow with her friend and opened Vinnie's thread again.

Vinnie: . . .

Fantastic. He was still thinking. Anna unbuttoned the fasteners of her dress and lifted it over her head. Its tailored fit wouldn't allow for it to go over her hips. She left the dress on the bed and strode into the bathroom to turn on the tub. She'd requested this room specifically for the tub. The idea of soaking in it held a lot of appeal, especially with Vinnie in the tub with her. Now she would be using it to get the tension out of her body.

Hot water filled the tub and the room with steam, fogging up the mirrors. Anna added one of the oils that were on the bathroom counter. She winced as she pulled off the adhesive bra cups and threw them in the trash. Thankfully her skin didn't look that irritated. The harsh lights washed out her pale skin. She looked at herself in the reflection of the mirror over her shoulder.

After Vinnie mentioned her freckles, she noticed them more. The black ink off her tattoo peeked out over her sheer red lingerie.

Vinnie hadn't finished whatever his thought was, as his response was still buried within the obnoxious blinking dots.

Using a makeup wipe, she prepared to clean the glittery patterns that adorned her face but paused. She wanted another picture of this. Framing herself carefully, she snapped a few selfies of just her face. The last thing she needed was to take a nude photo and have her account get hacked. Anna wasn't under the false impression that she was famous, but she had a professional reputation, and professional women weren't allowed sex scandals, unless you were a certain level of famous, or rather, infamous.

She scrubbed her face clean then rubbed a moisturizer into her skin. Turning off the water, she switched on the jets in the tub. She wanted a drink. Walking naked back into her room, she examined the minibar offerings before settling on one of the less acidic wines. *It would do the job; she was already tipsy*. She pulled out the small bottle alongside a bottle of water.

The tub had enough of an edge to set the bottles on, so she wrapped her phone in a hand towel and set it down with her drinks. She slowly stepped into the tub of hot water, gooseflesh racing up her legs and down her back. Gingerly, she lowered herself into the tub, the water coming up to her chest. She sighed in relief as she picked out her hairpins and dropped them into a pile between sips of wine.

Washing her hair was not on the agenda for the night, so after getting the last of the pins out, she tied her hair into a messy bun. Her brief peace was interrupted by the buzzing of her phone. She methodically dried her hands, looking at the icon. It was Vinnie.

She answered it and put him on speakerphone. "Hello again."

"Sorry. I shouldn't have hung up." He sounded dejected.

"My assumption was that you lost signal. I wouldn't have admitted to hanging up."

He sighed. "You're angry."

She paused before answering. Angry? No. Annoyed and wound up? Yes. "Annoyed would be more accurate. I'm unhappy knowing I was hung up on and about my text not being returned."

"I…I can call you tomorrow, it's late."

"I am soaking in a hot bath, drinking wine, and wondering why you aren't here with me." Anna rolled her shoulders and drew in a long slow breath.

"Well, that's an image." He sounded breathless.

"I'm not sending you a picture." Anna smirked, finishing off her mini wine bottle.

He chuckled. "You shouldn't; digital data is forever."

Anna wanted to play and she didn't want to ask what drama had made him hang up and not answer her text. Her head was light, and Preston had infuriated her. She wanted to lose herself in something more pleasurable. "You should come. I have a key waiting for you at the front desk."

Vinnie cleared his throat. "Tempting offer and I do need to talk to you."

"I don't want to talk." She lowered her tone and purred out what she wanted. "I want you here with me. I want you to make good on what we started earlier today."

"Anna. I need to talk to you." He sounded more irritated than interested.

She muted her phone and screamed into the hand towel, clenching and unclenching her hands before tapping her touchscreen to unmute herself. She couldn't keep the stress out of her tone. "Vinnie, I am exhausted from this event. I had an ex-lover try to convince me to go to bed with him so he could cheat on his pregnant wife. I am more than tipsy. I am naked, horny, and I want you. Do you really want to just talk?"

"Want and need are by definition different."

Anna groaned. "What happened? What on earth could have happened at your niece's birthday party?"

"Kass found out about the book." Vinnie sighed, the air reverbing through the phone.

That was different from drama. That was a problem. She didn't want spoilers getting out about the book prior to its release. "How did she find out?"

"One of her coworkers got an arc copy of my book. She recognized the story from how her coworker described it."

"Well, discussing it prior to the release date announcement is a breach of the arc contract."

"Do you think I care about that right now? The contract?" he growled.

She arched her eyebrow even though he couldn't see her. "You should. That contract protects your work."

"My work? Anna, Kass was in tears. She was really hurt by it. I should have thought about her feelings before I pursued this. How did I not think about the consequences?"

"Come to the hotel and talk with me. I need…"

"If you think I'm going to sleep with you right…"

"I'm not a hormonal teenager trying to get fucked! I'm a goddamn professional!" She cut him off. "I'm not discussing this further until I have sobered up some, and we can come up with a game plan together."

"I.. I'm sorry."

They were both quiet. Neither of them were known for speaking rashly. She was also very sure that this was the first time her real temper had eeked out in front of him. Anna could imagine how torn up he was right now. As much as she was agitated about his avoidance, she hated hearing him like this. He hadn't wanted his family to find out about the book. Knowing his brother's temper, Mat probably yelled at Vinnie and ruined Lizzie's party. Vinnie would feel guilty about that. His world was crashing around him and she was pushing him further out of his comfort zone.

"Don't be sorry. Just come up here. I promise I'll be wearing clothes. We'll figure it out."

More silence.

"I have a couple of things to take care of before I can go anywhere. Can you get me a digital copy of the book? Kass wants to read it."

Anna caught sight of her reflection in the mirror again, and she hated how hurt she looked right now. "I'll send you the pdf file. I would prefer it if we speak tonight."

"Sorry. I have things to finish. I'll see you for breakfast tomorrow, I'll have something ready for you when you get home."

"When I get to Rex's house, which is not my home," she corrected, lowering her shoulders and breathing slowly to reign in her runaway anger. "Don't bother cooking for me. The hotel offers breakfast. I'll see you when I get back in the afternoon, and we can assess things from there." She hung up before she said anything else that she might regret with a cooler head.

First things first. She sent the requested pdf to Vinnie's email as requested. She put her phone down and rolled her shoulders again, trying to get the tension out. It wasn't working. Of course, it wasn't working. She'd been expecting to get laid, not to be dealing with family drama and have Vinnie shut down completely.

Her finger traced over her screen and down through her apps until she tapped on Tinder. She swiped left on the first few profiles that came up, as she was only half serious about this potential hall pass she was going to give herself. The fourth profile that came up struck her as oddly familiar, so she paused and lifted her phone. Oh, it was the person from the elevator…They were on this floor. Maybe…

It was best not to make life decisions when emotions were high, but then again…

Chapter 10:
Paint The Story In Techicolor

Symbolism is Good, but Use Caution

October 15th; 50 Days Until…

He was fucking moron. A moron counting down the hours until his inevitable death at the hands of either his sister-in-law or his not-girlfriend. He supposed it all depended on who got to him first. Vinnie had emailed the PDF of the book to Kass last night after Anna sent it to him. Kass texted him this morning, letting him know that she planned to read the book in its entirety today, and that they'd go from there.

Kass was mad at him for the book, but Anna was mad at him for worrying about how Kass was reacting to the book, and he couldn't figure out what to do with himself. He'd driven to the club to help out, but Leila had kicked him out. He'd forgotten they were hosting a ladies-only night, and he wasn't welcome. Out of habit, he started writing out ideas for a second book, but his thoughts kept wandering to his not-girlfriend editor. Anna: self-assured, pretty, professional, and far out of his league. But apparently when intoxicated, not out of the realm of possibly sleeping together, as far as she was concerned. No, she'd been sober before the gala when they… Vinnie shook his head to keep his brain away from that track. He didn't need any other distractions.

He sipped from his coffee cup and glanced down at his notes, which had devolved into a description of Anna in the butterfly-backed dress. He should have gone to see Anna last night. She was right to be angry.

Crash!

He jumped at the sound of something breaking in the kitchen, rushing to investigate. There was a mouse somewhere in the house, and he was hoping to trap it before Anna found out.

"Fucking shit." Jane was kneeling in the kitchen, picking up the pieces of the broken plate.

Vinnie folded his arms over his chest. "I always thought Nathan taught us to cuss."

Her mismatched eyes were unreadable as always, but she nodded. "Guilty as charged. Being around Rex kept my language a bit cleaner, but I wasn't ever good about not swearing around you and your brother."

"I'll get the trashcan."

"Why?" She questioned as she finished gathering the pieces.

There was a fairly simple answer to that ridiculous question. "To put the broken pieces in. A plate isn't any good broken."

Jane gripped the pieces, almost protecting them. "It isn't too broken. I can put it back together, there are only four pieces."

"We have more plates. We don't need all of them." Vinnie didn't understand why she was reacting this way. It was just a plate.

"I don't want to throw Rex's things away."

"Okay, suit yourself," He shrugged.

She retrieved the glue from Rex's cluttered desk. She applied the glue and held the pieces together. Her eyes wandered back to him as if she sensed him watching her. "How was Elizabeth's party?"

It was so odd to hear Lizzie's full name. He couldn't remember the last time anyone called her anything other than Lizzie, or one of her many, many nicknames. "It was good. You didn't ask Rex?"

"He slept in late and had things to do in town all day. We didn't really talk much this morning before he left." She focused on the plate shards in her hands. "It sounded like Mat was with you guys when you got back. Are they getting along better?"

"I don't know, I wasn't with them. I had other things to do after Lizzie's party, so Mat gave him a ride home."

If Mat and Rex weren't fighting, that was a positive sign. Nothing surprised him more than an old dog learning a new trick. Maybe that long drive back from Galveston was all they needed? Now if they could all get into one room, perhaps they could get some answers out of Jane and come to a better understanding of each other. Their broken little family could get put back together. None of them had grown up easy, and it was bound to cause friction when emotions got high.

"They weren't yelling, so that's a good sign. Mat inherited Nathan's temper, that's for sure. I remember…"

"Mat is nothing like Nathan! Nothing!"

Jane's eyes were wide, startled at his outburst. Quickly, she offered clarification. "No, I didn't mean Mat is violent. I just meant he gets loud when he gets angry. I know he wouldn't hurt anyone. I'm sorry, I didn't mean for it to sound like that."

"At least he doesn't look like Nathan. I got that honor," Vinnie growled. "Lucky fucking me. Looks and a callous nature."

"Vinnie, there's nothing callous about you. And you don't look like him." Jane released the two pieces of the plate to grab another one, but they fell apart.

"I've seen pictures, but thanks for the empathetic lie." Vinnie snorted, pointing to her project. "Looks like that plate is done for."

"Maybe it just needs different glue." Jane shrugged, examining the bottle of glue. "You said you had other things to do last night. Were you helping Anna with something?"

"It's not really any of your business now, is it?" He shouldn't be acting like this. They were finally having a conversation and he was antagonizing her.

Jane went back to Rex's desk for another type of glue. "I suppose it's not. For what it's worth, I like Anna. She's kind, but with backbone. From what I understand Kass is wonderful too, just a little more domestic. You boys found good partners. I'm glad of that."

"We both got lucky. Mat'll keep Kass for the long haul. Anna's out of my league, but I'll be happy while I have her." Vinnie forced the lie out, he wasn't explaining anything to Jane. She didn't deserve the truth. She wasn't forthcoming with them, so he'd match her energy.

"Pretty bad fight, huh?" Jane went into the kitchen and retrieved a bottle of water. "You look to the right when you lie." She explained on her way back to the table. "Probably overcompensating because you know most people look down and to the left when they lie. The trick is to think about a truth when you're telling the lie. Let your expressions match your thoughts and keep your mouth moving."

"Grifter insight 101?"

"More like a 202 class, but you seem like you'd pick up on advanced techniques." Jane smiled and shoved her hands in her pockets. "You learn like me, quick. Read it or hear it and it sticks in your brain somewhere so you can pull it up like a card catalog. Mat always learned the hard way."

Vinnie was hyper aware his brother learned the hard way, but he learned the way Jane did? That he didn't know. Hell, Rex probably didn't know either. Jane had voluntarily told him something about herself as she saw it reflected in him. He never thought for a moment that he was like Jane. Nathan hated that Mat looked like Jane, and he'd yell at Mat for it, a lot. But he'd never heard anything similar about himself. Vinnie just always assumed he was his monster father all over again, but unlike his father, he managed to keep the worst traits at bay. Most of the time.

He wanted to know more, but if he pressed her, she'd shut down. She closed herself off whenever she was pushed. "Did you take college classes at the prison?"

She nodded. "I did. It won't mean anything once I get my new ID's. That degree is linked to Jane Doe."

"How did you keep your identity concealed?" He always wondered how she concealed her identity and now was as good a time as any to ask.

"My prints weren't on file anywhere, and I didn't have any ID on me when I got caught. It's what I was going to..."

The front door opened and both he and Jane looked towards the sound. Anna strode in, wearing jeans and a t-shirt, a garment bag over her arm and a bag in her hand. What nearly knocked Vinnie off his feet was the asymmetrical bob she was now sporting. She glanced at them, then paced toward the bedroom.

"I got a haircut like that before I pulled my last job," Jane commented.

"Well, she's not a criminal, so..." He trailed off, contemplating if he wanted to chase Anna into the bedroom.

"I cut it for practical reasons. I needed it to fit under a wig. But I also wanted to see something different when I looked in the mirror."

So much for not chasing Anna into the bedroom. On one hand, he didn't want to have this fight, but on the other hand, realistically, it was time to close the book on their charade. Kass knew about the book, and the rest of the family would find out soon. It would devolve into every bit of the disaster he always knew it would. Maybe if he could convince Anna to have a public breakup with him, he could get a little sympathy. But she certainly didn't owe him anything.

Vinnie had gotten so far ahead of himself yesterday, kissing her in the heat of the moment. He'd crashed into reality, acknowledging that he had feelings for her. Anna was attracted to him sexually, she'd said as much, but he'd somehow missed the beyond-friendship feelings he'd developed for her. If everything hadn't happened the way it had, they would have slept together and that would have been that. Anna would have gotten him out of her veins and he wouldn't have a place in her life. He hadn't missed her obvious signs of arousal when he helped with her shoes yesterday, but his own forwardness had caught him off guard.

Fire and passion weren't normal for him. That extremely uncomfortable conversation between himself and Mat hadn't been far off from reality. Leila had been the only person he'd slept with and again, while the experience hadn't been unpleasant, it hadn't been the connection he thought it should have been. He cared for Leila, and took his time with her, but the physical reaction had been just that – a reaction – not an intersection of feelings and experiences. With Anna, there was something there that hadn't been before, and he wasn't sure what to do with it.

"It sounds like she's packing." Thankfully Jane interrupted his spiraling train of thought.

"Right. Thank you."

Vinnie rapped his knuckles against the door and waited until Anna gave him permission to enter. He closed the door behind him. She wasn't in the midst of packing, but her closet door was ajar and one of her bags was open on the bed. She was a person of single focus, so he wasn't sure what stopped her. He noticed she was touching the stained glass butterfly that he adhered to the window.

"So…" He wasn't sure where to begin. Was this their goodbye? He wouldn't blame her. He acted so strangely last night. What kind of man turns down a naked woman in a tub? Him, apparently.

"Was this here before?" she asked, still examining the trinket.

Vinnie shoved his hands in his pockets. "I bought it this morning. It's nothing special. I saw it and thought of your dress from last night."

The aforementioned dress was hanging in its bag on the closet door. The hotel tag caught his attention. It had been dry cleaned this morning, possibly a rental like the other dresses he'd seen her in.

"I'm sure the colors are prettier than I can see. It looks gray and black to me," she dismissed.

"It is gray and black. I know you can see those colors accurately. It was the only one like it, but I thought it fit." He willed himself to elaborate on their situation. To talk about anything other than the small gift she now looked annoyed with.

"It's nice for the room." Anna kept her back to him.

He cleared his throat. "I bought it for you actually."

"Why?"

"It was that or the 'live-laugh-love' coffee cup and I thought the butterfly was prettier."

Anna sighed and turned to face him. Her new haircut suited her. It was styled with casual waves, but he could picture it sleek and straight, resting above her shoulders. He wasn't sure if she would be able to pull it back.

"Your haircut looks good. It suits you. Although, statistically, 70% of women opt for a drastic haircut after a break-up, so this doesn't bode well for our future partnership."

Her nails were different as well, the new manicure fading from red at the cuticles to black at the tips. They contrasted her highlighted hair as she tugged at the longer side. "You have statistics on women getting haircuts after breakups?"

"I have found it to be accurate, but in fairness it's anecdotal data at best," he conceded.

"Because you work at a strip club."

"Yes, that." Vinnie leaned his back against the door and motioned between them. "So, is this the end of this?"

It would be for the best. He never should have gotten her involved in the first place. It was ridiculous to pretend like they were something they weren't. There was no tale, no matter how tall, where someone like Anna stayed with someone like him. She was confident, professional, upstanding, and rich.

Movie quotes about kitchen boys and princesses echoed in his brain.

"Why is that your assumption?" She closed the bag on the bed and put it back in the closet. Her blue eyes were piercing as she prodded. "I cut my hair and get my nails done, so you conclude that I'm done with you?"

He looked away from her. "More going off the evidence from how I treated you last night."

"Fair." Anna opened the door. "It's nice outside, come on."

Vinnie didn't want to leave the room. In a closed room, there was less opportunity for eavesdropping. He didn't want an audience for this. But despite his feelings on the situation, he followed her out to the patio. Jane wasn't at the table where he'd left her.

Once they were outside, Anna turned her face up to the sun, a soft smile curling over her lips. This felt like a trap. She stretched her arms over her head then bent at the waist. "I hate going to the gym. I hate every part of working out, but it's annoying to not have an outlet here."

He sat down in one of the patio chairs. "I have a treadmill in the garage if you want to use that."

"Do you?" She turned, smooth as a dancer on her bare feet, with pale pink painted toes. "I could have saved myself almost a month of frustration if I had just asked you. Funny how communication works."

"You're mad that I wouldn't come up and talk to you last night, not…" He trailed off as the realization hit him between the eyes. He was, indeed, a fucking moron.

"It's been a while since I've been rejected so thoroughly, but no, I'm not angry with you over not sleeping with me." Anna laughed and perched herself on the end of his patio chair. She continued her explanation. "Don't misunderstand, I am not happy with you being unwilling to come talk to me last night. I wanted to help you. It's my job to help you, and again, I genuinely like you as a person. I want to see you succeed. You not trusting me to do my literal job is irritating."

He sat up, moving his legs off to the side to make room for her. "Sorry. I shouldn't have speculated about your state of mind." A car honked as it passed by the house, and Vinnie waved without recognizing it. One of Rex's friends no doubt.

Anna's hand was soft and smelled like almond lotion as she cupped his cheek and chin to get his attention back on her. "Hello, you. Penny for your thoughts."

"They're worth more than that. My editor told me so." He wasn't one for being casually touched, but there was something so comforting and familiar about Anna's.

"I did." She was smiling again, and once they made eye contact, she put her hands on her knees. "So, talk to me. How bad was it? You weren't very forthcoming last night."

"Kass didn't tell Mat or anyone else. She's gonna read the book today and let me know if she's not comfortable with it."

"Alright, not too bad then. At least it didn't ruin Lizzie's party. Kass sent me a picture of her with the stuffed horse I had sent to her. And she didn't let on that she was upset at that point."

He cracked his knuckles. "She likes to scare you in person. But there is one other thing, and this is the one that you aren't going to like."

Her eyebrow quirked up.

"She wants to have a say in editing out things that make her uncomfortable." He nearly spoke the sentence as a word. He'd said it so fast that Anna blinked as she deciphered the mess of words.

Now she looked mad. "You can't make promises like that! The first copies have gone out to the arc readers, the drafts have gone to the printers, and we are two months out from your release date. A launch like yours isn't something we can change at the drop of a coin. I suppose I should be thankful that you didn't tell her that you'd pull it if she insisted."

Vinnie cleared his throat, wishing he had water to drink, a cigarette to smoke, or a cyanide pill to take.

Anna drew in a very long breath, then paused, then exhaled through her nose for the same count. "Vinnie. I have thousands of dollars wrapped up in this project. I have my reputation attached to this project. You and I have a written contract in regards to this project. I can alter it so some of the royalties will go to Kass and her family, but we cannot pull it."

"Money doesn't fix everything." He put his fingers to his temples. "You can't just give her money and make her magically happy with the situation. Kass is my family and she's really upset about this. I can't ignore her feelings."

"I'm not asking you to ignore her feelings, but you should have thought about her reaction before you submitted the book to be published. Why would you send it to a publishing house if you hadn't considered the outcome of her finding out?"

"Because I didn't think it was good enough," he muttered.

"What?"

"I didn't think it was good enough! I didn't think anything I wrote would be good enough! I thought I would turn it in, it would get rejected, and I'd move on." He clenched his fists, nails imprinting his palms. "I just needed to know that it wasn't worth reading. But then you liked it, and I didn't know how to pull away from that feeling."

It was hard to talk and his throat was tight. He swallowed and forced down the lump in his throat. His body was starting to shake, and he inhaled sharply. Part of him was worried he was going to break down, and the other part of him kinda wanted to, so he'd stop himself from talking.

"Anna, you believed in me. You encouraged me. I wasn't a weirdo or a criminal to you. I was a writer and one worthy of taking a risk on. You looked at me like I was smart and not just a smartass. You don't get annoyed when I ramble, and you don't hurt me. I got addicted to this good feeling that you create in my chest, and I didn't know how to slow anything down." He heaved in more air. "I'm sorry. I don't know what to do. I don't want to hurt my family, but I don't want to hurt you either."

Anna's hands covered his clenched fists. "Take another breath." When he complied, she continued in that quiet tone he associated with all of their long talks. "I assure you that you are worthy of being heard. I am sorry you were made to feel that way."

He turned his hands over and threaded their hands together, but he wasn't sure what to say. His mind was racing, but there was nothing logical running on the hamster wheel in his skull.

"I suppose we can wait until she finishes the book and go from there. Maybe it'll be okay with her, and we don't need to be so upset about this." She squeezed his hands.

Vinnie felt his phone vibrate in his pocket. With his luck, it would be Kass telling him to pull the book. But then it could just be an email for male enhancement or crypto-currency bullshit.

"Is your phone set to taser? I felt that through your leg."

He chuckled despite everything. "I got used to it. I used it as an alarm that wouldn't wake Lizzie when she was napping."

"You're good with her," Anna complimented. "That's one of the things that I noticed straight away. You treat her like she's yours."

He pulled his hands away and pulled his phone out. "Well, the likelihood of having kids of myself dwindles by the day, so she's basically the sole carrier of our bloodline."

"I think you'd be a great father."

Between Anna's kind words and the text alert from Kass, Vinnie was sure his brain was about to short circuit. There was only so much he could take in such a short span of time. "Thank you for the sentiment. But I'm lacking a key element needed for the creation of children, and as an ex-con, adoption is an unlikely option."

He unlocked his phone screen and sighed. "It's a text from Kass."
Anna inclined her head, "Do you want to be alone?"
"Honestly, your company is the most comforting place I've ever found."
They both jumped at his confession, but Anna recovered first. "Then I'll stay."
Vinnie touched the thread but closed his eyes. He didn't want to hurt his family, but didn't want to make Anna mad and have her wash her hands of him.
"You can do this," she encouraged. "I won't go anywhere until we figure out a game plan."
"Okay."
The phone felt like it weighed ten times what it normally did; it was hot to the touch. He was misinterpreting his senses. It was only hot on the screen. Smartphones didn't work like that.

Kass: I want to be pissed. But it's really good.
Kass: Mat needs to know about it, and so does Rex
Kass: Thanks for making me look nicer than I was
Kass: Still not happy about it. But be proud of this

Vinnie: Thank you Kass. We'll figure out a day

Kass: Also that spicy scene -_-
Kass: I can't believe you guys talked about that

Vinnie: I assure you, we did not.
Vinnie: It was research and I was NOT thinking about you two

Kass: LOL GOOD

Vinnie: It was really only the premise and a few splashes

Kass: I noticed. Really colorful splashes tho -_^

Vinnie: I try. Love you sis.

The weight that came off his shoulder made him laugh out loud, and even with the risk of sounding crazy, he couldn't stop laughing. Anna looked expectantly at him. He was trying to catch his breath, so he simply handed over his unlocked phone.
"Well, that's the best-case scenario, I suppose."
"Until Mat knocks me out on the lawn, yes," Vinnie coughed, recovering from his laughing fit.

Anna was unimpressed. "Maybe we have the discussion in public? I don't like the idea of you getting hit."

She set his phone on the arm of the chair, and he caught her hand, giving it a soft squeeze. He wasn't sure how to start this conversation or if he even should. His emotions were high and this might be a rash decision, but he wanted it. He wanted to know if that slimmest of possibilities was within reach.

"I'm not worried about Mat hitting me. His punches are shit, and it wouldn't be the first time I've sported a black eye. Might make a good author photo."

Anna was still holding his hand, but she shook her head. "The current photo you have is good."

"But a black eye would add so much character." He leaned forward and pressed a kiss on her knuckles.

"This isn't getting you out of trouble. You hung up on me."

"And assumed you only wanted me to come over for sex. Yes, I know how much trouble I'm in for that." He kept their fingers entwined, but toyed with a lock of her newly shortened hair with his free hand. "This really does suit you. Reminds me of Marilyn Monroe without her signature curls."

"Mhmmm." Anna was giving him an 'oh-come-on' look, but her eyes were smiling. The corners of her eyes turned up, a dead giveaway for actual joy.

"Okay, I'm still in trouble here if comparing you to one of the most iconic beauties in history didn't work. I'm going to have to get more creative."

"If we were dating, you would have to get much more creative," she reminded him, resting her freehand on his knee. "Currently, we are doing business together, which would require one sincere apology and a trip to HR, considering your current position inside of my personal space."

He smirked, "Would that trip to HR include an account of last night?"

"Oh, I see we've moved on to blackmail."

God, that hundred-watt smile on her face kept him right on the edge of not being able to form a retort. The sun was setting behind her, purples and dark blue streaking across the upper sky as the deepening reds and oranges painted the lower half. He wanted to point it out to her, but he also didn't want to divert her attention away. Idly, he wondered how expensive a pair of glasses to help her see in true colors would be. A Christmas gift, maybe? *Stop. She always had him losing his train of thought.*

"No, just creative bargaining."

"So if you're bargaining..." Anna bit down on her lower lip before smirking. "What are you after, Mr. Goodroe?"

"This, Miss Kane, I am after this." He fought back against the voice in his head telling him that she was an impossible dream. "Anna, if there is even a ghost of a chance for us to be more than a show, then I want it. I want us."

"Fucking finally," Anna sighed and pulled him in for a kiss.

Vinnie tangled his fingers into her hair, content for a moment before pulling her fully onto his lap. After a few minutes of breathless entanglement, he shifted slightly and pressed his forehead to hers.

He tried to calm his breathing down, but he was softly panting as he questioned. "You aren't going to kill me if I need to take this slow, are you?"

She groaned but rubbed her nose against his. She motioned for him to get up with her. "Just be worth the wait and we'll call it even. Come on, I need to lay down, I'm exhausted. I slept like hell last night, and I'm hung-over."

They walked inside hand and hand. As they passed the table, Vinnie noticed the plate Jane had been repairing was back in one piece. The still wet ceramic glue had filled in the cracks, looking almost gold in the dying light.

Chapter 11: Character Growth

Small Moments Have Meaning

October 23rd, 47 Days Until…

Anna grimaced, watching Vinnie argue with Mat in the backyard. Neither had thrown a punch yet, but she was waiting for it. Judging by Mat's expression, it wouldn't be much longer. Rex was outside with them as well, whereas Jane was wherever she went when she didn't want to be seen.

"I tried to keep Lizzie awake the whole way here. They wouldn't fight if she was awake." Kass shook her head, before fanning herself. "Is it hot in here? It feels super warm. Am I crazy?"

"The heater kicked on some time last night. It was almost ninety when Rex woke up. He fought with it for a while, but he thinks it's gonna need to be replaced."

Anna was miserable and wanted to open the windows for the breeze, but with Lizzie sleeping and the brothers fighting outside, it was best to suffer with the fans.

"So much for making homemade lasagna. If I turn the oven on, it'll make it worse. New plan, but still Italian, 'cause I am in the mood for pasta. If I'm cooking, it's my choice."

Anna was confused. "They're going to eat together after that?"

Kass leaned to her right, presumably so she could get a better look at what was happening in the backyard. "I mean, probably. They stopped mid-punch when my dad showed up unexpectedly."

"That was after you and Mat first met, correct?" Anna asked.

Kass walked to the pantry. "Was that in the book? I don't remember reading that."

"No, your father told that story at your wedding."

The younger woman paused and looked at Anna over her shoulder, "Oh, he did, didn't he? I completely forgot about that. Sorry."

"Truthfully, I feel like I should apologize to you. I should have pushed back more on the book when Vinnie told me it was somewhat based on something that happened in his family. I am sorry for the part I played in all of this tension."

Kass nodded. "Thank you. It is what it is at this point. I can't decide if Jane coming back was a blessing in disguise or a curse. It's more stress, but it's also a distraction from all that." She motioned towards the lawn as Mat landed a punch on Vinnie.

Anna winced, that hit looked incredibly painful. "Are you sure…"

"I am. They need to get it out." Kass fidgeted with her hands as she moved away from the line of sight. "It's not the healthiest way to work things out, and deep down they know that too. But with how they grew up, sometimes this is how it is. After the violence, they can start talking through the hard part."

"Did you grow up around this kind of thing?"

"Fighting? Not really. I grew up in the country, so there were scuffles but not quite to this level."

"Does it scare you?" Anna hadn't grown up around any of the 'rough and tumble,' as Vinnie described it. While scared was an extreme word to use, she didn't know how else to describe her discomfort. She purposely turned her back on the scene outside.

"'Scared' would be a strong word, but then again, if I didn't know them I probably would be. It'll be alright, I promise." Kass acted older than her age. The calm in her voice carried an authority that caught Anna off guard. Whether it was the responsibility Kass had taken on partially raising her younger sibling, her current role of mother, or her job as a nurse, it gave the young woman a level of authority and calm in her voice.

"How can I help?" Anna needed a distraction.

Kass pointed to the top shelf of the pantry, "Can you grab two jars of canned tomatoes and a jar of peppers?" She had a box of spaghetti noodles and a store-bought can of mushrooms in her hands.

Anna chuckled. "It pays to be tall sometimes."

"I'm jealous. It sucks being short," Kass complained as Anna stretched to reach the glass jars. "While those three are outside working things out, we can make dinner. At minimum, Lizzie's gonna have to eat and spaghetti is an easy dish."

Kass tied back her auburn hair, and they took turns washing their hands at the sink. Kass grabbed two pots, and a pan, putting them on the stove. Anna examined the jars in her hands. Kass must have canned these herself.

They were labeled with her neat, delicate script. Anna bought jars of salsa before, but she never thought about canned peppers by themselves.

"I can't wait to get into our own house. I want to plant a garden in the spring, and Lizzie is going a little stir crazy without a yard to play in." She poured water into the pot and placed it on the stove.

"I'm sure my apartment is cramped with three people living in it."

Kass' cheeks tinged pink from embarrassment. "Oh, no, I'm sorry. I wasn't complaining. Mat and I are so grateful. I'm just looking forward to the next step."

"I didn't take any offense. And I'm just as eager to be back in my apartment as you are to be out of it." Anna assured her. "Did you want the tomatoes and peppers in the other pot?"

"If you could. If the seals are too tight, there's a jar opener in the third drawer in the cabinet to the right of the sink."

It felt odd to be cooking. Anna never needed the skill prior, and, to be honest, her attempts with Rex were abysmal. She didn't like it when she was bad at something. In the past, she either pushed herself to the breaking point to be good at whatever it was or simply decided it wasn't for her and dropped it. While self-sufficiency demanded the skill be acquired, her lack of patience and many bank account balances made take-out an easy choice.

"So, I have to ask. How much did Vinnie freak out about that tattoo of yours? I just saw it when you stretched to get the jars," Kass asked, pulling out a package of hamburger meat.

Anna almost commented about how he'd only seen it in passing, but remembered she and Vinnie decided to keep their prior not-dating relationship a secret, as they were now dating.

She didn't want to admit that they hadn't slept together, but she wasn't sure why he might freak out about her tattoo. He mentioned that it was a reference to one of his favorite shows, but she really wasn't familiar with it. The almost-tramp-stamp was just an interesting quote one of her fellow English majors had suggested. Her own handwriting was forever inked on the left on her lower back. *How could she explain this without giving too much away?*

Anna glanced behind her to make sure Jane hadn't materialized, or Lizzie had woken up. "He commented on it, but I'm not familiar with the show he mentioned. Another person suggested it when I got it. I thought it was just about writing and editing. "

"Really? I'm surprised he didn't keep the two of you in bed for hours watching the whole thing. Although it's not really pillow talk tv. There's a lot of trauma."

"Pillow talk hasn't really entered our conversations yet." Anna blushed. She hadn't meant to be so blunt. She needed more coffee.

"Oh." Kass looked surprised, then her face got even redder than it had been before. "OH! Oh my goodness, I am sorry." She looked around as well, her voice dropping to a conspiratorial volume. "It's nothing to be ashamed of. I'd only slept with one guy before Mat."

Anna couldn't stop her own laughter at the thought of being a near-virgin when she met Vinnie. She didn't throw herself at anyone she bumped into, but she certainly wasn't as picky to only have one previous lover.

As the realization dawned on Kass as to why Anna was laughing, Kass' blush got even deeper, and she started laughing herself. "Oh god, I can't know that!" She squealed, red-faced. "I thought he'd slept with Leila when they were together."

That wasn't Anna's to tell, but she didn't want Kass to think what she was currently thinking. "He did, but from what we discussed, he wasn't completely comfortable with the situation. So we are taking it painfully slow."

"So what Jane walked in on was…"

"Our first kiss," Anna supplied.

"Rex made it sound much more scandalous." Kass threw her hands up in exasperation. "What is it with this house and interrupted kisses? That happened with me and Mat too. Of course, it happened at the barbeque we were throwing for Lizzie, and it was my friend that interrupted, which had to be less embarrassing than having his mother walk in. But at the time, as far as we knew, his mother had just up and left, which is kinda what actually happened." She arranged the hamburger on the pan, and the meat sizzled. "Did you get the story about why she never reached out? Mat wants to know, but he hasn't tried the easiest solution, aka, talking to her."

She suddenly knew why Kass and Vinnie got along so well. They both told stories like they were trying to beat the sand in an hourglass. Anna blinked and tried to respond to the relevant part. "She hasn't been very forthcoming with any details. Honestly, I know she's here, but I rarely see her. Sometimes it feels like she's a ghost."

"I feel like I'm a ghost, so that's accurate."

Kass and Anna both jumped, turning to see Jane standing at the kitchen island.

She tugged at the front pockets of her hoodie and glanced out the patio doors. "It sounds like they're still *discussing* things. Would you like some help? I can go back to Rex's room when they come back in. Or I can just grab the water I need. It's too warm."

Anna wasn't sure what to do, and with one look at Kass, it was obvious she was having the same dilemma. The younger woman recovered quicker. "Um, there's garlic bread in the freezer if you want to grab two loaves. Do you know where the pans are?"

Jane nodded. The silence that settled in the kitchen was decidedly uncomfortable. The packages of bread crinkled, the metal pan hit the counter, and even the spray of the pressurized cooking oil was amplified in the quiet.

"I stayed away because the job I pulled was on Jim, the guy Nathan and Rex were working for and who Mat and Vinnie eventually worked for. He was and is dangerous, and that's why I'm staying out of sight," Jane explained simply, indicating the lack of emotion in her tone was likely deliberate.

"I think you should explain that to them. They deserve to hear it from you." Kass kept her eyes on the pan of meat in front of her.

Anna sprinkled spices into the tomatoes and preppers, following the recipe that Kass had wordlessly set out for her. Kass was right. Both Vinnie and Mat deserved the truth from Jane. *But what if it put them in danger?* Kass had known the family longer and was naturally more overprotective over all of them. She had a daughter to consider on top of everything else. Anna felt like she was watching a car crash in slow motion.

"Why do you think it would put them in danger now? Just the association with you? Or are they still connected to this Jim person somehow?" Anna asked, because she needed to know. She didn't want to put herself in danger. The idea of Vinnie having a past was one thing, but if he were currently involved, then she couldn't be involved with him. Had she jumped the gun by moving into a relationship with him?

Kass folded her arms over her chest. "I know that for a fact they aren't involved with him anymore. Mat owed him money, but he paid that off shortly after Lizzie was born."

Jane put the bread in the oven. "I want to talk to them, I do. But every time I try, I make things worse. I'm not trying to be their mother, I know I don't have that right. I should have stayed away."

"Why didn't you?" Kass aggressively stirred the pot with the tomatoes. "I know it's not my place to ask, but I'm gonna anyway. Why did you come back if you were so worried about being found?"

Jane glanced towards the living room and then back to them. "I…" Her eyes focused on Anna for a long moment, as if she was considering her words more carefully because she was in the room. "I hid something here and I needed it. I was planning on being in and out before Rex got home, but he surprised me."

"Does he know that?" Anna questioned. "He seems to be under the impression you came back for him."

Anna couldn't see the exact color of Jane's eyes, but she could tell they were mismatched in the same way Lizzie's were. Had that familial connection been the thing that stopped Jane from leaving that day?

She knew that Lizzie had been the first person to see Jane.

"Rex, god help him, knows me better than anyone. He knows better than to assume that he's the reason I appeared out of nowhere."

"What did you hide here? We found the letters at the cabin. Why didn't you hide everything together?" Kass pressed as Anna watched the amiable woman bristle over the fact that Jane still hadn't answered the question.

"Never put everything in one place. Rule number five of Crime. You never know when your hiding spot might get discovered," Rex interrupted, entering from the patio without the brothers.

Kass looked expectantly at him.

"They're cleaning up in the garage and Mat is getting your kit from the car," Rex explained.

"Seriously?" Her tone was now exasperated. "You didn't think to step in at that point?"

Anna's stomach clenched, now legitimately worried about Vinnie.

"Mat found a piece of glass on the ground with his arm. They're both fine."

"Why is it always my husband?" Kass massaged her forehead.

"Because he's got the luck of someone who flipped off a fae in a past life," Jane quipped, and all eyes were on her again. She shifted on her feet and turned on her heel. "I'm gonna go lie down."

Anna might have tried to stop her, since Jane still hadn't answered their question, but Mat and Vinnie came through the door.

"Don't bleed on the floor, Rex'll make us pull up the carpet," Vinnie admonished.

Mat snarled, "Fuck all the way off! I've got half a coke bottle in my arm!"

"That piece is barely half an inch long. Sister Christian, come get your drama queen husband."

Anna realized the isolated way she'd grown up was less normal than the craziness of having a family. She also realized that no one reacted to Jane, and as expected, the woman was gone.

October 30th; 40days until…

Vinnie watched Anna and Kass play with Lizzie on the lawn. The little girl, dressed as Evelyn from The Mummy, was squealing and trying to keep her empty candy bucket away from the adults.

"Most kids are princesses at her age." Rex snickered.

Vinnie shrugged. "She's kinda a princess if you follow the second movie."

"The first one was better."

"The first one is always better, except for siblings. The second one is always better in that case."

Mat, who was double-checking Lizzie's candy, flipped him off from where he was sitting at the table.

Vinnie laughed. "See, can't even talk and perform basic tasks at the same time."

"Fuck off." Mat threw a piece at him, but Rex caught it mid-air and unwrapped it. Mat scoffed. "Are you seriously eating your granddaughter's candy?"

"You know better than to throw a Twix bar in my direction." Rex put the bite-sized candy in his mouth. "Think you'd be happy to lose a piece or two."

"Kass told him half of it needs to stay here." Vinnie snapped a picture of Kass tossing Lizzie in the air.

"Take anything you want. She's ain't gonna know the difference. She'll be unconscious before we hit the end of the road with all the runnin' 'round she did." Mat leaned back in the dining chair, apparently finished for the moment.

"Did you get a picture of the three of ya together?" Rex questioned.

Mat nodded. "Yeah, Anna and Vinnie both got pictures when we got here."

Vinnie had given his brother all kinds of shit for being dressed like Brendon Friazer's character from the '90s movie. Kass' costume mirrored her daughters. The pictures were great. He made a mental note to send a couple to Rex and Kass.

Mat glanced into the living room. "Where's *she* at?"

"My room," Rex answered, knowing the 'she' that Mat was referring to. "She'll come out when you guys leave unless you want to talk to her."

"Naw. But make sure she knows that if Vinnie wants her to go to his book thing, then it's fine if we're both there." Mat stood and made his way outside.

"Typical. He leaves me to finish," Vinnie commented dryly as he separated the candy into two bags.

Rex shook his head. "The sad part is, if they talked, I think it'd get a lot better."

"She's got to actually answer questions in order for it to be talking," He pointed out.

"It's not easy for her."

"Growth is hard," Vinnie snipped, shooing Rex toward the door. "Go hang out with your granddaughter before they take off. I'll clean up the rest of this crafting mess."

Vinnie added a handful of the candy back into the bag that was going home with his niece. Sighing, he retrieved the trash can to sweep the glitter off the table.

"Thank you for getting him to go out there. He misses Lizzie. I don't know if he actually wants to move to the cabin."

Vinnie looked up at Jane before returning to his task. "We're gonna have to put a bell on you. He wants to move to the cabin because he wants you safe. He doesn't want to lose you again. You should be flattered by that."

"Flattered isn't the word I would use. Feels like I'm stealing him away from the rest of his family."

"Then make an effort. Answer our questions instead of dodging them."

She shifted on her feet. Rex hadn't ever mentioned her age, and he was sure that whatever was written on his and Mat's birth certificates wasn't accurate, as her date of birth was listed differently on each of them. He didn't know how old his mother actually was. She was likely younger than Rex, but how much younger was the question. She might not even be in her fifties yet, unless she was aging more gracefully than her time in prison and smoking habit should have allowed for. But it was as if the weight of the years hit her all at once as she attempted to hold his gaze and couldn't.

"I've never been good at being still – physically or metaphorically. It's not easy for me to answer some of those questions. It brings up a lot of difficult memories."

He wrapped a ring of duct tape around his hand, sticky side out, to pick up the remnants of the glitter. "Well, you could try therapy. It's helpful."

Jane's eyes kept wandering out to the patio, making sure no one else was coming inside. She assisted him with cleaning the table. "Did you do that? Therapy?"

"It was required in my case." Vinnie refused to look up at her, but when he reached for the paper scraps near her, she laid her hand over his left hand, where a long scar on the back of his hand narrowed to a shorter line on his palm.

"When did…"

Vinnie turned her hand over and tapped her index finger where an angry, jagged scar ran the length of it. "You first."

They locked eyes, both unwilling to talk about the origins of those physical marks. She pulled her hand away, relenting. "You're right. I don't have a right to ask that."

He shrugged. This is why he wanted Mat to be a part of this. Mat would start jawing and make it easier. It felt like he was playing chess with Jane right now, but neither of them were willing to give up any pawns to gain ground.

“Rex said you graduated near the top of your class. Why didn’t you go to college? You were always so smart. You learned to read before Mat did. He pretended, but you were really reading at four.”

Vinnie didn’t want to talk about this, but maybe if he put himself out there a bit, she’d match it. “We were already running errands for Jim by the time I was sixteen. He liked to have minors pick up his escorts. Less worried about them running off with them and the money.”

“He’d a fucking murderer. You know that right?”

Vinnie nearly laughed at the statement. It was impossible to not know that. There was no way to get the kind of power that Jim had without putting heads on spikes, so to speak. Jane’s clenched fist interrupted his of thought. One of her hands was in her pocket, but the other was clenched so tightly her knuckles were turning white.

It was personal. She hated Jim. Why? Vinnie’s brain ran through scenarios from bad to worse. This was the first flash of anger he’d seen from Jane, the first unintentional tell that he’d caught. What had Jim done to her?

The patio door opened and Lizzie came barreling in with Mat on her heels.

“OH helloes!” The three year old skidded up to Jane. “You is here! I members you.”

“I like your costume.” Jane smiled softly, but didn’t get any closer. Her eyes darted to Mat, but he remained quiet. “Are you an adventurer?”

“Issa li-bear-air-e-an.” Lizzie sounded the word out carefully. She’d practiced it over and over before going out tonight. “You Gam-pa Rex’s fend.”

A single tear ran down Jane’s cheek. “I am.”

“Oh no. Issa okay.” Lizzie grabbed Jane’s leg. “We can hug. I makes you feel better.”

Mat cleared his throat, and Vinnie braced for the rebuke. “Lizzie, you should give Miss Jane a big hug, she looks like she needs it.”

“Okays!”

Jane knelt down, and Lizzie threw her arms around the older woman’s shoulders, patting the back of Jane’s neck.

“Issa okay. Ita be okay. We can cry a little. Ita be okay dough.”

Vinnie was stunned. Mat was tense, but he wasn’t getting in the way. Vinnie watched as Jane gingerly hugged Lizzie back.

“Issa okay. E’erything bees okay. I says so. Okays deep b’eaths.” The little girl comforted before wiggling away as Jane relented her hold on the girl.

Jane’s face was streaked with tears, and Lizzie awkwardly wiped at her face, trying to help. “Deep b’eaths, for big feels.”

Jane forced a smile, but her whole body was trembling. "Thank you, Elizabeth."

"No, no, jus Lizzie. I not in t'ouble."

"Lizzie then. Thank you." Jane attempted to get back to her feet but almost fell forward.

Vinnie managed to grab her upper arm and hoist her up with one hand. Jane was lighter than he thought she'd be. "You okay?"

"I'm good. You guys have a good night." Jane excused herself back to Rex's room.

"GOOD NIGHTS!" Lizzie yelled before skipping back to Mat. "Daddy, she has big feels. I helps her b'eaths."

Mat swooped Lizzie her up in his arms. "You did great, Little Lady. Where's Momma, huh? We gotta watch Charlie Brown before we go back to that apartment."

Kass, Anna, and Rex entered from the patio door to join them. "I heard Charlie Brown. Are you ready to watch the movie?" Kass questioned.

"Yes, Momma! Yes!" Lizzie held her arms out for Kass and Mat handed her over.

"You okay?" she inquired. Mat simply nodded and kissed the top of her head, making Kass smile. "Alright, let's put the movie."

Anna slipped into the kitchen to get a cup of coffee. She had an overseas zoom call starting at ten, and she'd need the caffeine. After Mat and Kass went home, he was going to The Playhouse to help Leila. The club would no doubt be at capacity, but she told him to wait to come in until after he was done celebrating with his family. Speaking of family, Vinnie might not want to go after Jane, but someone should.

He tapped Rex on the shoulder. "Mat let Lizzie hug Jane, and she went to your room upset."

"Thanks, Kid."

"Yup." Vinnie.

Rex told them to start the movie without him, he'd be right back.

The scent of vanilla and coffee filled his nostrils as Anna offered him a cup to match hers. She was wearing the Halloween sweater he'd picked out for her. She'd nearly paired the gaudy orange sweater with a pair of pink sleep pants, but he stopped her and made sure she matched. The light in her eyes was instantaneous. Such a small thing, but it obviously meant a lot to her.

He took a sip from the cup. "Thank you."

"You've got work after this, I know you're going to need it. How long is this movie? I want to make sure I have time to change."

"About a half an hour. You've never seen it?" he asked, then shook his head at Anna's smirk. "Of course, you haven't. You had money instead of a childhood."

She pinched his side as she breezed by him, pausing at the chess game she and Rex had been playing for over a week, and moving her Rook. "Come on. Show me what I'm missing."

"Auntee Anna, you sits here!" Lizzie waved. "Uncle Vee-nee yous too! Movies time!"

November 20th; 19 Days Until…

Anna balanced the box she was carrying and shifted away from Vinnie when he tried to take it from her. "Go get a heavy box. I have this one."

Vinnie smirked and caged her in the corner of the entryway, one arm on either side of her head. He leaned into the box in her arms, pressing her to the wall. "Now what are you going to do? You are trapped."

"I'm holding a box, so there's only so much I can do." She lifted an eyebrow. "The question is, what are you going to do to me since I'm helpless?"

"You're a lot of things, but I don't think helpless has ever been on that list, Darlin'." Rex shook his head. He had moved up to his cabin in Kansas with Jane last week and was only down here for a week to help with Mat and Kass' move. "Think you love birds could keep walking?"

"Sorry, Rex." they both muttered.

Anna's cheeks warmed, embarrassed to get caught. Thankfully, neither of them had said anything too racy. Vinnie let her go by, and she took the box to the kitchen, since it was marked with an orange sticker.

There would be no more tripping over people after tonight. Mat and Kass had gotten the keys to their house on Friday. Anna had paid movers to have everything from her apartment moved into their new house by five that night. Her things were put back into her apartment yesterday after it had been professionally cleaned.

She'd boxed up all of her things that were at Rex's, and she'd dropped them off this morning to be put away by the organizer she hired. Had she paid too much to have it done so quickly? Absolutely. Was it going to be worth it to go home to her apartment and her cat who she'd missed far more than she expected to? Absolutely. Tonight, she was going to sit on her chaise, read, and sip whiskey while Jackal snuggled next to her.

She was going to take a long shower in her own bathroom, lower the blinds, walk upstairs naked, and lay on her bed under the skylight. Vinnie had to work at the club tonight. As much as she would have loved his company, she couldn't help but be ecstatic at the prospect of being alone. Having her own space for more than just her few sleeping hours sounded like pure bliss.

Kass had food in slow cookers in the kitchen to feed everyone as they moved in the last of their things from the storage unit, but Anna was going to eat light. Tonight she was ordering from her favorite Korean restaurant. Maybe she wanted soju instead of whiskey?

"You need a water?" Kass offered her a bottle.

Anna took it gratefully. "Almost done. It has to feel good to be in your own space."

"It does." She grinned back then pointed at the counter. "The green cooker has the vegetarian chili. I almost forgot this morning, I would have felt awful."

"I would have survived on your mac and cheese." She took another long drink of water and the lights flickered. Both women paused and when there was no thud, cursing, or further flickering they both sighed. "Lizzie's room?"

"Probably. Mat framed the drop ceiling last night according to the plans Vinnie left. We'll see how loud it gets."

"As long as there are no punches thrown, Vinnie's release party is in two weeks and I need him in one piece."

"Mat will behave, I already warned him. I'm so excited for Vinnie's party. Thank you for the gift card to that boutique for my dress. They gave me a discount because you do much business with them and with that gift card, I only owed them fifty dollars."

Anna wanted to go shopping with Kass to get to know her better, but she hadn't been able to get away from work. She'd reached out to the store and requested that they help Kass find a full outfit and act like the gift card and fifty dollars covered whatever the total was. Anna would make up the difference later. Kass was independent and Anna didn't want to overstep.

"I wish I could have gone with you, but my office has been busier than normal with my assistant quitting."

"Yikes. Did she give any warning?"

Anna wanted to curse a blue streak that no, Bailey hadn't given her a single fucking hour of warning, but Lizzie was around here somewhere.

"No, she simply stopped coming in and mailed back her keys. Not that it mattered, I had the locks changed."

Kass stirred the contents of one of the slow cookers, so Anna followed suit, not wanting to carry any more boxes for a few minutes.

They were almost done unloading, and it was only two o'clock. Rex was setting up the grill outside on the back patio. He laughed, joking that he couldn't, in good conscience, grill tofu, but he could grill eggplant for her. Admittedly, she was going to miss talking to Rex at night. He was great at chess, and he was still winning by a game. She'd get ahead of him at some point. Maybe she could teach him to play online with her?

Kass interrupted Anna's train of thought. "How long does it usually take you to find an assistant?"

"I think Alysha and I took about a month to find Bailey. But Alysha had been my assistant for almost four years, and they weren't comparable."

Kass snapped her fingers. "Vinnie's mentioned her. She's running one of your imprints, the POC one right?"

Anna smiled. "Yes, Alysha is running the imprint specifically focused on black voices. And she's going to make it more successful than any forecast I could have given my board."

"Can I ask you something?" She looked right and left, probably checking for Lizzie.

Anna trepidatiously nodded. "Sure."

"How many copies of Vinnie's book do you think are gonna sell? Realistically."

Anna laughed; she was relieved for a factual question. "With his current presales, between sixty and seventy thousand copies sold on release day, and closer to a hundred with ebook sales."

"Oh. That's a lot of books." Kass blinked. "Is that normal for an author's first book?"

"It's higher than average by about thirty thousand copies. We've run a good marketing campaign on it, and his co-workers have been creating a buzz on social media." Anna chuckled. Only Vinnie could have his adult entertainment employees pushing his Rated-R Hallmark book without a lick of shame. Publicity like that couldn't be bought.

"They all love him at the club." Kass stretched her arms over her head. "He's such a sweetie. I couldn't believe that he owned The Playhouse when we met. But somehow, he makes it work."

Anna appreciated how Vinnie spoke about his co-workers as if the club was an office or a restaurant. "I think it's the level of respect he gives them. They aren't used to it."

"He wants to be everyone's brother." Kass giggled, "Well, not yours."

She took a long drink from her water bottle. *No, he certainly didn't.* They made eye contact and both started laughing. Somewhere in the house, Lizzie echoed their laughter.

"She's with Violet on the porch. The screen's closed, but the door's open."

"That was nice of her to come and help."

"She's being *extra* nice. Lizzie's gonna have a sleepover with Auntie Violet and Tia Leila tonight, so Mat and I can have the house to ourselves."

"Well, the house does have three bedrooms." Anna covered her eyes in embarrassment. "I'm very tired. Sorry."

Kass waved her off then lowered her voice. "That vasectomy part of the book was based in reality. And it *comes* in handy, if you'll pardon the innuendo." Her cheeks were pink at the admission, but she didn't look like she regretted saying it.

Mat, as if knowing they were talking about him, strode into the kitchen without a shirt. "Hey, Sweetheart, we're almost done with everything. Rex is gonna run to town; you want him to grab you anything?"

Kass had put her bottle of water to her lips immediately and simply shook her head, making Mat chuckle.

"I'm going to make sure all the boxes are out of the truck." Anna made herself scarce, catching Kass' giggles as she rounded the corner. She almost ran into Vinnie, and she flattened her hands to his chest, pushing him away from the kitchen. "Oh hello. Go."

"Um, hi. Go? Is there a fire? Something more dangerous?" He adjusted his glasses and looked down at her.

Anna forced him further back. "Mat's in the kitchen shirtless, and I'm pretty sure Kass just put him on her personal menu."

"Really?" That devilish grin appeared on Vinnie's face, and Anna covered his mouth to keep him from hollering at his brother. They stumbled backwards into the open coat closet.

Anna clicked her tongue. "Let them have some fun. They haven't had any privacy in months. I think we can give them a little privacy in their own kitchen."

Vinnie reclined against the closet wall. "Mat'll get her off in that kitchen if she lets him. He'll keep her quiet because he knows Violet's outside with Lizzie, but if he thinks he can get away with it he will. There's food in the kitchen that I want to eat. I don't want *that* going on until I leave."

"I think Kass will make him wait until they have a little privacy, considering that Lizzie's going to be with Violet and Leila tonight." Anna rolled her eyes. "I know I'm going to enjoy having some alone time tonight."

Slam!

Vinnie had reached past her and flattened his hand on the folding closet door, shutting them inside. There was a sliver of light at the bottom of the door, but otherwise, they were in total darkness.

Anna opened her mouth to ask what he was doing, but he reversed their positions in the completely empty closet and pinned her to the wall. She'd worn flats and he was in boots, which gave him more height on her than normal.

"Anna, dear Anna." His voice lowered as he whispered in her ear. "Whatever do you need alone time for?"

"Vinnie."

He grabbed her arms and pinned them over her head as his mouth found hers, all tongues and teeth, she desperately tried to keep herself quiet as their exploration continued in heated urgency. After leaving her breathless, he kissed her cheek, and the click of his glasses and shift of fabric indicated that he'd pocketed his glasses. That phrase 'it wasn't a fight until someone lost their glasses' was different between them. Vinnie pocketed his glasses whenever he was getting more serious about any situation – including his exploration of her.

The past month had been filled with quiet, urgent, and somehow tempered exploration. But they hadn't slept together. It was as if he needed to know everything about how she'd react before he'd move on to the next step. She wanted him in her apartment. She wanted him all to herself, and she wanted him to fucking let go with her.

His mouth left a featherlight trail up her neck, soft as a whisper, without a mark in his wake. "Sweet Anna, that wasn't an answer." The vibration of his voice in her ear made her yelp, but he captured the sound by kissing her again.

Outside of the closet, Lizzie was chattering about going to town with Violet and Rex, and they both froze. Vinnie pressed his forehead to hers until the front door slammed closed. Anna's arms started to burn, and she turned her wrists trying to indicate that she needed to move. But Vinnie didn't release her arms. Instead, he kissed the other side of her neck.

"Anna, why do you need alone time?" His tongue flicked against her ear, and she couldn't stop her groan of frustration.

She couldn't move her arms, but she could move her legs. She snaked her leg around his waist pulling them flush. She turned her head and purred, "I want to get myself off imagining it's you."

Vinnie growled and found her mouth again as he released her arms. He hoisted her onto his hips with one arm, the other hand tangling in her hair.

Growling was new and very good. Anna wrapped her legs fully around him. He could hold her while doing this. Oh, he was going to be so, so good at this.

"I just saw them." Kass was outside the closet, and as someone pulled to open the door, Anna kicked it closed.

"What the fuck, man!?! Knock it off. I'm gonna be the first one that has sex in my own fucking house!"

"MATHEW!"

"Naw. You two have two damn minutes to get out of my fucking closet. How long have you been in there? Vinnie only needs three minutes. Ouch! Shit, Kass don't pinch me with your nails."

"We'll see you two on the back porch in a minute," Kass called out, no doubt dragging Mat away by the arm.

Anna's face was undoubtedly red as they awkwardly disentangled, but she pulled Vinnie down for one more kiss. "My apartment will have none of these interruptions. None. We will be alone."

He reached behind himself and opened the closet door. They both blinked, letting their eyes adjust. He pulled his glasses out of his shirt pocket and cleaned them on his shirt before returning them to his face.

"Your hair is a mess." She smirked and ruffled it to make it look more presentable.

"I think I did more damage." He returned the favor, taking his time to make sure her hair was laying in a manner he liked.

They shared a sweeter kiss and as they exited the closet, the front door swung back up and Violet was standing there.

"Is the second girlfriend that you've had come out of the closet?" Violet grinned.

Anna wasn't sure how Vinnie would react to that, but he simply put himself between her and Violet. "This one's mine, back off." His words were sharp but his tone was teasing.

"That was a short trip," Anna commented. They hadn't been in there that long had they?

Violet pulled a set of keys off the hook by the door. "Need to move Kass' car so we can get out. I woulda grabbed them sooner, but I heard a thud in the closet. I know he thinks closets are romantic spaces."

"Just go." Vinnie pointed to the door, and Violet left laughing. He crowded back into Anna's space. "Yes, that part was true. I locked Violet and Leila in a closet so they'd confess their feelings."

Chapter 12: Payoff Your Tension

The Moment They've Waited For, But…

December 2nd; 7 Days Until…

Vinnie sighed in frustration as he attempted to fasten his cufflinks. This was a simple task, and he was a man capable of simple tasks like fastening his cufflinks. He missed the buttonhole for the third time, and the metal adornment slipped out of his fingers. A metallic tink sounded as and it hit the floor.

"Are you fucking kidding me right now!?! Fucking shit!"

Mat laughed as he appeared in the doorway and retrieved the cufflink from the floor. "Calm down now. Come 'ere." He motioned for Vinnie to step closer.

Vinnie wordlessly held out his right arm and let Mat affix the wayward cuff. "Thank you." His eyes never left the floor.

"Stop it. You just need the one done?"

Vinnie held up his opposite wrist, turning it to show the other one already affixed.

"'K. Where's your good watch?" He picked up the item from where Vinnie had left it on the counter. Mat made sure the clasp was locked and took a step back to examine him further. "Red tie huh? We're gonna look like Christmas elves side by side."

Mat's tie was emerald green, Kass' favorite color and no doubt the color she'd picked for this evening's semi-formal event.

"Well one of us looks like a Christmas elf, and one of us is normal height."

"Fuck off."

"I leave for two minutes to check on Rex, and you two are already squabbling. Knock it off." Kass leaned, in the doorway admonishing them. "You both look great. I like the matching suits."

"It was his idea." They replied, nearly in sync.

Kass rolled her eyes before walking away. Technically, she was right. They did nearly match, both in charcoal gray suits with black button-up shirts. The only major difference was Mat's green tie to match Kass' tea-length, vintage inspired cocktail dress and his garnet-red tie to match whatever Anna was wearing. She'd taken his tie with her when she picked out her dress to make sure they matched.

"Let's get hustling, you two, before someone decides to steal the limo Anna sent over," Rex called out, unseen.

Vinnie took another deep breath and stared at his own reflection in the mirror. He looked good tonight. He looked the part of a successful writer.

After looking at the initial sales this morning, he was extremely grateful that Anna had an accounting team to keep track of it. The number had been overwhelming.

"You got this," Mat assured him. "Seriously. You did the work, and you're getting recognized."

"Yeah, I just had to plagiarize what I saw." He straightened his jacket, but Mat smacked the back of his shoulder. "The hell?"

"Stop selling yourself fucking short. You did good. And you're good enough for Anna. I know you've been in a mind spiral, thinking she's out of your league, but she sees you. Hold your fucking head up. Come on." Mat motioned for him to follow.

"OOOO! Uncle Veenee, yous and Daddy looks like cha'mings p'ince." Lizzie waved excitedly, already in her pajamas on the couch. Becki was here watching her for the evening, and her son, Tobi, was already fast asleep on the recliner.

"Thanks, Nugget." He picked her up for a hug. "You be good for Aunt Becki, okay?"

"Momma 'n' Daddy al'eady tells me." She gave him a kiss on the cheek. "Is okay, 'cause I says so!"

"Only because you say so."

He handed Lizzie to Mat and walked outside to get some air. Rex was already on the porch in a black, tailored suit. "That one's new."

"Your girl is very insistent about things being a certain way," Rex gruffed, but rolled his shoulders back proudly. "Jane says she's proud of ya. Knows things are gonna go well tonight."

"It's just a party. Just a celebration."

"Got that advice on repeat, huh?" Rex snickered.

Vinnie hated that Rex was right. Anna had repeated that phrase over and over yesterday, trying to get him to relax about being the center of attention at tonight's events. "Yeah, yeah. I think Christmas is gonna be the most stressful thing left this month."

"You're not worried about the big TV interview next week?"

"I'm less worried about that than I am about Mat and Jane being under the same roof for an extended amount of time over the holiday as they try to deal with each other."

Rex shook his head, "It's almost like one of them inherited an extremely stubborn nature from the other."

"Funny how that works. That old generational warning of 'hope you get one just like you' applies with those two." Vinnie rolled his eyes.

"Suppose it does," Rex patted him on the shoulder. "I'm proud of you, Vinnie. I really am. Ya did good, kid." He might have more but the door opened as Kass and Mat came out onto the porch.

"Don't move, Becki's gonna get a picture of us." Kass spun on her heel, motioning for them to turn towards the open door.

Becki, who had Lizzie on her hip, was holding Kass' phone while Lizzie held hers. "Say cheese!"

"CHEEZZZEEEE!" Lizzie squealed, waving her hands at them.

Becki took a few pictures with both phones, before handing Kass her phone back. "Vinnie, Leila said they are closing the club at eleven tonight, and she expects to see you all there for the afterparty."

"This really isn't as big of a deal as y'all are making it." Vinnie rubbed the back of his neck. Who made this kind of a fuss over a book? His family extended family, that's who.

"It's a big *freaking* deal." Mat caught himself from swearing as he corrected Vinnie.

They waved goodbye to Lizzie and Becki, and the driver opened the door to the limo, where Anna was already waiting for them.

"Well look at that, this car comes with a lady in a red dress." Rex chuckled, pushing Vinnie to go in first so he'd end up beside Anna on the rounded bench seat. Mat, Kass, and Rex entered after, getting situated as the doors were closed behind them.

It was more than a red dress. It had a similar off-shoulder cut to Kass' dress, but it was a floor-length, garnet-red gown, the fabric seemingly infused with glitter which sparkled under the overhead lights. Her hair had been curled and pinned back, revealing the elegant butterfly cuff earring adorning her right ear.

She offered Vinnie her hand and as he took it, she smiled at him. "Oh, hello."

"Hi," He managed, swallowing hard, to keep his composure.

"Help yourselves to some champaign. The cork is just resting there. I didn't want to take any chances." She motioned to the bottle in the ice bucket and the glasses on the counter.

"I got it." Mat pulled the bottle out of the ice and started pouring, giving the first glass to Vinnie, then handing them out to everyone else. "You wanna make a speech? Man of the hour and all that."

Vinnie needed to learn the phrase 'not really' in other languages. Maybe if he said it in not-English his brother would get the hint and stop putting him on the spot. But this was a big moment for him, he should say something.

Statistically, speeches were made by the person being honored or by someone close to the person. He looked around at his family, sitting in the limo with him. Other than Lizzie, the people he was closest to at the moment were the most important people in his life.

Rex who raised him, Mat who survived hell with him, Kass who brought encouragement into their lives with Lizzie in tow, and Anna who he loved... *Loved?*

Vinnie whipped his head around to look at Anna, who had her head cocked to one side, no doubt trying to figure out what he was thinking. Anna, who'd taken a chance on him, kept him focused, and pushed him. Anna, who hadn't hurt him, even when she was angry and had been patient as he figured out how to get closer to her. She didn't push him to get more physical than he was comfortable with and didn't mock him for being 'not like other guys.'

At no point did Anna treat him like he was broken or not normal, whatever the fuck normal was. Anna, who kissed him like he was the only one on her mind – without trepidation but also without pressure. She was always ready with a cup of coffee, an ear to listen to whatever was racing in his head, and she didn't mind his rambling. He loved her.

She slipped her free hand into his.

"Do you want me to say something?" she offered, cutting his potential mental spiral short.

"No, I can." He kissed her cheek. "Thank you for all of this."

"You're welcome."

Vinnie straightened his shoulders and looked at his family again. "Thank you all for everything. For supporting me, and for not actually breaking my jaw or my fingers Mat. I wish I had more words, but I guess I put them all down on paper already. Thank you. Just thank you."

"Cheers!" Mat's voice overpowered the rest as they clinked glasses and all took a sip. "To Vinnie, the published and successful author!"

"To Vinnie!"

Anna touched his shoulder and leaned closer to him, kissing his cheek. "I'm so proud of you. I hope you have a good time tonight."

"Just stay close and it'll be perfect."

Now, he just had to figure out how to tell her that he loved her without freaking her out. Maybe she felt the same way? Maybe?

Was it possible that he could have a happy ending? If he was writing his own story, he was in charge of the ending. The past was the past, and he wasn't going to let it interfere with his future.

December 9th; 0 Days Until…

Vinnie held the door for Anna as they entered her apartment after a day that should have ended hours earlier. They both kicked off their shoes, and he helped her get out of her coat so he could hang it up.

Anna picked up a yowling Jackal, cuddling the cat to her chest. "Are you going back home tonight?"

"At 12:45 in the morning, I probably should." He stopped short of what he wanted to say. He wanted to ask to stay. After a week of wrapping his head around what was about to be his new career and a round of radio/podcast interviews, he was finally alone with Anna for more than an hour or two. And he needed more than an hour or two. There was nothing on their schedules until his interview tomorrow evening, as Anna had her office closed for construction.

Vinnie finally had her all to himself. He'd waited long enough for this, he loved her and he wanted her. He finally had someone where those things ran parallel. He cared about her and was attracted to her, but he was a little unnerved about putting those thoughts into words and actions. The amount of erotica he'd consumed in the last week at breakneck speed was laughable.

Anna stepped into her tiny kitchen to set out a bowl for Jackal and opened her fridge door to get a bottle of water for herself. "Coffee, tea, or water?"

"Maybe whiskey?" His brain was spinning. He could handle this. He'd gotten in her space before. She wasn't shy about encouraging him or telling him no if she wasn't in the mood. He didn't need to worry about mixed signals.

"Sure. But it's kind of late." She had her back to him as ice cubes rattled into twin tumblers.

He cleared his throat. "I was thinking, I could stay, if that's alright with you." Vinnie wasn't a virgin, or a prude. Please see his resume working at a fucking strip club. But he wasn't as sure of himself as to know what to say. Not exactly sexually alluring to ask point-blank.

Anna glanced at him over her shoulder and gave him a sly smile before pouring their drinks. "I'd love that." She handed him one glass and held onto the other, clinking them together.

Her eyes never left his as she took a slow sip from her drink. He downed the contents of his in one gulp.

She took his glass back and set them on the counter, leaning against it, and gazing up at him. "You would pick the one day when I'm wearing plain things under my clothes. I've been waiting, you know. Any other day, you would have something prettier to unwrap."

Vinnie chuckled and crowded into her space, cradling her face in both hands. "I assure you, I am both disinterested in your undergarments, however plain, and very interested in what is beneath them. And while I am so appreciative of your patience with me, my apologies for making you wait. Tonight, let me make amends for any frustrations you've suffered."

Their first kiss was drawn out, slow and deliberate as her arms wrapped around his neck to pull him closer, which he certainly didn't fight. The minutes ticked by and Jackal's nails clicked across the tile floor as she made herself scarce. He tasted the whiskey and spice that he'd learned was pure Anna, and he couldn't get enough of it. The soft moan she graced him with only made him greedy for more.

Her hands were quick, sliding down from his shoulders and working to unbutton his dress shirt. He was glad for his lack of tie, as it wasn't in the way, but regretted not having it as the idea of her being at his mercy gave him a rush of ideas. He nipped at her neck, careful not to leave a mark, but he couldn't help himself from exploring further as she exposed her throat to him. She untucked both of his shirts and her cool, soft hands made him shiver without permission.

"Sorry. Always cold," She chuckled breathlessly as she pushed up at his shirts to get them out of her way. He took a sharp breath as he froze. Her hands were still under his clothes, but she paused, waiting for him to explain his reaction. "What is it? Talk to me."

His lips found her again, but his hands had dropped to his sides. One of her hands remained still, while the other rubbed his back, silently encouraging him to communicate.

"Stop or pause?" She questioned as he pressed his forehead to hers.

"Pause." He breathed in slowly and explained, "You have freckles that dance across your back. I have marks that aren't as whimsical."

She cupped his face with her hands. "I promise that they will not make me want you less. You walked a long road before we met, and those marks mean you survived." She pulled him down for another kiss, her foot rubbing up and down his calf. "We can go upstairs, and I can make it dark if you want. Or we can take a shower together, and I can show you how much I don't give a shit about those scars while I get on my knees."

Fuck, he wished she had room on her counter for him to put her up on it, but limitation aside, he wanted to get closer. He gripped her hips, lifting her in a swift motion and spun around, crashing them against the wall next to her bathroom. The wall should give him enough leverage to do as he desired.

She wrapped her legs around his waist, a desperate sound escaping her as he kneaded her ass with both hands. "Fucking hell." She tried to move – create more friction, but he held her still. The near growl from her as she attempted to to move again only gave him more confidence in his decision. Her breath puffed against his flesh. "Please."

"Please what?" He knew what she wanted, but was desperate to hear her say it. "Anna, please what?"

"Let me move or get me off." Her teeth were clenched and she shifted against him again.

He knew she could balance herself between his body and the wall, so he let go of her ass. His hands made quick work of the single button on her skirt and instead of moving his hands down, he slid them up her ribcage and over her head to divest her of her top in one bold move. It left her in the flesh colored plain bra and a startled expression. Her nails dug into his shoulders as he explored her exposed skin with his tongue.

He listened for changes in her breathing as he moved, waiting to hear the hitch before she whined. If he could live in the sound of her desperation, he would. His left hand palmed the outside of her thigh, her silken, soft skin covered in gooseflesh.

She tangled her fingers in his hair, tugging at it, not enough to hurt, just enough to be insistent. "Kiss me."

"No." He had other plans. Kissing her might distract him. He ignored her frustrated complaint and gripped her thigh, forcing her legs far enough apart to get her where he wanted her. The angle was awkward, but he got his right hand between them. Without giving her time to realize what he was doing, he moved her panties to the side with his thumb and thrust two fingers into her already wet opening.

A shiver ran through her body, and he molded himself to her as close as he could without restricting his own movements. He had a fervent need to feel her reactions. To know he was pleasing her. He dragged his fingers in and out of her, finding a rhythm as he held her still by her hip. A choked plea for him to bury himself inside of her and grant them both release further inflamed his motivation for restraint.

"No," he ordered. "Be still. I want to experience every moment of me getting you off. Your hands have been busy while you've been thinking of me. Now I'm going to show you how inferior that was."

Her blue eyes were wide but full of fire, and she gave him a slight nod. "Prove it."

If he hadn't been so single-minded in his task, he might have changed tactics. Fuck, he wanted her, but not yet. He needed this. He needed to watch, hear, learn, and experience her without his own release getting in the way. He mouthed her collarbone, grazing his teeth over her pulse point. The elevated thumping against his lips only increased as he flexed his fingers deeper inside her.

The little room she had to move, she used, rolling her back against the wall and trying to match his pace. A string of obscenities fell from her lips as he added a third finger but slowed his speed to a languorous pace, his thumb tracing a path over her clit. She flexed her hips, moving her legs wider apart, and he was confident he didn't need to hold them open.

"Arms over your head," he demanded. She complied, breathing heavier, chest heaving for air. Gripping both of her wrists with one hand, he trailed his tongue over the shell of her ear, fingers never increasing their speed. "That's a good girl. I want to hear you scream. I want to feel you dripping. When I get you off with my hand, that's only the beginning. I'm fucking famished and you will be the sweetest thing that's ever been on my tongue."

Her whine, that delicious whine, nearly buckled his knees as it escaped her. He increased his speed, driving his fingers deeper. Her tremor started where his fingers were buried in her, but it enveloped her whole frame, hips, arms, and heartbeat as she screeched his name. Her volume didn't disguise the wet sounds of her release, his fingers sinking deeper as she opened more fully, riding out her pleasure.

"One," Vinnie angled his neck to catch her in a brutal kiss, tongues battling for control until he mercilessly curled his fingers inside of her. Her mouth fell agape as his movements increased in speed, beckoning her to come for him again.

He grunted, unable to keep himself quiet as he tested her limits. Her cunt started to pulse but he slowed down, chuckling as he tormented her.

"Vinnie," she whimpered, trying to stimulate herself, chest against his chest.

"No, no. Feet on the floor, I want to worship you and earn my meal." He removed his fingers completely and her hips rocked forward, trying to follow.

Her legs were trembling as she unhooked them from his waist and stood on the ground. His eyes never left Anna's as he sucked off his fingers. Her tongue darted out to her lips, and he captured her in another wild kiss as he rolled up her skirt.

Fully clothed, he knelt in front of her, trailing his index fingers up her legs and hooking her underwear and dragging them down as he kissed her thighs. He looked up, wanting an image of her to keep before he took off his glasses. Flushed face, mussed hair, bra on but one strap hanging down, skirt scrunched up, and her absolutely wanting him to continue. He put his glasses in his shirt pocket, took it off and rolled it over itself before tossing it towards the door. He didn't want to break his glasses.

Her nails drug against his scalp, her manicure just pointed enough to make it dangerous. He continued to kiss her long legs, whispering filthy poetry into her pale skin.

Let him die drinking from her. He'd surrender to his fate. The first touch of his tongue on her clit made her curse in more than one language. Vinnie kneaded her flesh, enticing her down and over him as his tongue coaxed more from her. He wanted her in ecstasy, lapping then sucking, denying her the gratification, never keeping a rhythm long enough for her to tip over the edge.

"Fuck, Vinnie. I'm gonna be ruined for anyone else." The breathless confession made him hard enough that pure determination was all that kept him dragging her down and burying himself inside of her.

"Good." He slipped two-fingers back inside of her, turning his wrist and giving her more friction as he resumed tormenting her with just the tip of his tongue.

"So goddamn good. Jesus, I thought I'd have to teach you. Fuck, was I wrong. Please, don't stop. I'm so close." She rocked against his tongue and fingers, chasing her pleasure and using him for what she wanted.

Oh, and he'd let her use him. She started to shake again, but he withdrew his fingers. The guttural sound of disappointment was replaced with one of ecstasy as he molded his mouth to her flesh, devouring her as he promised he would, like a man starved for a meal that he'd waited an eternity for. Now he could have his fill.

Her whole body quivered as she ascended to her release, but other than panting to catch her stolen breath, she uttered not a sound.

"Two." He wiped his mouth on his forearm as he stood up to be close to her.

He nuzzled against her neck, content to bask in her satisfaction. The idea that he could undo her like this elated him in a way couldn't explain. It likely had something to do with how often men strove to know their partners wanted only them in the most carnal of ways. A throw-back to the more primitive…

"Get out of your head."

Anna pulled him down for a kiss. "Shower or bed? Not done with you yet. I haven't even gotten started with you. You've got too many clothes on."

"A shower sounds like fun, but condoms and showers sound like a disaster." He placed kisses across her shoulders, keeping her close.

"Well, I'm clean. Haven't been with anyone in almost a year, and I have an IUD. So if you're comfortable with it, I think we can live a little dangerously." She palmed the front of his pants before using her index and middle fingers to frame his dick as they moved up and down.

Vinnie bit down on the inside of his cheek to get some of his blood back into his brain.

"I want you." Anna purred, still stroking him, "how do I get to have you?" .

"Bed. I…" He lost his place for a moment, confidence gone. He'd just had her mewling for mercy and praising his name, but he'd plotted that part of this encounter and now there was uncertainty. If he couldn't control everything and if he…

Anna pushed her hands under his undershirt, fingers light over his skin. "You aren't going to disappoint me. I'll get your glasses so you don't trip up the stairs."

She bumped by him and retrieved his shirt, slipping his glasses back on for him. She smiled and took his hand. "Come on, remember my skylight? Think of how beautiful you're gonna look naked under the moonlight."

"Beautiful is not an adjective that I'd apply to myself." He shifted on his feet.

Anna used her free hand to unhook her bra and toss it across her apartment, then shimmied out of her skirt. "I would. Come 'ere."

Naked except for her watch, she was the picture of confidence, beckoning him to her again. Saying no to her in such an unguarded state wasn't going to happen. He embraced her, resting in her touch despite the state of his arousal, sharing slow and deliberate kisses.

"Go upstairs. I'll join you in just a minute."

Vinnie kissed her knuckles and headed up the stairs, slightly confused as to what Anna was doing until he heard her call for Jackal.

"Here, sweet girl. You're gonna hang out in the bathroom."

The shades that covered the apartment's massive windows had already lowered on their timer, and the city skyline was no more than a hint of an outline. He'd seen Anna's bedroom from the living room, as you could look straight up into it from the chaise, but he'd never been up here. The lights turned on automatically as he stepped up the stairs, but dimmed almost immediately.

The room, however, remained illuminated by the skylight over Anna's bed. Awkward as he felt being up there alone, he sat down on the bed and craned his neck to see the moon glowing brightly through the clear skylight. Footfalls, nearly undetectable, drew his attention back to the stairs and Anna, still naked, hung a black robe on the hook by the stairs.

"Beautiful in the moonlight," she confirmed and sat on his lap, sliding his glasses off and setting them on the nightstand by the bed. As if she hadn't been putty in his hands a few minutes ago, here she was – as cool and collected as ever.

Hands in his hair, and her mouth on his, he let her lead them in a languid kiss. His hands wandered up Anna's smooth back, enjoying the shiver he felt in response.

"Don't distract me now," she admonished, as she caught his face again.

This close, he could see her siren song eyes, like water teasing a sailor to come in and drown. Far apart from the frenzy downstairs, Anna's motions were restrained and delicate as she motioned for him to put his arms up so she could remove his shirt. He allowed her to continue but closed his eyes.

Anna leaned in close. "I will not ask. And I will not speculate about any marks I see. Your body is a wonder for its survival, nothing to be ashamed of, ever."

Those soothing words made him feel more exposed than losing clothes ever could. He took her left hand and moved it to one of the scars on his chest, and she inclined her head, placing a kiss there.

Anna had the hands of an experienced lover. Bold and patient. There was no fearfulness or shyness in her touch. "Can I do for you what you did for me?"

It never occurred to him that she'd ask permission before proceeding. Obviously, a person could withdraw consent at any point during an encounter, and that was paramount to respect. He hadn't been given a chance to say one way or the other last time. There wasn't regret in what he'd done with Leila, but he hadn't been entirely in control of the situation.

Anna shifted her hips to get his attention. "Come on back, love."

"I am concerned that if you do I..." He ground his teeth together, not wanting to admit his worry about the situation.

She put her finger to his lips. "If you finish quickly, I don't care. I promise it's nothing to be embarrassed about. This isn't going to be the only time we do this. We're going to learn about each other, what we like and what we don't. So can I do for you what you did for me? Or would you like something else?"

Vinnie surged forward and kissed her, attempting to show her physically how meaningful her words were to him.

He flipped their positions and put her on her back. The moonlight reflected off her skin and her blonde hair looked starlight kissed.

"Something else then." She smiled at him, wicked as the first recorded sin.

He kissed the column of her neck, one hand palming her breast while the other traced circles on her hip. A gasp from Anna assured him that he was on the right track again. He swirled his tongue at the dip of her collarbone and made a path to her chest, catching her taut nipple in his mouth. He'd never considered himself especially religious, but here in her bed, he was devout, praising any god listening as he suckled her.

Anna inhaled sharply as he switched his mouth to her other breast, and his hand drew a line from her hip to her still wet-pussy. He was fucking intoxicated by her, shamelessly lifting her hips to meet his fingers, her smoldering eyes fixed on him.

He mapped her luxurious skin until he nipped at her hip bone.

"You're going to kill me."

Maneuvering himself partially off the bed, he seized her ass, hauling her to his waiting mouth. He flattened his tongue over her slit and she moaned pressing herself closer and clutching the comforter beneath her. Continuing his ministrations, he kept testing patterns and rhythms until she started to shiver, and her pulse jumped. He pulled away before she came.

The sound that came out of Anna was between a hiss and groan, and her hand moved to her own body, but he intercepted her. He gripped her hand and swept her upright, putting her hands on his belt. She murmured words of encouragement as she undid the button and zipper, helping him rid himself of his remaining clothes.

Her hands were quick, encircling his cock and stroking him with a firm pressure that made him bend at the waist. He was lightheaded, he needed to breathe.

"I want to ride you. Please let me, Vinnie. I want to get myself off riding you."

He wasn't in a position to make any decisions, let alone discuss the semantics of positions. She had him so painfully erect that he simply nodded, not trusting his voice. Anna tugged, his hand forcing him back down on the bed while reaching into the nightstand and pulling something out of the drawer. After straddling him, she rocked side to side, teasing him with her damp curls as she stroked him with her free hand.

She placed a small vibrator in his open hand. He'd seen enough of them that he recognized the shape. "If you're worried about me not having a good time, you can use that. But you aren't going to need it, I'm already so close. You make me feel so good. I want to cum on you and I want to feel you cum in me. Still good?"

"Yes."

"Good boy."

Dear fucking god, his dick twitched at just those words as she impaled herself on him. She felt like hot velvet around him, and he tried to think about anything to get himself under control, but it was useless. There was only her. A wicked goddess, masquerading as a woman in succulent, heated flesh. Ravenous and unbound, hunting for pleasure wherever she could find it. Any exaltation would be meaningless by comparison. He felt drugged. Addicted after only one hit.

She grasped his empty hand and clamped it on her hip. Primal energy flooded his system, and he thrust into her without restraint, rocking to meet her rhythm. He tightened his grip, pulling her forward and back to increase the pace. She rolled her hips and teased her own tits as she rode him without mercy.

This was a raw connection, heady and slick as they crashed against each other. His heartbeat thudded in his eardrums as he moaned, wordlessly surrendering to the searing wet heat he was buried in. Stroke for stroke they matched intensities, chasing that bliss and not giving a fuck about the world outside.

Anna braced her hand on his chest, nails scratching a path of exquisite torture. She flexed around him, her walls clenching down and sending a spark down his spine. His back arched trying to claim her further without putting her beneath him. He wanted her over him, toying and torturing herself with his cock.

"Jesus Christ, Anna." His voice was hoarse, too overwhelmed to praise her the way he wanted to. Breathtaking and primal, he wanted more. More of her, more of this. "Fuck, I can't…"

The pulsing of her cunt was too much, he growled and rammed into her despite being beneath her. Instead of fighting him, Anna molded her body to his grinding against him and burying him deeper. His vision got spotty, his whole-body convulsing as he spilled inside of her without warning. He gulped for air afterward, vaguely aware of two things. Anna was still on top of him, and she was still shaking.

"Three." She nuzzled his neck, planting soft kisses and caressing his chest.

He attempted to catch his breath, blood still pounding in his veins. *Oh shit. Fuck, that was incredible. Had she gotten off?* Time was an illusion in moments like these and he couldn't see the clock to know if he'd drawn it out enough for her to be satisfied.

"Still good?" Anna's soft voice pulled him back to her.

Vinnie turned on his side. Her brilliant eyes inquisitive, as he hadn't formed any words to respond to her question.

He pushed himself up on his elbow while pressing his thumb to the toy in his hand to activate it. The vibration was a low hum in the quiet room. Anna opened her mouth, but he pressed it against her clit and all that came out was a strangled sound.

He grazed the toy over her delicate flesh, mouth claiming her as he stimulated her with a whisper of pressure. She was drenched, body twisting as if trying to escape the torture, but no, that wouldn't do.

"I…I…Please…I…" Anna was begging as he continued touching her.

"Let me watch you come undone." He brushed his nose against her cheek. "The next time you use this, I want you to think of my voice. My hands. Of me. I want you to cum for me. You are so fucking beautiful like this."

Her body quivered a full head-to-toe shudder as her mouth opened, but no sound escaped as she rode out her orgasm. One futile attempt to close her legs, which he denied her, and she let out a small whimper as he pulled the toy away.

He let his hand roam over her body as her breathing evened out. "Three."

"Four," she corrected, with a breathless chuckle.

Vinnie gathered Anna in his arms, nuzzling her sweat-dampened hair. *Fuck she smelled so good.* He entwined their legs and sighed. "If I interrupted your counting abilities, I will put a feather in my cap."

She turned in his arms so they were nose to nose. She pressed a kiss so chaste to his lips, it was criminal given their state of undress and recent activities. "You think I didn't get off riding you? I think I get the feather for being such a good lay. You didn't notice when I came around you."

He started to laugh, but stopped himself. He didn't want her to think he was laughing at her.

"You are amazing. I mean, you're amazing without the sex, but this moves you up a tier."

Vinnie couldn't keep from laughing at her assessment. He wanted this. Wanted to stay here with her. This could be his life. Anna could be his future. His forever. He couldn't say anything like that right. He didn't trust himself to find the right words, better to run with the joke Anna made. "I'm up a tier? Wait, more importantly, you have a tier system? I'm competitive, I'm going to need to know where I rank overall."

A giggle and smart-ass answer was what he expected, but Anna's face got serious. Her fingers brushed over his temples and tangled in his hair. Her breathing got uneven, not in a good way.

"Anna, are you alright? I'm sorry, I didn't mean too…"

"Shhh." She shushed him, putting his hand on her cheek. "I think you are in a tier all your own. I have other things to say, but I don't have the words yet. Just know that you are…You are what I need in my life. Let me keep you for a while, okay? Don't run off."

Her eyes had misted over, and he pressed his forehead to hers, offering her a promise. "I would never. Nothing could make me run from you."

Sleep was needed. Breakfast in the morning. The interview tomorrow and after that…He stopped himself from telling her that he loved her. He didn't want her to misinterpret his sincerity for pillow talk. Vinnie was going to get through the interview, steal Anna away for dinner, and tell her that he loved her.

The blonde wiggled in his arms, insisting that she clean up and let her cat out of the bathroom. She was all he wanted. Vinnie let her get up from the bed and put on his glasses, so he could watch her pull on her robe.

Anna grinned at him, "What?"

"Anna, I think this is the happiest I've ever been. Kinda waitin' for the other shoe to fall."

"There's nothing to worry about. We're both happy and whatever comes next we'll handle it together." With a quick kiss on his forehead, she disappeared down the stairs.

Whatever came next, they would handle it together. After his mother reappeared from the dead, he couldn't think of anything else that could be so cataclysmic.

December 9th

"Does this look alright? I feel like it's too much." Vinnie fussed with his tie.

He'd never been uncomfortable with wearing suits, but this one felt constrictive. Of course, it might be due to the 'whys' associated with its donning rather than the donning of the suit itself.

Anna moved over to him, her heels clacking against the tile floor. "You look great." She inclined her head to the side, straightening his tie as she smiled. "I think these are good colors together."

"Considering your mismatching lavender jacket and baby-blue pants, that's not reassuring."

She looked down at her own outfit. "What? I hung up the set together so I wouldn't -" She stopped as he started snickering and bopped his chest with the back of her hand. "You aren't funny."

"I beg to differ. You find me quite humorous most of the time." Focusing on Anna was easier than thinking about the impending interview. She kept him grounded and calm. He was anything but those things right now. He tried to replay what they'd rehearsed, but it kept being interrupted by images of last night in her bed. *No, no. He could not think about that right now.*

"She only laughs 'cause she thinks you're hot." Alysha breezed in with three coffees, keeping one of the iced options for herself and offering them the other two.

"What are you doing here?" Anna was clearly shocked to see her former assistant.

"I heard Bailey quit, and I figured you could use another pair of hands handling Mr. A-hole Walthers given everything. Take the coffee and thank me for bringing my magic back into your life today." Alysha smirked as they both took a cup.

"I am always grateful for your magic. Thank you for this." Anna took the other iced one and handed him the hot one. "I think you should have gotten him a tea though."

"Are you nervous? Why?" Alysha swept her hair behind her shoulder.

Vinnie sipped from his coffee and grimaced as it burned his tongue. "I've never fared well with public speaking."

"You talk all the time," Alysha argued.

"Not with cameras on me."

"What does that matter?"

"Because anything new can be intimidating." Anna interrupted the impending verbal spat and checked her phone. "We've got about ten miuntes until we need to be on set. Why don't you sit down and try to relax?"

"Did you know that sitting is considered the new smoking in office culture?" Vinnie flexed his foot; even his shoes felt tight. "In fact, the 25% of Americans that sit more than eight hours a day have a 147% increased risk of heart attack or stroke in comparison to the 56% of people that make a point to be active."

Alysha arched her eyebrow. "So, you don't want to sit?"

"No, I want a cigarette." He set his coffee down on the coffee table and began pacing.

"Alysha, could you please go make sure they are running on time on set for me?" Anna requested.

"On it. Calm down, Vinnie. Nobody watches the Friday night slot anyway." She walked out of the green room, coffee in hand.

Anna fell in line with Vinnie's pacing and slipped her hand into his, bringing him to stop. "Take a deep breath. I have prepared you with every question that I can ever remember being brought up in one of his interviews."

"But what if..." He bit the inside of his cheek. Anna knew all about his past, but it could still be sensationalized. What if this guy brought up that he'd gone to prison? What if it derailed the entire interview?

As if reading his mind, Anna attempted to reassure him. "Preston knows the prison stuff is off the table. I've warned him personally, and I know his boss."

"You do plan for everything."

She smirked, "That is what you pay me for."

He gripped her hand more tightly. "It's more than that and you know it."

"You're going to be fine. I promise. Sit down with me."

They both sat on the couch and he took a long, cleansing breath. *Anna was right, everything was going to be fine.* He couldn't live in fear of his past mistakes forever. But still, something in the air felt off-kilter.

"What if *Preston* does it anyway? The infamous Preston Walthers does get ad revenue from shock value."

"You say, 'I don't know what that has to do with the book, why do you ask?' and then chuckle with a superior look."

"And how exactly do I look superior?"

Anna arched her eyebrow. "Don't play dumb. It's the look you give Mat when you think he's being an idiot."

He looked at her over his glasses and thought about the last dumb thing his brother had done.

"Perfect." She touched the side of his face. "Just like that. Dismiss whatever sputtering he does after by listing some facts about how many successful people have been arrested or gone to jail."

He closed his eyes and covered her hand with his, relaxing a little. "Thank you."

"It's my job to prepare you for interviews like this."

"No." He sighed heavily, silently begging her to understand. The interview hardly mattered. It was about who she was to him and how she made him feel. The realness of this was so new but somehow felt comfortable and familiar. He'd woken up next to her this morning, certain he loved her. His family liked her, and she liked them. She wanted him. If he didn't achieve anything else, he had her. Anna thought he was worthy of her.

No one had ever been so intimately his, and he'd been never so intimately someone else's.

He fought against his urge to ramble about all the things that he'd been thinking and settled for the conversation they were having at this moment. If he could only learn to turn his brain off. "Thank you for not treating me like I'm less, or like I'm crazy when I start spewing nonsense."

She kissed him softly, taking care not to bump his glasses. "There is nothing *less* about you, and you certainly aren't crazy. You are one of the brightest, most creative, and most caring people I've ever met. You know how important you are to me and I'm pretty damn picky about my partners."

"What if he brings up my mother?" Or worse, what if it led to Mat getting bent out of shape about Jane again if the interviewer brought her up? Christmas wasn't that far away and all he wanted was some kind of peace in his family. He wanted them all to get along, despite the conflicts.

"Is there anything official anywhere about her?"

"I don't think so."

"Then he won't know." Anna's answer was matter-of-fact; she was in work mode again. She powered her phone back on and sipped her coffee through the bright-orange straw. "You'll be fine. I know you can do this."

Vinnie tugged at his sleeves and mentally reviewed the answers they'd gone over at lunch earlier that day. He needed to focus on the characters: what made them likable, relatable, what their driving forces were, and above all—avoid spoilers.

He knew the real story and the fictitious version backwards and forwards. As long as he didn't accidentally call one of the characters the name of the person he'd based them on, he'd be fine. *Fantastic, new fear unlocked.* His phone went off and he flipped it over, seeing the text message from Rex.

Rex: Jane and I are watching at the cabin. You'll be great

He responded and showed the message to Anna. "I suppose I have no choice but to do a good job now."

"Can't argue with Rex." Anna smiled. "I'm glad they're watching. This is important for you."

The door opened and he jumped as Alysha motioned for him to follow her. "They want to touch up your makeup, make sure you don't glow in the dark."

"We both know that's a lost cause." He stood up and Anna reached for his phone. "I think you have a much better phone than me." He smirked but handed it to her anyway.

"Phones and cameras are a recipe for disaster. I'm assuming you'd rather have me hold it than someone on set." She was right. He wouldn't want the risk of anyone else messing with it when he wasn't around.

He squeezed Anna's hand one more time, then followed Alysha out of the green room. He absent-mindedly gripped his car keys in his pocket; he probably should have left those with Anna too.

"Preston's a dick. If he brings Anna up, talk about her as an editor only. They slept together once, and he sniffs after her like a dog all the time." Alysha was at least six inches shorter, but Vinnie had to stretch out his strides to keep up with her pace. "If he thinks you two are dating, he'll wanna measure sticks."

He paused. "She's never mentioned that."

Alysha rolled her eyes. "She never talks about any of her past lovers. Once you're out, you're out. She's not a bed notch marker, but she's not about attachments. You're the longest relationship she's had in five years, and I'm not sure when you two blurred the lines."

"Who said we blurred the lines?"

She barked out a laugh. "Sir, she was giving you fuck-me eyes the whole time we were in the green room. Can't wait to give her hell about it. You'll be fine. Go knock it out the park."

Vincent Goodroe, son of a thief and grifter, ex-criminal, and former co-owner of a strip club stared at his reflection in the mirror as the artist touched up his makeup. Now the title above his head was bestselling author, with a book to be movie-adapted the following year. Did those new titles change who he was? Did they erase what he'd done?

"You know how important you are to me, and I'm pretty damn picky about my partners." Anna's words echoed in his head and he clung onto them. Even if everything crashed and burned, he had her.

Preston Walthers was every part the entitled asshole that Vinnie had expected. A livestream of the interview was on the news station's social media site, a fact that was brought up more than twice. Preston was attempting to make Vinnie unsettled by disclosing the potential size of the audience. It didn't work. They weren't in front of him, so Vinnie could ignore it.

There was no studio audience, only the crew on site and Anna standing by the main camera he was supposed to look at. She would nod and give him hand signals to curb him if his answers got long. They were in the middle of the last commercial break when Preston glanced over at Anna.

"I swear she ages in reverse. Wish she was showing more skin though. She's got a body like milk." The creepy way he spoke when the cameras stopped was unnerving. The TV persona was not who Preston was, but that wasn't a shock.

Vinnie cracked his knuckles but kept his tone even. "I think she looks professional. She's been an amazing editor and advocate to get my book out into the world."

"From experience, I can assure you she's better in bed than she is at anything else."

This was why Alysha told him that Anna had slept with Preston. It was to prep him so this didn't affect the interview. The information had been given so he didn't do anything stupid. Vinnie wasn't stupid.

"Not exactly an appropriate way to speak about a business contact." Vinnie shifted his eyes, the countdown to be back on air had started at thirty seconds.

Preston chuckled. "Give it a month or two and she'll go down easy. She fucks chicks too, so she doesn't exactly have standards."

He was not going to talk about Anna that way. There was a hum in Vinnie's ears, "Don't talk about her that way. Ever. Again," He warned.

The countdown was at ten, and Vinnie wasn't sure if it was Preston's smirk or the reshuffling of his cards that made his blood run cold. Vinnie looked at Anna in her lavender suit, who was motioning for him to smile, which he did.

"And now, it's time for the personal questions. The audience has been flooding them into the chat. Username, *Hannahsmadeofstars*, wants to know if you have someone special in your life." Preston's fake grin was back on for the camera.

Vinnie didn't want to lie, although Anna might want him to, given all the press he might be doing. "I have someone very special in my life. Hoping to keep her in the long-term."

"Oh no, that's hard for the ladies to know I'm sure. Here's another audience question, Username, *Noeditbuttonforlife,* says...now feel free not to answer this one if it's too personal..."

"I'm obviously an open book. I'm a writer."

They both gave the obligatory fake laugh as the laugh track played, stopping as the cameraman gave the signal.

"Well, they wanted to know if it's true that you used to own a strip club?"

Vinnie paused while the gasp effect sounded, but put a smirk on his face. "Guilty as charged. I co-owned The Playhouse for years and still help manage it."

Preston tapped his cards on the desk. Why did this feel like a bull pawing the ground? "So Vincent, speaking of guilty as charged..."

Vinnie braced himself for the prison question. He was going to play it off. Everything would be fine. Anna knew he'd been to prison when he was a young adult. He rolled his shoulders, remembering the answer he'd rehearsed for this.

Preston's expression changed to the falsely solemn one he used when reading about a story about a natural disaster.

Anna knew Vinnie wasn't going to let this dickhead make him less than because he'd done a year in prison for illegal weapons. That had been a bump in the road, not a defining moment.

"I just want to know, how hard was it for you when you killed your father at only ten years old?"

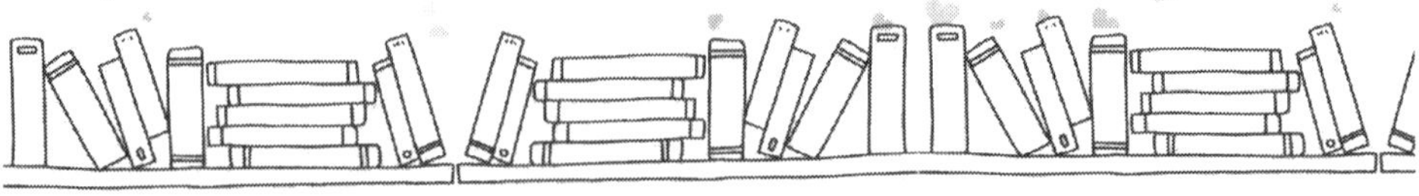

Chapter 13: Conflict Not Easily Solved

The Thing Money Can't Fix

December 9th

"I just want to know, how hard was it for you when you killed your father at only ten years old?"

There absolute horror and pain on Vinnie's face. The camera behind her moved. Someone on the crew was yelling. Alysha said her name. Anna turned her head and Alysha was saying something, but she couldn't hear anything even though the woman's lips were moving. There was pressure compressing her lungs. It was hard to breathe.

Then Anna could hear everything, like the volume had cranked up from one to eleven. She resisted the urge to cover her ears. Everything was so loud. She gasped, drawing in a sharp breath.

"Commercial! Go to commercial!"

Slam. Metal on metal. A door?

Anna looked back for Vinnie, but the chair he'd been sitting in was empty and Preston… Preston was smiling as he talked to his crew.

"You should have held the commercial, and focused on him running. *That* would have been a clip." He sounded disappointed. He was fucking disappointed.

"Anna."

Anna wasn't sure who said her name, but she marched up onto the set, her heels impacting the stage with an echo.

"It's just business, Anna. You know you would have used it to market, if you'd figured…"

He didn't get to finish the sentence. Anna balled her fist and stuck Preston in the face, nearly losing her balance with the momentum. There was a sickening crack from his nose and the blood that gushed from the impact felt wet on her knuckles.

"My nose! You psychotic bitch!" Preston's words were muffled by his hands covering his mouth and nose.

"Anna! Go. Go!" Alysha shoved her forward and pointed in the direction of one of the stage doors. "Vinnie went that way."

Alysha was hot on her heels as they wove through the studio to get to the parking garage, and Anna skidded to a stop. The space Vinnie had parked in was empty. He'd circled the lower level three times to get a spot close to the elevator so she wouldn't have to walk too far in her heels. She pressed her hand to her heart, it was beating so hard – she could feel the pulsing in her eardrums.

Anna didn't hit people. She'd never physically assaulted anyone in her life, and Preston certainly wasn't worth the complications. He wasn't worth it, but he'd hurt Vinnie. Her stomach felt like it had a cannon ball in it. The physical ache of what just happened was catching up to her. This would be so bad, the press would be focused on her hitting Preston and Vinnie's novel would be overshadowed by…*Oh my god, Vinnie!* She swallowed down the scream that threatened to spill out.

"Where do you think he'd go?" Alysha asked.

Anna shook her head, because she didn't know. She wasn't sure where he'd go other than away. "I'm not sure."

"Call him. Vinnie can't be good right now." Alysha trailed off as Anna wordlessly held up Vinnie's phone. " Oh shit. Do you want to try your apartment? It's close, and he has a key. I can drive."

"Sure." She swallowed the lump in her throat and followed Alysha to her car. Vinnie had driven them here.

They reached Alysha's beat-up Honda, and she grabbed the bags that were sitting in the passenger seat, squishing them between two car seats in the back. Anna stared at the carseats. Lizzie loved riding with Vinnie and telling him stories as they drove places.

"Sorry, had my nephews last night to help out my sister. They're so messy."

"It's fine. I appreciate your help." Anna felt so numb. Her ears felt like they were plugged with water.

Anna sat in the passenger seat, and Alysha climbed in and put the key in the ignition. Anna couldn't get her thoughts to still. She couldn't think of next steps. Couldn't figure out what she should be doing next.

"Holy fuck, you punched Preston! You fucking broke his nose!" Alysha pulled out of the garage, describing in detail what felt fuzzy to Anna.

She looked down at her left hand. There was blood on her knuckles, and it stained her pants. "Pull over, please." She clenched her jaw and breathed through her nose.

Alysha pulled over and Anna managed to throw the door open so she could vomit.

"Oh hun. It's gonna be okay." Alysha rubbed her back. "We'll find him. I'm sure he's pacing in your apartment, breaking down facts about cliffhanger interviews and clickbait headlines with Jackal."

Anna coughed a few more times, spitting to get the taste of bile out of her mouth. She took a bottle of mouthwash out of her purse, swished some in her mouth, and spit again. "I'm good. You can keep going."

Alysha pulled up to her building and Anna started to get out.

"Do you want me to come up with you?"

Anna shook her head. "If he's here, it's best if it's just me. I'll text you later."

"Deal. But um…get that hand looked at before too long. You tucked your thumb, it might be broken." Her brown eyes were full of concern. She clearly didn't want to leave.

"It'll be okay, Alysha. Thank you for everything today. I don't know what I would have done without you."

"No sweat. Take care of you too."

"I will."

Anna walked into the building, her heels creating a familiar echo of against the tiled floor as she reached the elevator. *Please be here. Please be here where it's safe for you.* She gripped his phone in her hand. Her left hand was starting to throb. It was fine. Later. She'd handle it later.

She opened her apartment door and was greeted by silence. Jackal was asleep on the chaise by the window, and the dishes from the snack she and Vinnie shared earlier were still in the sink. The air in the apartment was hollow. She didn't need to check upstairs. He wasn't here.

Toeing off her shoes, she went upstairs just to be sure, but only her messy bed greeted her. Vinnie had tried to make the bed in the morning, but she's teased that they were going to mess it up again after the interview and not to bother. A lump formed in her throat as she picked up his discarded shirt from the floor. He hadn't been able to keep his eyes off her when she'd worn it as they ate breakfast.

She should feel more. She should be more upset. She should be angry. She should be crying. The world felt muted, like she was experiencing it through frosted glass.

It wasn't enough. Being here wasn't enough. She was failing him.

She needed to do something, anything, to find him. Where could he have gone? Rex's house? The Playhouse? Mat and Kass' home? The cabin? Some hidden place he'd never mentioned to her? Where would she even begin?

Thumping back down the stairs, her hand started to ache. It hurt all the way to her wrist and her thumb was swelling. She needed medical attention. But she wasn't worried about herself.

What if he was in the parking garage? He'd broken down all the statistics of how much safer the parking structure would be during a hurricane due to its construction. He might feel safe there. Anna put her heels back on and made her way down to where her car was parked. Her car was there, but not Vinnie's. He wasn't here.

She had tried to get him alone almost every day after she'd moved back into her apartment, but she was mindful of his limits. He'd wanted to go slow and was embarrassed about admitting it. She'd assured him that she didn't mind waiting for him to be ready for the physical aspects. As much as she wanted him, she refused to be a regret in the dark when they parted ways. November had been so damn busy, and they'd barely seen each other alone. So many stolen kisses by their cars right here. So much time wasted and now what if…

A car honked, the sound amplified in the concrete structure. Anna jumped, moving out of the way of the BMW and the annoyed man motioning for her to get out of his way.

The logical part of her brain was being drowned out by her paranoid 'what if's.' She went to the security desk and inquired if Vinnie's car had been caught by the cameras. Eric was a fan of Vinnie's car; the two always chatted when they saw each other. He skimmed the footage but didn't see Vinnie or his car. When he asked Anna if everything was alright, she lied and said she was fine.

The elevator ride felt longer than normal. The hallway seemed darker. She unlocked her apartment door, kicked off her shoes, and set her keys down on the counter. All of these things she'd done a thousand times, but they felt lonely now. She was lonely being alone in her own space. What could she do? How could she fix this?

She sat down next to Jackal and pulled her cat up onto her lap. The black feline didn't even stir. Vinnie's phone was lighting up with alerts, incoming calls, and texts. His family didn't know she had his phone. She should call one of them. She should have done that first. Why hadn't she done that first? She should call one of them…Rex. She needed to call Rex. That's who Vinnie would go to.

Scrolling through her contacts, she tapped Rex's number and left it on speakerphone.

"He with you?" No greeting, only Rex's strained voice with the simple question.

Anna cleared her throat, "No. I was hoping he reached out to you somehow."

"His phone's going to voicemail."

"I have his phone. I took it before the interview started." Her jaw twitched. She wasn't going to start crying. Crying wasn't going to solve anything.

"Makes sense. I'm already on the road. Mat and I will start turning over some lesser known rocks of his. You could reach out to Leila. Her and Violet mighta heard from him."

Leila made sense, but it didn't feel like enough. Anna wanted to get ahead of Vinnie, get more people looking for him. "Don't you have a friend who's a Texas Ranger? I think I met him at Mat and Kass' wedding. Maybe he could put out an alert for Vinnie's car?"

"Darlin' I appreciate where your head's at, but it's not a good idea. Like it or not, Vinnie's a criminal first and a person second when it comes to johnny-law. If he's actin' off, then it might end badly."

Anna could hear the click of a turn signal.

"He's probably at my place in Houston. Mat's gonna be out looking for him. Best thing you can do is sit tight. You're a place he'd go to hide. Wouldn't surprise me if he shows up there soon."

"You don't think he'd head to you? At the cabin?"

"Anna, you've gotten closer to Vinnie than anyone I've ever seen other than his brother. But let me assure you right now, there's no way he's in any state for that nine/ten hour drive."

"But…"

"If he is headed that way, then Jane's up there."

Anna bit her cheek. Jane was the last person that Vinnie would want to see. "I can't imagine she's who he'd want to see."

Her phone beeped. Kass was calling her.

"Might be what he needs though. Both of 'em are runners." Rex cleared his throat. "Either way, I'm sure that's not the case. Sure he's on his way to you. You're the best thing he's ever had. Just keep that in mind with what you know now. I'll see you…"

The call disconnected abruptly, Vinnie mentioned the signal wasn't great by Rex's cabin. Anna looked at the incoming call, and she tapped it without really wanting to.

"Anna?" Kass' voice was soft, unsteady.

"Hi Kass. Are you alright?" That felt ridiculous to ask. Of course she wasn't alright. None of them were. Was Mat freaking out? Was that why she was whispering?

"As alright as I can be. I'm in Lizzie's room. I just wanted to be near her. Ya know?"

Anna really didn't.

Going to someone else for comfort was a foreign thought. Physicality was one thing, but she solved things on her own. But Vinnie made her see things could be different. She could belong to someone.

After she'd slept with Vinnie last night, she looked into his eyes and his perception of her was crystal clear. She hadn't looked like a conquest or a fling. In his eyes, she'd looked like forever. She'd never been anyone's forever, and it had never occurred to her to want to be.

She clenched her fist and yelped.

"Are you okay? What happened?"

"I think I might have broken my thumb."

"How did you do that?"

Anna let out a slow breath. "I punched Preston in the face."

Kass whooped on the other side of the line before catching herself. "Good for you! He deserved it! Wait, have you been seen? Did you go get your hand looked at, I mean? I had this case in one of my classes where we talked about how boxers can get fractures in their wrists when they're first learning proper form. Does your wrist hurt? I'm sure your hand is swollen, how bad is the swelling? Twice the size of your other hand? Not quite that bad?"

"Um…"

"Sorry too many questions way too fast. You know what? Mat's gonna leave and start driving around. Would it be okay if I came to see you with Lizzie? I can look at your hand, and I won't have to be alone." Kass' voice cracked and she took a shaky breath. "Vinnie is like a brother to me. I'm so worried about him."

Anna's instinct was to decline, but she didn't want to be alone. She wanted to be with people that cared about Vinnie as much as she did.

It had only been three hours since the interview, but it felt like half a day had passed. Anna had her office's main line ported to her cell phone, just in case Vinnie called there instead of calling her directly. She'd answered two spam calls, hoping it might be him calling from a payphone. If anyone could find one, it would have been Vinnie. The second spam caller tried to get aggressive, and Anna had cussed him out in more than just English.

The momentary release of rage had unclenched her stomach enough that she'd managed to drink a bit of water.

She wanted coffee, but didn't dare add a stimulant to her system. As good as whiskey sounded, she needed to stay sober.

What if he'd gotten into a car accident? Or gotten pulled over? Would being in a jail cell be safer at this point? At least she'd know where he was and she could help him. Why had he run? Where was he? What if the worst happened? What if he…

Her apartment buzzer sounded and Anna's screech startled Jackal, who glared at her through half opened eyes.

"How can you sleep through all of this?"

The black cat yawned and curled back into a ball.

Anna opened the door to let Kass and Lizzie into her apartment. Lizzie was sound asleep, and the young mother shrugged off her bag to lay her daughter in the oversized chair Anna pointed to.

"She sleeps like the dead." Kass kissed her daughter's head and put a blanket over her.

Anna was still in the kitchen, her hand on the refrigerator door. "Would you like some water?" Her own voice sounded hoarse, like she'd been yelling, but she hadn't. She'd just sat on the chaise, petting Jackal and silently begging for a key to turn in the lock. But it hadn't. Where was he?

"Sure." Kass checked her phone. "Mat stopped by Bree's place and she hasn't seen him. Did you get a hold of Leila?"

"She called me. He wasn't at The Playhouse, but they're keeping an eye out." Anna handed her a bottle of water and winced as she grabbed one for herself.

Kass stepped closer and looked at her hand. "You need to go to the hospital. Your thumb's at least very sprained, but I'd put money on a fracture as swollen as it is."

"I'm not leaving until we know where Vinnie is. He might come here and if I'm not here, he might…" Anna choked on the words and covered her mouth, dropping the bottle to the ground. Tears rolled down her cheeks, but she was still desperate to hold it together. That car of his was light. If he crashed it, he could be dying. She let out a desperate sound despite herself.

Kass put her arms around her. "Anna, he'll be okay. We'll find him. Everyone's looking for him and he's gonna be fine."

Anna gasped in a breath and pushed Kass away. "I can't, please. I just can't right now." She was shaking, but she refused to break down. Being a blubbering mess wasn't efficient. It wasn't going to improve the situation.

Kass stepped away without hesitation. "No worries, I get it. Do you want to sit?"

"I want a fucking cigarette and to punch that asshole again." Anna growled and hit her counter, hissing in pain.

"Alright, that's enough self punishment for things that aren't our fault." Kass sighed, analyzing Anna's hands. "Have you washed your hands since everything happened?"

Anna shook her head and looked down at the blood still on her knuckles. She should have washed her hands, gotten this off.

Kass didn't say anything at first. She simply turned on the kitchen sink and slowly lathered the soap over Anna's knuckles. "Let's get you clean first. It's unlikely you broke your own skin with only one punch, but we don't want his blood on you. Have you ever punched anyone before?"

"Only when I took self-defense classes, but I was wearing gloves and hitting a foam mitt."

"Yeah. The glove would have stabilized your wrist and kept you from tucking your thumb, which, to reiterate, I am 99% sure you've broken. I'll be careful as I double check everything."

Anna wanted it to be comforting. She wanted the closeness to matter, but she felt empty. She watched the pink foam swirl down the drain. Was this all she had left of her time with Vinnie? She shouldn't be this dramatic. It wasn't helping. Being emotional wasn't going to fix anything. She needed a place to release her anger.

Was this her fault somehow? Had she put Vinnie in Preston's sights for a better story? If she'd kept Vinnie at arm's length, as a client, would Preston have dug so hard for dirt? No. Money was Preston's only motivator, and nothing she did would have changed what happened. Preston was an asshole, and Anna was not responsible for him.

"Can you wiggle your fingers?" Kass requested.

Anna silently did as she was told, but her thumb throbbed as she moved it.

"Okay, I'm gonna press on your fingertips to check your blood flow." Kass had gentle hands. She was a pediatric nurse, so gentleness was part of her daily job.

Where was Vinnie? He hadn't gone to Rex's house in Houston, not to the club, not to Mat and Kass' home, and not here. Where on Earth was he? Had he driven to Rex's cabin? Rex didn't think he'd be able to safely make that drive. But what if he'd tried it anyway?

"I wanna immobilize this a little since you want to stay here. I don't want you to hurt yourself anymore. Go ahead and sit down. Do you have a first aid kit?

Anna nodded and sat down on the chaise. "In the bathroom, bottom of the wood cabinet."

Kass returned in a few minutes, sitting next to Anna with a first aid kit she hadn't ever opened.After wrapping Anna's wrist, she elevated it on a pillow with a bag of frozen berries beneath it.

"I almost asked if you wanted a sticker," Kass muttered, more to herself than Anna.

Anna was silent as looked over the Houston skyline. She didn't know what to do. She was powerless. Tears pricked at her eyes, and she wiped them away with her uninjured hand.

Kass put away the supplies she used and washed the dishes in the sink – reflexively, most likely. She looked down at her phone before sitting down next to Anna. They were quiet for what felt like forever. It was only twenty minutes. Anna couldn't stop staring at the clock. How far could he have gotten? Out of the city? Or was he hiding somewhere? The thought of him alone in a dark place...

"They never told me the whole story about their father," Kass admitted.

Anna resisted the urge to pull her injured hand closer.

"I knew Nathan died in a fire, and that it was an accident, but they never said anything about Vinnie causing it. About six months after Lizzie was born, Mat had this awful nightmare about that night. He was thrashing and crying about how everything was his fault. He wouldn't look at me for ten minutes after I woke him." Kass drew in a long deep breath as her finger clutched the circular pendant she always wore. "Mat just sat on the edge of our bed staring at Lizzie, whispering that he'd never hurt her."

Vinnie was always so careful, so gentle, and so aware of the space he held. He was afraid of hurting someone.

Kass continued, "We went out on the patio after he started calming down. He told me that he'd started the fire that killed Nathan. I could tell he wasn't being completely honest, but I thought it was just too much for him to talk about. I had no idea... I figured they'd started it together. Pardon the pun, but they've always been thick as thieves."

Anna nodded, not trusting herself to speak.

Kass flattened her hands on her knees. "I can't imagine how scared they must have been."

The sob that had been at the back of her throat for hours finally erupted from Anna. She started to openly weep at her imagination's version of Vinnie as a terrified child, setting a fire to end his father's life. What had happened that night? What had happened after? Had Vinnie been with Mat after? Had he been alone?

Kass put her hand on her arm, and Anna turned into the other woman, crying into her shoulder. They were both a mess, holding each other at the shared pain of their loved one lost somewhere in the world.

Anna could only think about how alone Vinnie was. And how she wished he'd run to her instead of wherever he'd gone. *Please be safe. Please come back.*

Chapter 14: Sometimes Flashbacks

Jane, Nathan, and Forever Choices

December 9th; Kansas

"Son of a fucking whore!" Rex snarled as the show abruptly went to commercial. "I'll knock that asshole's teeth in."

Jane gripped her shirt over her heart. The camera had focused on Vinnie's face before the feed cut. His expression of terror made her think of him as the little boy she'd left behind instead of the man he was.

Rex was already up on his feet, searching for his cellphone, but she couldn't move.

The questions replayed, over and over in her head. The lead up to the drop had been obvious – baiting Vinnie with false scandals, then calming statements, and then the real controversy. That was a classic push and pull tactic to get a real reaction from a mark. And Vinnie's broken expression had been a true reaction.

"Yeah. I saw it. His phone's goin' to voicemail." Rex paced the living room, cellphone pressed to his ear by his shoulder. "I'm on my way down. I'm aware it's a nine-hour drive on the good end, but I'm not abandonin' him. I'll see you soon. Update me if you find him."

Jane pulled her knees to her chest, ignoring the pop and crack of her joints. That couldn't be true. Not Vinnie. Not her mischievous little learner, who always stole books when they went to the corner store. But it was true. There was no way, without training Vinnie could have faked that level of fear.

"Janey, I know I just got back, but I gotta get back to Houston. Vinnie's phone's off, and he's god-knows-fucking-where. I hate leaving you without a car. Gonna fix that when I get back. Keep your phone on you. I'll let you know when we find him."

Rex was almost out the door, as he asked, "Do you need anything before I leave?"

"Wait."

Rex paused by the door, expectantly awaiting her request.

She cleared her throat. "What did that asshole mean about Vinnie killing Nathan? It was a fire. There was a picture in the paper of the boys by a firetruck. I saw it."

"The fire isn't what killed him. That was the second thing that happened that night. Mat started the fire, trying to cover up what really happened."

Rex would stay and explain further if she asked him. But Rex was the only real parent her boys had ever known. He needed to go to Houston, and she needed to stay out of the way.

"Just go. It's in the past, no changin' it now. Vinnie needs you. We can talk about it when you're back."

He hugged her and disappeared out the door, gravel crackling under the tires as he disappeared down the driveway.

Jane watched the red of his tail lights get farther and farther away, until they vanished as Rex turned the corner by the end of the lake.

She walked away from the window and to the computer to use the search engine. Technology was a challenge she tackled while in prison. The way the world was now, she wasn't content to not comprehend the tools that were now at hand.

Vinnie had been ten when Nathan died, and his birthday was April 1st of '88. Jane typed Nathan Goodroe, fire, and 1998 into the search engine and waited for the results.

The third link was from The Houston Chronicle, the headline read "Local Man Dies in Fire; Children Survive." This was the article she remembered seeing when she was in prison. She clicked on it, scanning until she found the blurry picture of Mat and Vinnie huddled by the firetruck, sharing a blanket. After checking the date of this article, she added more parameters to her search.

The next relevant link was from the same paper. "Ten-Year-Old Shoots Father, Starts Fire to Cover Tracks". The first picture was of Vinnie without his glasses, looking angry.

"Fucking cops," she snarled.

Of course, Vinnie looked angry. She could imagine every part of his interrogation. He was the son of a career criminal. He wouldn't have gotten any leeway. They'd have taken his glasses away, claiming safety, and barked orders at him when he couldn't see. She could only guess how long they'd grilled him, trying to get him to admit whatever part he had in what happened that night. How long had he been alone in one of those cold, soundless interrogation rooms? How long was he questioned without a lawyer or Rex?

Jane took her pack of cloves and went out on the porch to smoke. Lola, her mother, had raised her with rules to ensure her survival in the world. There hadn't been the normal rules of looking both ways before crossing the street or checking the expiration dates on food. The first rule Lola had taught Jane was survival. It was the only rule that mattered, everything else was secondary.

She breathed out the smoke, watching it curl in the cold air. She'd always hated the cold. Her jaw trembled and she put the stick out in the ashtray, wrapping her arms around herself and letting out a sob. Survival was a crock of shit.

December 26, 1986

Jane sipped on the virgin drink with one hand on her belly, glaring at the frizzy-haired blonde in a mismatched outfit on Rex's arm. Rex and Nathan were both drunk out of their minds, laughing and jabbering about a job prior to the one they'd just pulled off. Nathan kept bringing up the casino, but Rex would change the subject and redirect. Even drunk and high, he was sharp. His intelligence was why she hadn't picked Rex as her mark. She liked him, but she'd keep her distance. His brilliant blue eyes saw far too much.

She lit a clove and held it in her hand, trying to break up the stink of cigarette smoke and marijuana fog. This dive bar on the backend of Housten's shittiest neighborhood was a focal point for under-the-table dealings. The rule in effect: no cops, ever.

This place was cleaner when Rocky owned it. The sleazebag that Jim gave it to was a moron. Jane had cleaned the register out twice without getting caught before she'd planned the casino job. She had to bring home money nightly, Nathan thought she was working a corner, and she wasn't going to give him a reason to think otherwise. She'd make sure some of the money from tonight got 'misplaced.' Nathan would assume he'd spent it and not question it. Shitty part of it was that he'd make Rex resplit the money, but that wasn't her problem. She had to have run money, just in case.

A sharp pain in her side made her wince. This baby boy had no respect for the woman who'd graciously decided not to kick him out. Jane needed to figure out where she could leave him once he was born. Nathan was explosive, and Jane didn't need another factor to complicate her plan. She'd tell everyone that he didn't make it and that would be that.

She cracked open a peanut and popped it into her mouth. She was hungry but Nathan wasn't going to want to leave anytime soon. She could try and leave without him. If they split up, she could eat and stash some of that money. They weren't too far...

"There is the woman that sees beyond this Earth." A wet, beer-scented kiss impacted against her cheek.

It took every ounce of her self-control not to rock the man's jaw. It might knock his crooked tooth back in place. He was always rambling about her eyes. Something about a story his grandmother used to tell. Jane growled, "Dale, when's the last time you showered?"

"Bitch, I'm too high to even care about taking your shit right now." He shook his glass at the bartender for a refill. "My girl's pregnant. Our kids are gonna be friends."

"Which girl? Your wife or one of the bitches that you tattoo for blow-jobs?"

He gulped down two swallows of his new beer as the insult went over his head. "My wife of course. She's pissed about not drinking, but looking forward to having a rugrat."

"I'm sure she is."

Dale leaned closer to her and she stiffened, shifting her foot and getting ready to sidestep. "I should give you a tattoo sometime. I'd do something pretty."

"Unless I'm there, you ain't doing shit, you fuckhead!" Nathan jerked Jane back to him by grabbing a fistful of her dress. "No one touches her unless she's working."

Nathan kissed the same cheek that Dale had. It gave Jane some satisfaction knowing he'd gotten the other man's slobber in his mouth. This was the perfect way to get out. "I'm tired."

Nathan sat on a barstool, forcing his leg between hers, and pulling her awkwardly up on his lap. "You don't want 'er right now anyway. She's fatter than she looks, weighs a ton. Wait 'til after the kid's born, then we can talk price."

She wanted to snap. Nathan didn't pimp her out, and no one ever would. She wanted to run out of the bar, steal a car, and disappear into the cold night. Maybe none of her plans were worth this. Patience was a learned trait and she was hanging on by old habits and training. Jane didn't want to be here.

Nathan and Dale were talking about something she should be listening to, but she couldn't stop looking at Rex and the girl he was with. The blonde twirled in front of him, her pink skirt going high enough to flash her black panties. She was trying to get Rex to dance with her, but he shook his head and motioned for her to come closer. Even drunk, he was so gentle.

Rex held onto the girl's hand and kissed her enthusiastically, but without forcing himself into her space. Their fingers were entwined, and Jane couldn't force herself to look away from the woman's mismatched painted nails and the silver ring on Rex's finger. The stupid smiles on their faces made a knot in her stomach. The morons were perfect for each other.

"If you tattoo anything on her, it's gonna be 'Goodroe' right..." Nathan ran a finger down Jane's neck, "...here so everyone knows she fucking mine."

She was going to vomit. "I need to pee, let me down."

"Come on..."

"I'll piss on your leg if you don't let me down!" she snapped, rushing away as Nathan and Dale laughed at her.

Jane slammed the metal door hard enough to shake all the stalls in the row. She gulped in deep breaths to keep from vomiting. She wasn't putting her face anywhere near that toilet. She didn't even want to piss in it. The alleyway outside was cleaner. But she didn't have a choice. Too much water tonight. Rex had kept a cup in her hand the whole trip back, reminding her to sip on it as they flew back to Texas. His protective nature had made him perfect for the role he played tonight, but it wasn't all acting. She hadn't missed his lack of speech when she was tying his tie, or when he was giving her long looks. He was a sucker for a pair of doe-eyes. If he wasn't so smart, he would have been the better choice. With him there would be less bobbing and weaving, fewer bruises, and he was overall a better human than Nathan. She could still feel the warmth from Rex's hand on the small of her back when they walked into the casino.

"Are you alright?"

She didn't recognize the voice on the other side of the closed door. "I'm fine. There's stalls open."

"Rex sent me in here to check on you."

Jane clenched her fists. Who the fuck did Rex think he was? She wasn't some fragile thing who needed nice words and protection. She shoved the door open and marched to the sink, knocking her shoulder into the other woman. "I'm fine. He doesn't need to worry."

"I didn't mind. You looked upset." The girl in the red top continued about how she could always tell when a man was the 'too rough' type, inquiring about Jane's safety. There was a high-pitched noise in Jane's ears, interrupting the other woman's words. "Plus, Nathan's kinda a pill when he gets high. Too rough for business."

Jane's hands were still under the water as the realization hit her. This bitch had slept with Nathan while she was with Rex. She turned off the water and shook her hands at the mirror.

"Well, if you're good, I'm gonna.."

Jane grabbed a fistfull of the other woman's jean jacket, jerking her away from the door and into the wall. She kicked the doorstop under the door to keep anyone from interrupting them. The blonde looked scared. *Good*. Jane wanted her scared.

"You fucked Nathan, huh?" Jane put her hand on the woman's shoulder, holding her against the wall.

"It's my job." Her bright blue eyes were wide. "It's your job too. Nathan said you..."

"Shut the hell up." Jane shook her head. "Nathan doesn't know shit about me. And now I'm findin' out that Rex doesn't know shit about you. How's it sittin' with 'im? You fuckin' his partner?"

"I," She swallowed, eyes darting to the left, "I told him. He didn't care."

Jane grinned at the quiver in her voice, "Well, that's a lie. You didn't tell him."

Someone tried to push open the door and then knocked.

"We're cleanin'! Come back in ten," Jane hollered, waiting until the footsteps moved away from the door. "Why didn't you tell him?"

"He knows what I do." She shifted her feet, boots crunching the dirt on the floor.

"I know he does. What's your name again? I forget."

"It's Gail. I should get back to Rex, tell him you're good." Gail attempted to move away from her again, but Jane pushed her back again.

"He can wait. I want to talk to you, Gail. Woman to woman. Nathan doesn't give a shit about anyone but Nathan. Rex, on the other hand, he likes you."

An unconscious smile started to appear on Gail's face. *Good.*

"That's the rough part. Rex lets you work, but I'll bet he doesn't like it. Let's try this again. How do you think he's gonna feel about you screwing Nathan?"

Gail's face fell. "Nathan said not to say anything. It didn't mean anything. I was just..."

"Doin' you job," Jane finished, tucking a lock of hair behind Gail's ear.

The woman was shaking. *Good.* If their position were reversed, Jane would have hit her opponent in the stomach as a distraction. Gail had more morals than Jane did. Good for fucking her. Jane wasn't one to let life play her. She played life.

"Nathan doesn't fire blanks. I know he tells y'all that, but it ain't true. I wouldn't be knocked up if it was."

Gail opened her mouth but closed it, fidgeting with her hands.

"You've been drinking water all night. Rex mentioned you love wine but you haven't had a drop tonight."

See everything. Lola McCroy had beat observance into her daughter like a Catholic Priest learned the sacraments. Jane noticed, more than once that Gail switching out her glass of wine for a cup of water. Rex wasn't paying attention, probably thought Gail had been drinking, and not giving it to the woman in the booth next to theirs.

Another knock on the door. "Janey, Gail? You gals doin' alright?" Rex questioned on the other side of the door.

"We're fine, Blue-Eyes. Your girl's helping me get cleaned up. Be out in a hop," Jane called out, putting her finger to Gail's lips to keep her quiet.

"Alright, shake a leg. Nathan wants food, we're gonna walk down to Waffle House."

Jane counted Rex's footfalls until she reached ten, then folded her arms over her chest. "So, you're having Nathan's kid. Shit, knockin' girls up gotta be the only thing other than safe crackin' that he's not a failure at. Are you gonna tell, Rex? Gonna lie? Tell him that it's his? Maybe get rid of it?"

A single tear ran down Gail's cheek and Jane brushed it away.

"Oh, no sweetie. You can't cry now. You already spilled the milk, can't get it back in the bottle now. You gotta decide what you're gonna do."

"I don't know whose it is," Gail admitted. "I can't tell, Rex. It'll hurt him."

"It will. You should disappear, save him the heartache."

A small sob escaped the blonde. *Good.*

Jane removed the wedge under the door with her foot and opened it. She motioned for Gail to follow. "Boys are waitin', come on."

October 4, 1987

The female officer's voice was muffled by the glass window.

"She's in the car with the baby. We're still waiting on another ambulance. She hasn't said much, other than asking for you to be called and refusing treatment. You're a family friend, correct?"

Jane coiled herself around Mat in the backseat of the car, trying to block out the red and blue strobe lights. The car smelled like gun oil, sweat, and dirt. She needed out. She couldn't be in this car, but she was trapped.

The doors were locked on the outside. It was her worst nightmare. Her name on a police report – *rule two: don't risk committing crimes you don't have to.* She shouldn't have done it.

She'd have to talk to the cops again. Repeat the story again, over and over, as they tried to trick her. Jane buried her nose in her son's hair, using him to calm herself down. Mat was safe. He was safe. Her stomach clenched. They were safe tonight, but what about tomorrow?

A tap on the glass caused Jane to lift her head. Rex Abster, Nathan's partner-in-crime, offered a wave from as he stood next to the officer. The door opened and, while she didn't trust herself to stand, Jane immediately swung her legs out and put her feet on the ground. If the cops wanted to cage her again, they were going to have to force her.

"Mrs. Goodroe…" The officer started, but Rex interrupted.

"It's Miss McCroy."

While it was nice to have her name not linked to Nathan, Rex could have let that go. The cops didn't have a record of her real name. Rex was too good for the world they operated in.

"Sorry, Miss McCroy. Your friend Rex is going to let you stay with him tonight. You can't go back to your apartment. We have to search for drugs," the officer explained, eyes never leaving her notepad.

"I need things for him." Jane shifted Mat in her arms. She needed to get back in the apartment, needed her IDs, and run money. She didn't have anything to finance her next move. She had months of savings hidden in a kickbox in the kitchen.

Rex lifted the duffle back in his hand. "I already went in with the officer and grabbed you some things. We can come back tomorrow after they give us the go-ahead."

She couldn't argue. It would look suspicious if she insisted on going back in on her own. Jane nodded and pushed herself out of the car on shaking legs. Rex looped his arm around her waist, making sure she was steady. His cornflower-blue eyes were full of concern for her. Why? Why did he care? She hadn't seen him in months.

Jane forced herself to speak. "I'm good. Thanks."

The officer held out her card, and Jane took it awkwardly as she juggled Mat. "Here's my card. Call me tomorrow, and we can take your victim statement. Don't let that asshole get away with this. You didn't deserve any of it."

Jane nodded again and let Rex lead her to his car, surprised when he opened the back door instead of the passenger door. She looked up inquisitively at him, and he explained quietly. "I don't have a carseat for Mat and you can't be in the front with him."

She climbed into the backseat, buckling herself in, as there were ten officers in her line of sight. There were so many eyes on her, so she kept her head down.

Mat was sound asleep; he'd cried himself out within the first hour of everything happening. Rex's car was running and warmer than the cop car had been. Jane glanced at the radio. It showed 9:15. Three hours? It had been three hours since she'd attempted to leave?

Rex got into the driver's seat, lifting his hand to the officer as they pulled away from the complex. "You okay, Janey?"

"I guess." She felt hollow, drained. Like she'd run for hours but hadn't gone anywhere.

"Cops are holding him overnight, at least. I called Larry, a lawyer friend of ours, and he's gonna try and get in to see Nathan. You told the cops he fell off the stairs, but your neighbor said he was chasing you. What the hell really happened?"

"I was leaving with Mat and he tried to push me down the stairs, so I shifted my weight and knocked him over the rail." Jane could hear herself explaining the series of events, but it was as if she was underwater. Her own words sounded so far away. Was she whispering? She didn't think she was whispering.

"Why were you leaving?"

The rhythmic click of the turn signal and the red flashing lights made her nauseous. She could only think of being trapped in the backseat of the cop car.

"He tried to kick me." Her jaw throbbed, as was bile crept up her throat. "Pull over. Now."

"Can't; in the middle of turning. Hold tight."

The car was decelerating but not fast enough. Jane attempted to roll down the window, but it stuck partway down. She leaned forward, desperate to keep Mat out of the path of her vomit as it splashed on the floor of the car and her shoes. Tears blurred her eyes and her throat burned. She waited for Rex to start yelling, but all she could hear was a hum in her ears, the car's engine, and Mat's crying.

The door beside her opened and, Rex's warm hands smoothed her hair away from her face. "It's okay. You're okay."

"I…I…I'm sorry. I…" Jane realized that it wasn't Mat crying, it was her. She was sobbing.

"Not worried about the car, it's seen worse." Rex held out his hands. "Hand me Mat, then you can shift over and get out on the other side. You can ride in the passenger seat. We're only a couple of miles from my house, and I'll drive slow."

Jane let Rex take Mat, toeing off her disgusting shoes and switching seats as requested.

"There's coffee in that thermos if you want to rinse your mouth out." Rex put the bag with her things in the trunk with one hand while holding Mat with the other.

She practically gargled with the coffee to get the acidic aftertaste out of her mouth. Rex waited for her to spit on the ground before handing Mat back. Rex turned the heat all the way up but rolled down his window. They listened to the radio in silence until they pulled into the driveway.

"You good to walk?"

"I puked, I didn't break my legs," Jane snipped, averting her eye.

Rex shrugged. "Alright then. I'll grab your bag, and we can get ya cleaned up."

As they entered the house, he pointed to the bathroom and smacked the wall before he turned the light on. "Sorry, it's finicky. Need to fix it. There's towels on the rack, and you can toss your clothes in the hamper. Clean clothes are in your bag here."

"Wait." Jane noticed the puke that was on Rex's shirt. How had that gotten there? She looked down, and sure enough, it was on Mat's blanket too. "You have…" She trailed off, pointing to his shirt.

"Well hell, that's nothin'." He grabbed the hem of his shirt, rolling it up from the bottom and pulling it over his head before tossing it in the open hamper. "Throw his blanket in there too. We'll wash everything together after your shower."

She looked up at Rex. She knew he had tattoos, but she never really looked at them before now. There was a Celtic cross on his right upper arm, with small green clovers hidden in the black knots. Over his heart was a Claddagh with a traditional triknot in the background and lettering she couldn't make out.

As Rex washed his hands at the sink, she noticed he had another one peaking just above the waistline of his pants – brass knuckles in black, with a shamrock cutout. On his left bicep, a gaudy mermaid with stars over the tits. It didn't look like Dale's work. Too shaky. Why was she drooling over his body-art? *Must be the hormones.*

Jane put Mat's blanket in the hamper, careful to not wake him.

"Let me snag the formula and a bottle, in case he wakes up." Rex put a bottle in his back pocket and set the formula outside of the bathroom. "There's shampoo and soap in there. Nothin' fancy, but it'll do the job." Rex took Mat from her, and Jane had to force herself to look away.

Nathan wasn't in the best shape, but Jane never dwelt on it. She wasn't with him for his looks. Rex, on the other hand, was in shape, and she could see his muscle definition on his stomach and back as he moved.

His chest tattoo read 'love, luck, and loyalty.' He also had a large angel, wielding a flaming sword detailing his back. That one was new.

"I didn't realize you had so many tattoos." She felt stupid the moment the statement slipped out.

He'd paused to pull a diaper out of the bag, and with Mat resting on his shoulder and one knee on the bathroom floor, he looked up at her with a sheepish grin. "Yeah, got addicted. Plus teenage rebellion and all that."

"My mother…" Jane snapped her mouth closed. *Rule three – never share past details. Never. You came from nowhere, you have no past.* Rex was still looking at her, so she fumbled out an answer. "She was strict, wouldn't have allowed them."

He smirked, his eyes lighting up with mischief. "Ah, but you always wanted one. See, the best part of being Catholic is if you screw up, you say some Hail Marys, kiss a priest's ass, and you're all good. "

She shrugged, not trusting herself to give an answer. "Rex, thank you for helping me," she called out, as he reached the door.

"Don't sweat it, Janey. I've got your back. We'll deal with tomorrow, tomorrow."

Jane nodded, and after Rex left the bathroom, she stripped and stumbled into the shower. The water was almost immediately hot and didn't smell like sulfur, which was a nice change. Nathan always showered before her, so her showers were lukewarm at best. She used a washcloth to scrub herself down with the bar of soap. The clean, outdoorsy scent she associated with Rex filled her nostrils.

Her hands slipped down to her stomach, framing it and rubbing her rounded bump. "Are you okay in there? I'm sorry if I messed you up. I'm not sure what to do with you or your brother. I got in too deep and now I'm stuck."

With Mat, she'd been sober her entire pregnancy, as she was gathering intel about Nathan, she and didn't want to risk her story unraveling. She hadn't known she was pregnant with Vinnie for almost two months, and she'd put Mat on formula so she could drink. Drinking made Nathan tolerable. He wanted to party all the time, and if she drank with him, he didn't want to fight.

Nathan ignored Mat for the most part, but when Jane told him she was pregnant again, he screamed at her to get rid of it. They'd been fighting tooth and nail about it since September. He told her he wasn't going to deal with another one, especially since she was whoring herself out and it wouldn't be his. She'd let him think whatever he wanted. Maybe it was better that way. If Nathan thought she was having another man's kid, maybe he'd let her go.

Jane hid the pregnancy at first, telling him she terminated it. He found out tonight that she hadn't and shit hit the fan. The retaliation was swift; he tried to kick her in the stomach, but she sidestepped him. In a fit of genuine fear, she grabbed Mat and the car keys running for the door. She was on the apartment stairs when she heard him rushing towards her. She knew Nathan fought dirty. He was going to push her down the stairs. As the thought flashed in her head, she crouched and avoided the incoming blow. She curled herself into a ball around Mat to protect him. Nathan was off-balance so Jane jerked her shoulder up, using her weight to send him over the side of the stairs.

She pressed her hands on the shower wall, forcing herself to center in the present. What was done was done. Jane turned off the water and toweled herself off, carefully avoiding the purple and yellow marks on her back and thighs. Rummaging through the bag, she grabbed the most comfortable clothes Rex had packed. She was pleasantly surprised that he hadn't forgotten anything other than, her hair ties. She combed through her wet tresses and left it down.

Her brain wouldn't stop flashing back to the apartment and Nathan. He'd hit the sidewalk below the stairs with a stomach-turning thud and Jane thought she'd killed him. His scream of pain had almost been a relief; she wanted him out of her way, not dead.

Rule two: don't commit crimes you don't have to.

There was never a moment when Lola's rules weren't running through Jane's head. She knew that this second boy was Nathan's; she hadn't slept with anyone else. Sometimes it was easier to give him what he wanted rather than put up a fight. Nathan was something she had to endure to get her revenge. As far as he knew, she was working a corner and it was anyone's guess who's kid this was. No man was going to raise another man's kid like his own, that's not how the world worked.

She shouldered the duffle bag and walked into the living room. Rex was sitting in a recliner with Mat on his bare chest, telling him a story about a forest spirit and an ax cutter. Jane retreated behind the wall so she wouldn't be seen.

"I think we need to find a safe place for your momma. If your dad has to do time over this, I think I'm gonna steal the both of you up to Kansas to hide. You'll like it up there – lots of trees, a lake, and a lot of quiet."

Jane hated the idea of putting her plan on hold, but maybe it would work to her advantage.

"Your momma's a special lady. You better be a good for her."

Rex couldn't have known she was listening; why was he talking like she mattered?

What would he gain by being nice to her? All she was to him was his partner's girl.

"I can take him back." She strode into the living room and held out her hands, "Give you a chance cleaned up."

"Sounds good. There's food in the fridge, so help yourself." Rex smiled as he handed off her son and disappeared into the bathroom.

Jane wasn't going to Kansas. She could steal Rex's car and…she realized she'd have to leave Mat behind if she ran. Couldn't run with a baby. She'd tried to run with him and failed. She just needed a little more time to figure things out. Maybe hiding with Rex for a spell wasn't such a bad idea.

April 1, 1989

Seven days. Seven days until Nathan was out of prison. Six days until Rex took her and the boys back to Houston. Jane's stomach knotted as she mapped the ten-hour car ride in her head. It felt like marching to an execution versus a homecoming. Nathan had been in prison for eighteen months for drug use and attempted assault.

Despite Rex's reassurances, Jane knew what was in store for her when she and Nathan were reunited. She should have run when the running was good.

Rex had snuck past her defenses, and she'd gotten used to his kindness. Jane scoffed at herself. It must've been the boys. Babies made women emotional wrecks, although, her own mother had gotten over it pretty quickly. Jane couldn't ever remember a time when Lola had mothered her the way she did her boys.

But she wasn't going to deceive herself. She wasn't good at being a mother. Every time she and Rex went to town and she saw other mothers fussing over their children, she realized how truly bad she was at it. Her boys got more affection and parenting from Rex than they did from her.

Maybe she could convince Rex to take her somewhere other than Houston. She wanted revenge, but was dealing with Nathan worth it? Was it worth putting the boys' lives in danger? Probably not, but she still wanted it. She wanted Jim dead for what he'd done to her. Jane wanted him to suffer.

Long-cons were all about patience, timing, planning, and a little luck, but they were also a recipe for disaster. One wrong move, and the complicated long-con and it would be ruined. A slip of the tongue could undo years of work, and she wouldn't have that. The plan was paused, but it was still going to be her masterpiece. Jim had killed Lola and her entire crew in one night. Jane had been left in the ashes, and she intended to be the person who ruined Jim's reputation and ended his life. She'd take everything from him like he'd taken everything from her.

But she wasn't of a single mind anymore. Staying here at the cabin had changed so much. She'd changed so much. Revenge or something else? Could she want a life that wasn't one Lola laid out for her? More than power and control? Could love be…?

Tonight was Vinnie's first birthday, and somehow all of her feelings had hit her at once. Looking at Rex through the fire of her son's birthday candles, she realized how much she had. Her boys were loved and safe. And she had a man, who treated her boys like they were precious, and her like she hung the moon. What if it wasn't worth it? What if what they had right at this moment was it?

In a moment of insanity, she told Rex that he could have anything he wanted from her as a thank you. He avoided her eyes and asked her if she could sing for him. He'd asked for a song with meaning between them. The song she sang the day they truly met. It took the breath out of her lungs. Why did he care so much?

She gathered the boys out of their bath, dressing them for bedtime, kissing them, and singing them their lullabies. Vinnie was already fast asleep, and Jane gathered him up in the wrap carrier that she'd made out of one of Rex's shirts. Mat was trying to stay awake, but his eyes were drooping.

"Can you help Momma, Sweet-boy?"

Mat nodded enthusiastically. "Yesh."

"Can you carry the tape recorder for me? We're gonna go sit with Uncle Rex for a bit."

Her toddler gripped the tape recorder as if his life depended on it, and she scooped him up to walk out to the porch.

The boys were both curled up on her while Rex played the chords on his guitar. She sang the way she had during the casino job, when she faked falling, and they pretended to be married. Her intention was to make him emotional, but she'd done it to herself. It made her think of how gentle he'd been with her, and the genuine concern in his voice. The way he stopped Nathan from hitting her. He got in the way of someone trying to hurt her. No one had ever just stood up for her. She always had to prove she was worthy of protection. Rex wasn't like Nathan. Rex wasn't like anyone she'd ever known.

She hadn't ever lived like this. Rex didn't care who the boy's father was. He loved them; he treated them like they were special. He never talked down to her or thought of her as a hooker. When she spoke he listened, sometimes too well. She wouldn't simply fade from his memory if she vanished. Jane took a deep breath in the quiet, pulling the air from the lake and the forest into her lungs. Real air was worth the sneezing, as Rex had told her over and over when her allergies got bad.

She couldn't think of anything to say, but she should. What if she told him what she was feeling? He clearly felt something for her. A man didn't treat a woman this kindly unless he had a use for her.

"You could have asked me for anything, Blue Eyes…and all you wanted was for me to sing you that silly little song."

Rex shifted on the patio chair next to her. He wasn't looking at her, and then he was. No one had ever looked at her the way he was. She could see herself in his eyes, how beautiful she was there. He actually cared. Her heart clenched. She cared about him too. Oh god, she'd fallen for him. She'd fallen for the partner of her patsy. What was wrong with her?

Rule five: Never get in too deep. It's a game.

"It's late. Should get those boys to bed." His voice cut into her train of thought.

"They're fine, mostly asleep anyhow. Your own fault for making this rocker far too comfortable." She cleared her throat. "Mat, tell your uncle good night."

Mat climbed over her and onto Rex, hugging him tightly. Jane bit down on the inside of her cheek, watching them together. This is what she wanted. Fuck the revenge. What had Lola ever done for her? She wasn't giving this up. Not Kansas and not Rex! She could learn domestic things: how to cook and clean, and all of it. Jane McCroy didn't fail at things. If she could have Rex, then maybe it didn't matter if she didn't complete her plan. What if her masterpiece was right in front of her?

Rex loved her, and she loved him. They were still dancing like that quiet moment at Christmas, but she could pull him to her, bring him the rest of the way in. Rex would see this was right. Nathan was an asshole who ruined everything in his wake. Nathan wasn't who she wanted around her babies. Rex was who she needed.

"Okay, that's enough lovin' on 'im. Get back up on Momma. There's my sweet boy." Mat barely moved, but Rex handed him over. Jane snuggled her son, who immediately tried to wake Vinnie. "Hey now, don't poke at your brother."

She got to the door and stopped. What if she could show him what a life the four of them would really look like? "You should come lay down with us."

Rex muttered for her to go in without him and that he'd see her in the morning.

His dismissal surprised her, but she heard the crack in his voice. There was something there. Maybe he needed a push.

"You sure you don't wanna lay down with us?"

Rex's voice was low. He was choked up. "I got something to take care of tonight. Go get some sleep, Janey."

"Okay then. G'night, Rex."

In the morning, she'd tell him. She'd tell him the truth point blank, and they'd be together. Jane wasn't going back to Houston or to Nathan. She and the boys were going to stay here in Kansas with Rex and be regular people. No more jobs and no more crime. They were going to have a happy life. Nothing could stop it.

September 29, 1993

"How late you gonna be out?" Nathan Goodroe's sleep-laden voice stopped Jane at the door.

Fuck. She thought he'd fallen asleep in his chair. She'd laced his beer. Glancing back, she saw the bottle by his chair was only half gone. Fantastic. This would be the one time he picked restraint.

"Not sure, depends on how fast I can get clients. We need another two hundred for rent by week's end." She pulled on her thigh-high boots. She bought them with the excuse that men wanted to see girls in 'pretty woman' boots. The real point was to hide tools. A bag might get lifted, but no one was taking her boots.

"That's bullshit. You paid him on the first for rent." He cleared his throat. "I 'member."

"I only gave him part of it. We didn't have it all. Your last job came up short."

She knew better than to turn her back on him. She truly did, after seven years of dealing with him, but sometimes she didn't act on her own intelligence. He jerked her into the wall by her ponytail, making her gasp in surprise.

"You fucked him, didn't you?" Nathan's breath stank of stale beer and menthol cigarettes.

Nearly gagging, she struggled to push him off. "No. And even if I did, it would be for rent. Not for fun."

"I think you always enjoy it, you whore." He twisted her hair, knowing how much it hurt her.

"Don't call me a whore."

The pain was instant. His backhand impacted her cheek as the back of her head slammed against the wall. She couldn't move, trapped between him and the door as he twisted her ponytail again. "I'll call you whatever the fuck," he spat, slapping her again, "I want."

"Don't hit Mommy."

Jane could see over Nathan's shoulder. Both of her boys were standing in the hallway. Mat had been the one to speak up, holding Vinnie's hand and trying to look brave.

"Stat-sis-ically, hitting only causes more vi-olence. No one learns from pains, it's too a negative an enforcement." Vinnie's more timid voice echoed after his brother. "Please don't hurt Mom."

"You are some kind of freak! Fucking bastard, thinking you're smartest one in the fucking room. I'll fucking teach you a word! Come 'ere, Vincent." Nathan motioned for Vinnie to come closer, but Mat stepped in front of Vinnie, putting himself between his father and his brother.

"Matty, take your brother and both of you go to bed," Jane ordered the boys, making sure they were behind the door before she turned her attention to Nathan. "Baby, let me get warmed up with you before I leave." She put her hands on his chest and leaned forward, placing a kiss on his cheek.

Nathan grumbled but let Jane lead him back to his chair, flopping down. Jane handed him the half-empty bottle. "Finish your beer while I get started."

He tipped his head back and guzzled down the contents before grabbing her chin and forcing her to look at him. "Your mouth is your prettiest hole, have I told ya that?"

Good. With his speech slurring even more, Jane knew it would only be a few more minutes before he passed out. "Charming." She rolled her eyes, unable to keep the comment to herself.

Making a show about getting him out of his pants, she only made it to his zipper before he started snoring. Thank god. She didn't want to have to strip to buy more time. She spat into his beer bottle, added some water to it, and placed it back on the end table. He'd think he passed out and forgot.

Jane opened the door to the room the boys shared. It was the biggest room in the trailer and the only room with a lock. They were both on Vinnie's bed, both covering Vinnie's ears. They jumped up to greet her when they realized it was her.

"Mommy!" Mat bounded down and hugged her leg in contrast to Vinnie, who was waiting for her to come to him.

"It's okay, boys. Everything is okay." She sat down next to Vinnie and kissed the top of his head. "You both need to try and go back to sleep."

"Is dad mad?"

Vinnie answered his brother's question before Jane could. "Dad's always mad."

"Don't worry about dad. Just get back under your covers. It'll all be alright in the morning." She shooed Mat back towards his bed when the phone rang, stopped, and rang again.

"Wrong number," Vinnie parroted. He'd heard her say it enough to Nathan.

She nodded and kissed Mat's forehead first, then Vinnie's. "Yup. Wrong number. You boys stay in bed and I'll be back in the morning."

"Before dad's awake?" Vinnie's lower lip quivered.

"I'll protect you if she isn't, Vinnie. I gots you," Mat volunteered as he squeezed his tattered stuffed dog.

Jane smoothed the hair from Vinnie's forehead. "It'll be okay, Night-bug. Sooner than you think, everything is gonna be different."

"Promise?"

"I promise."

Jane gave them another round of kisses, checked on Nathan to make sure he was still unconscious, then dashed out the door. Her boots clomped on the trailer stairs as she raced to get to the payphone within the ten-minute requirement.

Thankfully, no one was using the payphone and she dug into her right boot to pull out the needed change. She punched the number in, letting it ring twice, then hung up to complete the signal.

The payphone didn't make through the first ring as she jerked it off the hook. "What? What's going on? We talked yesterday. You shouldn't be calling me again this soon."

The male on the other side of the line sighed. "We gotta move up the timetable."

"Why? And how much of a move up?"

"It's gotta be the first."

Jane's heart stopped in her chest. "The fucking first?!? That's in two days!"

There was noise in the background, a slot machine's clatter of a jackpot being hit. The voice lowered, breathing intensifying. He must be cupping the phone to his face. "Jim's getting a new security system installed. If we don't run it on the first, there'll be twice the cameras, and we will be totally fucked. We can't run it with the tech he's adding. It's the first or we're scrapping."

"To hell with scrapping! I have invested seven years setting up this con for *this* payoff. I'm going to ruin him. If we need to run it on the first, then I'll be ready on the first." Jane glanced around the empty parking lot, she'd forgotten to control her volume.

"Okay. I'll meet you at this time tomorrow at the Rusty Nail. Are you sure about this Jane? If we don't get away with this..."

"Jim'll put my head on a spike, I know." Jane knew. She knew the consequences, and she knew exactly how brutal Jim could be when he wanted to be.

"Jane, he'll kill everyone you know. I know you don't care too much about your old man, but you better think of a hiding spot for your boys, just in case."

The line went dead, and Jane put the phone back on the cradle. She paced the length of the sidewalk in front of the trailer park office three times before making her decision. It was now or never, and she'd picked now.

Four years ago, she'd looked in Rex's eyes, and watched as he'd lied to her about loving her and sent her back to Nathan because of some twisted sense of honor. He'd picked a fight with Nathan every time she had a shiner. Rex regretted sending her back; she could see it. The night he rejected her, she told him there would be a moment when he begged her to stay, and she wouldn't be able to. She had a distinct feeling that they were coming to that moment soon. She couldn't stop this now. It was time for revenge, and after her perfect plan was complete, it would be Shangri-la. Finally, paradise, hopefully for all four of them, but if not, for her and the boys for sure.

All she had to do was drive all night to get to Rex's cabin. It wasn't the first time she'd gone a day without sleeping. A few loose ends to tie up, and she could hit the road.

Jane let herself back into the trailer and went straight to the fridge, pulling out four beers. She took the boy's liquid allergy medicine and set it next to the drinks on the counter. Twist cap beers had been godsent for her sanity. She added the medicine to all four of them, resealed them, and put them in the fridge, then took the rest out and set them on the floor by the trash.

Nathan only drank cold beer. This should give her at least a day before he noticed her gone. Maybe even two.

She grabbed the notepad she normally wrote grocery lists on and left Nathan a note. *Took the boys to Dale and Cindy's to get them out of your hair. See you tonight.*

Her left hand cramped, and she shook it out before signing the note. She hated writing everything with her non-dominate hand.

Rule Number Seven: No papertrail. Nothing traceable.

Jane went to her bedroom, unlocked the wheels of the bedframe and pushed it towards the wall, careful not to make noise. She knocked her knuckles on the boards until she heard a hollow tone answer back so she could retrieve. The kickbox had seven years of savings and the fake IDs she needed for her con.

There were butterflies in her stomach. It was over, this hell of living with Nathan Goodroe was fucking over. He was never gonna black her eyes, bruise her ribs, or scare her boys ever again. They were free after she pulled this off.

I hope you're watching over me Lola. I'm gonna ruin Jim for you. I hope you get a chuckle out of it in purgatory. Your legacy set this up, and I'm finally gonna pull the trigger.

Jane put everything back in place and packed a bag. She wanted the pictures of the boys growing up, but she had to travel light. She shouldn't take the risk. *Wait!* She'd put a kickbox in at the cabin. She could leave everything there with notes, just in case. Jane wanted them to know who she was if it all went south. It wasn't going to, but it was asking for trouble to not leave the 'worst case' notes.

What about the camera? She'd picked up a video camera on a whim. Had she deleted everything from the last surveillance run? There wasn't time to think things through anymore. She needed to get on the road. Whatever wasn't needed she'd just burn.

She slipped into the boys' room. Vinnie was still sleeping, but Mat woke up instantly, looking frightened. "No worries, Sweet-Boy, it's just me. Can you get you and your brother's backpacks ready? We're gonna go see Uncle Rex."

Despite wiping the sleep from his eyes. Mat was immediately excited, "Really?"

"Really. Get both of your bags ready for a week's visit, okay?"

"Are we going to the cabin?"

"Sure are." She kissed the top of his head. "Get packed up quick, then wake Vinnie after you're done packing. Both need to pee before we leave. Make sure you tie Vinnie's shoes. He hasn't quite got it yet. I'll come back in here to get you. Wait in here 'til then, understand?"

Mat fidgeted with his hands. "Are we sneaking by dad?"

"Yup. That's why we need to be very quiet."

"Okay, Momma."

Jane left the room and triple-checked her duffle bag as she made a phone call.

A cough came before the shop's greeting, "Triple Threat Tattoos. This is Dale."

"Hey, it's Jane."

"Jane, the beautiful siren. How can I help you tonight?" His leering smile was audible.

She bit the inside of her cheek. She had no time for his fucking nonsense. "I need you to cover for me. I'm going out of town with the boys and I don't want Nathan on my heels. I left 'im a note, saying that the boys are with you and Cindy."

Dale sighed. "He's a pain in my ass when you do this."

"I'll swing by with five hundred for your trouble."

"An even grand."

Jane rolled her eyes, "Seventy-fifty, and I'll tell Cindy I gave you five if she asks." she countered.

"Done deal. When you swinging by?"

"Fifteen or so."

"Lights'll be on for you, baby-girl."

She hung up the phone and looked around. Nothing else she needed here. Nathan grumbled his sleep and grunted mid-snore. All the saints in heaven's mercies – to never hear that sound again would be a gift all in itself.

She put Dale's money in her boot to make the drop easier. Both boys were up with their backpacks on as she reentered their room. Poor Vinnie, rocking on his feet and hair a mess, clearly half awake.

Mat was zipping up Vinnie's jacket. "We're ready Momma."

"We sure fucking are."

December 10th, Kansas

The slam of a car door startled Jane awake. She'd fallen asleep on the couch, waiting by the phone as the past replayed in technicolor. She blinked at the clock. Her vision was blurry, but she could make out the 3:30. It was too early for Rex to be back.

When heavy footfalls approached the porch steps and a key positioned in the lock,

Jane reached for the poker on the fireplace to defend herself if needed. Whoever she expected to come through the door, it wasn't Vinnie. He looked half manic, eyes red, breathing heavy.

"Vinnie," She called out softly, worried she'd startle him more than he already looked.

Vinnie looked right, left, and then, as if there had been a delay in his hearing, he turned toward her. "Where's Rex?"

"He drove to Houston to find you. They've been calling." She set the poker down on the hearth, taking a step closer. "Did you drive straight here?"

"Too many miles. Had to stop for gas. Didn't know he was gone. Shouldn't have come here. Shouldn't have…" He let out a pained sound and stumbled backward into the door. "I'm tired. I'm so sorry.

Jane got close enough to him to touch his shoulder.

He was so much taller than she was. Where had his height come from? Certainly not her or Nathan. She felt shorter than normal next to him. "You don't have anything to be sorry for. Come sit."

She caught one of his hands, noticing his knuckles were broken and bloody with mud on his hands.

"Are you hurt? What happened to your hand?"

"Glass went through it. The bottle broke when Mat got hurt so bad." Vinnie trailed off shaking his head violently. "No, that's not now. That was before. Now is…Now was…Had to change a flat, bolts were stuck."

"Alright. That makes sense."

"I never make any sense. I go on and on about nonsense. It's irritating." His voice cracked, but he allowed Jane to guide him to the living room.

Jane got him to sit on the couch. "You aren't irritating. You're just smarter than most people can handle."

Vinnie looked so lost. He was wearing the same shirt and pants from the interview, but his jacket and tie were missing.

"I'm going to get you some water, and then I'm going to clean up your hands. Okay?"

He didn't answer, but he didn't object and that was good enough for now. She retrieved the first aid kit from the bathroom, a bowl with water, a towel, and two bottles of water. After setting out the items she needed, she grabbed one of the dining chairs and brought it with her so she could sit.

"We need to get your hands clean. Can you put them in the bowl for me?"

Vinnie's eyes were unfocused, but he complied. Some of the water splashed onto the floor and her socks. He allowed her to pat his hands dry with the towel. There was no resistance as she moved his limbs.

Jane offered him one of the water bottles. "You should try and drink some water."

"I didn't tell Anna." Vinnie's voice was hoarse. "The record was sealed; I was a juvenile. She didn't know I was a killer. A monster."

She wanted to comfort him, but she didn't want to overstep. The choices she made all those years ago negated her title.

She wasn't his mother, just the woman who gave birth to him, not his parent. Her hands twitched. Maybe she could hold his hands?

"I never told her that I loved her. I should have known better than to expect a happy ending. This is what I deserve for what I did. She won't look at me the same way ever again. I can't face her. I can't ever go back."

Jane laid her hands over his, desperate to make him stop berating himself.

Tears dripped off Vinnie's face. "Mom. I don't know what to do."

Mom. He called her mom. She hadn't heard that title in more than two decades. The last time she heard it, he'd been half asleep as she tucked him and Mat into their bed at Rex's cabin.

A sob ripped out of her throat, and she hugged him tightly before she could stop herself. Vinnie wasn't one for hugs, even when he was little, and it seemed now was no different. His hands remained in his lap as his body shook. God, she wanted to take this pain away from him.

She tried to get through to him. Reassure him. "Vinnie, you aren't a monster. Whatever you did, it doesn't make you a monster."

"I killed him. I killed Nathan." His voice was barely audible.

Jane tried to comfort him as best she could, but when he pushed her away, she let him. She sat next to him on the couch. "I'm sure you didn't have a choice."

"But I still did it. Anna…I can't go back. I can't ever go back to her." He sniffled, eyes still unfocused.

She put the bottle of water in his hands and grabbed the box of tissues on the end table, setting them closer. Blowing her own nose, she took a shuddering breath.

"Vinnie, you can't run away from this."

"That's fucking rich coming from you," he growled, fists clenched over his thighs.

That stung. It was well deserved, but it still stung.

Vinnie pocketed his glasses and wiped off his face.

Jane cleared her throat. "I'm sorry, I should have killed him when I had the chance. I've always regretted it, and now I regret it even more."

"What are you talking about? When did that happen?"

"You and Mat were already at Rex's cabin. It was the night I disappeared. Everything had gone sideways, but I almost did it before getting caught. I should have done it."

"I thought getting caught was why you disappeared." Vinnie looked truly confused.

She interlocked her fingers and drew in a long breath.

Rule Four: Never admit to what you don't have to.

Shut-up, Lola! Those rules were for your benefit and no one else's. Jane thought angrily at her own mother as she looked at her son. "Let me try and explain with the whole truth," she began.

October 1, 1993

Fucking shit! Jane beat her fists into the steering wheel over and over again, until her hands throbbed from the punishment. She wanted to scream, but couldn't. No matter how hard she tried to make some kind of noise, nothing would come out. It was as if someone was gripping her throat, cutting off her airway.

The take was still in the bag next to her, metaphorically covered with the blood of her co-conspirator. She'd heard the three muffled gunshots in a row, changed the direction she'd been walking in, and broke out into a dead run before blending into the crowd. Her wig and clothes were in the bathroom trash can, so she'd been able to slip out of the building, but they still had her face on camera. His people had an image of her damn face.

It had been perfect. The job had gone perfectly. Not a line out of place, until she'd rounded the corner, and looked straight into the newly installed camera in the south hallway. Jim had begun the installation of the security system early, and she had walked full-face into it. No screeching alarms, no flashing lights – criminals didn't call the cops. Criminals shot thieves in the back of the head and concealed them in concrete. But Jim wasn't a common criminal. He didn't just kill people who screwed him; he killed everyone connected to the person who dared to cross him. Then he killed the one that actually crossed him.

The boys were safe. They were with Rex. But safe for how long?

Jim would turn Houston inside out, looking for what was in the bag sitting in the passenger seat.

Money plates, flawless copies of twenty-dollar bill printing plates, which on their own were worthless, but not when you had the formula to make the paper for money. Lola had stolen papers. Well, not stolen – copied. Stolen things were searched for, but no one knew about copied things. In her youth, Lola had infiltrated the Pentagon. What Lola had copied were the plans for updating US currency for the next twenty years, including the printing and fabric formulas.

Jane had laid the foundations through one of her mother's old contacts. The formula was up for use if the plates could be provided. She'd paid the counterfeiter to start on the plates, using Jim's name as the interested buyer. Then she put the rumor in a couple of ears that Jim was the one to trust. Give him a couple thousand, and he'd make you ten times that in a week. Then, as the buzz grew louder, she set up the meeting for the formula to be sold rather than looking for partnership.

The trap was set, and Jim took the bait and the plates. He'd shelled out over a million for those plates and only half of it had been his money. The rest was from other criminals – men and women who wouldn't take the failure well. It was fucking perfect, until it wasn't.

Jim would rip through anyone associated with whoever took it from him. He'd be looking for the counterfeits to surface. Jane couldn't finish her plan. She had a buyer set up for both the plates and the formula, but she couldn't get out of Houston to get to him. Jim would hear about it, recognize her description, and come for her. Her thoughts flashed back to the house she'd grown up in. The unwelcomed memory appeared behind her eyes. Rooms littered with bodies as she belly crawled in the dark, tapping on floorboards, looking for a stash of money with a fake ID for her.

The scream she'd been holding back finally escaped, the sound echoing in the chamber of her car. Tears streamed down her face. How could she have gotten caught? How could she have been so stupid as to look up at that fucking camera?

She had to run. Everyone knew that Nathan was a bastard, and it wouldn't surprise anyone that she left. She could get the boys and run with Rex…Rex who worked with Jim, and could have found out what was in Jim's safe through the grapevine. Rex, who knew how to re-wire security systems, play a crowd, and was the partner of a safecracker. Rex would be in the crosshairs if they took off together. Mat and Vinnie wouldn't be spared if Jim thought Nathan and Rex were involved, and neither would she. She had to vanish alone.

The boys were with Rex, and surely, he wouldn't take them back to Nathan if she was gone. They would be safe in Kansas. She had to disappear. And she had to disappear alone.

The safest place she could think of, and the last place Jim would look for her was the place she least wanted to be in: prison.

Jim's ego wouldn't let him believe that someone who pulled one over on him would get caught. So she would get caught.

Rule number one: survive.

Before she got caught, she had to tie up any remaining loose ends. She drove to the closest airport and switched cars for one that was in long-term parking.

She carefully wiped down the entire car with alcohol while keeping her face covered. She might be behind bars for more than a year or two, and she needed a place to hide her take. Nathan might lose the trailer, or worse, find it somehow. He'd be loud about it, and it would be over for all of them. Rex's house would be perfect. Rex didn't like change, and he'd be there for at least a couple of years.

She picked the lock his door and let herself into Rex's house. She had to do this fast.

She couldn't risk anything looking out of place. As she paced, her eyes fell on the painting of the cabin, and she nodded to herself. She took it off the wall and found the spiked hammer Rex used on steaks to put a hole in the wall. The hole needed to be the size of her fist for the bag to fit, but she hesitated before putting it in.

She never took a purse on a job, but she'd forgotten to leave her ID at the cabin. It was still in her wallet. The only things in the wallet were her ID, a little cash, and a picture of Mat and Vinnie from last Christmas. The cash was fine, but she should burn the other two things. Not burning them would be a liability. Her fingers clenched the picture of her boys, grinning broadly for the camera. She didn't want to burn it. Without giving herself any more time to think it through, she shoved her wallet into the bag and put it into the hole in the wall.

It hadn't taken her long to patch the wall. Rex always had supplies, and Jane had seen him patch plenty of walls after Nathan lost his temper. She hung the painting up to cover the patch. It was done. The take was hidden, the boys were safe, and now she just needed to commit a crime and get caught. Her foot tapped against the floor. She'd be in a cage, but it would be worth it. She'd spent seven years in hell, what was a handful more? And bonus, it wouldn't be with Nathan Goodroe. That bastard…

That bastard, who might convince Rex to give the boys back. Without having her as an intermediary, what would happen to them? Nathan had such a temper, he might hurt them if she wasn't there to take it. Rex wouldn't give them back. There was no way he'd give them back. Jane bit down on her thumb. *But what if he did?*

She parked the car at the liquor store around the corner from the trailer park and walked home. No keys, so she picked the lock.

She was on fire tonight. Nathan was still snoring; it was as if she'd only been gone a couple of hours versus a couple of days. He kept a gun in the drawer of the end table, and it was always loaded. Jane lost count of how many times she'd drilled it into the boys to not touch that table or anything in it.

It was heavy in her hand. She was a grifter, so she'd shot at people but she'd never killed anyone.

Rule number two: Don't commit a crime you don't have to.

Maybe this was the better crime to commit. She was a documented battered woman, so if she killed him, no one would blame her. It would be self-defense, wouldn't it? He was drugged though, the medicine and alcohol in his system would throw up red flags. She might be in prison longer than she planned, or be executed.

If she killed him, she could one-hundred percent guarantee the boys would be safe with Rex, but it might cost her, her life.

Rule Number One: Survive.

It was too heavy. The gun was too heavy in her hands. She couldn't do it. She just couldn't risk the cops throwing her in a cage for the rest of her life. Rex surely wouldn't bring the boys back to Nathan. They'd be safe until she came back. Carefully wiping the gun off, she put it back in the drawer.

"I hope you choke to death, you fucking bastard." Jane growled at the sleeping man.

Nathan didn't even flinch and resumed his snoring.

December 10th; Kansas

She wiped the tears from her face, trying to compose herself. She could have saved her son from this pain. Why hadn't she been strong enough to follow through? "I'm so sorry. I wish to god I would have just pulled the trigger, saved you all this pain."

"Why did you go to prison for so long? The truth." Vinnie finally took a drink of water.

"The car I stole had a gun in the trunk, with a filed-off serial number and silencer attached. Unbelievably, it wasn't linked to any murders, but since I refused to cooperate with my real name or anything else, they sentenced me to the max and denied me parole because I wouldn't crack."

"Why didn't you ever reach out? You could have reached out. Rex thought you died, Mat was lost without you, and I didn't even remember you." He blew his nose, hands still shaking.

"Fear. First, it was fear of Jim figuring it out somehow. Then I just...the years kept passing by and I didn't know how to reach out. I saw in the paper that Nathan died in a fire, and I knew you'd be safe with Rex. I thought maybe it would be for the better."

"How could it possibly be for the better? We needed you."

"It was too hard to go back and face you. I didn't want to admit to the things I did out of selfishness when I should have been focusing on you and your brother." Jane stood and retrieved the picture she'd gone back to Rex's for and handed it to Vinnie.

"I don't understand."

"I missed everything of you and Mat growing up from those little boys to the men you are now because I ran. I ran and I didn't look back. I didn't trust the people I loved to be there." She explained further, hoping to keep him from repeating the past.

"It cost me my whole life. I can never get it back. All for a take that's meaningless now. Except for that memory. That picture of you and your brother was the actual reason I dared to go back to Rex's. I wanted to take it and vanish. I didn't and don't deserve to be let back in by you or anyone else. Why Rex is letting me stay is beyond my understanding."

Jane took the picture from him and clasped his hands in hers.

"Vinnie, I can't tell you how to live your life or what to do. But please, do not walk away from Anna before you go talk to her. Do not give up your life because of fear. I can't change anything that happened between me and Rex or make up for any of the time I lost with you and Mat." She swallowed the lump that formed in her throat. "The two of you may hate me for the rest of your lives, and I've accepted that."

"I don't hate you." Vinnie confessed. He still looked so lost.

A tear rolled down her face, and she had to take a deep breath to keep herself from breaking down. "I'm glad. I need to call Rex and tell him you're here. And you should call Anna."

"I don't have my phone. And even if I did, I'm scared she won't answer."

"Alright. What if we went back to Houston together?"

He shifted on the couch. "I'm not sure I could drive all the way back. I'm not doing great."

"I can drive us. I've done that drive on adrenaline and coffee." She smiled, trying to encourage him. "I'll even stop for chicken nuggets."

"Huh?"

"Right, you said you were too young to remember. It's the only thing you and Mat ever wanted when we went out to eat. You two would lose your minds every time we passed a Mcdonald's."

Vinnie chuckled, but there wasn't any joy in it. "Figures. Let me use the bathroom and we can head out. Might as well get it over with."

Jane touched his shoulder as he passed her. "Maybe. It'll be okay for you."

"Not sure how that could be the case, but thank you."

She retrieved her cellphone and hit the programmed number for Rex. It rang three times before a sleepy voice, who was not Rex, answered.

"Yeah?"

"I was looking for Rex?" Jane wondered if she'd put his number in this thing wrong.

"It's Mat, Jane."

She nodded, despite him not being about to see her. "Oh. Is Rex okay?"

"He needed some shut-eye. You good?" Mat sounded exhausted. There was a woman's voice in the background. Had to be Kass.

"Vinnie's here with me."

"Thank fucking god! Is he okay?" The relief in his voice was overwhelming.

"He's not great, but we're gonna start driving back to Houston in a few minutes." Jane walked to the bedroom she shared with Rex and put a bag together as Mat relayed her message to his wife.

"Get him to sleep if you can. He gets off when he doesn't sleep. Plus, he isn't gonna be able to take his meds on time, so that's not great for him either."

She couldn't stop the tears that rolled down her cheeks. "Mat, you did such a good job taking care of him when you two were little. I'm sorry. For everything. Even if you can't forgive me, I want you to know I'm sorry. I'd like the chance to talk to you about everything that happened, nothing off the table."

There was a long pause. It felt like an eternity before he spoke again. "Just get him home and we can figure out the rest out later."

"Alright."

"Alright. Drive safe, Jane. Look forward to seeing both of you."

The line went dead, and Jane finished packing, making sure to grab Anna's mail she'd accidentally packed so it could be returned to the woman. Vinnie was waiting for her at the front door.

"What if she doesn't want me anymore?"

Jane wanted to give him the optimism that Rex or Kass would have, or sarcasm like Mat would have, but that wasn't who she was. She just saw things as they were.

"If Anna doesn't want you because of your past, then it's better you know now."

Chapter 15: The Real Resolution

These Two Really Need To Talk

December 10th; Houston

It was pouring rain. *Oh the poetic metaphor bullshit be praised.* Anna sat on her chaise, wearing Vinnie's black shirt and her suit pants from yesterday, watching the water pelt the windows. Her injured hand rested on Jackal, who was oblivious to her owner's turmoil. It felt so empty in her apartment. Despite the assurance from Mat that Vinnie was in one piece and on his way back from Kansas with Jane, she was worried. Her phone lit up and she flipped it over to check her messages.

Alysha: How's the hand?

Anna: Hairline fracture.
Anna: Fun fact. Our lawyers work for the same firm.
Anna: He's suing me & pressing assault charges
Anna: The officer just left

Alysha: What a dick.

Anna: It'll be fine. I want to know who unsealed those records.

Alysha: Understandable. How's Vinnie?

Anna: Mat said he's alright

Alysha: Good. Let me know if you need anything
Alysha: Also keep ice on that hand Rhonda Rousey

Jackel yawned and arched her back as she stretched, hopping down from the couch and trotting across the apartment. Anna closed her eyes, thinking the feline was going to eat, only to be startled by a loud yowl.

"What? You have food and water. What else could you possibly need?" She glanced over and noticed that Jackal was sitting in front of the door, her tail swishing back and forth on the floor.

The door handle turned and the deadbolt unlocked. Jackal yowled again as Vinnie walked into her apartment with an envelope in his hand. "Hey, pretty girl."

He looked like a wreck, and while he closed the door, he proceeded no further than her foyer.

Anna nearly tripped over her own feet getting up off her chaise, running to Vinnie, and throwing her arms around him.

For lack of a better way to describe it, it was as if his entire body sighed as he picked her up and hugged her tighter. They didn't speak for several minutes, they just stood there holding each other.

Anna wasn't a super emotional person, but she was having trouble speaking and knew he'd need words. "I was so worried about you."

He still hadn't put her back on her feet. At her admission, he squeezed her even tighter, another shaky breath escaping him.

"Get your shoes off. Come inside, I'll get us some coffee and we can talk." She patted his back.

Vinnie wouldn't even look at her, so she stayed next to him until he kicked off his shoes. "I don't think I can be trusted with hot beverages right now."

She tugged his hand so he'd follow her. He was disconnected from her. How had so much changed in less than twenty-four hours? She sat on the opposite side of the chaise, the tension in his frame a practical scream for space. It was the last thing Anna wanted, but she forced herself to hold back. "Penny for your thoughts?"

"My thoughts are worth more than that, you should ask my editor." He reflexively responded, with a muted smile.

"There you are." She smiled softly. "I was worried you were too upset for our joke."

Vinnie clasped and unclasped his hands, wringing them together. His knee started bouncing as his heel moved up and down. "In the early 1990s there was a spike in child abuse, ranging from malnutrition to violence. It reached a rate of 15 per 1000 on average. There aren't a lot of statistics about abused children who commit parenticide. I didn't even know that was a word until I was in court."

He shifted uncomfortably, his eyes everywhere but on her.

Anna wanted to make him feel better, but she also needed to let him get through what he was trying to put into words.

"My father, Nathan… wasn't good."

She didn't want to put him through this. He was so upset, and he shaking to the point that she could feel the chaise vibrating "Vinnie, you don't need to…"

"I do though. I need to explain things. You… you deserve to know."

"Okay. I'm right here, I'm listening."

"Nathan was always angry, even angrier when he'd been drinking. Some of it…it was my fault. I would run my mouth. Sometimes I couldn't help it. I had to say whatever was on my mind, I had to get it out." Vinnie started talking faster, as if desperate to explain the whys of the situation. "He hit me sometimes, but usually, it was Mat. He hurt Mat a lot, but it was always my fault… Nathan would get mad at me, but Mat would distract him, get between us."

"Vinnie…" Anna's chest felt heavy as he continued. Why the hell was he blaming himself? She squeezed his hand, trying to pull him back to her, but he was almost disassociating as he continued.

"I could have taken it. I really could have. This one night, Nathan was on a tear. Not sure what I did, but he was coming right for me. Mat called him an asshole and Nathan… He hit Mat with a bottle…I remember the sound of it shattering." Vinnie swallowed, trying to gather himself to finish. "Mat just dropped to the ground, like a rock to the bottom of a pool. I thought he was dead. I was so scared."

She covered her mouth to keep from making a sound. She didn't trust herself not to break down if she tried to speak.

"Nathan didn't care, just sat back down in his chair and lit a cigarette. Mat finally made a sound, so I cleaned him up and put him to bed. I wanted to call someone. Mat kept telling me he was fine, when he wasn't. I knew that if I didn't do something, Nathan was going to kill us. I know I should have called the cops, but I didn't think they'd help."

Vinnie took his glasses off and set them on the coffee table. He let go of her hand and flattened his palms against his legs.

Tears dripping off Anna's cheeks. All the angry scars that had littered Vinnie's body, she'd assumed, they were from his criminal days. They weren't. They were from his childhood.

"He was obsessed with his gun and he was paranoid, so it was always loaded in an end table by his favorite chair. Nathan was sleeping and I got the gun out of the end table, but then he woke up. I fell back onto some glass and it went through my hand."

She'd noticed that scar, but hadn't let herself dwell on it.

"I didn't drop the gun though. Nathan tried to take it away, but I was too quick for him and I hid in me and Mat's room. Thought I'd be safe in there, but Nathan kicked the door in. There was a hammer in his hand. He said he was gonna put us both down the hard way. I fell off Mat's bed and onto the ground. I couldn't get up. My body wouldn't move."

His voice broke, the rest of the words spilled out in a sob as he covered his face with his hands. "I pointed the gun at him and kept squeezing the trigger until I was out of bullets. Mat was yelling at me, and I could hear Nathan choking, but I didn't care. I didn't care that I killed him. I'm a fucking monster!"

Anna forced his hands away from his face and wrapped her body around his. She cradled his head to her shoulder, smoothing his hair, whispering to him as she rocked with him. "Stop. Just stop. You did nothing wrong. You were scared and desperate. You thought he was going to kill you and your brother. You were defending yourself. You were trying to stay alive. Vinnie, Vinnie, you are not a monster."

"But I.." He tried to force her away, but she wasn't having it.

She caught his face in her hands, forcing him to look at her and wiping his tears away, "Nothing you or Mat did would have merited what he did to you. Nothing. You did not deserve the things he did to you. What he did to you and your brother was wrong. I am so sorry that you went through that. I am sorry for what he did to you, for how he made you feel, for everything you were made to endure. It was not your fault. It was his fault for doing it to you."

He let out a sob, but his arms were limp at his sides as he pressed their foreheads together. "Anna, I swear, I'd never hurt you. I wouldn't."

"Shh. Shh. Vinnie, I know you'd never hurt me." She moved one of his hands to the small of her back. "You are nothing like him. Nothing."

Trepidatiously, he wrapped his arms around her and rested his head against the crook of her neck. His unsteady breathing puffed air against her skin. "I love you so much. I don't want to be alone. Please don't leave me. "

Leaving him alone was the last thing she was doing. Sweet Vinnie, who never deserved any of this pain. Life was so cruel sometimes. If nothing else, she would be his safe place. Oh, to be his forever. To keep him forever and be his home. "I'm not going anywhere. You are safe with me. Nothing will change that. I promise, Vinnie, you are safe."

Anna held him while he cried. She couldn't make out everything he was saying, but she wasn't going to let him go until he started to calm down.

The storm raged outside, the thunder rattling the glass. He slumped into her shoulder, drawing a shuddering breath.

"Thank you for not making me leave."

She kissed the side of his head, it was all she could reach with the angle she was at. "You're the one who left, silly. Thank you for coming back and trusting me."

"Not like you didn't get the headline," he huffed.

"Headlines are clicks, I always want the meat of a story."

Vinnie shifted, pulling away from her slightly, "You can't eat meat, it makes you sick."

Anna arched her eyebrow. He was making jokes at a time like this?

"Please just go with it. I need the humor to decompress."

She pressed her forhead to his. "You think you're so funny."

"Alysha says you think I'm funny because you think I'm hot." His soft chuckle and small smile gave her a little hope.

"You are hot." She kissed his forehead. "You also need a shower and probably some food. Have you eaten since yesterday?"

"Please don't cook for me. I've been through a lot of trauma in the last twenty-four hours."

Anna smacked his arm but hissed in pain at the impact, pulling her left hand to her chest.

"What did you do?" He gingerly examined the bandage on her hand, as if just noticing it. "This is a cast? How did you get hurt?"

"I may have punched Preston in the face after you bolted. And I don't know how to throw a punch properly, so my thumb was tucked under my fingers and it broke." She felt uncomfortable with how concerned he was looking at her hand. "It's fine. It's only a hairline fracture."

Vinnie started laughing and Anna tried to get up, but he held on.

"Let me up, please."

"No! You defended my honor. You're my knight in shining armor." He was grinning at her.

Anna picked up his glasses and put them back on him. "Ah, yes, an ineffective puncher to the rescue."

"You can rescue me anytime. I am in constant need of it."

He kissed her, and Anna could still taste the salt from his tears. So she held onto him a little longer before patting his arm with her right hand. "Okay. What do you want for dinner? You need to eat."

"My mother bought me chicken nuggets for lunch." Vinnie started laughing again. "I was asleep when she went through the drive-thru, and she ordered me chicken nuggets. I guess I liked them when I was a kid."

Anna arched her eyebrow. Mother was a new word.

"So Jane is being referred to as your mother now? You're comfortable with that?"

"Yes. No. Maybe? Not sure yet. We talked a bit on the way back to Houston. Mat's said he'd talk to her too."

She climbed off of Vinnie's lap and motioned for him to follow her. "Shower. You need a shower. And I'll order us some food."

He nodded. "Yeah, I probably smell like I need a shower."

"I love you, but you do." She smirked and unlocked her phone to figure out what to order as the bathroom door closed behind Vinnie. She leaned her hip against her counter. *Wait, what had she just said?!?*

The door immediately re-opened and Vinnie was staring at her. "I realize that it might have been a more casual use of the phrase. But at the risk of emotional damage, did you just say that you loved me?"

Anna nodded because she had just said that she loved him, and she'd meant it.

"Cool. Just making sure I wasn't hallucinating." Vinnie closed the bathroom door, then opened it again.

Why did this feel like a game of whack-a-mole?

"So, I don't chicken out. Although technically I did say it in the midst of my sobbing a few minutes ago, and I felt it for certain last night when we were together. But also, before that, when we were in the limo going to my party was when I realized how much I cared about you. And I wanted to tell you before, but it felt awkward, and then I didn't want you to think it was pillow..." He trailed off as Anna walked up to him and put her uninjured hand in his. "Thank you. I was spiraling."

"Just a bit. And not one bit casually – I love you."

He grinned and kissed her again. "I love you."

"Thank you. Now, shower. You need to take care of yourself."

Vinnie gave her a mock salute and disappeared into the bathroom. Anna walked over to the paperwork he'd brought in with him. It was just a piece of mail that must have gone to Rex's by mistake.

She opened the envelope, finding her Birth Certificate, which had taken her almost the whole year to get a copy of. She read the contents, and sure enough, her mother was listed, but John Doe was written on the father line. Short of a DNA investigation, she wasn't going to have a family outside of the one she had with Vinnie, and that was just fine with her.

December 24; Houston

Christmas was Vinnie's favorite holiday. Surprising someone he cared about with something they would like made him smile. Kass had explained to him that his love language was giving gifts, so it made sense that it made him so happy. It was the way he naturally wanted to express love to others.

Speaking of love, Anna was sitting with his mother at the island while Rex teased the two about staying out of his kitchen for everyone's safety. They were waiting on Mat, Kass, and Lizzie before starting dinner. He put the last touches on the handmade stockings that Kass had put their initials on last year. The two new stockings with the gold-threaded letters "JEA" and "ALK." He picked on Kass about getting Jane's initials wrong, but she said that Jane's driver's license said "Abster" so she used the "A."

"Sorry to derail Christmas at the cabin. I feel bad, but I can't leave the state until the trial." Anna sipped on her hot chocolate.

"I can't believe that asshole pressed charges." Jane remarked

Vinnie chuckled. "To be fair, she broke his nose. Anna Lauren Kane, fighter extraordinaire.".

"Not with a broken thumb, I'm not."

Rex stirred the dish on the stove. "He earned it. Wish someone caught that on video."

"No. No evidence," Jane chided him, then turned to Anna shaking her head. "You hear this? He's like a rookie. Forgot everything about the game after I left."

"I went straight-ish and raised your kids, ya convict." Rex waved his spatula at Jane.

"Always complaining." Jane rolled her eyes.

Anna leaned back against Vinnie, and he kissed the top of her head. He tapping her nose to get her attention, before the thought slipped his mind again. "I meant to ask you, is this pushing back your international travel?"

She looked up at him. "No, waiting to get documentation so I can have my passport reissued is what's holding that up." She turned back to Jane, "Thank you for getting my birth certificate back to me."

"I just feel bad I accidentally took it."

"I thought you didn't know who your parents were. I would think that would make it a challenge." Rex leaned back against the counter.

Anna shrugged. "Difficult, but not impossible. I knew my birthday, that I was born in Texas, and Emily only changed my last name, so I just had to call every hospital in Texas with my date of birth and first and middle names."

"Aren't there a lot of hospitals in Texas?" Jane questioned sipping from her own mug.

"Over 500 currently," Vinnie supplied. "But fewer in 1987."

"Yes, but still a lot." Anna checked on her phone before putting it into her pocket. "Once I had my live birth record with my mother's name, 'Abigail Harrington', on it, I was able to request my adoption paperwork, and the state issued me a new certificate. So, not terribly challenging, just a lot of hoops."

Rex had turned his attention fully to Anna. "What was that name again?"

Vinnie's eyebrow went up but stayed quiet. If Rex recognized a name, it wasn't always a good thing.

"Abigail Harrington."

"You wouldn't happen to know her birthday off-hand would you?" Rex adjusted his glasses.

Anna pulled out her phone. "I scanned the certificate, so I can check real fast. Why, was she part of your secret organization?" She joked as she opened her scanning app.

"Maybe."

"Oh." Anna's finger swiped faster across her phone and Vinnie rubbed her shoulder. "Here is February 14, 1965."

"Well shit." Rex snickered. "Small world."

Jane now looked curious. "Do you know her?"

"Yeah, I did. She went by Gail. I was with her when I met you."

Jane sipped from her mug. "The blonde that couldn't match her clothes?"

"Be nice, she was colorblind." Rex clicked his tongue.

"You dated my birth mother? How did you meet?"

"Oh…" Rex folded his hands and let out a long breath. "She was, um, working, when we met."

Anna blinked, before sighing heavily. "Was she a prostitute?"

"Yes, but to be fair to her we dated for five 'r six months in…" He trailed off doing math in his head. "Casino job was…before Mat was born in '87, …so 86. I dated her in 1986."

"Oh."

Vinnie looked down at Anna, who was mirroring Rex's prior math calculation expression. "You okay?" He whispered in her ear and she nodded in response.

Anna snapped her fingers. "I was born in September of 1987, but I was a preemie, so I think that takes you off the hook."

Rex gruffed an uncomfortable laugh. "Sorry Darlin', I know she wasn't always careful with clients before I met her, so it's likely she went back to that way after she left."

"If I ever really wanna know, I'll get a DNA test done."

Mat crashed through the door with a squealing Lizzie in tow, and that was the end of the conversation, but Vinnie felt Jane's eyes on him. Vinnie wasn't one to miss things, but Jane had obviously caught something the rest of them had missed.

They managed to wrestle Lizzie into eating a little before letting her tear through all her presents. Kass was arguing about everyone being too generous, and Mat picked on Anna about having to set a price limit next year to keep her spending in check.

Everyone was relaxing in the living room when Jane excused herself to go out to smoke and motioned with her head for Vinnie to follow. He shut the door behind them and she lit a clove, offering it to him, but he shook his head.

Jane took a long drag on it, letting the smoke curl into the air.

"Is there a problem?" he finally asked, making eye contact with his mother. The stress was pouring off of her. Why was she so stressed?

"Nathan slept with Gail too, in December of '86. And when Mat was born at thirty-nine weeks, they thought he was a preemie because he was so small." She took another drag of her clove.

It took exactly a second for him to add up the equation that she laid out.

"Fuck! Are you sure? Like 100% sure, sure?"

"I kinda ran her off because I knew she slept with Nathan and that it would hurt Rex."

They were standing side by side in the chilly night air as the implication hung around them.

Vinnie was positive he was going to have a nervous breakdown. "Can I ever catch a fucking break? Do you think this is him getting revenge from the grave? Like 'ha ha, you killed me so I'm gonna pull strings in the universe and get you to fuck your half-sister.'"

"Don't panic yet. You just need to get DNA tested." Jane flicked off the ash, the red embers blowing with the breeze. "She could be Rex's or anyone else she slept with. How Rex never caught anything from her is a miracle."

"Hey, tone down the sex worker shaming. Let me have my crisis in peace, please." Vinnie buried his face in his hands.

The sliding door opened, and Mat let himself out onto the patio. "What crisis now? We should be done with those now. We've hit all soap opera tropes: accidental kid, someone back from the dead, a murder, a re-connection love story. I'm pretty damn sure the only one we didn't hit is the surprise sibling. And I know that's not..."

Mat groaned and covered his face with his hands for a moment, before leaning against the side of the house. "What did I miss? Did you have a kid in prison or something?"

Anna's laughter carried through the glass, and Vinnie couldn't stop staring at her. *What if…*

Jane put her clove out in the ashtray and interrupted his train of thought. "DNA test first. Panic later."

"Seriously, the *hell* did I miss?"

"Nathan slept with Anna's birth mother," Jane supplied.

Oh now, she wanted to be up front answers.

Mat still looked confused, "So?"

"Anna's older than me dumbass." Vinnie spelled out the problem for his brother, "She was born in September and Nathan slept with her mother in December."

"Oh fuck!"

"Yes, that exactly."

December 26; Houston

Vinnie was sitting in Anna's office, watching her sign for the courier package. After Lizzie had passed out from running sprints around all of them, Rex had put two and two together about Anna's potential parentage. And since the toddler was unconscious, they had a civil adult conversation about the whole thing. Also the moon turned into cheese. Christmas Eve had been a bit tense after the bombshell. Anna had excused herself earlier as and much as he hated to, Vinnie let her go and have space. He'd basically spent the rest of the evening trying not to panic about the situation and failing. Mat sprinkled in a lot of swearing, and Rex was eerily quiet.

Vinnie never had a particular interest in visiting Nathan's grave, but he was not above going to spit on it after this was all over.

Anna click-clacked back into her office with lunch in one hand and the papers in the other. She set their lunch down on one side of her desk and sat on her couch with the documents in her hands.

"If I ask you how you got those results back in less than ten hours, are you going to tell me it was money?" He sat next to her but left a person's worth of space between them.

She smirked at him but set the envelope down on her coffee table. "The last time I had a family was in 2005 when Emily died. I'm nervous to open this. The worst case would, of course, be that we are blood relatives."

"We'll have to have a destination wedding in Arkansas."

She pursed her lips. "Not laughing."

"I'm sorry. We've established that I use gallows humor as a crutch." He rubbed the back of his neck.

Anna nodded and pushed the envelope forward and back on the table. "The less upsetting scenario, but still an uncomfortable one, would be if Rex is my father. Especially knowing that your mother ran my mother off in a fit of jealousy."

"I don't remember her using that word in the story." Vinnie arched his eyebrow.

She chuckled dryly. "We need to work on your understanding of subtext. Also, we need to get permission to write her story because it is fascinating."

"She'll never let you do it."

"What if we set it in high fantasy? You could write a magic system. There could even be dragons."

Vinnie tapped the envelope. "I feel like you're stalling for some reason."

"I've been on my own for so long that it feels strange to be part of a family." Anna picked it up and started unsealing it. "Here goes nothing, or everything, in our case, I guess."

She pulled out the reports and her eyes scanned them quickly. As much as Vinnie wanted to look over her shoulder, he knew he shouldn't. Anna yipped and covered her mouth with her casted hand.

He didn't know what that yip meant. His mind was spiraling down the worst reality. "You don't need to tell me everything. I just need to know if it's the worst-case scenario."

"It's not." Anna reached for him, and he pulled her into a hug with a grateful sigh.

They hadn't had any physical contact since Christmas Eve and, while he wasn't touch-centered, not being able to touch her was brutal. It was necessary space, until they learned Anna's parentage, but god, he'd never been so desperate to have someone in his arms.

Anna's voice was soft as she relayed the rest of the information. "I'm Rex's daughter."

"Holy fuck." Vinnie kissed the top of her head. "Do you think that means I should ask his permission before I ask you to marry me?"

Anna leaned back away from him, but poked her finger against his chest. "If you ask anyone about marrying me, it better be me. And if you're going to ask me to marry you, then I think we have a few details to work out."

"Such as?"

"I'm planning on traveling most of next year."

"After your court case is settled?" He smirked.

"I have money, so it's an inconvenience at most. Do you have a passport?"

"Yes, I got one in October. What else?"

Anna picked at her manicure. "I want kids."

"I like kids." He grinned, tracing an infinity symbol on her knee.

"I'm slowing down my work schedule, but not stopping. I do not plan on leaving my director's position. I want to keep growing the company as a whole. And I wouldn't change my professional name."

Vinnie cocked his head to the side. "What about me has ever indicated that I would want to uphold the traditional roles or make you any less the center of attention? I like watching you."

"Oh, I know." She flashed a seductive smile at him, biting her lower lip to keep from laughing.

"Do not distract me. I meant I like watching you be in charge. Wait, that didn't help me." He tried to refocus. "So traveling, kids, keep working, and what else?"

"I'm sure there are other things. But those are the major ones I think we'd need to cover when we have the marriage conversation."

"Okay."

Before Anna could react, he shifted from on the couch to kneel in front of her, still holding her hand. "I'm formally requesting permission to ask you to marry me. I just need to know when I'm getting my first royalty check, so I can get you a ring that's worthy of you. Would that be alright?"

Anna caught his face in her hands. "You get your check on Friday. And I don't give a fuck what the ring looks like. The answer will be yes."

He pressed their foreheads together. "It'll be yes *when* I ask?"

"We could get married *on* Friday for all I care." That hundred-watt smile that she only seemed to flash when they were together, broke out on her face.

Vinnie captured her in a long kiss. "Let me woo you a little. Also, I don't think you want your thumb in a cast for pictures."

"Courthouse."

"Seriously?"

"Yes." Anna nodded. "I just want you and me and our family."

Chapter 16: Romcoms End in HEA

Sometimes Happily Ever After Happens

January 28th; Houston

Anna had never been one to get excited about fancy parties. They were simply a part of her job. They were fun from time to time, but her happiest times were in more intimate settings. She'd lived her whole life having things, money, and a little bit of power. But that whole time, she'd missed out on having a full-time family.

She didn't fault Emily for her lack of what the world would have considered mothering. Emily wasn't the warmest person, but Anna had never felt neglected. Emily Kane had taken Anna in when she'd had nothing and laid the world at her feet.

She wasn't giving up her job, or any kind of nonsense like that. Anna's job was important to her. What she did at the publishing office was important. If she hadn't had the job she did, she wouldn't have met Vinnie when she met him. Vinnie wouldn't ever ask her to quit or scale back her job.

Vinnie's first royalty check had been deposited into his bank account on a Friday morning, and that Friday evening, while at dinner, he proposed. She said yes, but couldn't stop laughing, which was embarrassing. Most of the restaurant was confused as to why her reaction was more laughter than crying.

They had, of course, told the whole family that night and everyone was just as excited for them.

Anna had been serious about a courthouse wedding; she wanted something simple, clean, and to be done with it. The only person she wanted here who couldn't attend was her friend Minji, but getting her here from Korea was not going to happen.

Her friend was expecting her first child and wasn't taking any chances.

Seoul was on the itinerary for post-wedding travel, so they'd reconnect where it was easier for the expectant mother. Stretching over and grabbing her phone, Anna made a note in her calendar to have a gold ring made for Minji's baby gift.

Since her apartment was around the corner from the courthouse, Anna was getting ready at home. Alysha had disappeared to go check on the boys, who were getting ready in her office downstairs. There was a soft knock on the door, and Anna stepped out of the bathroom to answer it. Alysha had a key, so it wouldn't be her. Oh, maybe it was Kass' friend Dara that offered to be the photographer for the day. Anna opened the door, surprised to see Rex standing there with Dara.

"That's quite a dress, Darlin'," he complimented.

Anna smoothed the tule shirt. "Thank you. It's more bridal than I planned on, but I thought it was pretty." Dara had already snapped a few pictures.

"Well, Vinnie thinks you're wearing a white suit for some reason."

She moved to let them come inside, as she explained, "I may have convinced him that I was, so I could surprise him."

The lace, off-shoulder bodice of her dress had a soft romantic look, which matched perfectly with the vintage rose hair piece she'd found.

Dara let out a low whistle. "You have a view to kill for. I hope you know that you and Vinnie are coming back up here with me to get pictures with the sunset."

Jackal darted around the corner, and Anna picked her up without thinking about it. "Oh, I bet I just got your black fur on me."

Anna didn't miss the clicking of the camera but tried to ignore it and look natural. She hated having her picture taken.

"Dara wanted to get a few pictures of the two of us together." Rex looked so uncomfortable. Since he found out that she was indeed his daughter, he kept looking like he wanted to say something, but always stopped himself.

Anna put Jackal back on the floor. "I have an idea. Let's try this." She walked over to her two-person table and tapped it, indicating for him to sit as she retrieved her chessboard.

"That's a fantastic idea!" Dara agreed, looking around the apartment. "Can I stand on your stairs?"

"Of course, whatever makes it easier." Anna nodded, setting up the board with Rex helping. "If my hands are moving I can forget the crowd."

He held out her queen. "You might just get that from me. Hate being still for too long. Did I win our last game?"

"We haven't finished our last game." She slid over his Rook.

"'Suppose we should make it look like your winning, with it bein' your day and all."

"I can win all on my own, I don't need any pity." She smiled and he echoed it. "We can just play for a bit while she takes pictures."

Rex made an affirming sound as they continued to set up the pieces. "Gail never did tell me about you. I didn't know."

"I know you didn't. You would have been in my life if you'd known." This was an easier way for them to have this talk, even with another person in the room. Dara was likely just trying to get shots and wasn't listening.

"You did more than alright for yourself." He moved one of his pawns in a reckless way. He wasn't concentrating.

Anna took the pawn, holding it in her fingers. "I think things happened the way they were supposed to. If you had been raising me, you probably wouldn't have taken in Mat and Vinnie. They needed you. You were where you needed to be, and I was where I needed to be."

They moved pieces on the board, as the white noise system in her apartment played soft music. Rex finally responded with a gruff agreement. "Suppose you're right."

"I am. And I'm glad to have you in my life now. You're pretty amazing."

"If you say so."

"I do say so." She smirked, brushing a wayward lock of hair away from her face. She'd need to touch up her hair before going downstairs.

Rex took one of her pawns. "Think you're slacking here. I'mma beat ya easy."

"Well, I'm getting married today, so you have the advantage of my distraction." Before she could make her next move, he grabbed her hand and gave it a squeeze.

"You make a lovely bride."

Anna blushed, unable to help it.

"That's the shot!" Dara laughed, and they both looked up at her, hanging halfway over the railing.

Anna turned her head quickly, unable to look at how the other woman was situated near the edge.

"Not a fan of heights, eh?"

"Definitely not."

The door opened, and Alysha let herself in with Kass and Lizzie in tow. "WE HAVA GIFFS!!"

The toddler raced up to Anna, nearly colliding with the table, but Rex blocked Lizzie with his hand.

Lizzie held up a small flat box, "Iss fors you! Uncle Veenee says so."

Anna took it from her, clueless as to what it could be. Mat had their rings. Inside the box was an infinity symbol necklace with their birthstones set into it. It was simple and beautiful.

"Can I help you with it?" Kass asked.

"Sure." Anna reached for her phone out of habit.

"There's a fountain out front, and I will chuck your phone into it." Alysha threatened as Kass fastened the necklace around Anna's neck.

"All set on the necklace. Alysha, do you have any hairpins? I want to secure a couple of her curls."

"Here, move. I know this girl's fine baby hair." Alysha secured the hair piece into Anna's curls. "Lookin' good."

Anna wasn't used to being the center of attention like this. She was used to being able to shift attention to a project, not having it be centered on her.

"I suppose we should get this show on the road." Rex stood up.

"Yeah we gots to hussles!" Lizzie stamped her feet excitedly as they all started towards the door.

Dara was clicking pictures behind them as they exited the apartment. Anna was locking the door when Alysha grabbed her hand, lowering her voice to tease Anna. "Look at that, only 27 days late on your New Years' Resolution."

"It's only been a year?" Anna laughed out loud. " I feel like I've lived a whole lifetime."

Rex was holding the elevator for them. "Those Goodroes will do it to you."

Vincent Goodroe had been a lot of things in his life, but married man wasn't a title he thought he'd ever have. Being a published author had been hard to believe, as impossible as that would have sounded just a year ago. He'd spent so much of his life in fear and letting things happen to him rather than taking action. The owner of the strip club he'd gone to on his birthday asked him if he wanted in on an opportunity; sure. That guy's wife needed Vinnie's help to get her out of marriage; no problem. Keep working at the strip club even after his sort-of relationship ended; might as well. Help his brother with whatever he needed help with, including his niece; with pleasure. But all those things happened to him instead of him making decisions.

In contrast, Vinnie had written a book and sent it in to be reviewed. He had made that decision. When he'd met Anna, who encouraged him to pursue it, he had put in the work for himself. He completed the manuscript, survived the editing process, and he got to celebrate the results. He faced one of the darkest moments of his life and came out the other side in one piece.

Most importantly, he got the girl, er, woman. Anna, who never thought of him as someone's whatever. To her, he was the first part of the sentence and never a dependent clause. She loved him. He couldn't stop the smile from crossing his features with the knowledge of that.

Jane's voice broke through the quiet. "Is he alright?"

"He's good, but he'll write a whole book in his head if you leave him alone long enough." Mat chuckled.

Vinnie rolled his eyes and finished knotting his tie as he fake laughed. "Har, har. He thinks he's a comedian."

"You hang out with my wife too much. She says that all the time."

Two quick taps on the door and Kass, Rex, and Lizzie came into Anna's office. "We're all ready to go!" Kass clapped her hands, then continued. "Vinnie, you stay put and face the window. The rest of us are clearing out so they can have their first look alone."

"He just doesn't want us to see him cry," Mat snickered.

Rex waved, gesturing for them to leave the room. "Pretty sure we've got plenty of evidence of you crying at your own wedding. Better watch out," he warned

"Daddy! Wanna flys!"

Mat patted Vinnie's shoulder as he walked by. "See ya in a few. Remember, you're good enough for her, even if you are an ass."

"Thanks," Vinnie deadpanned, watching his brother scoop up Lizzie and toss her up in the air.

Jane squeezed his hand and began to leave, but Vinnie held on for a moment. Concern was evident in her eyes. "You okay?"

Vinnie pulled her into a hug. "Thank you for telling me not to run. You were there when I really needed you to be."

"I'm glad I was." His mother hugged him back before pulling away and leaving, hand and hand with Rex.

Kass leaned in the doorway, a smirk on her face.

He arched his eyebrow at his sister-in-law. "Are you blocking the door? You're shorter than Anna; it won't work."

She stuck out her tongue. "Brat. No, I just wanted to tell you something real quick."

"As always, I am all ears for my favorite sister."

"Still your only sister," She rolled her eyes.

"All the easier for me not to play favorites."

Kass grabbed his hands and looked up at him, a giant grin on her face. "You have everything waiting on the other side of that door, and despite the fact that you never thought you'd have it, you do. You have a love story that's all yours."

Vinnie blinked. This girl, who had inadvertently wound up entangled in his brother's life, had started the chain reaction that had gotten him here. If it hadn't been for Kass walking into Mat's life with Lizzie, then his brother would have remained alone. Vinnie would still be focused on The Playhouse and likely would have stayed in that life until he died. Kass had been the first half of the book with his brother, and Anna had started the half of the book that was his.

He pulled the auburn-haired girl into a hug. "Thanks for making a rash decision, keeping Lizzie, and not killing me for writing it down."

"You're welcome. Time to start the next book. I think it'll be just as good, or who knows, maybe even better." She hugged him back before waving her hands in front of her face to keep from tearing up as she slipped out of the room.

Dara came in and assessed the room, opening the blinds, and tapping her foot on the tile. "Thoughts on going back upstairs?"

"We are running short on time," he confirmed by looking at his watch. "We also met in this room, if that helps."

"A little." She turned off the overhead light and snapped a few pictures of the empty room. "This is better. Lights off then, just the sun through the windows. Walk backward to the doorway then stop."

Vinnie felt a little silly, but Dara knew what she was doing. She'd captured every sappy moment from Mat and Kass' wedding with perfection, so he trusted her.

"Put your left hand out behind you," Dara instructed.

"You turn too." Alysha sounded just as happy. "See you in a bit."

"Thank you." Anna was choked up, her voice softer than normal.

Vinnie didn't trust himself to speak, so he simply squeezed her hand and she echoed it. Dara was taking pictures, perched on the empty space of what would be an internal window once construction was completed.

"Alright. Both of you close your eyes, then turn to face each other and hold hands. Take your time, it's not a race."

More shudder clicks and as he turned and felt the breeze of Anna turning. Her hands found his and she entwined their fingers.

"Thank you for the necklace."

"Wanted to give you at least one surprise today." Vinnie took a deep breath in and couldn't help himself. "I love you."

"I love you." He could hear the smile in Anna's voice. The smile that was his and his alone. The one that always made him feel like everything would be alright.

Dara cleared her throat and gave the next order. “Okay lovebirds. Gonna open those eyes on three. One. Two. Three.”

Vinnie opened his eyes and looked right into Anna’s.

“Hello, you.”

“Hi.”

The End

Epilogue: Don't Need it? Don't Add It

One More Moment

December 24th, 2017

Family was a funny thing – hard to gain and far too easy to lose. This cabin had been the backdrop of falling in love, losing love, healing from the past, and celebrating the future.

Rex never could have imagined the path that life had taken him on. As a snot-nosed twelve-year-old, Nathan James Goodroe had kept Rexton Lawrence Abster from getting his ass kicked by a bigger kid, and they were thick as thieves from that moment forward. From skipping classes to chasing skirts to fighting outside of bars to running jobs for one of Houston's prominent criminal enterprises, they'd done it all together. Rex had thought of crime as a means to an end. Make a little money to make a life. But Nathan had gotten seduced by that life. Nathan developed an addiction to any habit that got near him, while Rex stuck to ink on his skin and movies in his collection. They probably would have gone back and forth, getting into shit until one of them died, but then there was Jane.

Jane Elizabeth McCroy, with her dark hair, mismatched eyes, and far more smarts then she ever let on about. She'd watched them for a couple of months before zeroing in on Nathan as her mark. She hadn't planned on staying with him for more than a job, but she saw how fast Nathan cracked a safe, and she knew she could use that. She hadn't intended for either of those pink plus signs or how much Rex changed her view of the world. But even with boys that she loved, sometimes people don't make the right choices.

Sometimes bad choices were circumstances. Oftentimes bad choices were people, and Natalie Bahman had been a bad choice for Mathew James Goodroe. It was impossible to know that a moody thirteen-year-old girl was going to turn into a manipulative woman who didn't care who got hurt in her wake as long as she got what she wanted. The first time Rex heard Natalie yell at Mat for being too stupid to not know why she was mad at him, he'd warned his nephew that she was trouble, but teenage hormones overrode good sense all too often. Married at eighteen and divorced while in jail, Mathew should have known to stay away from his ex-wife, but sometimes sex was bigger selling point than love. Sex with one woman leading to the pregnancy of another, was an impossible twist so it was on brand for Mathew's lousy luck.

Life could be described as a dose of faith, a dose of timing, or in the case of Kassarah Grace Shatan, it was the moment of faith that led to the world's worst timing. However, flying in the face of the worst circumstance, she found a way to turn the situation into a charmed life with a baby girl and a man who learned to love himself just a bit with her encouragement. Her green eyes could see the slimmest measure of light and pull it into the darkest corner, turning a cynic into a believer. A story so incredible that no one would believe the facts unless they were presented as fiction.

Fiction was an escape for Vincent James Goodroe. It was his way to tune out the world. From simple movies as a child with coke-bottle thick glass to tomes of science fiction as a teenager, Vinnie never wanted to stay in the world he lived in for very long. He was a constant source of trivia and general knowledge, but he kept himself hidden in plain sight. The embodiment of 'sure I can help,' he never looked out for himself, too frightened to take a risk on himself. But taking a risk was often the only way to make a life.

Risk was a calculation, and Anna Lauren Kane knew how to evaluate human risk and make it work for her. A seasoned loner, the idea of family was so foreign that her assistant was her closest tether to a personal life. Born a secret, raised with money, and pulled back to family by the most unbelievable of stories.

Elizabeth Grace Goodroe – the unbelievable little girl whose existence had brought them all together. The granddaughter who lit up his life and...

"Hey, Blue-Eyes, you still with us?" Jane teased from the hearth. "You've been muttering to yourself for a good ten minutes there."

Rex cleared his throat. "You coulda said somethin'."

"I just did." She caught his hand in hers and kissed his knuckles. "Kass texted me. They should be here any minute."

He nodded, eyes wandering to framed wedding photos of two smiling families hanging on the wall: a group photo with all of them, including the normally camera-shy Jane, joyfully facing forward. Family. Simple as that, and it didn't get much better.

The front door opened, letting in a blast of cold air, and Anna pulled herself closer to Vinnie.

"She's out like a light, Kassie."

"Don't call me Kassie." Kass swatted Mat on his back and closed the door behind her. "Let's put Lizzie down upstairs, and we'll be back down."

Mat was toeing off his boots. "I'm tired. It was a long drive up here from Mason."

"I brought whiskey from my private stock," Anna offered.

"We'll be down in a couple of minutes." Mat chuckled as Jane came around the corner. "Hey."

"Here, I can take her upstairs. Go get a drink and sit with your brother and Rex," she offered as Mat handed over Lizzie.

"Careful, she's gettin' big."

"They always do."

"Coffee on the pot, Rex?" Kass asked, taking off her jacket.

"It's decaf, but we got it, darlin'." Rex nodded, accepting the side hug from her as she passed by him to get to the kitchen.

Vinnie kissed Anna's temple. "What am I helping you build tonight?" he asked his brother.

"Just a bike. Should be simple as a shot in the dark." Mat knocked on the doorframe as he sauntered back into the living room, clinking his tumbler against Vinnie's where it sat on its coaster.

Anna motioned to the chessboard. "Are you going to make your next move tonight? Or is this game on hold until after Christmas?"

Rex smirked at her. "Why? Did you want me to let you win for Christmas?"

"You seem to be forgetting our record. I am currently up on wins between us."

"You so sure about that?"

Vinnie waved a tissue between them. "Christmas truce. I swear, the two of you are so damn competitive. It's almost like you're related. Ouch!" Vinnie jumped. "Kass, Anna's pinching me."

"Don't be a goof, and you won't get pinched." Kass chuckled and picked up Anna's cup. "Do you want me to warm yours up before I take a drink of mine?"

Anna shook her head. "No thank you, I'm drinking tea."

Kass' eyebrow shot up and she sniffed Anna's drink. "Ginger and lemon? That's a good one for the stomach."

"Mhmm." Anna's lips were pressed in a line, and she reached to retrieve her cup. "Thank you for the recipe."

"Are you sick?" Mat questioned. "You drink more coffee than my wife, and her cup is glued to her hand. Ouch! Jesus. Rex, did you pull both of 'em aside at our weddings and teach 'em how to pinch?"

Rex snickered and took a sip from his own cup as Jane slipped back into the room, whiskey tumbler in hand. She sat back on the fireplace hearth.

"Do you need to get anything from your car?" Vinnie questioned Mat.

Mat nodded. "Yeah, but I'm gonna sip this first. Your wife has the best taste."

Vinnie kissed the back of Anna's hand. "She does."

"You are the expectation to the rule," Mat pointed out.

Vinnie opened his mouth, but Kass interrupted. "No, no. It's Christmas. We're being *nice*."

Rex stood and stretched, cracking his back. "I suppose we should all get to helping with getting Christmas ready for the little one before it gets too late."

It was a flurry of activity, getting out stockings, stuffing them, and hanging them on the fireplace. Kass took pictures as the brothers built Lizzie's bike. With the presents all under the tree and all the adults relaxing, Anna excused herself for a moment and came back with a gift wrapped in black. She handed it to Vinnie and sat down, giving him a little space on the couch.

"Can't open anything until Christmas," Jane admonished.

"Wife rules. What are you gonna do?" Vinnie turned the package over a few times. "It's not really a gift. It's just the proof copy of my second book."

Anna sipped her tea and ran her toe along Vinnie's knee. He caught her foot and attempted to put it in his lap, but she slipped away. "Open it first," she insisted.

"It's his story this time, right?" Mat asked.

Anna's smile was slightly cryptic. "His story to tell."

"I think she's not giving hints," Kass observed.

Rex nodded, although he was pretty sure that was Anna's keeping-a-secret smile. What was she up to now?

Vinnie's eyebrow was arched, but he slowly unwrapped the paper. "Should I wait until Christmas?" he teased.

"If you ever want to unwrap me again, you'll open it now." Anna folded her arms over her chest as the rest of the cabin erupted in laughter.

"Understood." Vinnie finished unwrapping the item, but if it was a book, it was solid black. A proof copy maybe? Vinnie's eyes were wide as he looked at it. Suddenly, he launched off the couch, nearly tackling Anna, hugging her and laughing.

Anna was laughing along with him. "You flipped it over. No one else knows what's going on."

Vinnie, seemingly unable to hear her, simply squeezed her tighter and kissed her face over and over.

"Vinnie." Anna caught his face in her hands. "Tell our family."

Our family. That was music to Rex's ears. Anna still struggled with feeling like she was a part of their ragtag little crew. 'Our family' was the best thing to hear.

Vinnie was grinning ear to ear as he handed Rex the item. It was a shadow box with a framed message. "There's going to be a new character in our love story."

"You know, the likelihood of twins is higher with older pregnant women. According to a study…"

"Oh, I remember that one from my classes."

"I'm buying your kid a drum set, just so you know."

"I had nothing to do with Lizzie's keyboard, don't punish me!"

"Congratulations!"

"Congratulations!"

About the Author

Katharine Sweet is a happily married dog mom with two sweet pups and is an avid reader. She hails from Michigan where her days are powered by good coffee, hockey, nerd culture, and (when possible) the perfect new hairstyle. Katharine has been writing and storytelling for as long as she can remember. She loves the way that stories can not only pull you in but also help you connect. On paper, Katharine's deep interest in human character and her sharp wit gives her a unique voice that draws you into her work. Although she admittedly loves horror and suspense, her friends would describe her as bottled sunshine and someone with unbridled kindness.

Check out more from the author and find her social media:
www.sweettaleswithspice.com/links

Also by Author

Love Is…

Book One of the Goodroe Brother's Duet

Gram Satan's Rated-R Cookbook

A Humorous companion cookbook to the Goodroe Brother Books
Exclusively on Kindle

Made in the USA
Monee, IL
14 July 2024

61336990R00187